"This story definitely leaves the reader with a great deal of introspection."

—*Rendezvous*

"All of Cramer's characters are fully realized, and his love of the Appalachians comes shining through. This is a fine first novel."

—*Booklist* (starred review)

"Elegant and quirky, Cramer's debut novel is a sophisticated find, dancing with imaginative phrasing and wit."

—*The Parable Group*

"Mr. Cramer masterfully introduces a variety of characters and makes you feel like you know each one intimately. . . . Please, do yourself a favor and read this book."

—*Christian Bookshelf Book Review*

"*Sutter's Cross* will rouse feelings of compassion as well as indignation. Drawing strong comparisons to Jesus Christ, Cramer gives the reader plenty of food for thought. One would never guess this is his first novel."

—*MyShelf.com*

BAD GROUND

W. DALE CRAMER

BETHANYHOUSE
Minneapolis, Minnesota

Published by Bethany House Publishers
11400 Hampshire Avenue South
Bloomington, Minnesota 55438

Bethany House Publishers is a Division of
Baker Book House Company, Grand Rapids, Michigan.

Printed in the United States of America

ISBN 0-7394-4461-1

For Terry Hadaway

who knows why, or should.

Books by W. Dale Cramer

Sutter's Cross

Bad Ground

BAD GROUND

CHAPTER I

A boy afraid of the dark; a man afraid of the light.

Be anxious for nothing," his mother said, and then she went on to a better place and left the seventeen-year-old boy by himself, with nothing. The car died, and her treatments swallowed the rent money even before that final trip to the hospital. For the last month of her life, Jeremy lived with Uncle Walter and Aunt Anna and their three rotten kids, and it had not worked out. It wasn't their fault; he knew that. Living apart from his mother for the first time in his life, he went for short visits and saw the pain consume her in stages. In the beginning his young heart begged for a miracle; in the end, for relief. Even if Walter and Anna's house had been a haven of peace and comfort, it would still have been eclipsed by his mother's demise.

The day before the funeral Anna gave him the letter his mother had left for him. He went down to the creek to get away from the twins, sat up against the trunk of a poplar tree, and read.

Dear Jeremy,
    I've written this letter a thousand times and there's never enough room to say all I want, so I won't. I'll just tell you what I need to. I

know my leaving will be harder on you than it is on me, but I can't help that. You're what's left of me and Tom. Knowing that, even while I'm dying, fills me up with a kind of light. After what happened to your dad all I ever wanted to do was keep you safe, and I know now it was a wrong thing. I was so scared.

But I'm not afraid anymore. The Lord has brought me to a whole new place on the other side of fear and I can see forever, like that time up at Eagle Rock. It's like that when you're close to death—all the unimportant stuff just sort of falls away and you know what's real. I know now what I have to ask you to do, and I'm glad I won't be there to see it. When the time is right I want you to go find your uncle Aiden, and when you find him, stay with him. He'll try to run you off, but don't you let him. Do whatever it takes to stay with him. You have something I couldn't give him, and he has something I couldn't give you. I won't tell you what—you'll just have to find out from each other. When you find it, you'll know. Until then, don't tell him about this letter. It might take a while, but whatever happens stay the course and remember he's your father's only brother.

I'll see that Anna understands. You just go.

I love you with all my heart.

Mom

When he had finished reading he folded the letter and put it back into the envelope, then took it out and read it again. While the letter was printed neatly on two pages of his mother's pale blue stationery and every word was clear, he didn't make it back to the house for three hours. He couldn't get his mind around it. Written weeks earlier, when she still had the strength to think and write, her letter contained the dying wisdom of a woman who could not possibly mean him harm, but it was the wisdom of another world. Jeremy had inherited much of his mother's native insight, though in her last weeks she had gone beyond him, into a peace and understanding that lay outside the experience of a seventeen-year-old boy. Her instructions were perfectly plain; he understood *what* he was to do, he just didn't know *why*. The only thing she had left up to him was the timing.

When the time is right, she said. He could almost hear her voice telling him, "You'll know."

At the funeral the next day Jeremy overheard part of a conversation between three gray-haired men who had separated themselves from the crowd for a quick cigarette.

". . . the other one—you know, the one that lived. I heard he went back to mining as soon as he was able. Never missed a lick," the tall, thin one said.

"Oh yeah! Whatever happened to him?" the slick one asked. He looked like a used car salesman.

Jeremy knew the third old man, the one with the deep voice. He was a deacon in Walter and Anna's church, and he sang in the choir.

"I talked to a old boy that knows him, not two weeks ago. Said he was working a hard-rock tunnel for Murlyn & Pratt someplace down around Atlanta."

Jeremy's heart raced. Now, at precisely this time, on the heels of his mother's last request, news of his lost uncle was almost prophetic. He hadn't seen Uncle Aiden for ten years—not since the accident. Nobody had. Jeremy remembered him, but he didn't know how much of the memory was shaped by pictures he'd grown up with, snapshots of his father and Aiden together— before. He recalled odd incidents, fragments of stories, the sound of laughter, and the way his father had smiled when he was around Uncle Aiden. The light that came into his eyes.

In the sunlit darkness of his mother's funeral, news of Aiden opened a door onto the world and laid a question on Jeremy's mind: Did he have the kind of faith it would take to fling himself whole into the void? There was only one problem.

Fear.

He had never faced anything alone.

For the last ten years, in the absence of his father, his mother had kept him safe. Above all else, she had kept him safe. After his father's death Julie had gathered Jeremy tightly under her wing like a mother hen, shielding him. She had tucked him in at night and awakened him in the morning with prayers for his safety, for God's protection, for angels to hover over her only son and see that no harm came to him. She took him to church every time the doors were open; the people he'd grown up with at church formed a shell around him. Even at school he had not made a single friend outside of the kids he knew from church—partly because he didn't hide his faith, but also because he didn't participate in anything. His mother wouldn't let him go out for sports. Football and baseball were too dangerous, and he couldn't make it to practice anyway because he sacked groceries in the afternoons to help make ends meet. She had insulated him against the world the same way she'd insulated him against the snow when he was little, wrapping him in so many layers he couldn't move.

But now her voice reached out to him through the handwritten words on the pale blue page, and told him to go, to leave the only home, the only comfort, the only protection he knew. *Find your uncle,* she said, and it felt strangely like a court sentence, like banishment. Worst of all, she had left him no room for debate, no way to ask *why.* He slipped away from the funeral service to take his mother's letter from his wallet and read it again, though he had memorized it by now. He searched desperately for a loophole, but his mother had shaped these words, on this page, for him alone, while her warm soul still moved her hand, and she had left no question about what he was to do. *Just go,* she said. It contradicted everything she had said and done before, yet there it was, and it filled him with an impossible dread.

The crippling fear would not go away—he knew this—and might even grow stronger with time, as his mother's voice faded. He knew that if he did not go now, he might never do it.

The time was right.

When he got back to Walter and Anna's he looked up Murlyn & Pratt in the phone book, called them and told them he was a miner looking for work somewhere close to Atlanta. They gave him an address and told him how to find the place. He wrote a brief note and left it on the hall table for Anna the next morning before daylight—just a good-bye, for he had seen in Anna's eyes that she knew. His mother had said Anna would be told, and his mother, as always, had kept her word. He slipped out the back door with a duffel bag and sixty-three dollars.

Jeremy could have taken a bus from the mountains of eastern Tennessee down to Atlanta, but bus rides cost money, which was why the shaggy-haired boy in the baggy jeans ended up hitching a ride with a farmer in a pickup truck. The old man, wearing overalls and a CAT cap and spitting tobacco juice out the window at regular intervals, had obviously picked up Jeremy to have somebody to talk to, but Jeremy didn't say a whole lot. He didn't have to. Mostly he stared out the window, nodding occasionally, laughing when it was called for, now and then priming the pump with a question about the old man's farm or his coon dogs or his new Santa Gertrudis bull. He wanted to talk, so Jeremy listened. Mile after mile the hardwood forests of the Great Smokies hunched over the twisting two-lane highway, filtering the light so that Jeremy felt as if he had rolled down through the mountains in an endless green tunnel full of words. The old farmer prattled all the way down to Benton, where he was going to look at a used hay baler.

Two rides later Jeremy found himself just short of Chatsworth, Georgia, where, because the sun was about to go down, he shouldered his duffel bag, turned aside from the road and headed uphill into the woods to look for a place to camp. Alone in the world, he was in no particular hurry, and everything he owned was in the duffel bag.

The hills around Chatsworth were round and tree-covered like the mountains back home. But these were just hills, oddly steep, rising precipitously like dull teeth, a last barrier before the mountains receded into the flatlands. Ten minutes of climbing brought Jeremy to a level spot where a shelf of rock stuck out far enough to provide shelter in case it rained during the night. It was here he dropped his bag, where he could see nothing but woods around him.

Rummaging through his duffel bag for a plastic jug, he cut across the hill until he found a trickle of a brook and filled the jug. With the last of the daylight he foraged several armloads of dry firewood and used his feet to sweep the leaves back so the fire wouldn't spread, then built a small campfire. He sat cross-legged in front of the little rock shelf and ate a dinner of peanut butter and crackers, washing it down with spring water. Lying back against his bag with his hands folded behind his head, he watched a screech owl shake and ruffle itself awake, listened to the squirrels skittering through the leaves, and felt the evening trickle into the valley. Dim memories of his father came to him here, memories of camping in places like this when he was very small. He could almost hear his father's voice, talking softly, his face hanging in the firelight, about life and work and fishing.

But as the light failed, the realization pressed in upon him: he was utterly alone. Fear tiptoed in on the darkness and he listened hard, his ears tuned to catch the slightest rustling and turn it into footsteps. To distract himself, he tugged an old Bible from his bag and opened it. It had been his mother's; the margins were littered with her cramped handwriting, and every worn page bore underlines and brackets and other signs of her passing. She had told him once that you could tell a lot about a person by looking at the dirty parts in their Bible, then she had laughed and shown him places she'd visited so many times that the pages were smudged brown and worried soft—dirty.

Closing the book, he parted his hands and let it fall open naturally so that it showed him, of its own accord, the place she had visited most often, right in the middle. It was the dirtiest place, and he knew the underlined words without having to read them. He had last heard them when he was standing beside her bed in the hospital. With his forearm resting on the rail so he could hold her soft, spent hand, he had finally asked her the most pressing question.

"Aren't you afraid?"

She had smiled then, and there was pain in it. She spoke in that unnaturally high, breathy voice that came near the end.

"Not anymore," she said. She squeezed his hand with the little strength she had left. "But I know about pain now, and I know it can only go so far. It's not the dying that scares you, it's the not knowing." And then she had quoted the words from the place she visited most often, speaking them to Jeremy as if she owned them, and looking straight through him.

Raising the Bible up against his face now, he pressed his nose into it and breathed deeply. He could still smell her there, faintly. Sitting cross-legged, he tilted the book toward the campfire to catch the flickering light and read the words: *"Yea, though I walk through the valley of the shadow of death, I will fear no evil: for Thou art with me."*

The valley of the shadow. He had gone into it with her, and though he knew she was safe now and beyond the pain, he felt that he had not entirely found his own way out again. He wasn't sure he ever would.

For a long time he sat searching out the dirty pages, the familiar places his mother's hands had smudged with repeated visits, reading until his eyelids grew heavy.

Burrowed into his sleeping bag, he slept as one who has no place else to be, and the stars kissed his sleep like a mother.

South of Atlanta, a machine the size of a house churned its way through the earth. Two hundred feet underground, the monster cored a perfectly round hole, ripping and tearing through solid granite, emitting a steady stream of gravel. All about the machine and its vast support structure far beneath the surface, helmeted men moved ghostlike through a haze of dust, Cimmerians, oblivious to the noise.

The impossible earth-shattering, soul-grinding noise.

Menendez didn't seem big enough to scream a scream that could rise above such a roar.

Snake heard it first. He and Griff were standing on the trailing gear fifty feet behind the machine, talking in abbreviated sentences, cupped hands around mouths, shouting into each other's ear.

The operator must have heard it too, because the machine stopped with the flip of a switch, everything groaning to a halt in a matter of seconds. Framed by this new and shocking silence, it was truly an admirable scream. Men scuttled like ants from a kicked anthill—running, climbing, pointing, shouting—all moving up and forward.

Snake knew his men, and he knew what had happened even

before he went up the ladder to the conveyor: Menendez had snagged his hand in a roller. Stopping at the base of the steel ladder, Snake grabbed Ripley by the shirtsleeve and whispered something to him. The electrician nodded and headed for the motor control cabinet as Snake started up the ladder.

By the time he got there four men had already gathered around Menendez, who was kneeling on the catwalk with his left arm jammed up to the shoulder underneath the conveyor belt. Sweat poured from his pale face. His scream dropped to an agonized moan as he squirmed for a position to ease the pressure on his crushed arm.

Snake squatted next to him and peered under the conveyor, studying the arm, the thick black belt, the steel roller. He took off his helmet and rubbed his bald head. Burn scars had replaced much of Snake's scalp, and he kept the remaining tufts of hair shaved. The left side of his head, the side facing Menendez, was missing an ear, and the skin graft covering the left side of his face and merging with his scarred scalp had a distinctly reptilian appearance. His mouth was a lipless slit, and the shrinking of scar tissue had given his eyes a peculiar slant.

"You're lucky it wasn't the end roller," Snake said. "You'd be hamburger."

"Or missing an arm," Griff added. Even grizzled old Griff winced at the thought.

Nanny Grubs, a mule of a man, knelt behind Menendez with an arm around his chest, trying to help him hold his weight off the trapped arm. Over Menendez's shoulder Nanny asked, "Boss, you want us to cut the belt?"

Snake shook his head. "The company gets paid for footage, Nanny—a hundred dollars an inch. It would take an hour to get another belt in here and fit it. One hour of downtime works out to six thousand dollars that the company isn't making, while you keep drawing your wages. You think he's worth six grand, Nanny? He's kind of small." He looked Menendez full in the face. The man was fighting to remain conscious, his eyes threatening to roll back. Black hair splayed down his forehead and drops of sweat dangled from the ends.

"I'll tell you what, amigo," Snake grunted, pushing himself to his feet, "I'm about tired of this. This is the third time in two weeks you've got yourself or somebody else in a bind, all because you don't listen. I told you to keep your hands away from the rollers. You can adjust them with a hammer—I don't understand why you need to get your fingers in the way."

Questioning glances ricocheted between the men.

Snake leaned a palm against an angle-iron post, thumbing the switch box mounted on the face of it. On the front of the switch box were two buttons, one red and one green—the stop-start buttons for the conveyor. Glancing at his boots, at the ceiling, then back toward the trailing gear, feigning an internal debate, Snake was pretty sure nobody else saw Ripley step out from the big gray cabinet down on the control deck and give him the okay sign. Ripley's handlebar mustache lifted in a wry grin.

A drop of water plopped into a puddle in the bottom, and the sound echoed off the walls. Snake looked at Griff. His mouth twitched; his thumb toyed with the green button.

"What do you say, Griff? Let's just run his sorry hide on through and see what comes out the other side."

Menendez's head jerked upright, his eyes widened and his mouth flew open. Griff, shaking his head no, started to reach for Snake's arm, but before he could take a step the thumb surged into the button and the conveyor jolted to life.

The belt, now running in reverse, spit Menendez out on top of Nanny and then shut down as quickly as it had started up. Nanny whooped and tumbled backward with Menendez; Geech and Travis jumped across the conveyor to help but collided with each other and went down in a tangled pile on top of Nanny. Griff collapsed on the catwalk in a fit of laughter, and Menendez, after one piercing wail, took a deep, shuddering breath and passed out cold.

By the time they got Menendez down off of the machine and onto the flatcar for the long ride out of the tunnel, he was conscious again and railing steadily. From the shrillness of his voice and the jabbing finger of his good hand, Snake could tell the venomous flood would have been immensely entertaining, not to mention educational, if he'd been able to understand Spanish. Both bones in Menendez's forearm were broken, his wrist bent at a peculiar angle. He cradled it gingerly across his chest when the loki stopped at the bottom of the vertical shaft and he had to get up and walk over to the man-lift, the lightweight, rickety cage that served as an elevator. When the man-lift clattered to a stop at the top of the two-hundred-foot shaft, Snake escorted Menendez across the yard to the front of the machine shop, where the paramedics took over and made him lie down on a gurney. Just before they loaded him into the ambulance he switched to English—probably, Snake figured, because he had exhausted his vast store of Spanish profanity.

"You *crazy*, Snakeface! You need to get you some help, man! You *loco*! You the devil! I hope your dog dies! God will *get* you one day, you—"

The tirade was snuffed in midsentence when Snake leaned over, grabbed the sides of the gurney, and went nose to nose with him.

"God already got me," Snake hissed. His misshapen nostrils flared, his scar-sloped eyes raged and he tapped the broken wrist with a forefinger. "You think this is bad? I'll tell you what, amigo—you go to hell. And after you fight your way back from hell, then we'll talk. *Then* we'll have something in common."

He let go and straightened up, breathing heavily, eyes smoldering.

Waving the gurney on, he snapped at the stunned paramedics, "Get him out of here!"

As the ambulance drove away, he could hear Menendez through the closed doors, railing afresh, "I QUIT, Snakeface! You can *have* this stinking job! I QUIIIIIIT!"

Snake stood there for a long time after the ambulance left, listening to the night. The yard was quiet except for the gentle clattering of granite chips pouring in waves onto the slag pile and the rhythmic thumping of the tray lift like an industrial heartbeat in the night, steady and hard. He couldn't feel it, but he knew there must be a light breeze because he didn't smell the sewage treatment plant across the way. The air was fresh for a change, but it didn't help his mood.

Something had wounded him. Menendez's words had impaled him, without warning, unleashing the rage he tried so hard to suppress.

"God will get you."

Tom.

Tom had said that to him years ago. More than once. *Tom.* Even now, the memory struck remorse into his chest and pumped it inexorably to his limbs. He felt heavy. Jamming his hands into his pockets he started walking, away from the hole, avoiding the company of friends and brothers, for they would dull the pain and drown the memory in laughter, and he did not want that now. Sometimes, when it came over him late at night, he wanted only to carry the pain and let it carry him. It was the least he could do. It was all he could do.

Beyond the lay-down yard he walked, following the horseshoe curve of the perimeter road, past the hog house and the office trailers, past mountains of pipe and giant reels of cable, past a junkyard of what looked like broken and rusty dinosaur parts, around by the entry gate and back up the slight rise toward the treatment plant, not knowing where he was going. Just walking. Remembering.

In darkness he walked toward the flame.

The ten-foot-high flame sprouted from the conical roof of a squat, round, concrete structure nestled in the gentle slope at the near edge of the plant. It had always been there, lashing delicately and continuously at the night sky. He had seen it from a distance, wondered about it absently, but had never been drawn to it until now, when he walked toward it precisely because he was not thinking of it. His mind was elsewhere, watching Tom make a perfect cast through the morning mist on a lake a hundred miles and a lifetime away, and hearing that clear, guileless laugh when a bass rose to take the twitching lure. It was some elemental thing, deeper than a thought process, that drew Snake to the flame. He stopped in the road a few paces from the round green building, staring up at it. The flame stared back.

He had adored Tom, though he never quite understood him. Tom was the sort nobody ever played practical jokes on because nothing bothered him. When they short-sheeted his bunk at summer camp he just lay down on top of the sheet and went right to sleep. Fishing, he had the patience of a stone, working the john-boat into every creek mouth and around every stump, casting into every hole with the expectant eyes of a child, even after a long day without so much as a nibble. When the jocks at school roughed up "Tooty" Potimkin in the hallway until he spilled the contents of the mysterious gym bag he always carried, it was Tom who stepped in without a word, without confrontation of any kind, and calmly helped Tooty pick up his seashells and put them back in the bag. Hundreds of them. By the time he'd finished, the jocks were all gone. If you asked him, Tom would shrug and say his attitude came from his faith in God—a faith he seemed to wear like an old pair of jeans—but Snake fervently hoped it had been a delusion. If Tom's God was real, He would almost certainly have a bone to pick with Snake.

Listen! Your brother's blood cries out to me from the ground.

Snake stared at the flame, drawn, as all men are, by the mystery at the heart of the living fire, and repulsed, as few are, by having once known fire in its swollen wrath. The flame licked at the darkness; shards of blue and orange and pale yellow intertwined, leaped upward, snapped off and disappeared. Like lives.

When the shift ended, Snake pulled a slouch hat hard down on his head and threw on a long-sleeved shirt before he left the hog house.

His truck was the newest one in the gravel parking lot, a charcoal gray king cab with all the bells and whistles. He told the guys he bought the truck with all the money he saved by staying away from women, and there was more than a little truth in it. He loved the smell of the leather seats and the rich sound of the stereo system. He'd never had a truck with a CD player before. He could close the doors and roll up the dark-tinted windows, crank up Jackson Browne or Van Morrison and escape for a while.

Always the old stuff. He had no patience with what passed for music these days. Like so many other things, he'd outgrown it somehow. In the burn unit he had fallen into an abyss where the need for one more breath became the pinpoint focus of his considerable will, and the outer layers of his life had peeled away along with his face. After that, after all that, he simply had no interest in pop music made by dancing people with microphones glued to their heads and fireworks in the background. Likewise, much of what passed for country music had become transparently commercial—the clichéd, repetitive lyrics insulting his intelligence in the same way as daytime television. He couldn't quite say why, but he knew it had something to do with adversity, with knowing what it took to stay alive. He wanted to tell them all to stop their whining. If you're gonna be dumb, you gotta be tough.

This particular night he went straight for Linda Ronstadt. It was that kind of night. He needed to bleed and he knew she could make the cut.

The ice-blue LED lights of the dashboard clock clicked over to midnight on the way home, reminding him he needed a few groceries. The big grocery store stayed open all night, which suited him perfectly. After midnight there were seldom more than two or three people in the whole place, and he could avoid them easily enough. But he couldn't avoid the plump young girl working the only open register. She tried to look at him once, but couldn't manage it. Keeping his face down and his hat brim low to make it easier on her, he swiped his debit card and took his bags without a word, without a touch. Even the doors moved out of his way as he escaped into the night.

Snake lived in an old brick three-story office building that had been converted to apartments when the shifting tides of society left it awash on the outskirts of prosperity. The current landlords had bought it cheaply years ago, remodeled it and rented it out, mostly to the students of a small college just up the road. Pulling into the parking lot, he passed Geech's old pickup truck and fishing boat, parked side by side. Geech lived by himself on the first floor of the same building, though on the opposite side of the stairwell.

The elevator didn't work. From the layers of peeling, dry-rotted masking tape on the hand-lettered *Out of Order* sign, Snake figured it hadn't worked since the lawyers abandoned the original office space. Exhausted, he trudged up to the third floor.

Inside his apartment he bolted the door, took off his hat,

popped open a beer and picked up the remote, but after one pass through the channels he gave up and turned off the television. He started to put on a record, then changed his mind; sometimes silence demanded to be heard. He picked up a log he'd been thinking about carving on. It had cured long enough, and he'd taken it to work the night before and sawed the bottom flat. It looked like a small stick of firewood cut in half, but an upraised limb nearly as thick as the trunk rose out of it, and the angle and proportion of the limb held a potential for something unusual. He would make something of it as soon as he decided. Sitting on the edge of a chair and placing a trash can between his feet, he started shaving away the bark. It didn't take long to peel the limb clean, only he still could not see what he would make of it. His heart was in it but his mind was not, and it was not in his nature to begin a thing without knowing how it would end.

Finally, he sighed and shoved both the log and the trash can under the desk, turned off the lights, and stood at the window watching the night creatures flit like moths through a pool of streetlight: a lurching wino whose feet could never quite catch up with his center of gravity; a streetwalker in high-heeled white boots flinging obscene gestures after a man in a black Lincoln who slowed and said something and sped away; a wiry, streetwise dog pacing confidently through the light, watching his flanks; a dark cat flowing quickly across the lit ground to merge with the sheltering darkness of a weeded lot. A dry smile flickered across Snake's face when it occurred to him that, though he had something in common with all of them, the creature who stirred the strongest feeling of kinship was the cat.

But there was no comfort in it. He gave up and went to bed, pulling the covers up over his head to try and shut out the light from the streetlamp.

CHAPTER 2

A far country.

Jeremy awoke with the birds before dawn, and the first thing that came to his mind was his mother: the way she had always greeted the day. Poking his head out of the sleeping bag he whispered, "Morning, God."

After choking down a few more peanut butter crackers and an apple he rolled his sleeping bag, brushed his teeth, poured the remainder of the water on the embers of last night's fire, shouldered his bag and picked his way back down the hill by the first purple light.

Back out on the highway a steady stream of cars and trucks passed him by. Struggling up a long hill with the strap chafing at his shoulder he wondered why nobody would pick him up, but he figured most of them were on their way to work at the textile mills and didn't have time for hitchhikers. And then he realized what he must look like in the dawning light, wearing grungy, slept-in clothes. By the time the sun winked through the trees he had given up holding out his thumb, shortened his stride and settled into a pace that his legs could handle for the long haul. Already he was discovering the therapeutic value of distance, second only to time for healing wounds. He was young, and the world lay wide in front of him, terrifying and exhilarating.

A pearl white Lexus roared past with its brake lights glaring, slowed, and pulled half off the road as it stopped. The man behind the wheel motioned hurriedly. Jeremy unslung his bag as he broke into a trot to catch up. After the standard short exchange revealed that the man was going all the way to Atlanta, Jeremy tossed his bag in the back seat and climbed in.

Perry looked like something from a catalog—tightly groomed hair, starched white shirt tailored to fit his chiseled frame, power tie, high-dollar slacks and shoes, teeth flashing impossibly white against a well-maintained tan. He had an uncommon energy about him, constantly drumming his fingers on the steering wheel in time to Miles Davis. As they rolled smoothly southward, he asked Jeremy all about himself—where he was from, why he had left, all about his mother's illness, the fiasco at Walter and Anna's and what he planned to do with his life.

Jeremy shrugged. "I haven't really thought much about what to do after I find my uncle," he said. Sometimes a person needed to go through a door to find out what was on the other side of it. "I guess I'll have to get a job somewhere."

"What do you do?"

Another shrug. He could do pretty much anything anybody showed him how to do, but Perry's starched collar, the power tie, the slightly sad and condescending smile all said a green kid out of Tennessee with no diploma and no skills was destined to wear a paper hat and take orders for burgers through a headset. Jeremy wasn't about to post "bag boy" as his occupation.

"I like working with my hands," he said. "I worked on a new office building last summer."

"Really? Doing what? Electrical? Plumbing?" Perry was relentless. He looked straight ahead with a knowing smile.

Jeremy stared out the window for a minute, expressionless, remembering the blue hard hat he had worn. Everybody had to be classified: pipe fitters and plumbers wore red, electricians yellow, carpenters gray, supervision white. Laborers—common laborers, those who swept floors and set up scaffolding and dug ditches and hauled away debris—wore blue. The guys on the job said you could tell a man's IQ by the color of his hat. Jeremy took a secret delight in recalling what old Henry had told him once about a particularly abusive white-hat.

"The man wants you to know he's smarter than you," Henry had told him in a conspiratorial whisper, then tapped his own hard hat with a forefinger. *"But if he's wearing a plastic bucket on his head, you and me both know—he ain't no genius either."*

"I was just a laborer," Jeremy finally said. "But it paid pretty good, for a summer job."

The condescending smile stayed, although Perry didn't pursue the subject any further. They passed a sign bearing the words *Welcome to White, Georgia,* followed immediately by a sign reducing the speed limit to 35.

Perry tapped the brakes, disengaging the cruise control. "These little towns are all speed traps," he said. "Hey, you hungry? How about some breakfast? I'm buying."

"Well, yeah, I guess I could eat a bite." Jeremy could always eat a bite.

Buddy's White Restaurant, the sign on the roof of the old frame building said, and the double entendre wasn't lost on Jeremy, though Perry didn't seem to notice. He had no detectable accent; Jeremy figured he grew up someplace else. He definitely wasn't from around here.

Buddy's White Restaurant obviously hadn't changed in years, with its black-and-white checkerboard floor, Formica tabletops, and red vinyl stools on chrome pedestals at the counter. Two of

the seats wore duct-tape patches. Jeremy ordered a stack of pancakes and a Coke. Perry scanned a menu heavy on eggs, bacon,
Streak-O-Lean, pork chops and hash browns, everything fried.

"Would you happen to have raisin bran?" he asked the waitress, whose pencil poised unmoving above her pad.

She pursed her lips, shook her head.

"How about oatmeal?" Perry said, trying again. "The old-fashioned, five-minute kind."

Another small shake of the head.

"English muffin?"

"I can do that," she said, her pencil stirring.

"Whole wheat?"

"Ahh . . . no."

"All right, then. An English muffin, strawberry preserves, no
butter, and a glass of orange juice."

"No coffee?"

"I don't *do* coffee." He said it a little too emphatically, as if she
should have known. As soon as she left the table Perry turned his
attention back to Jeremy.

"So tell me about this uncle of yours, Jeremy. What does he
do?"

"He's a miner."

"In Atlanta? I didn't know there was any coal around Atlanta.
Maybe up in the mountains or in north Alabama, but not in
Atlanta."

"It's not coal mining, it's hard-rock tunneling. Like highway
tunnels and stuff. It's what my dad did until he got killed."

"Yes, you mentioned that your father was dead, but you never
said how. What happened to him? Cave-in?"

Jeremy shook his head. "There was an explosion, that's all I
really know. I don't think he was even underground when it happened."

"How long ago was this?"

"Ten years. Uncle Aiden got burned too. He left town after he got out of the hospital and never came back. He wasn't married or anything, so I guess he just decided to book."

"Like you."

Not exactly, but Jeremy figured his mother's letter was none of Perry's business. He nodded. "Yeah, like me, I guess. I don't know a whole lot about him, really. Mom never talked about him." This was true, and it had left Jeremy with an uneasy feeling. His mother had never been one to talk about people behind their backs; if she didn't like somebody she just didn't talk about them at all, and she didn't talk about Aiden. It was as if he had died along with Jeremy's dad.

"You haven't seen him in ten years?"

"No."

"You haven't talked to him? He doesn't know you're coming?"

"No."

"How do you know he'll take you in?"

Jeremy shrugged. "I don't."

"So you're all alone—completely alone in the world, at seventeen? Wow, that's tough." There was a look of genuine compassion in Perry's eyes, and he laid his hand softly on top of Jeremy's as he spoke.

The gesture took Jeremy by surprise. He wasn't sure it meant anything at all, and at that precise moment the waitress arrived to break the tension, sliding a plate of pancakes in front of him. It gave him an excuse to retract his hand, and it gave him something to look at besides Perry. He was away from home now, out of his element. He expected to encounter new things, strange people, and he didn't want to misinterpret them. Best not to overreact.

Back on the road the talk turned to baseball and the Braves' chances in the playoffs without a real first baseman, and Jeremy forgot his momentary discomfort in Buddy's White Restaurant—dismissed it as an illusion, a misunderstanding. But an hour later, as they approached the city, Perry grew quiet and thoughtful.

"Jeremy," he said at last, "what if you can't find your uncle? What if he doesn't want you? You don't have any money or any prospects of any kind, do you?"

"I, uh . . . I don't know. I guess I haven't really thought it out. Why?"

"Well, I was just thinking. I like you. You're a good kid. A bright kid."

Jeremy smiled.

"I'd say it's about time you caught a break."

"I heard *that*," Jeremy puffed.

"And I was thinking, I've got this big place in town and I'm all alone in it. You could stay with me if you like. There's a lot of space—you could have your own room, no strings. You could maybe go back and finish school."

Jeremy didn't move, didn't speak, but alarm bells were clanging in his head. He had no idea how to react. He had a nasty suspicion that there were indeed some strings attached, but he was a young country boy, short on clues. The only thing he knew for certain was that he didn't know much. Distrustful of his own suspicions, he squirmed and tried to think.

Perry spoke quietly. "What do you say, Jeremy? You and me. I think we could be good together." Smiling, he reached over and laid his hand casually on Jeremy's thigh.

Jeremy stared at the hand, wondering briefly if he'd unconsciously said or done anything to mislead this man. He cleared his throat.

"Please take your hand off of me," he said, and his voice shook.

"What are you afraid of, Jeremy? I would never hurt you."
Perry was still smiling, and his hand squeezed Jeremy's thigh.

"Please move your hand," Jeremy repeated. He heard the quavering panic in his own voice. The next thing he heard, to his great surprise, was his own voice praying loudly for deliverance from this evil. And he kept on, because he was afraid if he didn't keep praying he might start crying.

Anger flashed in Perry's face, and he jerked his hand away. Gripping the wheel tightly he whipped the car to the right, into the emergency lane, and skidded to a stop next to the concrete retaining wall. Cars whizzed by at seventy miles an hour a few feet away, rocking the Lexus in their backwash.

"Get out," he said.

Jeremy stared at him, blinked. They had almost reached downtown Atlanta, a long, long way from Jeremy's comfort zone. He had seen glimpses of the skyline over the trees ahead.

"GET OUT!" Perry yelled.

Jeremy opened the door and stepped out of the air-conditioned car into a wave of August heat. He was reaching for the back door when the Lexus screeched away and merged into the traffic, disappearing in seconds.

With his duffel bag.

He chased after it for a few steps, waving his arms and shouting, but the Lexus was gone, just like that. Cars whipped by and hamburger wrappers trotted past his feet until finally he took a deep breath, shoved his hands into his pockets, and started walking. He knew better than to try to hitch a ride on the expressway, especially in the middle of a city, so he headed for the exit ramp a half mile ahead. The August sun assaulted him, tiny pieces of grit lashed the back of his neck in the wake of the passing cars, and exhaust fumes burned his eyes. Straight overhead the sky was white with haze, but the horizon was an odd shade of brown.

It was a strange land, vast and complex and pitiless. Jeremy had met his first great obstacle and suffered his first crushing defeat, so he did the only thing he could: he put one foot in front of the other. One thing at a time—one simple thing. Get off the expressway, then worry about what to do next. He tried not to think about his duffel bag, his few changes of clothes, his meager possessions.

His mother's Bible.

He had still felt attached, somehow, even adrift in the wide world, so long as he'd had his duffel bag with him, a portable slice of home. Now he felt like a snail without its shell, lost and vulnerable. At least he still had the sixty-three dollars in his wallet; he had managed to get this far without spending a penny.

South. When he finally got off the expressway he knew he was on the north side of town, and he needed to get to the south side.

He'd never been to Atlanta. This was his first ground-level view, walking south on a street humming with life on a scale he had never encountered, sleek European cars dodging between service trucks laden with tool bins and pipe and ladders, hardhats and suits headed for lunch at fast-food restaurants, people walking, running, riding bikes, everything moving, everybody going someplace. He passed a construction site and watched through the fence for a bit as a big track-hoe clawed chunks of concrete from the remaining half of a dead building that reminded him of the bombing site in Oklahoma City. The big diesel puffed and rumbled, the bucket swung, and a load of jagged concrete and steel crashed grinding and creaking into the back of a dump truck. Two hardhats stood next to the fence sharing a blueprint, watching the past crumble, planning the future.

Jeremy kept his hands in his pockets and moved on. Uncle Walter had once told him you have to be careful in the city; there are muggers on every corner, and if you keep your hands in your pockets they leave you alone because they think you might have a gun.

He passed warehouses, tire places, auto shops advertising an expertise in Bavarian imports, wrought-iron manufacturers, antique dealers, palm readers, squat old clapboard houses, and every so often a beautiful old stone or brick church building with stained-glass windows. Settled as they were between the industrial concerns at the city's edge, the venerable churches spoke to something deep inside Jeremy. They too looked sadly out of place.

After a mile or so the road crossed the railroad tracks and started up a long hill between two tall chain link fences. Behind the fences on either side lay the huge ponds, the manicured lawns, and the maze of pipe that made up the city waterworks. Topping the rise, Jeremy got his first clear view of the entire city skyline. He stopped and stared at it for a long time. It was a daunting sight, a jagged picket fence at the edge of the world.

Just beyond the waterworks the D.O.T. was tearing up part of the street. Striped barrels cordoned off a lane; one guy wrestled with a jackhammer while two others in orange vests leaned on shovels and told each other jokes in the shade of an oak tree. Jeremy fished the piece of paper from his pocket and read the directions he had written down, the path to his uncle. The street names on his piece of paper made no sense to him without a point of reference. In desperation he walked right up to the two guys leaning on their shovels.

"Um, excuse me," he said. "I'm a little off track and I was wondering if one of y'all could tell me how to get to Sweetbriar Creek."

The dark-skinned guy shook his head, shrugged. "I don't know too much about dat." He talked like Justin Wilson, the Cajun cook on TV.

The other one, a tall, thin guy with sunken cheeks, said, "What's it close to?"

Jeremy handed him the piece of paper. He pushed his hard hat back and studied it for a minute, then whistled.

"You ain't off track, Gomer, you're a lost ball in a wheat field. You need to get to Moreland Avenue. You're on the wrong side of town."

Jeremy nodded, swallowed. "Okay. Can you tell me how to get there?"

The tall man began to point and rattle off a list of street names and places to turn. Jeremy was immediately lost, but he kept on nodding as if he understood. He gathered only that it was a long way and that it was generally south and east. The dark-skinned guy watched his face, read his confusion and interrupted.

"You got a ride?" he asked.

Jeremy shook his head, reluctantly.

"You got money?"

"Some."

"Then you best gid you a taxi and tell him to take you there, boy. Don't you mess wi' dat city."

"How far is it?" Jeremy asked.

The Cajun shrugged. "Maybe only eight mile, or six like the crow fly—but you ain' no crow. Kid like you? You go down there by yo'self alone, you gid yo butt whupped and yo chicken took."

"He's right," the tall one said. "Take a cab. Probably cost you a bundle, but it'll be worth it in the long run."

Jeremy bit his lip, folded the piece of paper and stuck it back in his pocket. "Thanks," he said. "I might just do that." But the money was the only thing between him and starvation; he would cling to it like a life preserver. He walked south, putting one foot in front of the other.

What Snake had always liked about the Asian couple down-stairs was that they were quiet. He knew nothing else about them, apart from the fact that the man ran out with a book bag every morning, presumably to the local college. Snake rarely saw the woman; now and then he might get a glimpse of her from the window, crossing the lot with a bag of groceries. She had blue-black hair not quite to the shoulders and she was pretty, in a por-celain sort of way, but she held herself very closely. She was always very businesslike in her straight dresses and flat shoes, walking quickly and without any sort of feminine flair, slightly stoop-shouldered, never raising her face, never looking about. She seemed somehow concave. Snake mentally dubbed her the China Girl and catalogued her as a curious recluse like himself. Beyond that, he rarely thought about her at all.

Until that morning.

The man—her husband, or whatever he was—usually came home right before Snake left for work; Snake would hear the echo of his footsteps on the stairs and the turning of his key around two in the afternoon. Apart from the front door noises reverberating up the hollow stairwell, the Asian couple never made a sound, never cranked up the volume on the stereo or TV, never shouted at each other like a young American couple would have done.

But on this particular morning Snake awoke to the sound of furniture grinding across the floor downstairs. He thought at first they were moving out. Apartment dwellers are transient by defi-nition; somebody was always coming or going. While dragging himself out of bed and putting on a pot of coffee he heard more noises, loud voices. He looked out the window expecting to see a moving van, but there was none. There was only a young guy in shorts and sneakers raising the lift gate on an empty two-ton stake-bed truck, climbing in and driving off. Snake shrugged and went to get dressed.

He had poured a second cup of coffee and sat down on the couch to look at the half log he wanted to carve when the first glissando came rippling up through the concrete to tell him what had been delivered on the truck. He rolled his eyes. The bane of a swing-shift miner's existence, the very worst thing imaginable, was a pianist in the apartment downstairs. This would probably mean war.

He tried to concentrate on the carving, but the piano made it impossible, so he finally gave it up. He was about to go get the broom so he could thump on the floor with the handle when it dawned on him that what he was hearing was very good. He didn't know if it was good because it had been filtered through concrete or because of some peculiar acoustic property of the old building, but the sound coming up to him seemed, at least to his untrained ear, stunningly, extraordinarily beautiful.

Somehow he knew it was the girl. It was the China Girl, not her husband. The music rising through the floor was classical. Snake had no knowledge of classical music, but he was on intimate terms with melancholy. The notes dipped and climbed and chased each other all over the sky like a flock of swallows; there was nothing sad about the music itself, but there was something in the playing of it that his soul recognized immediately, though if you had asked him he could not have described it in a lifetime. The melancholy came from the ends of the pianist's fingers, rose up through the floor and pierced him like an ice pick.

He sat very still for a long time, his middle finger keeping time on the arm of the chair. Then, very gently, so as not to make a noise, he lay down on the floor and put his good ear to the rug. The slowing of a trill, the exquisite spaces between the notes, that one little note left hanging out there all by itself at the end—these things reached him, and they turned inside him like drill steel. No, it couldn't be the man—the stern-faced marionette Snake had seen coming home from the college with such rigid discipline on his thin lips and no-nonsense purpose in his stride—this was music plucked and resonating on the same steel wire that ran through Snake's marrow. He lay with his eyes closed, listening, while the coffee maker timed out and turned itself off.

The sign in front of the bank said ninety degrees at ten o'clock.

Jeremy had spent a summer in south Georgia once, when he was small and his mother had worked there briefly, and he knew the burnt-out end of August in Georgia could be malevolent. By midmorning a thin gray haze squatted on the land, obscuring the horizon and diffusing the light so that the bleached earth outshined the sky and assaulted squinting eyes from unexpected angles. A man working outside walked slowly, drank often and carried five pounds of sweat in his clothes from nine in the morning until dusk, when it dried to little white maps of salt. But these were only the physical effects. Sometimes the ninety-eight-degree days and eighty-degree nights would chain themselves together for a week or two in a relentless siege on the psyche. A Northerner tasting a Georgia August thought it to be the penalty for being a Southerner. A native thought of it as a fair price for not being a Yankee.

Jeremy worked his way down the winding streets of Atlanta, staying to the shadows when he could, turning always south and east, until he found himself on the relatively shady sidewalks in front of the Georgia Tech campus. Blocky student apartment buildings intermingled with old brick houses, the kind with two sets of steps—one going up onto the porch and the other at the outer edge of the lawn, descending through the retaining wall onto the sidewalk at street level. Magnolias and maples overhung the sidewalk, and the shade helped, but there was still not a breath of wind.

The sun burst in on him full force as he crossed the bridge over the expressway. Though too early for lunch, he had walked off his breakfast and was starving, so he stopped in at a big hamburger joint just across the bridge. The place looked interesting at first, but the people who took his order acted rude, yelling at him to have his money in his hand and make up his mind or get out of line. He felt as though he'd landed in New York, an impression reinforced by the observation that nobody else seemed to object to such treatment. The Cajun was right: this was a different world.

The hamburger tasted like shoe leather, so he followed it with a chili dog, washing it all down with roughly a gallon of Coke and lingering as long as possible in the air-conditioning before finally forcing himself back out onto the shimmering sidewalk.

Resuming his pattern of going a block or two south, then a block or two east, he saw that he was clearly going to skirt the worst of the ominous downtown cluster of skyscrapers, but now another problem arose. He felt queasy even before he left the hamburger joint, but now, out in the sun, the heat rippling from the concrete beat against him in waves and the chili dog did a breast-stroke across the sea of Coke in his stomach.

Squinting against the light, his head spinning, his stomach rumbling, he turned east on a narrow street and his feet thudded heavily downhill on the sidewalk. Tilting his head back to fight the impulse to hurl, he wasn't watching where he was going. He tripped over something and sprawled face forward on the side-walk. Rolling over, sitting up, rubbing a skinned place on his head, he noticed for the first time the line of ragged people hud-dled in a narrow strip of shade cast by the low retaining wall beside a parking lot. He had tripped over somebody's feet.

One of them was staring at him—a black man, probably forty years old, half bald, with a wild beard radiating from a pocked face. The face leaned forward out of the shadow and the man flowed smoothly onto all fours, creeping, dragging a black trash bag with him, until he was mere inches from Jeremy's face. His smell preceded him.

"You all right, bro?" he said. His eyes widened and his head tilted like a dog.

Jeremy nodded. "Just lost," he said.

"Where you want to go?" the man asked. He was missing a few teeth. His lips had to exaggerate a little to make the words come out right.

"Sweetbriar Creek."

The man looked down the street and his lips pushed up in thought until his nose wrinkled. He shook his head.

"You all alone?" he asked, and an eyebrow went up.

Jeremy nodded.

"I never heard of no Sweetbriar Creek. Let's go ax Big Game. He'll know."

The man rose to his feet clutching his garbage bag in a fist, the bottom of it swinging just clear of the ground. He was bare-footed and his feet were grimy. The seams of his pants were split up to his knees and they swished and flapped against each other as he swaggered down the sidewalk. Jeremy got to his feet and followed him, rubbing his head, checking his fingertips for blood. He noticed that the other people leaning back against the wall pulled their feet in to make way for the man with the garbage bag.

The wall beside them rose higher as they went down the sidewalk, then turned abruptly before they reached the street, revealing a small dirt lot carved out of the corner of the block with parking lots above it on two sides. Small trees planted in a neat row along the sidewalks shaded the figures of eight or ten homeless people, sleeping curled around their bundles. In the corner where the two walls met, a man in dreadlocks sat cross-legged talking to a very large blond-haired man whose forehead was crosshatched with scars. The big one looked like a TV wrestler.

"Big Game!" the garbage man said, holding out his fist to the man with the dreadlocks.

Dreadlocks rose to his feet, meeting the fist with his own while keeping his eyes on Jeremy.

"My man here needs to know how to get to, uh . . ." The garbage man looked at Jeremy.

"Sweetbriar Creek," Jeremy said. "There's a water treatment plant or something. It's off of Moreland Avenue."

"Oh, yeah, all right. Where you from, boy?"

Big Game was still smiling, but Jeremy sensed an ominous tone. Then he realized with a sinking feeling that the large man with the scars on his forehead had risen and moved quietly behind him, alongside the garbage man.

"Tennessee," Jeremy said, and the pitch of his voice went up a notch.

"*Ten*nessee," Big Game mimicked, feigning a rolling drawl and smiling at the garbage man. "You know he ain't lyin'. Tell by the way he says it—accent on the *Ten*." His eyes turned back to Jeremy as he edged closer and the smile changed, morphed into something unmistakably sinister. "You a long way from home, boy."

Jeremy wondered if it would do any good to throw up on him, and then he began to wonder if it would be possible to *keep* from throwing up on him. He risked a furtive glance, but there were no cops in sight.

"I might be persuaded to help you—for a price," Big Game said. "You got money?"

Jeremy nodded, pulled his wallet out. As he started to open it, Big Game snatched it from his hands, plucked out all the cash, and handed the empty wallet back to him, smiling. It happened so fast Jeremy didn't even have time to protest, not that it would have done any good.

"I guess that'll do." Big Game put his arm around Jeremy and guided him to the street. "This is Courtland," he said, pointing south. "Go down there until you see Highway 10, like in *Ten*nessee." He flashed a quick grin at his accomplices. "Then make a left and go all the way out until it dead-ends. That be Moreland."

It took all the courage Jeremy could muster to speak up. "That's all the money I got," he croaked.

"And we are very grateful," Big Game said with mock sincerity, placing a hand against his own chest. "Ain't that right, Bear?"

The blond bear grinned over Jeremy's shoulder. It was not a reassuring grin.

Big Game gave him a shove. "You run along now, *Ten*nessee, and be glad you still got your shoes."

Jeremy shuffled away, hoping to put some distance behind him before he blew his groceries. Several blocks away he sat down on a curb and pulled out his wallet, just so he could stare into it and try to get his mind around what had just happened. At least his mother's letter was still there, folded and in its place. The letter was the one thing he might have gone back for, perhaps the only thing larger than his fear.

After a while he stood up, put away his wallet and pushed on. In his pockets he discovered the three dollars and change he'd gotten back when he bought lunch, and it was enough to stand between him and utter despair. He wasn't completely broke—yet—but he was starting to think the Cajun he'd met this morning was some kind of prophet. As he trudged up the sidewalk he replayed all the evil that had befallen him already, in one short day since leaving home, and he suddenly felt more alone than he ever had before in his life.

"Be anxious for nothing," he said out loud, but the words rang hollow. God and Mother, at least in that bleak moment, seemed as far away as home.

CHAPTER 3

Giants in the earth.

J eremy's face glowed red, sunburn stung the back of his neck, and sweat soaked his clothes all the way to his shoes. The nausea had finally abated, but he still felt light-headed. He had put nearly a mile between himself and Big Game before it occurred to him that he couldn't trust a mugger's directions. Pulling the wilted paper from his pocket, he read it again. According to the directions he'd gotten from Murlyn & Pratt, the place couldn't be far from I-285. At least that was a clue.

A jogger passed him, a thirty-something guy in shorts and T-shirt, wiping his face with a towel. He nodded to Jeremy as he passed, and Jeremy's instincts told him this guy was all right. Besides, he was beyond the downtown area now—there were houses here, with grass around them. The neighborhood seemed marginally safer.

"Hey!" Jeremy shouted, and the man turned around, keeping his legs pumping even as he stopped. "Excuse me, but could you tell me which way it is to, uh—" he checked his directions again—"Moreland Avenue and I-285?"

Running in place, the sweat-drenched jogger pointed east.

"Moreland is that way, a mile or two. Then you turn right."

"Thank you," Jeremy said. He winced at the sun, wiped his face with his shirttail.

The man kept bouncing, watching him. "Why don't you just take the bus?" he said, puffing. He scanned Jeremy from head to foot, a smile came into his eyes, and Jeremy knew he'd been appraised for the lost dog he was.

"There's a bus?" Jeremy's hand jingled the change in his front pocket. Why couldn't somebody have told him about the bus earlier?

The man grinned. "Sure, there's a bus. Just wait on that corner down there. It's air-conditioned too!" He laughed, shook his head and trotted away.

Jeremy watched the neighborhoods roll by. Most of the houses looked old, but some of them had been restored; the stores had been painted, the sidewalks were free of trash, and big old hickory, oak, and locust trees cast a deep shade along both sides of the street. After a few miles, however, the well-tended brick neighborhoods gave way to broken-down clapboard houses with weedy yards. He began to see government housing projects, used clothing stores, and pawnshops.

He kept watch out the window for I-285. After passing a couple of trucking places he happened to spot a street sign bearing a name he recognized from his piece of paper. He jumped up shouting, but the driver didn't pull over until he reached the bus stop a half mile farther down the road.

Jeremy trudged up the slow grade to Cobb's Mill Road, amazed at how a brief stint in the cool air of the bus could make the outside air feel even hotter. He took off his sweat-soaked T-shirt and hung it on his head, fanning it out behind to shade the sunburnt back of his neck.

On the corner of Cobb's Mill Road sat a store that looked like it might have been reclaimed from what was once a stable or chicken house, a plain white block building with a glass door and two solid picture windows cut into the side facing the street. There were bars on the door and windows, and the words PAY FIRST! had been stenciled right across the front of the tired old gas pumps. A fading hand-lettered sign on the roof read:

Boyle's Gro
Greeting Cards, Ammunition
Shoplifters Prosecuted

Jeremy pictured his parched body lying in the weeds dead of thirst with two dollars still in his pocket, and he wondered if there would ever in this life be a better use for his last two dollars than to go into Boyle's Gro and purchase the biggest bottle of Gatorade he could afford.

Joe Boyle looked like he should have had a cigar in his mouth, but he had a toothpick instead. Gray hair peppered his crew cut. His muscular, tattoo-covered forearms pinned a crossword puzzle to the glass countertop. He tapped slowly on the newspaper with the rubber end of a pencil and watched Jeremy like an inmate. The store held a disheveled mixture of everything imaginable, from bubble-gum cards to shotgun shells—everything except groceries. Boyle's Gro carried very few perishables, and the coolers all along the back wall made it clear that most of his profits came from the sale of beer.

Jeremy bought a football-sized Gatorade and sucked down half of it before pushing himself back out the door. While he was paying, he asked Joe Boyle if this was the road to the treatment plant.

"Yep," Joe said, and shifted the toothpick to the other side of his mouth.

"About how far is it?" Jeremy asked.

A casual shrug. "Mile or two. Just follow your nose."

There were nineteen cents remaining in Jeremy's pocket. He could feel Joe Boyle's eyes on the back of his rag-wrapped head as he walked away.

He saw no other stores on Cobb's Mill Road, just mildewed houses and double-wide trailers with piles of broken junk in the weeds out by the road. One house didn't even have any siding on it, just old weathered tar paper. He wondered how a house came to be like that. The owner must have stripped off the rotten clapboard and nailed up tar paper, planning on installing vinyl siding or something. But then he'd lost interest, or the loan hadn't come through, or he hadn't gotten the raise, and the house stayed half-dressed long enough for him to get used to it. The torn, curled corners and the faded gray color of the tar paper told Jeremy the house had been that way for years, but there were curtains in the windows and the grass was cut.

He rounded a bend and came upon a tiny strip mall containing only a spartan bail bondsman's office, a laundromat, and a pawnshop with a neon sign and bars on the windows. It was familiar territory. There would be a jail somewhere nearby, and not too far away would be the county line. People were pretty much the same everywhere; even back home, the county government always put the landfill, the sewage treatment plant, and the jail as close to someone *else's* backyard as geographically possible, because such things destroyed property values. He recalled his mother once telling him that hogs wouldn't use the bathroom near their trough if they could help it, and it made him laugh. Nobody but his mother would have said hogs *"use the bathroom."*

Every third lot was vacant, choked with weeds and blackberry brambles. Bent and rusty chain link fences lay half-buried, tangled in honeysuckle and ivy. Everywhere he looked he saw dark places, places where a man with bad intentions might wait for a kid like himself to wander within reach. He was fast becoming convinced that the wider world was full of traps and evil men in dark places, and he quickened his pace. A shadow flashed by and a 747 screamed low overhead, adding to this particular evil place the distinction of being directly under a landing pattern of one of the world's busiest airports.

After a while the trees cleared out on the right side of the road and grassy rolling hillsides showed through. Ten yards back from the road a high chain link fence with a coil of razor wire along the top extended for hundreds of yards in both directions. Inside the fence was a row of long low whitewashed block buildings with small barred windows up near the eaves, lined up like barracks across a dirt drive from what appeared to be a fair-sized house. It looked like a work camp of some sort, though Jeremy saw no sign on the locked gate, nor any guards patrolling.

The wine smell of fermenting garbage came to him about the time he topped a hill, and the trees on the left side opened out onto a landfill. Steel towers lined the edge of the trees, marching toward the horizon in a neat row, carrying high-voltage lines to the city. Through the haze he could still make out the distant skyline, and he stopped for a moment to gaze at it, proud of how far he had come in one day. Only then did it occur to him that if he didn't find his uncle he was about to be stranded a long way from home in a rough neighborhood with nothing but the clothes on his back and nineteen cents. Swallowing a lump of fear, he fixed his eyes on the road ahead, and walked.

At the bottom of a long hill curving down from the height of the landfill, the road crossed a concrete bridge over a creek. To his left, a little valley stretched into the distance, bordered on one side by the long straight-edged mountain of refuse that was the landfill and on the other by what had to be the sewage treatment plant. Round concrete skimmer ponds, pale green storage tanks and odd-shaped red brick buildings lay scattered along the rise on the right side of the valley, and a penetrating odor hung in the hot, still air. An isolated thunderstorm grumbled in the distance.

The creek coursing under the bridge on which he stood might have been pretty had it not been half choked by debris, tangled limbs fetched up against rocks and bridge pilings, and waist-deep acres of kudzu covering the sloped banks.

Parallel to the creek a gravel road ran through a gated fence and then split, forking like a horseshoe around both sides of a narrow valley bottom. The near end of the valley appeared to be some sort of industrial scrapyard full of painted steel cabinets, chunks of metal scarred by the smoke trails of torch and welder, and pipes—pipes and hoses of all shapes and sizes, bent and twisted and straight, stockpiled among the other debris. Lining the road down the left side of the valley sat a row of white trailers, some with wooden stairs on the end facing the road. One trailer, in the middle of the row, sat broadside to the road with a large deck in the center of it. Beyond the trailers was a fenced-in electrical switchyard, and beyond that, a large aluminum building the size of a warehouse. In the center of the valley the boom of a crane swung slowly to one side. When Jeremy's gaze returned to his immediate surroundings he finally spotted the yellow brick sign in the shade of a water oak beside the entry.

Sweetbriar Creek
Water Pollution Control Plant
City of Atlanta

Something about the place knotted his stomach with dread, but he was here, and he was out of options. He hitched up his jeans, put on his damp T-shirt, smoothed his hair back with his fingers and walked straight through the open gate, up to where the road split around the scrapyard. He turned right and followed the horseshoe road up into the treatment plant, figuring he would find somebody and start asking questions.

The stench was overpowering in the baked heat of midafternoon, and it didn't surprise him that nobody seemed to be out and about at such a time. He walked unchallenged in this strange place, up the slight grade past a round concrete pond where a steel screed revolved like the hand of a clock around a central tower, skimming the surface. When Jeremy came to the curious round building with the flame sprouting from its roof, he stopped.

He hadn't noticed the flame from a distance, pale and transparent as it was against the fierce afternoon light. But now it piqued his curiosity and he stopped to stare at it until he heard footsteps behind him.

Alarmed, he turned around expecting to be in trouble. The man approaching him wore a uniform of dark gray pants, light gray short-sleeve shirt with a nametag, and a matching gray cap with a waterworks emblem on the front. The nametag said *Gerald*.

"Can I help you?" the man asked. He seemed pleasant enough.

"I, uh . . ."

"You lost?"

"No, sir, I uh . . . I'm looking for my uncle."

"Ohhh, well, who's your uncle?"

"His name's Aiden. Aiden Prine."

The man scratched his head through his hat, squinted at the ground, shook his head.

"Don't know any Prine," he finally said. "He work for the city?"

"He's a miner."

"Oh! *That's* why I don't know him." He laughed. "He must be working in the hole—with the mining contractor over there. We don't see much of those guys. I been around here forever and I know most everybody with the city, but that tunnel—" he shook his head and laughed—"that's a whole nother world."

Jeremy shielded his eyes and surveyed the industrial wasteland between the treatment plant and the dump. The row of trailers he'd seen was now directly across the valley from him, maybe a couple football fields away. In the middle distance, in the center of the valley, sat the crane he had seen earlier, and next to it some kind of strange, inclined conveyor, shaped like a huge praying mantis, spitting gravel onto a pile. But he didn't see any hole.

"What tunnel?" he asked.

Gerald pointed for him. "See that ring of steel beams sticking up out of the ground in front of the crane?"

He still didn't understand until the crane throttled up, belched a cloud of diesel smoke, lifted a load of reinforcing rods from the yard, swung it around and dropped it neatly into the void inside the ring of rusty pilings. The crane paid out cable for ten or fifteen seconds before it slowed and stopped. The entrance to the tunnel went straight down.

"That shaft goes down about two hundred feet," Gerald said. "The miners blasted it out with dynamite, then they went horizontal and blew out a cavern big enough to build that machine of theirs. Must have been forty trucks rolled in here, all full of parts, and every bit of it went down that hole. Last I heard, that big machine done dug about a mile. Supposed to go five before they're done."

"Why?" Jeremy asked. He was still squinting at the hole. He only knew about railroad and highway tunnels. This one didn't appear to serve any purpose.

"Rain." Gerald pointed a thumb over his shoulder. "This treatment plant does fine as long as the weather's good, but when the streets dump a couple days of rainwater in with the sewage we can't handle it, and it ends up in Jackson Lake."

"Raw sewage?"

"Yeah, well it's been diluted a lot, but it's still sewage. A while back the city got some federal money for stuff like this, so the engineers decided to make a big hole in the ground to catch the overflow whenever it rains. Like a holding tank. Then, when it quits raining, we can pump it back out and process it. They're diggin' a great big outhouse is what they're doing." He laughed.

Jeremy chuckled too, just to be polite.

"Hey, you look kind of dogged out," Gerald said, and Jeremy took a glancing inventory of himself—dirty jeans, wrinkled, sweaty T-shirt, radiant sunburn. "Where'd you come from? I didn't see you drive in."

"Knoxville," Jeremy said. "I hitchhiked."

"You thumbed all the way from Knoxville?" He peeked around behind Jeremy as if something might be hidden there. "You're travelin' awful light. Where's your stuff?"

"I kind of lost it," Jeremy said.

"Huh. So all you got is them big-leg jeans and that . . . uh, what does that say, anyway?" He pointed at the front of Jeremy's T-shirt—two words emblazoned above a posterized picture of three guys with guitars on their shoulders.

"Deus Aderit," Jeremy said.

"What's that mean?"

"It's the name of a band."

Gerald shrugged. "Never heard of them."

"No, well, you probably wouldn't unless you're into Christian rock. My mom bought this shirt for me at a concert six months ago." *The last good day she ever had.*

"If you say so. I got to get back to work. I guess you're okay. Go ahead on down there and look for your uncle, but be careful— it's a bad place."

Jeremy groped for the rusty wall with his fingertips, white-knuckling the top edge of the steel even before he was close enough to see over it. The wall around the top of the shaft had been made by driving interlocking steel beams down to bedrock and then cutting off the tops five feet above the ground. The ragged bead of blue-black slag left by the cutting torch bit into his palms as he leaned forward, ever so cautiously, and peeked over into the hole.

His grip tightened all the way to his shoulders but he swallowed hard and stood his ground, forcing himself to look. The shaft was big enough to drop a whole house into it without even touching the sides. Near the top, the rock was white with granite dust, but little springs issued from a dozen cracks, their dark parabolas merging farther down in cool shadow. Two hundred feet down, in the dark, distant bottom he could make out a flatcar and a yellow diesel locomotive glistening with spray. An unseen floodlight cast a partial rainbow in the silver mist. It smelled like rain.

"WHAT DO YOU THINK YOU'RE DOING?!"

He shot back from the wall and spun around, snagging his T-shirt on the jagged steel. The voice belonged to a black giant of a man—at least six-five—with shoulders like a linebacker. He wore a miner's helmet of brown Bakelite with a brim all the way around. One hand balanced a pneumatic drill on his shoulder; the other held a coil of steel cable loosely at his side. The drill looked like it weighed more than Jeremy.

He froze. He didn't think he could outrun the man, and he couldn't think of anything to say. He just stood there.

"You rustling?" the man asked.

Jeremy's face registered his shock. "Oh, no! I wasn't gonna take anything, I swear! I was just looking!"

The big man bowed his head, hiding a chuckle behind his hat. He was still smiling a little when he looked up. "Rustling—looking for work. You looking for work?" He shifted the drill but made no move to put it down.

Be anxious for nothing. Jeremy scratched his neck, looked over at the hole, back at the man. Now that he was here, he wasn't sure what he wanted to do. He didn't even know if Uncle Aiden would remember him—or want anything to do with him. Either way, he needed money and it sounded like the big man was offering him a job.

"Maybe," he said.

"How old are you?" the man asked.

"Eighteen," he lied—but it was only a six-month lie, and he knew he would have to eat during those six months. Besides, his mother's death granted him a certain latitude; his age didn't seem important anymore.

"What can you do?"

His mind scrambled for a better answer than "laborer." Since then he had sacked groceries and helped old man Parks rebuild a motor.

"I'm a mechanic," he said.

Even the man's laugh was big. A gold tooth glinted in the sun. "Mechanic, huh? You're gonna have to learn to lie better than that if you want to be a miner, boy."

He turned his back on Jeremy and continued his trek toward the man-lift, still laughing, shaking his head. "Mechanic," he wheezed.

The opportunity was slipping away. Jeremy steeled himself and called out, "My uncle works here!"

The big man stopped, turned around. His head tilted and he adjusted the drill on his shoulder. "Who's your uncle?"

"His name's Aiden. Aiden Prine."

The man frowned for a minute, looking off to the side, then brightened.

"Prine! Yeah! You're talkin' about Snake! He's the walking boss on swing shift—they won't be here for another hour or so. So you just need to get signed in, right? Man, why didn't you tell me that up front? Just go to that office trailer over there and tell Meg who you are. She'll take care of everything."

Meg really did take care of everything. All Jeremy had to do was mention the name Aiden Prine and he was in. At first she snickered a little about Jeremy's low-slung baggy jeans, but it all seemed good-natured enough. She didn't even give him a hard time about not having any identification on him so long as he gave her a social security number; she just went ahead and put down whatever he told her, then issued him a pair of rubber boots and a blue hard hat.

He was disappointed about the hard hat. Blue. He wanted one of those helmets like the miners wore.

"Did you come in with Snake? I haven't seen him yet. Is he out on the site?"

"Uh, no, he . . . uh . . . I came by myself. He'll be here at the usual time. Is that okay?" Jeremy held his breath, hoping his little bluff would hold. He wasn't sure how Snake would react, but he knew he had to have this job.

"Hey, Snake doesn't have to ask me anything," Meg said, looking at her watch. "I just keep records. If he comes in at the usual time he should be here in about a half hour, but sometimes he's early. Pssh, sometimes I think he *lives* here. I guess you can go hang out in the hog house and meet the crew when they come in. Whatever."

Several trailers faced the gravel access road, and there was a big aluminum building down at the other end, but Jeremy didn't know a hog house from a hardware store. He put the blue hard hat on his head, stuck the boots under his arm and strolled casually down the road, blatantly conspicuous in his attempt to look inconspicuous.

Hearing someone approach from behind, he turned to see a gray-haired black man in a security guard uniform, gaining on him. The old man fell in step and greeted him with a question.

"Wha'd they say?"

Jeremy hadn't met this man before, had no recollection of a prior conversation, however brief, that might have led to this question. Alarms went off in his head at first, but the innocuous smile of the old man disarmed them.

"They said I could wait for Unc ... uh, Snake at the hog house."

"Oh, Snake! Yeah, he should be here any time now. I never seen you before. You a miner?"

Jeremy caught the motion of the old man's eyes, the brief glance at the new blue hard hat, and decided on instinct not to go there.

"I'm a mechanic," he said.

"Oh, okay. First time on a mining project?"

The gleam in the old man's eye had deepened toward mischievous. Jeremy began to suspect he'd already said something stupid.

"What makes you think that?"

"Well, partly it's those britches, but mostly it's because we just walked right past the hog house."

Jeremy climbed the steps to the wooden deck and poked his head through the door of the trailer. It smelled of stale sweat and urine. A community shower, a few toilet stalls and two stained sinks took up a third of the trailer's length; the rest served as a long dressing room with lockers lining both sides, a bench running down the middle. A barrel-chested man with thinning hair stood facing an open locker, changing clothes.

"Is this the hog house?" Jeremy's querulous voice changed octaves in the middle of the question.

The miner looked him over, his gaze pausing slightly at the baggy jeans. "Yeah, this is the hog house. Who are you?" He hung his pants in the locker.

"My name's Jeremy." He took a step into the trailer.

Griff glanced at the new blue hard hat. "You a new hire?"

He nodded. "Meg told me to come here."

The man shrugged, took off his T-shirt and put it in the locker. "I'm Griff—the shift boss. I'm in charge of what goes on in the hole anytime the walking boss ain't there." He pulled a grimy undershirt from the locker and put it on.

Coming in from the sunlight Jeremy's eyes struggled with the twilight inside the hog house, but when Griff lit a cigarette the glare of the lighter revealed a dozen tiny *X*s scattered across his stone face, like a cartoon character after a fight. He caught Jeremy staring.

"What?"

Jeremy didn't say anything; he just made a little *X* on his own face with a forefinger.

"Oh, the stitches. I had some rocks took out of my face this morning."

Jeremy's head tilted, his brow furrowed. "Rocks. How'd you get rocks—"

"Drilled into a miss-hole last year. Every couple months a batch of gravel works its way to the top and I have to go get 'em cut out."

"What's a miss-hole?"

Griff sighed. "You ask a lot of questions. You know anything about drilling and blasting?"

Jeremy shook his head.

"Not much to it. You drill a bunch of holes, you pack it, you shoot it. Then you muck out the loose rock and do it all over again." The jeans Griff stepped into shimmered with grease and rock dust. "Once in a while the dynamite in the bottom of a hole don't fire. It don't happen often, and usually it ain't no problem. Stuff's pretty stable—hard to set off without a cap. But sometimes your drill drifts back into the same hole, right on top of the mis-fire." He shrugged. "If you hit it just right the pressure sets it off and you eat the drill—end of story. I seen it tear a man's head clean off."

Jeremy swallowed.

Griff pulled up a dingy sock. "I got lucky—the drill missed me. But the rock shotgunned me pretty good." He chuckled. "Blew me clear across the shaft. When I come to, I had a rock the size of a baseball stuck in my neck." He leaned his head back and ran a finger down his neck to show Jeremy the jagged, doughy scar.

Jeremy turned the new hard hat in his hands as if he were looking for cracks. "Look, maybe I shouldn't . . . Do I . . . Will I have to run a drill?"

Griff snorted, "What, you want to live forever?" He grunted, tugging at a rubber boot. "Something's gotta kill you, sooner or later. Quick is the only way to go, boy. The *last* thing I want is to see it coming. I'll take the big flyswatter every time."

A tangle of footsteps clumped across the wooden deck. Several men shuffled into the trailer and edged past Griff to the lockers. The smallest one nodded toward Jeremy. "What's this, Griff? New meat?"

"Yeah, Geech. He thinks mining is dangerous. Imagine that." He tried to hide a grin.

Geech looked again, saw the expression on Jeremy's face.

"Hey, what you been telling him, Griff? He looks like he seen a ghost."

Griff stood up, tucking in his shirt. "He asked me about the stitches," he said and shrugged. "I told him."

Geech opened a locker. "Don't ever listen to Griff's war stories, kid. He's just a crusty old buzzard with some scars and a attitude. What's your name?"

"Jeremy."

"Germy?"

"No, *Jeremy.*" He said it louder the second time, but it was too late. The ripple of laughter told him he'd been tagged.

"You know, Germy, them jeans are gonna be trouble. Some places there's six inches of water in the bottom of the tunnel. No way you're gonna get all that tucked into your boots—and if you leave 'em out, they'll soak up water till they drag you down and drown you."

Another round of laughter. Even Jeremy laughed, nervously. It was a small thing, to laugh at himself with them, but it was the right thing. At least he knew that much. But Geech wasn't through, yet.

"So, Germy, what do you do?"

He twisted the hard hat, glanced at Griff. "I'm a mechanic," he mumbled.

Amid the ensuing laughter the door opened again, a small dog shot past Jeremy and a wraith of a man appeared in the door. Geech called out to him, "Yo, Biggins! The kid here is after your job. Says he's a mechanic!"

Biggins's khaki work shirt and pants hung loose on his wiry frame, seemingly without touching his body. A gray, sallow face spoke eloquently of thirty years of rock dust and hard liquor. He closed in on Jeremy, studying him through black horn-rimmed glasses. His breath smelled of chewing tobacco. He shook his head, snorted once, turned and walked out.

Jeremy heard a low growl and looked down to see the dog, some sort of scruffy terrier, sniffing at his shoes.

"Carl!" Geech shouted. "Get over here and leave Germy alone before he stomps you."

The dog trotted back between the legs of the men, jumped up and sat down on the bench, staring disdainfully at Jeremy.

On the way out, Griff stopped to check his watch in the doorway.

"Step it up, girls. The train leaves in ten minutes. Nanny, take—Germy, is it? Take Germy and get up a load of water and air line before you come in." He lit another cigarette and a cloud of smoke swirled after him as he left.

On his way to the hog house Snake stopped in at the office trailer to see Sonny, to give him the straight story about Menendez. There would be several different versions of the story circulating by now, enhanced by the guys on graveyard shift and altered by Meg, who didn't understand half of what she heard.

Sonny Bauer was the project manager, a middle-aged engineer whose jowly face, baggy eyes, and gruff manner had bought him a largely undeserved reputation for being hard-nosed. Snake liked him okay, for a project manager. The gruffness didn't faze Snake, but Sonny was an engineer and therefore capable of only limited understanding. Snake parked himself in the square chair in front of the desk until Sonny hung up the phone.

"So tell me what you did to Manny Menendez," Sonny said, cynicism writ large on his face.

Snake shrugged. "He got careless and caught his arm in a roller."

"I heard *you* broke his arm getting him out." Sonny took a big black cigar from a box on his desk and ran it slowly under his nose.

Snake shook his head. "His wrist was already broken. I just kind of ejected him from the roller, that's all. What's this all about?"

Sonny sat back, cigar in one hand, lighter in the other. "His wife came by here to pick up his stuff this morning. They're making noises about a lawsuit."

A shrug. "Okay." Snake's level stare didn't change.

"Well, you know, little things like that affect our insurance rates, Snake." He held the lighter to the cigar and puffed fire into it as he spoke. "Not to mention they tend to bring OSHA down on us. You really want those clowns breathing over your shoulder? You think we need handrails around the flatcar? Do your guys want to wear full face shields and dust masks all the time?"

"He's not gonna sue anybody, Sonny. That's just talk."

"Yeah, well you didn't see the look in his wife's eye. She sounded serious enough to me."

Snake leaned close to the desk. "Did you tell her about the bag of dope we found in his locker when we cleaned it out? Because I think that might have a bearing on his lawsuit when it goes to court, you know? Speaks to his state of mind, his ability to function and all that."

Sonny sat up, rolled his shoulders, contemplated his cigar. Personnel problems always made him nervous, and Snake assumed it was because there was no formula for it. You couldn't solve it with a calculator.

"There was dope in his locker?"

"There was if I say there was. If you like, I can produce nine credible witnesses who'll swear there was a pink rhinoceros in his locker—wearing makeup and a nose ring."

Sonny rested his chin on his fists and glared at Snake. "I think maybe you need to lighten up a bit," he finally said. "Are you okay?"

"I'm fine, chief." Snake turned away, purposefully studying the race chart on the wall, a large bar chart graphing the footage gained by the two mining shifts. Swing shift—Snake's crew—was represented by a red bar, and graveyard by blue. Day shift did only maintenance. Snake could tell at a glance his shift was ahead by almost a hundred feet.

"Don't get me wrong, Snake. I know you know your job, and I know these guys need a swift kick now and then. And if you keep going like you're going, the footage bonuses are going to make me and you both rich. I just think sometimes—" he waved the cigar cavalierly—"I just think you could lighten up a little, that's all."

Snake chewed on this for a few seconds, and then his jaw muscles started to flex.

"Let's talk about insurance rates," Snake said.

"Look, Snake—"

"No, let's talk about it. You brought it up, let's talk about it. Everybody knows the insurance rates are high. It's one of the major cost factors, and everybody knows why. What do they figure, a man a mile?" He already knew the answer.

Sonny nodded slightly, adjusted his paperweight. "Something like that."

"The insurance company knows, you know, I know, and the men down in that hole know, it's a *dangerous job*. Menendez was trouble. He didn't pay attention. *That's* what we can't afford, Sonny. A man like him is a liability, an accident waiting to happen. We got off light with just a broken arm—especially since it was his."

The scars on Snake's face underlined his words. The discussion was pretty much over. Sonny sniffed. There was a smirk on his lips, but he rolled the cigar in his fingers and kept his eyes there rather than look at Snake.

"Well," he said, "it still leaves us shorthanded. I guess it's a good thing you got your nephew to come on board."

"This is not happening," Snake growled. He clutched the paper in his hand—a copy of Jeremy's job application—and almost *ran* to the hog house. "This can*not* be happening."

He leaped up the steps, crossed the deck in two strides, jerked open the door and skidded into the hog house. The Jeremy in Snake's mind was seven years old, hated girls, and watched cartoons. The lanky kid standing in front of him now could almost look him straight in the eye.

"Jeremy?"

The kid nodded. He swallowed hard and flinched with his first glance at Snake's face, but at least he made eye contact. "Uncle Aiden?" There was a little tremor in his voice.

The name amused Nanny for some reason and he mumbled it over and over again to his locker—"Uncle Aiden, Uncle Aiden, Uncle Aiden . . ."—until Geech smacked him in the back of the head.

Snake glanced at his own reflection in the mirror over the sink. "Yeah, it's me. I guess we've both changed some. Good to see you," he said, and shook hands. "But what's *this* about?" he asked, brandishing Jeremy's sign-in sheet.

Jeremy shrugged. "They, uh, gave me a job. I guess I'm working here."

Snake shook his head. "I don't think so. Meg signed you in

because she thought I brought you here as a replacement for a guy that quit last night. You can't work here—you're just a kid! What did you do, run away from home? Does your mother know about this?"

Jeremy hesitated, glancing at the crew. He bit back words twice before he finally muttered, "Uncle Aiden, Mama's dead."

Snake blinked and recoiled in shock. "Oh! I, uh, I didn't . . . I'm sorry. Why didn't somebody—"

"We didn't know where you were. Nobody's heard from you since . . ."

Snake jerked his head toward the door. "Let's take a walk."

His hand shook as he folded the paper and stuck it in his shirt pocket. He tried to think, tried to focus and put facts in order as he walked slowly across the gravel road into the lay-down yard, looking for a place to sit.

Julie was dead. Technically, Jeremy was an orphan now, and Snake was his next of kin. *Tom's son.* He sat heavily on a banded bundle of pipe, put his face in his hands, and took several long deep breaths before he raised his hooded eyes to Jeremy.

"What happened?"

"To Mom? Breast cancer. They caught it late. Wasn't a whole lot they could do. She went quick."

Snake shook his head slowly. "I liked Julie. She deserved a better life than what she got." He kicked at the dirt for a bit, then said, "So what about school? Aren't you supposed to be in school?"

Jeremy shrugged, made a face. "Hasn't started yet, but it doesn't matter. I didn't even finish last year, what with Mom in the hospital and all. Ain't no big thing—I'm not accountant material anyway."

This sounded alarmingly like himself at the same age, but Snake wasn't about to say it. "Well, you're not miner material either, Jeremy. If you need help I'll do whatever I can, but you're not working here."

"I already got the job. You can't stop me."

"Oh yeah. I can stop you."

Jeremy's voice went up a note. "And what do I do then? Where do I go? I got nothing else! I gotta work somewhere, I don't see why it shouldn't be here!"

"You can live with Walter and Anna."

Jeremy rolled his eyes. "I already tried that. Cat hair in the mashed potatoes, Anna screeching at everybody, Walter holding forth on everything from catfish food to capital punishment, Norman whining all the time and the girls screaming and giggling and going through your stuff every time you turn your back."

Snake laughed out loud, and it felt good. Apparently Walter and Anna hadn't changed much in ten years. "Yeah, I hate it when Walter holds forth. I've never even seen the twins. Norman still fat?"

"Fatter than ever."

"I thought maybe he'd grow out of it." Snake sighed. "You still need to be in school. What are you, a senior now?"

"I would be." Jeremy shook his head. "Look, I'm not going back to school. That's out. I'm on my own now and I'm going to have to make a living. If I don't do it here I'll do it somewhere else. I'll live under a bridge if I have to, but I'm not going back. I guess it's up to you."

"Well, you're as *stubborn* as your old man, I'll give you that." Snake stared until Jeremy shifted his feet. He noted the skinny arms and thin chest, the light, sunburn-prone complexion, the pitifully sparse collection of whiskers on his lip and the smattering of acne on his chin.

"You don't belong here, Jeremy."

"I don't belong anywhere. You're the only family I got left

except for Walter and Anna. And Granny." His voice dropped with this last, and Snake understood. Snake's mother was on the list of Things Not To Be Discussed, and in any case they both knew she was not a factor.

"You don't understand," Snake said. "I'm sorry, but this is rough, dangerous work. Look, if you don't fit in at Walter and Anna's, if you can't cut it in high school, or if you can't handle flipping burgers—if any of those things doesn't work out, it's just a minor inconvenience and you can try again someplace else. But if you make a mistake *here*"—Snake jerked a thumb toward the shaft for emphasis—"you can ride out in a plastic bag. This is no place for a green kid."

"How old were you when you started mining?" Jeremy asked.

"That's not the point. It's not about age, it's about attitude. I can look at you and tell you're not cut out for mining. And while we're at it, I'm not buying for one minute that you're eighteen. This is a hard place, Jeremy, and the guys who work here are hard cases. Their hobbies are mostly illegal. If you see one of these guys wearing a tie, he's on his way to court."

But the boy would hold his ground; Snake could see it in his eyes. He realized with a sudden chill that they were Tom's eyes, and the argument was already lost. Tom had always been slow to make up his mind, but once he'd done it his eyes conveyed his resolve and announced with a calm finality that he would not be moved.

"If it's so bad, why are *you* still here?" Jeremy asked.

Snake turned away, gazing for a long moment at the flame across the way. It was a legitimate question, one he had thought about a lot over the years. He could have made a living a dozen other ways; he had always known that. Even Walter had offered him a job after the accident, working in a nice safe insurance office. The money would have been the same or better in the long run, but there was a pride here, in knowing how to do things ordinary people couldn't, holding dynamite in his hands and making it do his bidding, forging a path through solid rock. This was his home, and these men were his brothers. He had known it all at once ten years ago when he came back pink and stitched and disfigured, his hands atrophied to thin claws, his face half covered with serpentine partial-thickness skin grafts. They had instantly dubbed him Snake, and the compassion in the gesture was not lost on him. Living in the shadow of their own mortality, it was no small thing to forgive and accept a man who wore calamity in plain sight and forced them to treat it like family. It was a rare brand of grace. Maybe the only kind he would ever find.

"It's all I know," Snake said quietly.

"I can do this," Jeremy said.

His eyes said he *would* do it, even if it killed him. That was what Snake was afraid of. He stared at the kid, torn between this new sense of responsibility and an old, old fear.

"Why me, Jeremy? You haven't seen me since you were little. You can't possibly remember much about me."

A peculiar sadness settled on Jeremy as he avoided Snake's eyes, and for an instant Snake had a vague impression he was hiding something. But maybe not.

"I guess it was the laughs," Jeremy said.

"Laughs." Snake tilted his head, confused.

"The way Dad laughed when you were around. It's like you lit him up. All the laughter went out of the house when Dad died."

Snake stared at the ground. The boy's words were spears.

"You remember what you told me about that cat?" Jeremy said.

"What cat?" Snake kept his face down and spoke softly.

"You had a cat in your apartment back when I was a kid—"

"You're still a kid."

"—and you said he always left a pile on the kitchen floor while you were at work?"

Snake shook his head, blank.

"You told us how you would always chase him down, cram his nose in it and throw him out the window. You said you did that every day for, like, three months, and then one day you came home and the cat looked at you, looked at the pile, ran over and stuck his own nose in it and jumped out the window."

Snake chuckled, almost against his will.

"I believed that story," Jeremy said, unsmiling.

"So when did you begin to suspect that it was a lie?"

"About thirty seconds ago."

There was something uncomfortably penetrating in Jeremy's stare, and it forced Snake to look elsewhere. His men were filing out, roughhousing, ragging each other, heading for the shaft. They were louder even than usual, being careful not to pay any attention to Snake and Jeremy. Not a glance.

Snake sighed, drummed his fingers on the pipe.

"All right," he said finally, "you can try it for a while, but I'm not going to carry you. You can work topside, help out in the shop and the yard, bring supplies in on the flatbed. Biggins is the mechanic for swing shift and he's in charge topside, so you do whatever he tells you. Get Eldon to show you how to flag for him, and how to rig, and if you get a spare minute, learn to drive the loader."

"Thanks, Uncle Aiden."

"You won't be thanking me in a day or two. And call me Snake. Uncle Aiden's dead. You got a place to stay?"

CHAPTER 4

Eyes to see.

"Grab a couple four-by-fours," Nanny said, then he picked up two timbers himself and yelled something at the crane operator about fetching the spreader from the bottom of the shaft. The boards looked small in Nanny's powerful hands.

Jeremy shouldered two timbers and staggered under the load, trying to catch up. Nanny's long strides had already carried him halfway to the man-lift. A lump swelled in the boy's throat as he climbed the short stair to the platform jutting out over the abyss— a platform that reminded him vaguely of a gallows. His breath came fast and shallow, but he told himself it was because he was straining with the timbers. The rest of the crew was waiting there for the man-lift to trundle up from the depths to the landing so they could go to work. Snake spoke to Nanny when they arrived. He didn't even look at Jeremy.

Jeremy had seen the man-lift before, when he peeked into the hole that first time. It didn't look any safer now; a rickety cage with a sheet-steel bottom and chain link sides, rumbling up and down on a geared rail that looked way too frail for the load. Trying to hide his reluctance as he tested the floor, he padded carefully to the far end of the cage and stood with his back against the chain link, resting his timbers on end while Snake closed the gate.

Jeremy's mouth felt dry enough to spit sawdust. When the man-lift jolted into its slow, clattering descent he flinched and his hands flailed out for a grip on the chain link. One of the timbers fell over and slammed down next to Snake's foot. All eyes turned to Jeremy.

"Sorry." His voice broke over dry gravel.

"Hey, it's all right, Germy," Geech said, laughing. "I don't trust this thing my own self. I don't never put my full weight down on it."

Nanny tried not to look at the boy. Jeremy tried not to look down. He studied the craggy, blast-torn granite as the cage descended; a hundred shades of blue and gray shot through with startling white streaks. The grain of the rock came into ever sharper focus as the trickles of water merged to wash the granite clean. The cage thumped to a stop in misty twilight at the bottom of the shaft.

The crew piled onto the flatcar while Griff and Snake cranked the locomotive behind it. It didn't look like a train engine. Designed for mining, it was just a long yellow box, no higher than a man's shoulder, with a platform at the back big enough for two men to stand together at the controls. The diesel roared to life and swing shift chugged into the tunnel.

"What are we supposed to load pipe on if they've got the flatcar?" Jeremy asked, watching the loki leave.

"It'll be back," Nanny said. "They go in, day shift comes out. Maybe ten minutes."

The top of the shaft looked impossibly distant from two hundred feet down, like looking up at the sky through a gun barrel. Jeremy pictured himself trapped down here and felt a strange tightening in his chest. The lump in his throat felt like a lemon, and he fought back an urge to bolt, to climb back up to the world. He was glad when Nanny found the spreader right away and they headed back up to the nice open yard where he could breathe.

"Like this—now cinch it down so it don't slip. You don't want to be in the bottom of the shaft when a load of pipe slips the chokers and comes at you end-on." Nanny's big hands dominated the steel cables with ease. He laughed, for no apparent reason, and then explained. "Geech come close to gettin' cored that way one time when we was young like you. Pipe bit a chunk out of his hat."

"Is Geech, like, your brother or something?"

"Nah, we just worked together since forever. We was working together before I met Bobby Sue, before we had all them kids. He's like family, I guess."

"How'd you get a name like Nanny?" Jeremy asked. "That's kind of an odd name, for a man."

Nanny grinned and wiped his nose on his shirtsleeve. "It's short for my real name," he said. "My folks didn't get along too good and Daddy was bad to drink. They fought all the time, and the way I heard it they argued for nine months about what to name me. My aunt said they was still arguing about it even after I was born. Mama wanted to call me Smiley because that was her family's name, and Daddy wanted to call me Floyd, after his brother. The drugs they give her in the hospital made Mama kind of bold, so she told him she wasn't comin' home with the baby till he gave in. Daddy said okay. Aunt Bette says Mama's exact words were, 'All right then, it's unanimous—Smiley.' Daddy just nodded and never said another word about it, but when it come time to fill out the paper, he wrote *Unanimous Smiley Grubs*." He shrugged. "I guess Nanny is better."

Jeremy managed, somehow, not to laugh. "So why didn't they just change it later?"

Nanny's face darkened. "You don't change a thing after a man signs his name to it. It just ain't done." He finished tying off the load and straightened up, signaling the crane operator and heading for the man-lift.

The rumbling of the diesel reverberated from the walls as the loki pushed the flatcar through the tunnel. From the cab of the loki, the smooth, perfectly round interior of the tunnel looked like the inside of a pipe, except that it was big enough to hold a highway. A coating of dry gray-white dust, the residue of hard-rock mining, obscured the personality of the granite.

Jeremy focused on the big square floodlights hanging at too long intervals, high up on the ribs of the tunnel. His breathing came easier whenever they approached a light, but as they trundled past and their shadows swung around to blend with the darkness his grip tightened on the rail.

After they rounded a long bend he looked over his shoulder and saw that the entrance had disappeared beyond the curve. Ahead, the tunnel's throat narrowed in an infinite series of alternating rings of light and dark, like a huge banded snake, swallowing him. A vise tightened on his chest. From the distance he began to hear an ominous grumbling, a deeper sound than the roar of the diesel loki, a sound more felt than heard. Far ahead, the tunnel seemed to fade into a dense dust cloud out of which a handful of pale yellow lights twinkled. Jeremy breathed in short, shallow gasps.

"It's all right," Nanny said. "You get used to it after a while."

Vague shapes of steel beams began to appear in the halos of light scattered about the trailing gear, and the roaring grew. Jeremy had never heard anything remotely like it—a fearsome, grinding, hellish noise that penetrated the bones and drove out rational thought. Here and there he could make out the movements of men inside the cloud, but he couldn't make them human. He couldn't imagine getting used to it. He could feel his brain rattling in his head, and his hands left sweaty outlines on the rail.

Nanny braked the flatcar a few feet behind the trailing gear, which looked to Jeremy like nothing more than a wide flatcar half-covered with equipment and machinery he didn't understand. The machine itself was still out of sight, lost in the dusty air ahead. Nanny switched off the motor and swung down. Jeremy followed him. He could see half a dozen gray, helmeted men working in the thick haze, doing things he didn't understand.

Griff met them at the back of the trailing gear. He blew a cloud of cigarette smoke, and Jeremy watched it vibrate as it drifted, dancing on sound waves. He could feel the waves of sound passing through him.

With a series of hand gestures, Griff told Nanny he wanted Jeremy to unload the pipe.

Nanny jerked a thumb at Jeremy, pointed to his eyes, then forward, toward the machine. He wanted to show the kid around.

Griff nodded and tapped his watch as if to say "Make it quick." He glanced at Jeremy, chuckled, shook his head and disappeared up a ladder to the drill deck. Nanny motioned for Jeremy to follow.

As they toured the machine, Nanny pointed out various things, leaning close to Jeremy's ear and shouting as loud as he could. To a boy's eyes the machine and its trailing support structure was an impenetrable maze of hoses, wires, catwalks, conveyors, and massive hydraulic pistons, but Nanny managed to make some sense out of it. The whole operation moved through the earth basically like a train, in three sections.

The mining machine, of course, led the way. Holding itself in place with eight giant grippers—pads forced against the wall by huge hydraulic rams—the fifty-foot-long, eight-hundred-and-fifty-ton machine chewed through solid rock at the rate of six feet per hour and left behind a perfectly round hole large enough for a two-lane highway. Every hour, three hundred tons of shattered rock crawled out along one wall of the tunnel on a conveyor belt.

Thirty feet behind the machine was the first of two massive flatcars, train cars towed behind the machine with a thick steel hawser. The first flatcar was a double-decker, for the miners had welded a boxlike girder structure on top of it to make a deck up near the ceiling as a work platform for drilling anchors when they encountered loose rock.

Bringing up the rear was a second flatcar, as large as the first but without the overhead structure. This, the tail end of the trailing gear, was what Jeremy had seen first when they arrived.

After the nickel tour, Nanny sent Jeremy back to unload the pipe all by himself, and Jeremy began to think for the first time that he might survive—not that he could see the end of terror, but that he might be able to function in spite of it.

While Jeremy hauled pipe from the loki and stacked it on the trailing gear, Nanny and Geech parked themselves on wire reels opposite each other to grab a bite to eat. Nanny broke out a foil-wrapped bundle of Buffalo wings while Geech poured himself a plastic cup of soup from a thermos. They talked with their hands while they ate, never speaking a word—words were useless unless a man could read lips—and they didn't use regular sign language as far as Jeremy could tell. Yet they still seemed to understand each other perfectly. Nanny, after he had gnawed a chicken bone bare, would raise it up to eye level and toss it like a dart toward Geech's soup cup. He rung it once; a greasy bone landed with a splash in the middle of the cup, and a triumphant grin lit Nanny's face. Geech didn't seem to care. He plucked the bone out, threw it over his shoulder, and kept eating.

Jeremy watched, and absorbed. He understood very little about mining, or the workings of the machine, but he saw that men moved and worked and laughed and smoked and ate and made friends here while dogs and children slept, hundreds of feet above. If these men could do it, maybe he could too. Staying busy seemed to help. As long as he kept his mind occupied he might be able to hold the fear at arm's length. It would not go away, but maybe, just maybe, with a little effort, he could keep it at bay. He was very proud of having gotten this far. It was a man's job, unloading the pipe, and he felt like a man. Putting one foot in front of the other, he kept moving, but every time he returned to the loki for another piece of pipe his eyes strayed toward the shaft.

An hour later he was out of the tunnel and back up top feeling the humid weight of an August evening in a valley that trapped the heavy aromas of rancid garbage and raw sewage and stirred them together like stew in a bowl. He could almost see why a man might prefer the tunnel, once he got used to it. Underground, there was no smell except for the slightly acid sweetness of rock dust, and the temperature remained constant. Everything was constant; there was no day or night or hot or cold. It was always the same in the tunnel.

He reported to Biggins, who handed him a pick and shovel and told him to dig a ditch from the switchyard to the shaft. A hundred yards of crush-and-run lay in his path, a mixture of gravel and fine-ground granite compacted by rain and heavy machinery to a density approaching concrete. The baloney cable, the main power line for the machine, ran across to the shaft in a steel pipe as big as Jeremy's leg. The pipe lay on top of the ground, but crush-and-run had been humped over it to protect it where it crossed the road. The rest of the pipe was exposed to damage by heavy machinery, and Biggins wanted it buried.

Biggins was something of a linguist, in his own way. He reeled off intricate tapestries of earthy language every time he opened his mouth, and he had done it so profusely and for so long that the four-letter words had settled in and become the foundation of his whole speech pattern. Biggins told him to dig the ditch next to the pipe, embellishing each noun with an assortment of colorful adjectives. Jeremy managed to sift out that he wanted the ditch a foot wide and eighteen inches deep.

Even a kid of Jeremy's limited experience knew there were machines on the job capable of digging a ditch. He figured it was some kind of test, so he turned off his brain and started swinging the pick, pacing himself because he knew it would be a long night. But the pick was heavy, the ground hard, and before long the blue hard hat was falling off of his sweat-slick head every time he bent over. Biggins came by every ten or fifteen minutes, bird-dogging him.

"What's the holdup, Germy? You ain't done yet? What are you straightening up for? Get busy! Swing that pick, boy!" Biggins took a small man's delight in calling him Germy.

Jeremy knew how to dig a ditch. Old Henry had taught him that. Keep a steady pace, don't try to do too much too fast, and work in six-inch layers—break it, dig it, clean it, then break another six inches. Even digging a ditch, Henry told him, there ..was a right way and a wrong way. He had also taught Jeremy to

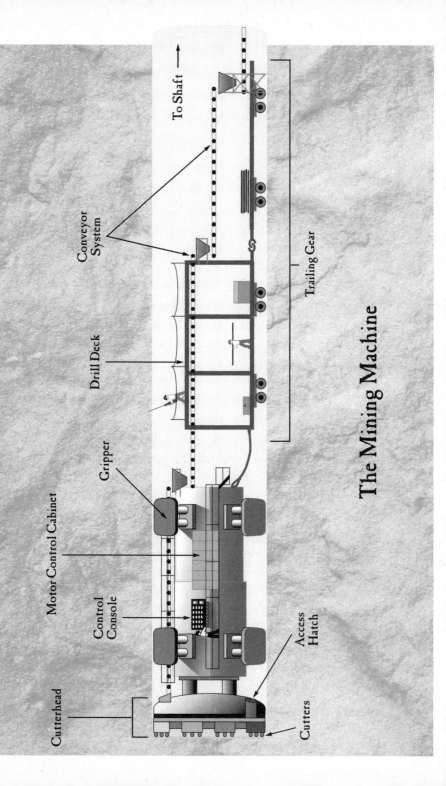

The Mining Machine

let his mind wander while his body worked, and he did so now, opening his memory like a book.

Henry hadn't been able to read or write, but there was an uncommon wisdom in his eyes, bought with bitter experience. He said he had *"eyes to see."*

Jeremy only worked with the old man for a few months, yet during that one summer he collected some things he would keep for the rest of his life. One of those things happened in the cab of the foreman's truck. Long before daylight, the foreman would pick up Jeremy first, then Henry, then drive for another hour and a half in the process of picking up the rest of the crew and getting to the jobsite in town. Henry watched for the truck every morning, silhouetted against the yellow light in the screen door of a crowded little clapboard house with a deep porch and cracked wooden steps. He would roll his big self onto the truck seat, clutching a bowl in his left hand while he pulled the door shut. The bowl was big, like a cake-mixing bowl, with wrinkled foil over the top. It didn't look that big in Henry's thick hands, but there must have been five scrambled eggs in it, a pile of bacon, and three or four homemade cat-head biscuits, buttered and loaded with fig preserves. Sometimes, even now, Jeremy could still smell them.

Henry always said, *"Mornin', boss. Mornin', young'un."* He always called Jeremy "young'un" but talked to him like he was *some*body. He had a face as comfortable as old shoes, perpetually raised eyebrows giving the impression that he was always smiling about something. Never looking directly at anyone, his face was long fixed in that resigned humility so common in black men

Henry's age, a humility that had been a survival skill back when a black man had to get humble or else, a humility learned from birth in a time when, as Henry said, *"a man could grow up knowin' all his life he wouldn't never be nothin' but a nigger."*

On those early mornings, Jeremy usually slept most of the long ride in to work, and he would awaken to the jostling, truck-door-slamming, laughing sounds of men rolling out for work. He could remember several mornings watching Henry walk off talking to somebody, rubbing his arm. Henry would rub his arm and shake his left hand like a dog shook a rabbit, the way a man would do when his arm was asleep, then he would flex his hand to chase the needles out of it. Jeremy's head had leaned heavy on Henry's shoulder when he fell asleep. Henry ate his breakfast one-handed rather than move and wake him up. Jeremy never mentioned it to him, never let on that he had noticed the small kindness—it wouldn't have been cool.

But he never forgot it. He was pretty sure he'd never dig another ditch as long as he lived without thinking about Henry.

The sun dipped behind the garbage dump, and darkness settled on the valley as Jeremy dug, but his mind and hands were occupied so that he hardly noticed. The yard was bathed in the bluish glow of the big square lights mounted high on poles—plenty of light for digging a ditch.

Leaning on his shovel, Jeremy had stopped to wipe the sweat out of his eyes with the tail of his T-shirt when he heard the crunch of footsteps behind him. He had broken and cleaned out the top six inches for about fifty feet.

When he got within range, Biggins went off like a grenade. "I thought I told you EIGHTEEN INCHES DEEP!"

Jeremy just stood there and took it while Biggins thundered and rained on him, pouring out a vile flood that would have dug the ditch on its own if it could have been harnessed.

When Biggins finally drew a breath, Jeremy mumbled, "I wasn't done with it."

"You *bet* you weren't done with it!" Biggins yelled and then launched into a whole new symphony of abuse. Neither of them heard the old security guard approach. All of a sudden he was just standing there beside Biggins, hands behind his back, listening, with that same slightly amused look on his face.

Biggins finally noticed the old man, did a double take and lost his rhythm. His tirade faltered and ground to an awkward halt.

"Wha'd they say?" the old man asked. He delivered the odd question so matter-of-factly that it knocked Biggins off track. Jeremy could see it on his face. Biggins frowned and bit his lip for a second, trying to come up with an answer for a question that didn't make any sense, but by the time he regained his balance he had forgotten Jeremy.

"You need something from me?" The angry eyes of Biggins now bored into the old security guard.

"No, I'm just listenin'," the guard said, fighting back the threat of a smile. He nodded toward Jeremy. "Go ahead."

But Biggins had been derailed, and he couldn't find the words again. He turned back to Jeremy and stammered for a couple seconds before he finally managed to yell, "Get back to work!" and stalked off toward the shop muttering to himself.

The security guard didn't look anything like Henry—he was older and smaller and lighter of skin—yet he had that same subversive quality in his eyes, as if he knew a great many things he wasn't telling. Nevertheless, Jeremy suspected that he was about half crazy.

"See you found yourself a friend," the old man said, his eyes indicating the retreating Biggins.

Jeremy punched the shovel into the loosened crush-and-run and leaned on it for a second.

"How did you do that?" he asked.

"What? Rattle old Biggins? Ain't nothin' to it. A fella like that can't stand no kind of light. He'll puff and blow so long as he's on his own ground, but let somebody look him in the eye and he'll lose his nerve every time. Seen it all my life."

"Yeah, well—thanks." Watching Biggins slam the office door, he meant it sincerely.

"You from around here, boy?"

"No sir, I'm from Tennessee, up east of Knoxville."

"Drive down today?" He was checking out Jeremy's fluorescent sunburn.

"Well, I hitchhiked. But yeah, I did just get here today."

"You thumbed all the way?" The old guard's eyes widened. "You a long way from home, child. God must be lookin' out for you."

Jeremy's head tilted and his shovel stopped. He didn't know what to say. He liked the old man, and he owed him for getting Biggins off his back, but at the same time he felt a little like a salmon after swimming a thousand miles upstream—all red and breathless.

"Are you a preacher, Mr. uh. . . ?"

The old man shook his head, laughed. "Moss Fisher, but just call me Moss. Everybody else does."

"You know, it's a funny thing," Jeremy said. "My mother took me to church from the day I was born, and I can't remember a time when I wasn't a Christian. But I *am* starting to wonder what God's got against me." He leaned on his shovel and scanned his surroundings. "A couple days ago I buried my mother, and since then it's like . . . I don't know, it's like I turned into Job or something. In less than a week I've lost everything. I'm a million miles from home and I'm down to my last nineteen cents, digging a ditch between the *stinking* garbage dump and the *stinking* sewage treatment plant"—he jabbed a forefinger for accent—"and taking abuse from some trash-mouthed psychotic just to keep a few dollars between me and the street. Since breakfast I've been hit on, poisoned, robbed, and hard-cussed, and now it looks like I get to dig ditches all night without any supper."

He stared over at the shaft, trying to think of a way to say exactly what he was feeling right now, when he heard the man-lift clattering up from the depths and remembered what Geech had said. It was perfect.

"I've always been a believer," Jeremy said, "but now that I think about it, I'm not sure I ever put my full weight down on it. When Mom was around, it just seemed like God was too. But here—" Jeremy swept an arm at the valley around him—"this has got to be what they mean when they say 'Godforsaken.'"

Moss Fisher ran a finger across his lips and met Jeremy's stare with thoughtful eyes. "You hungry?" he asked.

Jeremy shook his head and turned his attention back to the shovel, suddenly ashamed of having unloaded on somebody he just met.

"Okay," Moss said, then walked briskly away.

Jeremy thought he'd seen the last of him, but in a few minutes he reappeared carrying a brown paper sack and a can of Coke. Carl the terrier trotted along behind him. Jeremy wasted no time unwrapping a tomato sandwich and diving into it while Carl inspected the ditch.

"Might be a little acidy this late in the summer," Moss said, "but it'll eat."

Jeremy mumbled his thanks around a mouthful of sandwich.

Moss stared into the distance, watching the flame on the slope at the foot of the treatment plant. It had brightened with the onset of darkness.

"You know anything about this place?" Moss asked. "How it works?"

Jeremy shook his head, took another bite, and Moss launched into a casual explanation of the process. He explained how waste poured in through the diversion structure, and then an intricate web of pumps and conveyors pushed it through a long and complicated process where it was skimmed, settled, sifted, and sorted before being bombarded with chemicals and heat and then hauled off to the drying beds.

"See the two buildings up there on the right?" He pointed toward the far end of the plant, over near the entrance.

The buildings looked like all the other buildings in the plant except that a conveyor spanned the distance between them, from the ground floor on one building nearly to the top of the other, slanting upward like an escalator. A peaked roof of tin covered the length of the conveyor, presumably to keep the rain off of it. The steel supports underneath formed an unbroken line of Ws.

"That belt carries waste up to the drying ovens after it's been treated and heated and blasted with chemicals and wrung out. You're right, son—this place is about as low as it gets, and what's on that belt is the lowest of the low. But look in the bar joists underneath it."

Jeremy stared hard. The floodlights on the corners of the buildings lit the conveyor from several different angles so that he could see it fairly well even from a distance. There were plants entangled in the girders—good, rich, green, healthy plants, and lots of them, clustered under the girder for almost its entire length. They looked familiar, though in that strange place he couldn't make the connection until he saw a glint of red, and then another. His eyes narrowed.

"Tomatoes?"

"That's right," Moss said, and a wide smile spread across his face. "Biggest, prettiest tomatoes you ever saw."

Jeremy blinked, stopped chewing. His eyes went from the remains of the tomato sandwich he was eating, to the hanging plants, and then to Moss Fisher.

"Oh, NO!" Moss laughed, waving both hands at the sandwich. "Not *those*! That tomato came from my garden at home. I wouldn't do that to you, son."

Not completely convinced, but still hungry, Jeremy went ahead and washed down the last of his sandwich with the Coke.

"How did tomatoes get all the way up there?" he asked, pointing with his eyes. Most of the plants were suspended high in the air.

"They do it all by theirselves. The one thing we never been able to kill, no matter how we try, is tomato seeds. A little fertilizer falls off the belt now and then and gets stuck in the corners of the steel. Then a tomato seed, after all it's been through, falls off the belt on its way to the oven and lands up there in that little bit of manure, and it grows like crazy. If there's anything in the world that shouldn't be alive it's those tomatoes, but there they are."

"Cool," Jeremy said, tilting the can to drain the last of his Coke, then tossing it in the ditch. Carl pounced on the empty can, butted it up out of the ditch, kicked it and chased it across the yard toward the hog house.

"See?" Moss said quietly, watching Jeremy's face. "That's God. You can always find God, even in the low places—*especially* in the low places—if you know how to look."

"You *are* a preacher," Jeremy said.

"We all are." The old man laughed. "Everybody preaches something."

CHAPTER 5

How long, O Lord?

At the end of the shift Snake took Jeremy home, dragged him out of the truck, prodded him up to the third floor, showed him the shower, pulled out the sleeper sofa, and then went to bed himself. But he didn't sleep; he stared at the ceiling and tried to see a way out of this mess.

It was happening again. He was becoming a passenger in his own life. Lying on his back, alone, feeling trapped, his mind drifted back to his days in the burn unit. Not the first days—the swirling, dark miasma of confused nightmares and distant voices—but the middle weeks, after the initial crisis had passed. They cut back on his drugs when he left the intensive care unit. Thus began the time of pain.

He had lain on his back then too, only not by choice. Life itself, that which he had always driven before him and controlled with a smooth confidence, had turned literally in a flash and caught him in its teeth, lashed him to a hospital bed and tortured him without mercy. With what was left of his hands suspended from stainless steel poles, he would lie helpless and watch while the nurse pumped a syringe into a nodule on his IV tube, which had been attached to his right foot because it was the only good vein beneath unburned skin. Seductive and cruel, the morphine would spread like a warm tide until it reached his head and made him drowsy, whispering to him, crooking a finger and coaxing him to the edge of sleep.

Then it would pounce. As he peered over the threshold into a warm and comforting world, the gentle murmurings of the drug would swell to a grating roar and the dreamworld would shatter into white swords of flame as he faced the explosion all over again. His head would rock back, eyes and mouth fling wide, gasping, and the stainless steel bed would rattle with the force of his revulsion as his knees flew up and his skinless arms flailed wildly on their tethers.

Now, ten years later, he lay on his back in his apartment and strained to hear, again, the duplicitous whispering of fate. He hadn't asked for Jeremy to come here, but here he was, and he'd brought his father's eyes with him.

Tom was two years older than Aiden, but he had never been the leader. Aiden, with his bold and boundless curiosity, had always been the spark plug. Even as a child, Tom had been a mitigating influence. He was not timid; he was merely cautious, a gene which Aiden did not possess and could not understand.

Aiden's fragmented early memories told him that when he and Tom were children they had been more or less equal in their parents' eyes, although his charm might have even given him a slight edge over his quiet brother when they were very small. His father had ignored them both, waiting for them to grow into something useful, capable of work, and so the early years of nurturing had fallen almost exclusively to their mother. Even she had not been particularly demonstrative, but she'd had her moments. Sometimes, when the boys would charge through the house with bat and ball or fishing rod, she'd grab the nearest one on the fly and lift him off his feet in a spontaneous bear hug, then just as quickly let him go.

But sometimes, just sometimes, at the end of a boisterous evening, Aiden's mind would slow and he would go and sit by his mother's knee. She had the habit of reading her Bible for an hour before bedtime, sitting in her favorite chair and holding the Bible on her lap. Tom was as loyal as a dog—he would come whenever called—but Aiden had always been more of a cat and would seldom abandon his own pursuits until some need settled upon him. And then he would come, usually with a book or a baseball or a toy in his hands to occupy his eyes and allow him the dignity of distractedness as he leaned his head against his mother's knee. Her eyes stayed fixed on her Bible, but her hand would always search him out and rest gently on his head. She would curl a hank of hair about a finger and twirl it slowly round and round, absently scribing a little circle with her fingertip while he pretended not to notice. Though she also had her moments with Tom, he never saw his mother do exactly this with his brother. It was a small gift she gave only to Aiden. Sometimes they talked a little, but not often, and so much time had washed over the memories that now only one or two brief exchanges remained.

"What will happen to me?" he had asked her once. "What will it be like when I'm grown?" His insatiable curiosity had peeked into the future and seen only fog.

Her finger stopped twirling. He could hear the pages of her Bible crinkle as she smoothed them with the flat of her hand, and he could feel her eyes on him.

"I don't know," she said, and there was a sadness in her voice. "You're so independent, so self-reliant—I'm afraid for you. You always take the hard road, Aiden." And then she had said something else he could never quite remember word for word, but he knew the feel of it. It was something about how in the long run the hard road has its rewards if you can bear the carnage, the terrible toll on yourself and those closest to you, because eventually it will lead you back to where you began, and you will know the truth in ways inaccessible to the unbeaten, the unscarred.

Snake did not want Jeremy here. There was too much of Tom in the boy. He felt an uneasy sense of design in Jeremy's sudden appearance, as if fate actually possessed a hand and he could see it moving. Again. He had learned to *fear* the hand of fate, and a chill premonition had gripped him from the moment Jeremy arrived. He desperately wanted the boy gone, and yet at the same time, just as desperately, he wanted to take care of Tom's son, to see that no harm came to him.

The kid didn't even own a change of clothes. When he finally awoke around noon he had nothing to wear except the jeans and T-shirt he'd worn through the whole long day before, stiff with rock dust and still damp with cold sweat. Snake gave him something to wear, loaned him a wad of cash, wrote down directions to the Trading Post and handed him the keys to the truck.

"Why don't you come with me?" Jeremy asked.

"I don't shop," Snake said. "You gotta learn to take care of yourself. And don't think this is a free ride either. It'll be coming out of your first paycheck—if you last that long."

Nanny took Jeremy aside one night and said, "Don't let Biggins catch you loafing. Don't nobody expect you to know nothin' yet, but what you *can* do, do it like you was killin' snakes. Keep your mouth shut and do your job, and after a while it'll get better."

Doing a man's job at the tunnel every night was by far the hardest thing Jeremy had ever done and it pained him greatly, as stretching and growing always does. He knew his position was precarious, so he took orders from absolutely anybody and then put his shoulder to it, doing with a religious zeal whatever he was told to do.

At least Carl warmed up to him. The dog, who according to Geech was a pedigreed Border terrier, took to following Jeremy whenever he worked in the yard and shop, sniffing around, getting in the way of whatever Jeremy was doing, sometimes stealing tools or chewing the plastic handles off Biggins's screwdrivers. Sometimes he would ride down in the man-lift with the crew and go to work in the hole with Geech, but most of the time he preferred the relative quiet of the yard. He seemed to like the way Jeremy talked to him, and sometimes he would honor Jeremy with the gift of a dead rat.

Under the abrasive tutelage of Biggins, Jeremy gradually learned his way around. The mechanic shouted orders at him continually, prefacing every order with "GERMY!"

"GERMY! Get down the shaft and muck out under the tray lift!"

"GERMY! Sweep out the shop!"

"GERMY! Check the oil in the crane!"

"GERMY! WHERE'S MY TOOLBOX?!"

The toolbox haunted him. One of his responsibilities was following Biggins around like his personal bearer and keeping the big red toolbox within arm's reach at all times. Biggins would leave it wherever he'd been working last and then act like he couldn't remember. It was Germy's job to remember. Ten times a night he would hear the enraged roar, "GERMY! WHERE'S MY TOOLBOX?!" He would drop whatever he was doing and rush off to hunt the toolbox, going over all the places he'd seen Biggins working that night. It became second nature, no matter what else he was doing, to track the mechanic's movements, just so he'd know where to look.

Carl even got in on it. After a while, the dog heard the word *toolbox* so many times he apparently made the association. One night, during one of Biggins's toolbox tirades, Jeremy watched with growing fascination while Carl trotted straight out to the stacker conveyor where Biggins had been working, marched right up to the red toolbox, and barked at it. From then on, whenever Jeremy needed to find the toolbox, he would just tell Carl to find it and then follow him.

Living at home with his mother, Jeremy had never really been aware of personal space; it must have existed, but his mother's pathways and his own had always been so intertwined, they had always been so completely comfortable with each other, that the concept of personal space didn't seem to apply. Nor was there any personal space at Walter and Anna's house—not that he hadn't wished for it. But here, in his uncle's apartment, he became acutely aware of the strict limits of his own space and that required by Snake. For the first day or two they bumped awkwardly against each other with the strained politeness of distant kin. Jeremy bought his own bathroom stuff and kept it in a bag in the closet, leaving nothing of his on the counter. He used the closet next to the front door for the few clothes he purchased, and he was always careful to fold away the sleeper sofa the minute he got out of it. Later, after he started drawing paychecks, he would buy his own groceries and keep his sandwich meat on a separate shelf in the refrigerator.

Snake never quite told him these things; he had to figure them out for himself by watching for small flashes of irritation. Snake would jerk the dishwasher door a little too hard if he couldn't find a glass in the cabinet, or if Jeremy left his toothpaste on the counter he would toss it gruffly under the sink. But seldom was anything said.

In his apartment Snake was little more than a brooding presence. It was almost as though he had a split personality, with Jeremy being the only one who saw his dark side. At work, Snake was in command of his surroundings, and it wasn't just a title. He was knowledgeable and just, hard but fair; his men respected him, and they liked him. When he came home, however, his wounds seemed to surface, and all his private poisons, his doubts and insecurities and grudges, leaked out. Barricading himself in his dim fortress he would listen to his music, carve a little, drink a lot, and sleep too much. Though Jeremy had a thousand questions for the man who knew his father better than anyone alive, Snake had turned out to be someone he could not talk to.

Snake rarely watched television. One day—it was midmorning, nearly eleven o'clock, after breakfast, and he was bored—Jeremy picked up the remote and aimed it at the TV. Snake looked up from his carving and frowned.

"Don't do that," he said. The sound of a Bach sinfonia filtered up through the floor and into the silence between them.

"Why? I just wanted to—"

"Leave it off," Snake said. "I like the quiet. And there's nothing on in the daytime but saps and soaps. All those pretty people."

"Well, why do you have a TV if you're not—"

"Sports."

"But there aren't any games in the daytime, and we work every night."

"Right. So leave it off. *Okay?*"

Jeremy edged over to the stereo. The muffled sinfonia from

downstairs drew toward its conclusion. He recognized the piece but couldn't recall the number. His mother had played a lot of Bach—back when. He ran his finger over the face of the receiver. He could tell it was a nice unit, but he had no idea how nice until he reached up and started to turn it on.

"Leave that alone."

"What, the stereo?"

"Yes, the stereo. The vintage McIntosh 1900 receiver with the four-thousand-dollar Magnepan speakers. Yes. Leave it alone. It isn't yours."

"Oooo-kay." Jeremy's eyes widened and he pursed his lips, turning away from Snake. "Listen, I think I'm just gonna take a little, um—" he pointed both his thumbs at the door—"later, okay?"

"I leave here at two." Snake didn't look up as Jeremy eased out the door.

He found nothing to do outside either. There was an old, rusty, bent, netless basketball hoop at the far end of the parking lot, only he had no ball. Back home he could have found something to do. Back home he had friends.

Just beyond the parking lot stood a very old oak tree whose roots traveled twenty feet to buckle the edge of the asphalt. Having stood apart and alone its entire life, without competition from other trees, it had grown large and round and full. Thick, powerful limbs spread from its great trunk down low, at the height of a man. Jeremy walked up to it and studied it for a moment, its shape and structure. It was a fine, proud tree, and it rustled in a gentle breeze, calling to him. He wrapped his arms around a limb and hoisted himself up.

Climbing high, he found a solid perch in the very top branches and sat with his back to the main mast, looking out over the street. He felt safe and comfortable in the arms of the old tree, and he sat there for a long time watching and thinking before he took the letter from his wallet and unfolded it. After he had read it a couple of times he leaned his head back against the trunk and stared at the cotton ball clouds rushing across the sky.

"Whatever it takes," he whispered. "I don't know, Mom. I don't know how long I can do this."

Jeremy sensed an atmospheric change in the hog house on Friday night. Snake handed out paychecks at the beginning of the Friday night shift while the guys were dressing out, and the time-honored ritual of the check pool began. Jeremy didn't get in on it the first week because he didn't get paid; he wouldn't see a check until the end of the second week. But right away, starting with the check pool, he sensed the difference in a Friday night. These were uncomplicated men, most of them, with uncomplicated desires, and they moved in uncomplicated rhythms. They endured a greater load of stress and physical hardship during the week than most people. They knew this, and they were proud of it, so when the weekend arrived they stepped out from under their load and flung themselves onto the world with greater abandon than most people.

As soon as Snake started handing out checks the men scratched around and found pencils, then plastered check stubs against locker doors while they added the check number to the amount. They read the resulting five-digit number as a poker hand.

"Anybody beat trip fours?" Geech called out.

Nanny claimed a full house, but when Snake checked his math it turned out he didn't really have anything.

Luke McCluskey, sitting astraddle the bench, scratched his

head. "Does a straight flush beat three of a kind?" he asked.

"There ain't no flushes, Einstein," Travis answered. "There's only one suit."

"Okay, but don't a straight beat it?"

"I don't think so," Nanny said.

"Yes it does," Snake interjected, picking up Luke's check stub. He studied the figures for a minute, then nodded. "Yeah, Geech. He's got you beat."

Luke pumped a fist and pointed a finger at Geech, laughing— a customary gloat, part of his winnings. Geech grumbled, then pulled a five-dollar bill from his wallet, wadded it up and threw it at Luke, who snatched it from the air and blew him a kiss.

After everybody dropped their fives on Luke and he had counted them, he separated out a few bills and held them up.

"Yo, Germy!" he said. "You're low, aren't you?"

Jeremy didn't know what he meant. He turned a puzzled expression on Snake.

"Yeah, he's low," Snake said. "He's the new guy." Turning to Jeremy, he explained, "Whoever wins the check pool buys a couple cases of beer. The newest grunt has to go get it and have it here in the hog house, still cold, when shift's over."

"I can't buy beer," Jeremy said. He started to blurt out that he was underage, but he caught himself.

"Why not?" Luke asked. Other eyes turned toward Jeremy and an uncomfortable silence ensued.

Jeremy's mother had hated alcohol in all its forms. It was evil, she said. She refused to associate with anyone who wasn't a teeto-taler; wouldn't think of eating at a restaurant where they served wine. Jeremy was horrified. He didn't want to be anywhere near the stuff, let alone *buy* two whole cases of beer. He ventured a thin excuse.

"I, um . . . I don't have a car," he said.

Geech reached into the pocket of a pair of jeans hanging in his locker and tossed him a set of keys.

"Take my truck. Maybe somebody'll total it and I can sue 'em. Only way *I'll* ever get anything out of that rust-bucket."

"But I don't drink," Jeremy said, and several pairs of eyes blinked. They looked at him like he was speaking Russian.

"You don't have to drink it," Luke said. "You just have to go get it."

Snake grabbed Jeremy's shirtsleeve and dragged him, none too gently, toward the door. "Excuse us a minute, gentlemen," he said.

Outside, Snake turned on him. "What's this all about? You too good to go buy beer? Because if you are, you're too good to work here."

"I don't drink," Jeremy repeated.

Snake's face closed in. "I don't *care,* Jeremy! It's your job. It's Friday night, and the check pool is a time-honored tradition. When the Egyptians were building the pyramids they bought beer with the check pool money on Friday nights! And the low grunt had to go get it. Now, are you working here, or not?"

Jeremy looked away for a minute, feeling very alone. Even Carl turned his back and ran off leaping at a moth.

"Where do I go to get it?" he mumbled.

"Boyle's is the closest," Snake said. "That's where Luke always went."

Near the end of the shift, when it came time to go after the beer, Biggins stormed out of his office and told Jeremy to start cleaning up the shop, making sure all the tools were accounted for, hanging things up and sweeping the floor.

Jeremy looked at his watch.

"I can't," he stammered. The thought of refusing a direct order from Biggins filled him with dread, but he had to do it. "I'm supposed to go get beer. It's Friday night." The very words pained him a little bit.

Biggins opened his face to scream, but checked himself.

"Oh," he said. "Well, then you better get going."

Even Biggins wouldn't mess with tradition.

Jeremy worried about Joe Boyle all the way up to the store. By the time he got there he had considered all the possibilities and figured out that if Joe Boyle carded him there was absolutely nothing he could do about it. So when he got out of Geech's truck he squared his shoulders and stalked into Boyle's Gro as if he'd been buying two cases of beer here every Friday night for the last twenty years.

He plunked the cases up onto the counter and laid the bills on top of them. When Joe Boyle made eye contact, Jeremy nodded casually, once, without smiling. It was his best impression of how he thought a miner would act. Joe Boyle's eyes paused for a second on Jeremy's face, then he leaned over the counter and looked out into the parking lot.

"That's Geech's truck," he said. The truck was unique—a '65 Chevy with a blue hood, one fender coated with red primer, one with gray, a gun rack in the back glass with a four-foot level hung on it, and a *Harvard* decal underneath. "I see you found the treatment plant. You a miner?"

Jeremy froze, and a red terror rolled down from the top of his head. He had assumed Joe Boyle would either card him or he wouldn't; it hadn't occurred to him that Joe might just *ask* him if he was a minor. He wasn't prepared for the question. He flushed and gaped and was about to blurt out, "No! I'm eighteen, I swear!" when Joe Boyle rang up the sale and laid the change on the counter.

"Good people," Joe said. "Some of my best customers."

Joe Boyle's faith in the miners' drinking habits was vindicated when the crew poured into the hog house at the end of their shift and converted two cases of beer into a trash can full of empties in less than twenty minutes. Luke shoved one into Jeremy's hand, and the sly grin on his face widened when Jeremy quietly slipped it back into the case.

"What, you too good to drink with us?" Luke asked.

Jeremy shrugged. "I told you I don't drink."

Luke nudged Travis. "Little Germy don't drink."

"Leave'm alone," Travis said. "He don't have to drink if he don't want to." Travis was a little older and apparently didn't feel the need to compete as strongly as Luke.

But it was Travis who took up for Jeremy, and not Snake. It occurred to Jeremy that Snake didn't seem to care what he did, so long as he showed up for work on time and did his job. It was a hollow puzzlement to Jeremy, and it bothered him for a long time that night. What does blood mean?

The weekend turned out gray. A fine drizzle kept Jeremy indoors on Saturday, watching college football with Snake on his raggedy old TV. It was the first week of the college football season, and Snake switched channels with the remote whenever a commercial came on, following four games simultaneously while he picked at his carving. He kept the sound turned up pretty loud. Not surprising. Jeremy had already learned that most miners were hard of hearing. Every once in a while Snake would do something Jeremy couldn't figure out: he would mute the sound on the TV as if he had heard a noise and wanted to check it out. As far as Jeremy could tell there was never anything to hear.

Snake was quieter even than usual, like he was mad or something. Most of the time he drank himself to sleep after they got home from work, and Jeremy figured he probably woke up with a headache. He never seemed out of control but he drank a lot, and there had to be a price the next morning. This whole drinking thing was different than Jeremy had imagined. His mother had always said that alcohol was an intolerable evil, though somehow Snake's habit, in the context of his isolated lifestyle, seemed like a thing to be pitied. He seemed to need a sedative just to survive the hours away from the job, needed to knock himself out so that *something*, whatever it was, would go away and leave him alone. Jeremy wanted to talk to him about it, yet he knew better than to approach Snake out of pity; that would have pulled his pin for sure.

Snake sat on the edge of the couch with the corner of the newspaper-covered coffee table drawn close so that the carving sat between his knees among its own shavings. There were lots of carvings around—on the stereo shelves, on the shelf in the closet, on the windowsills, on Snake's dresser—some finished and some not. There were carvings of wizards and angels and leprechauns and unicorns, even a couple of demons and dragons, all of them very well done and intricately detailed. There were two hanging on the wall next to the door that had been carved from half logs like the one Snake was working on now. Most of the bark remained, but faces stared out from the heart of each log—long, blank, stoic faces like the king and queen in a deck of cards, carved in striking detail and symmetry, staring coldly from a recess in the heart of what otherwise looked like firewood. Jeremy saw real talent in the carvings, and given the unhurried focus Snake lavished on the pieces, it didn't surprise him.

But there was something different about this new piece. A limb raised itself for nearly a foot, angling up out of the half log like an arm. The piece was larger than anything else Snake had carved, and the shape remained a mystery, even though he'd already cleared the bark from the limb and begun shaping. It looked a bit like a hand and forearm rising from the raw log, but it was still very rough.

Jeremy, watching him work, asked him a question or two about his carvings, but Snake wouldn't give him more than a yes or no, and sometimes not even that. He must have pushed it a little too far because Snake finally answered one of his questions by stomping off into the bedroom. When he came back he was carrying a big laundry basket loaded down with the week's dirty work clothes.

"Here," he said, thumping the basket down at Jeremy's feet and handing him a roll of quarters. "Earn your keep. The machines are in the basement. Use a cup of that soap and set the machine to warm for colored, hot for whites."

So Jeremy spent Saturday afternoon stuck in the basement of the old apartment building, looking out a dirty little window at the rain and listening to clothes tumble. While he was there the Asian lady from downstairs came in to do her laundry. She was very quiet and demure, nodding politely when she entered and then turning to her work, sorting clothes. When Jeremy took his first load out of the dryer and started to fold them, she watched him and covered a smile with her fingers.

She rose from her seat and stood beside him at the folding table.

"I show you," she said without looking directly at him. With an efficiency bordering on magic, she smoothed and folded the entire basket of clothes in a minute or two, her hands flying automatically through the task. Then she nodded again and sat back down. She seemed very nice and in some small way reminded him of his mother with her quiet efficiency.

"Are you the one who plays the piano sometimes?" he asked.

She looked up then, and made eye contact for the first time. Her eyes smiled.

"I play," she said, and having found a common patch of ground, they began to talk. They laughed at themselves when she tried to teach him her name, Chuan, for the best his Southern mouth would do was *Swan*. Nor would her Chinese palate wrap around the word *y'all*.

He liked talking to her, listening to her. She was old—at least thirty—and he found he could talk to her as easily as he had talked to his mother. He talked about his mother. She told him about her home, and how sometimes in the winter the setting sun would reflect from the snowcapped mountains on both sides so that from the recesses of the valley it appeared there were two broad sunsets full of fire and mystery, one to the east and one to the west. She was a comfort to Jeremy, partly because her loneliness was as cavernous as his own.

CHAPTER 6

One part breath of God.

In the South the passage of time during the green months is marked by flowers. It's a ubiquitous marking, one that can be found anywhere, in any kind of neighborhood, along any country road, so that anyone who grows up there has but to look around to know what month it is. From the first frost-cracking emergence of crocus and daffodil, through the blinding white blossoming of Bradford pear trees, the dense carpets of bright pink thrift dressing up drainage ditches at the ends of driveways and the delicate mist of redbuds tinting the edges of meadows, the short, spectacular profusion of dogwoods and azaleas at Easter, the weather warms and fades quickly into summer. June is the month of the mimosa, delicate salmon pink flowers on banks of pea green fronds leaning over blacktop roads, while drifts of honeysuckle weigh down pasture fences out in the sunshine. The heat of midsummer belongs to the leggy orange day lilies and spindly crape myrtles with their burnt pink clusters hanging like grapes against deep green foliage. The crape myrtles are everywhere, defying the sun, growing darker and more intense as the summer boils them down, reduces them.

After the first cool snap, the blossoms fall from the crape

myrtles and no one notices their passing. One day they are just gone, like the dogwoods and mimosas before them. A little peach tone sneaks into the tired leaves of the dogwoods sometime in late September, and then autumn is at hand.

It was in that time, after the last of the flowers, when Jeremy found the church, quite by accident. He woke up early one Sunday, ate breakfast, showered, stowed his blankets and sat on the couch wondering what to do. Snake was still asleep, so he was afraid to turn on the TV, and the stereo was off-limits. He slipped quietly out the door and went for a walk.

The cool autumn morning had shrouded the world in a light fog, matching the grayness that had crept into Jeremy's soul. The weeks had shown him no mercy; he felt farther from home and more alone than ever. With every passing day the thought weighed more heavily on his mind that he could always just go home. He had given it his best effort. He had tried to stay with Snake, but his mother could not have known what it would be like. Surely she would not have wanted this life for her son. Surely she would understand if he gave it up, packed it in and went back home to the people and comfort that he knew. Wavering, and depressed by his inability to decide, he walked a few blocks down the street to the railroad bridge, wormed his way through a fence and climbed up the steep bank to the tracks.

The tracks curved slowly out of sight in the mist. He decided to follow them, swinging his arms and stepping from crosstie to crosstie the way he had done as a kid, going nowhere, for no particular reason. The tracks ran on the edge of a low ridge, beside a matted little patch of woods on the high side where the thick shadows made him quicken his pace, and above another dingy neighborhood of gray houses on the low side, too old and small and run-down for decent folks. He didn't like the look of the place, and was about to turn around and go back when he heard singing.

He had forgotten it was Sunday. He heard the singing first, then spotted the church up ahead, nearly out of sight beneath the bend in the tracks. It was an old white frame church with a grave-yard next to it, the way churches used to be back home, except that it was run-down and one of the stained-glass windows had been replaced with plywood. He found himself moving again, drawn almost unconsciously down the tracks, stepping from tie to tie until he stood at the apex of the curving ridge above the church. Sitting down on the steel rail, he propped his arms on his knees and just listened for a while. He didn't recognize the song, or even understand the words from where he sat, but it didn't mat-ter. There was something in it, in the raising of voices in unison to reach for something beyond themselves, something at once unknowable and undeniable, something Jeremy needed like food, like sunlight.

By the time he wobbled his way down the kudzu bank, his boots and jeans were soaked to the knees from the night rain and morning mist collected on the vines. Crossing the street, he started to tuck in his T-shirt, but then he took stock of himself and thought, *What's the use?*

The singing stopped before he reached the top of the church steps, so he moved to the side and waited a few minutes, figuring he wasn't dressed for a grand entrance. When he heard the singing start up again he slipped through the doors and stopped, suddenly paralyzed by what he saw. The church he had always attended with his mother, the conservative little brick church in the hills where he grew up, where he knew everybody and they sang the same songs his grandmother had sung and where the preacher wore a suit and pounded a pulpit—well, this was not that church.

The music director, if Jeremy was guessing right about which one was the director, stood where the pulpit would have been if there'd been a pulpit. He looked to be maybe twenty-five, was small and thin and Asian—Jeremy guessed Vietnamese—had a sixties retro shoulder-length hairstyle complete with bangs, and wore a royal blue bowling shirt with his name embroidered over the pocket, carpenter jeans, and flame-red high-top tennis shoes. He sang and played lead guitar while the drummer, a skinny, middle-aged black guy who grinned constantly, apparently proud of the gap where his two front teeth should have been, pounded exuberantly on a set of drums. Beside the drummer, a tall, dapper, elderly gentleman in a neatly tailored, gray three-piece suit stood ramrod straight with no expression on his face and laid down impeccable rhythm licks on a bass guitar. Behind them, five black women and one portly red-haired white girl in choir robes swayed and clapped and sang backup. The congregation, altogether no more than a hundred people, a mix of black, white, Hispanic, and Asian, sang with the abandon of old and dear friends.

Jeremy stood at the rear and took it in. He started to ease out the door, thinking he'd stumbled into the Twilight Zone, when he hesitated. Instead, he stayed to listen for a minute, alone at the back, because there was something here. Jeremy didn't know the songs, but the words seemed to be saying the same things the old hymns had said, only in different words and with different sounds. He listened a little longer and began to hear an astonishing harmony, a oneness that transcended music. And underneath the harmony was a freedom of soul, an uninhibited joy radiating from these people. There was one man whose slumping posture, slack face, baggy eyes and general heaviness of form led Jeremy to believe he was mentally retarded. The man was dancing, swinging his ample behind back and forth as he swayed and bobbed awkwardly to the music, a wide, childlike smile on his face. The man next to him, who appeared way too old to be his father, tried once or twice to curb his enthusiasm with a hand on a shoulder, but the dancer ignored him until he gave up.

Jeremy wanted to slip into a pew at the rear, to stay awhile, to see more of this, except he felt absurdly conspicuous all alone so he moved down farther and blended in at the back of the crowd. The majority of them, he couldn't help noticing, were dressed no better than he was.

The Hispanic man who stepped onto the dais next didn't look or act like a preacher—at least not what Jeremy had always thought of as a preacher. Short and stocky, he wore plain clothes— short-sleeve shirt, no jacket—and he didn't appear to know anything about how to run a worship service. He spoke clearly but softly, so that everyone had to listen closely. The first thing he did was to ask if anyone needed prayer, and people spoke up, one after another. It was the usual stuff: a sick aunt, an upcoming surgery, a death in the family, a son overseas. Then he prayed, but first he got down on his knees right there on the dais, clasping his hands in front of him like a child. As far as Jeremy could recall, the pastor remembered every single request.

When the prayer was over he stood back up and, without any sort of preamble, began reading the creation story from the book of Genesis. While he was reading, Jeremy caught an odd fluttering of movement and realized suddenly that there was a man sitting in a chair facing the front row and translating the spoken words into sign language. The rapid train of fluid gestures held Jeremy's attention for a full minute before it dawned on him that the hands belonged to Moss Fisher. The old security guard didn't look the same without his uniform, yet the same lively face animated all his gestures as he talked with his hands.

The speaker finished reading the creation story, and afterward Jeremy fully expected him to throw down the theory of evolution and stomp on it, which was what had always happened in church before whenever the subject of creation came up. But he didn't do that. Instead, the speaker started pointing out things Jeremy hadn't really thought about, and describing them in a kind of poetic language he'd never heard applied to the Bible. He talked softly about how God's voice sent brilliant whiteness firing out of a blackness that had no prior knowledge of light, how He hung the sun and moon with a whisper, painted crimson sunsets and ice-blue oceans, wrought rivers of silver fishes and endless rippling fields of grass, hurricanes and butterflies and elephants and snow, all with nothing more than the sound of His voice.

"In the beginning, he was God the Wordsmith," the speaker said, "and He saw that it was good. But then He came to man. And when He decided to make a man, He did not speak him into being. He picked up a handful of dirt instead." The speaker knelt and scooped at the hardwood floor with his hand. Rising, he brought his closed fist close to his mouth.

"He blew into the dirt, like this," he said. His cheeks puffed, and Jeremy could hear the hiss as he exhaled into his fist. Opening his hand slowly, palm up, he said, "And there was a living, breathing man. The first one. It was the first time God ever got His hands dirty, the first time He started with something instead of nothing, and the first time He ever breathed His own life into something like that. It was then, when He made man, that He stopped being God the Wordsmith, and He became God the Father."

Jeremy watched, fascinated, as Moss spooled off the sign language, and listened as the soft-spoken pastor explained how every person who ever existed was one part dust and one part breath of God.

"If there is anger in you," he said, "if there is selfishness and lust and strife, that is the voice of the dust. But if there is love and joy and peace, that is the breath of God."

After the service Moss caught up to Jeremy right away, likely having spotted him through the sparse crowd, and introduced him to a dozen people whose names Jeremy would never remember, except for the retarded boy and Mr. Flippen, the weather-beaten old man who did, in fact, turn out to be the boy's father. Jeremy said hello to the boy, who might have been as tall as Jeremy if he hadn't slumped so. He didn't answer at all, but kept his sagging eyes on his father and worked his mouth like a toothless old man chewing gum.

"Donny don't talk," his father said. "Never has. He knows what you're saying, though."

For no apparent reason, Donny suddenly broke into a silly grin, grunted loudly, and pushed heavily into his father's shoulder, shoving him toward the door.

A stumpy, elderly black lady waddled up to Jeremy and, leaning over a pocketbook the size of a pillow, looked him up and down without a trace of a smile.

"Jeremy, I'd like you to meet my wife, Pearl," Moss said.

"Pleased to meet you, Miss Pearl."

She pointed at Jeremy's ribs and turned on Moss. "Who been feeding him?" she demanded. She didn't wait for an answer. "You comin' home with me, young'un. *I'll* put some meat on them bones. *Sarah!*" she shouted, her attention suddenly diverted, and waddled away, already talking to somebody else.

Jeremy stammered, recovered, and said, "I don't know, Moss. I can't just barge in—"

"Heh," Moss laughed. "Sure you can. It's no use to argue with that woman. I haven't won an argument since nineteen sixty-eight, and I still think she lost that one on purpose. She's meaner than a onion sack full of water moccasins, but she sure can cook."

Pearl Fisher could cook. She threw down a Sunday dinner of fried chicken, mashed potatoes and milk gravy, homegrown tomatoes, black-eyed peas and collard greens, and served it up with hot cracklin' corn bread and iced tea.

Jeremy almost cried.

Afterward he and Moss sat out on the front porch and watched life roll down the street, leaning back in their rocking chairs because they were both too full to sit up straight.

"Sure can cook," Moss repeated with a sigh.

"Heard that," Jeremy agreed. "What was that preacher's name again? I forgot it already."

"Emilio Estrada. He's from Colombia. Good man."

Jeremy nodded. "I loved listening to him. Has he got like a Ph.D. or something? What a teacher. I never heard anybody explain things the way he did."

Moss laughed that grandfather laugh of his, then said, "Yeah, he's got a education all right. Used to run cocaine for a living. They say he was real good with a knife. One night down in Florida he proved it, and he ended up doing eight years in the state pen."

"Emilio?"

"Yep. He was one tough hombre. But God got hold of him while he was in prison, turned him around. Spent the last half of his time reading and studying and talking to the other inmates. Started his own little church in there, they say. When he got out he couldn't go back to Colombia, so he came here. Now he spends most of his time working with Hispanics in the federal pen over on Boulevard."

"Why couldn't he go back to Colombia?"

"Well, the week after he got caught the DEA got his boss, so his people all thought Emilio sold him out. He didn't, but he couldn't prove it."

"That just doesn't sound like the man I heard talking this morning," Jeremy said.

"It's not. That was then, this is now. Before and after."

"Hey, it was kind of a shock to see you up there signing this morning. I didn't know you could do that."

"Oh yeah. I talk best with my hands."

"How many deaf people do you have in that little church?"

"None. Least none I know of."

Jeremy turned and stared at him for a minute. "None? Then why do you do it?"

Moss shrugged. "Just in case, I guess. I figure if any deaf people come there, we'll be ready."

"How long you been doing it?"

"Seventeen years."

Jeremy found himself staring again.

"Seventeen? And nobody, in all that time—"

"Not a one. Well, there was my brother at first. That's how I got started doing it. My brother was deaf. Fact is, he had a lot of problems. I grew up talking to him all the time, 'cause he taught me to sign as quick as he learned it, way back when we were kids. Seventeen years ago he read something about Jesus, and the next thing I know I'm signing for the church. I believe the Lord led me right straight to it."

Moss grinned and rubbed the top of his head, remembering.

"Heh, hadn't been for me translating for Ralph, I doubt either one of us would've ever seen the light. I been signing ever since, I guess because I don't know how to do nothin' else. You might say it's my calling. You gotta give what you got."

"What happened to your brother?"

"Oh, Ralph went on ahead fifteen years ago. He had a lot of

problems," he repeated. The smile faded from Moss's face, and he stared at his fingers.

"And you've been signing at the same church all this time without a single person there who knows what you're saying?"

"Oh, they all know what I'm saying. They can hear. But then, the words ain't mine, are they? The words belong to the preacher. What *I'm* saying is kind of different from the words." Moss leaned closer to Jeremy, and his brown hands began to speak along with what he was saying. It came so natural to Moss that Jeremy wasn't sure if he knew he was doing it.

"We say things with who we are and what we do. How we live. As I said before, everybody preaches *something,* whether he means to or not, and he don't even have to open his mouth to do it. My big brother helped me find God, and God showed me who I was supposed to be. Ever since then, that's who I am. Talking with my hands—that's just part of who I am."

"Yeah, but Moss, seventeen years?"

"Well, it was the last thing I knew God told me to do, and I figure if I just keep right on, sooner or later He'll show me the why of it. You're young, Jeremy. You got to learn to be patient, to wait on the Lord. You got to have *long* faith."

CHAPTER 7

Battle scars.

Jeremy took over all the little menial tasks for Biggins, anything beneath Biggins's dignity, anything Biggins didn't like to do. He learned how to clean greasy parts in the mineral spirits tank and how to remove paint with a sandblaster. Biggins never cut him any slack, watched him like a hawk and pounced on the smallest mistake, so it was inevitable that Jeremy would sooner or later make a beauty of a mistake. He was only trying to keep busy; he didn't know a sandblaster could ruin a camshaft. When Biggins saw it, he sandblasted Jeremy with an astonishing array of colorful words before condemning him to move a mountain of pipe, piece by piece, from one end of the yard to the other. Ripley, the electrician, stood watching this slow parade of torture one night from the open bay of the shop, twisting a toothpick beneath his prodigious mustache.

"How come you don't just move all that pipe with the loader?" he asked Biggins.

Biggins pushed his horn-rims up and gave Ripley a none-of-your-business glare. "'Cause I don't want to," he snapped.

"Oh. It's like that. Well, he's about half done and he don't appear to be tiring of it. What are you gonna have him do when he's finished?"

"I'm gonna tell him to move it back," Biggins said.

Owing to the peculiar acoustics of the shop and the quiet of the night, Jeremy heard this exchange quite clearly from across the road. On his next trip past the shop he shouldered two lengths of pipe instead of the usual one.

Sometimes there were little breaks in the monotony. Two or three times a night, Jeremy would drive a load of supplies in on the loki. His stomach still knotted up anytime he had to go underground, but anything was better than Biggins. The best nights of all were when Biggins showed up badly hung over, or still drunk, and didn't have the energy to harass Jeremy. A couple times a week, Biggins would simply forget the mindless busywork of hand-carrying pipe from one place to another, nor would he scream for Germy to go find his toolbox. Jeremy avoided him then. He would go to the bottom of the shaft to muck out around the tray lift. It was one of his routine jobs, clearing the accumulation of spillage around the vertical conveyor before it built up enough to cause a jam, and when he was finished he wouldn't report back to Biggins in the shop. Instead, he would hang around the yard and find something to do on his own. Biggins had a little plywood office with a desk and a chair in the back corner of the shop, and on hangover nights he would retreat there and kick back behind a closed door to sleep it off.

It was on hangover nights that the crane operator taught Jeremy how to drive the loader. Eldon had learned to operate a crane at the age of fifteen, working on an offshore oil rig, but it had been more like the discovery of an innate gift than the learning of a trade. He was a natural.

The big loader on the mining project, the one they used for moving virtually anything, Eldon called "the Grove." He said it was the biggest rubber-tired loader made; the tires towered above Jeremy's head. Sitting in the cab, Jeremy felt like he was twenty feet off the ground. Eldon let him crank up the Grove and drive it around, warning him to stay off the bucket controls for the time being.

After a couple nights of driving around and getting used to it, Jeremy parked the Grove in front of the hog house, where Eldon showed him how to raise and lower and tilt the bucket. Jeremy puffed and grimaced when the steel arms jolted spastically up and down, slamming the bucket into the ground and jerking up again hard enough to rock the whole rig on its huge tires.

Then Eldon took the controls.

"Chill for a minute, Germy. Look, you gotta finesse her a little." In Eldon's hands the bucket eased up and down and tilted back and forth with a smooth grace, as if the whole machine were an extension of his body. "See, use your fingers. She's not a shovel; she's an instrument. Play her with your fingers and wrists, not your shoulders."

Eldon laughed and pushed his hard hat to the back of his head. He wore a black hard hat with a Falcon emblem on the front. It had been given to him as a safety award while working on the Georgia Dome.

"You been workin' with that schizoid Biggins too long, Germy. He thinks you gotta hard-cuss everything to make it work. Not so, Grasshopper. You must become one with it."

Jeremy learned a thing or two about industrial-strength cussing the following night when he drove up to the shop in the Grove with a load of cutting wheels. He was grinning, sitting all high and proud in the driver's seat—until he pushed the wrong lever and dumped six four-hundred-pound cutting wheels onto the concrete apron of Biggins's shop from a height of five feet. When the thunder stopped, the verbal thrashing began.

Biggins roundly cussed him, then took him off the Grove and put him to work mopping the tobacco-stained concrete floor of the machine shop, and in that awkward hour nearly everybody on the project stopped by to gawk and grin for a second. Nobody could recall ever seeing the shop floor mopped. Swept maybe, but not mopped. It was a new concept, and singularly humiliating. Every time Biggins walked within spitting distance of Jeremy's mop he added to the tobacco stains.

A week later Ripley made a big crock pot full of gumbo in his trailer, and all the yard help sat around in the machine shop for a while, eating out of styrofoam bowls. When Jeremy sat down with his bowl he bowed his head and mumbled his thanks, out of long habit, and when he looked up he saw that all eyes were on him. Conversations had come to a sudden halt, and they all sat with spoons poised, not sure how to deal with a kid who said grace over his food—in public. It was not the sort of thing anybody, even Biggins, would challenge, but the looks told Jeremy they were uncomfortable with it.

Biggins helped himself to seconds. Settling down on a gangbox with his bowl, Biggins grunted his approval of the electrician's cooking, yet even the gruff compliment was liberally seasoned with his trademark profanity.

Jeremy just couldn't leave it alone.

"Do you really have to take the Lord's name in vain over a bowl of soup?" He spoke timidly, mumbling into his gumbo, but Biggins must have caught part of it because his head snapped up and a predatory gleam came into his eye. It got very quiet. The others stopped talking, stopped moving, and watched Biggins with a kind of gleeful anticipation.

"Say what?" Biggins asked.

Jeremy was in it now, and there was no going back. "My mother always said that kind of talk was ignorant and low, and that any man with any education at all could find better words to use," he said, his voice growing stronger in the conviction that his mother had been right.

"Your mother." Biggins smiled, stuck his spoon in his bowl, and regarded Jeremy thoughtfully. "You know," he said, "I never really thought about it before. You're right, Germy. I don't have to use them words. I done it without thinking about it, and I'm sure I could do better if I just took a minute to think up some better ones." And then he proceeded to rattle off a lengthy list of alternatives, all considerably more toxic than the originals. Ripley and Eldon both thought it was hysterical.

"Very intelligent," Jeremy said, after the laughter died down.

Biggins's eyes narrowed, and a sneer curled his lip. He let out a derisive snort.

"You know, Germy, you remind me of a hippie girl I run into in the airport when I come back from Nam. She was about your age. Got off the plane and there she was, standing in the waiting area wearing them sweet little hip-hugger jeans with the knees blowed out and a peace sign"—he tapped his forehead—"painted right here. She didn't know me. She was just looking for uniforms. And let me tell you, that stringy little haybag was loaded for bear, buddy. Got right up in my face and turned plumb purple, and screamed, 'BABY-KILLER! BABY-KILLER! BABY-KILLER!'"

For a second Biggins looked into his styrofoam bowl and stirred his gumbo. Nobody said anything. When he looked up again a cold hatred narrowed his eyes.

"That girl didn't have no right." He pointed his spoon at

Jeremy as if he'd been her accomplice, though the incident he described took place before Jeremy was born. "She stayed here, in a nice safe dormitory that her daddy paid for, piled up with her long-haired, pot-smokin', war-protestin', slick-talkin', draft-deferred boyfriend while I belly-crawled over the bodies of my buddies. . . ." He wiped his mouth with a greasy hand as his voice trailed off. There was a glimmer of something unbearable in his eyes—only a glimmer, but enough to make Jeremy look away.

"You could hear the chest wounds," he muttered, "when you put your knee down." He shook his head, hesitated for a long moment.

"*Baby-killer,* she called me." He snorted, pointed a finger at Jeremy. "I looked her right in her little bloodshot eye and told her I never killed no more'n I could eat."

Eldon choked on his gumbo and rocked forward, gripping his knees, wheezing with laughter. Ripley spit out a mouthful of Coke and grabbed a rag to wipe his mustache.

Jeremy didn't laugh; he'd seen the look on Biggins's face.

Biggins just sat there shaking his head and mumbling to himself. "No right," he muttered.

But, oddly enough, in the days to come, Biggins actually tried to modify his speech patterns—at least when Jeremy was around. He still called him Germy, still treated him like an unwanted stepchild, but his language was curiously mitigated for a while. Jeremy started to hear words like *flipping* and *dad-blasted,* and even the word *doggone* once. The sheer absurdity of such a word coming from Biggins had caused a ripple of laughter, so he didn't try that one again.

The whole experiment lasted less than a week. Doomed to failure from the start, a civil tongue trying to survive in Biggins's head would eventually have starved and died anyway. It was inevitable. No one could figure out why he attempted it in the first place, since the frustration of constantly checking himself raised his legendary irritability to new and dizzying heights. Most of the men admitted a strange sense of relief when Jeremy finally did something to break the dam.

Biggins was a pack rat—a hardcore, incurable, indiscriminate, prodigious collector of junk. Anything he thought might one day come in handy, or could be repaired, or had once been valuable whether it could be repaired or not, or might one day be a collector's item—anything at all—he quickly claimed and tossed in the back of his truck. And so it was that he stopped on the side of the road on his way to work one afternoon to look at a painted metal lounge chair somebody had thrown away. It was lying mortally wounded in the tall grass with its white legs sticking up, and it would doubtless have died and been recycled where it lay had not Biggins spotted it and pulled off the road. He turned the wrought-iron beauty over and examined it, top and bottom, and stroked his chin. There was a lot of rust, which had eaten through a weld in a place or two. The legs were bent, the prop for the back broken off. But the wrought iron looked pretty, what he could see of it, and none of the chair's problems were insurmountable for a man who had access to sandblasters, welders, a shop full of scrap metal, and a few cans of paint. So he hefted it into the back of his truck and went on to work.

By nightfall Jeremy had caught up on all of his chores and began casting about for something to pass the time. Things were going smoothly underground. Ripley had just laid in a fresh reel of cable, the cutting wheels remained fine and sharp, and a night's supply of water and air line had already gone in on the loki. Jeremy had finished mucking out under the tray lift and was presently knocking down the slag pile with the loader—an utterly useless thing to do, but he liked to play with the loader and the practice was already turning him into a decent operator.

Over the guttural rumble of the loader's diesel, Jeremy heard someone shout, "Germy!"

Biggins flagged him down and sent him out to the parking lot to fetch the lounge chair from the back of his truck—using the loader. From Jeremy's point of view it was a rare opportunity. Biggins had never acknowledged his growing competence with the loader and almost never gave him a job to do that involved driving the big machine. Totally apart from the fact that he hadn't heard any of the more egregious obscenities out of Biggins in nearly a week, he was now being sent to the parking lot *with the loader,* right in between everybody's personal vehicles. It was a small but extraordinary act of faith, and a clear sign that Jeremy had climbed a notch in the irascible old mechanic's estimation.

He was careful. Because a goodwill gesture from Biggins was by definition a watershed event, Jeremy was supremely cautious, crawling into the parking lot with the bucket low so he could see everything. Before he climbed down to go after the chair, he made sure to lock the wheels down. He lifted the rusty old lounge chair out of the back of Biggins's truck without so much as touching the sides, then laid it in the bucket of the loader as delicately as if it were a newborn baby. He climbed up into the cab of the Grove, shifted gently into reverse, and eased back out of the lot very slowly.

Once clear of the cars, he turned the loader and roared back down the road in front of the office trailers with the throttle wide open in celebration, but he made sure to slow it down well before reaching the shop. Biggins stood waiting in the rectangle of fluorescent light spilling from the bay's door. Jeremy rolled to a soft stop, killed the engine, locked the brakes, climbed down and walked around front to stand next to Biggins and stare into an empty bucket.

The chair was gone.

Panic rising in his throat, Jeremy stammered, frantically retracing the steps in his mind. Nothing had gone wrong. Absolutely nothing. But then he recalled the way the loader, on its big rubber tires, had rocked and jostled and bounced when it was coming back down the washboard road, and he remembered the low angle of the bucket, and a sickening possibility occurred to him. He stared hard into the darkness. Sure enough, a hundred yards down the road he could barely make out the outline of Carl, standing in the middle of the road sniffing at something very oddly shaped. There were one or two spires of bent metal showing white above the gravel, but mostly what was there had conformed itself to the shallow rut as if it had been run over by a very large front-end loader.

Biggins was next to figure out what had happened. It couldn't have been timed worse, as far as Jeremy was concerned. Snake and Geech had just come up from the hole with Ripley, and Eldon had sauntered over with them to see what was going on at the shop. The four of them arrived just as Biggins was looking for his prize chair.

Squinting into the night, Biggins put the puzzle together very quickly. A week's worth of pent-up, frustrated obscenities welled up and cracked the dam. His mouth hung open and he only sputtered at first, but then the crack widened and the dam let go. He broke into a run—actually started *running* down the road toward the mangled chair, the way a sane person might have done if a child had been run over—and as he ran he let fly with a unified body of professional-grade profanity, so focused and intense that Jeremy pictured it snuffing out entire constellations on its way to punching a new hole in the universe.

"Dude!" Eldon said. "He's flipped! Germy, I don't know what you did to turn his crank, but if I was you I think I'd bust a move right about now."

Snake sucked a tooth. Said nothing.

The temperature dropped precipitously at night, and Jeremy took to wearing a light jacket, which helped to pad his shoulder against the tons of pipe he carried night after night in the wake of Biggins's wrath. True to his word, Biggins was making him move the pile of pipe back to where it had been in the first place. But Jeremy was young, and the twenty-foot lengths of pipe got lighter as his shoulders and back tightened and his legs grew accustomed to endless marching from one end of the job to the other. He appealed to Snake several times, away from the job, asking if there wasn't some way he could get away from Biggins for a while. Snake told him to keep his mouth shut and do what he was told.

So he was hauling pipe. He shouldered a length from the pile in the semidarkness near the sludge pond and carried it down the road past the shop, past the switchyard, past the hog house, all the way down to the growing pile in the lay-down yard where he dropped it down from his shoulder, slid it onto the pile, and went back for another.

He heard a sharp *crack* as he passed the shop and saw that Ripley and Eldon were playing with the rifle again. Eldon kept the little Ruger .22 carbine in his truck, and would bring it out sometimes when the work was caught up and things were quiet. He'd pull his truck around to the dark side of the shop and point the headlights across the creek toward the vast wall of mingled garbage and dirt that was the landfill, and he and Ripley would take turns picking off rats.

On his way back past them with another length of pipe, Jeremy stopped for a minute to watch. He was about to ask if he could take a crack at it when Biggins stepped out the door and saw him.

"GERMY! What are you doing standing around, boy? You got pipe to tote! Get to it!"

Jeremy had shouldered his load, turned away and headed for the lay-down yard when he heard footsteps. Travis, who had forgotten his dinner and come up to fetch it from his locker, fell in with him while Biggins yelled at his back. Travis was a man of few words, but something in his perpetually slitted eyes and the pugnacious set of his chin warned of danger. They walked several yards side by side in silence before Travis spoke.

"Anytime you want to take him down, I got your back," he said, and then he turned up the steps of the hog house before Jeremy could think to respond.

Jeremy didn't know quite what to make of it, but it made him feel a little twinge of pride, knowing somebody had at least noticed him, saw what he was going through and was on his side. He slid his load onto the growing pipe pile, then picked up a piece of gravel and sent it skipping and pinging across the junk in the lay-down yard.

"Wha'd they say?" Moss had come out to make his evening rounds. Jeremy hadn't heard him approach.

"I didn't even get a chance to ask," Jeremy said, staring down the road. "Biggins caught me."

The rifle cracked again, and somebody whooped. It sounded like Eldon.

"I see," Moss said. "They shooting rats again?"

Jeremy nodded. "Yeah. They get to do whatever they want when they're caught up. Must be nice."

"Well, Eldon and Ripley work for subcontractors. They don't

get their paycheck from the mining company, so the rules ain't the same."

"They don't work for *Biggins*. That's the difference. That man's crazy, Moss."

Moss cocked his head sideways.

"You having trouble with Biggins again?"

There was something odd about the old man, some quality of childish innocence or ageless wisdom—one or the other, or both, Jeremy could not tell. Whatever it was, it surrounded Moss like an aura, swallowing wrath and fear and suspicion with deceptive ease, and so Jeremy told him about his ups and downs with Biggins. He spilled the whole story, how every time he started to build a little trust something would happen to mess it up and he'd end up back on the pipe pile. He told him about Biggins's disturbing Vietnam memories and the abortive attempt at cleaning up his language.

"The man just doesn't make any sense," Jeremy huffed.

"Yeah, he does," Moss said quietly. "I guess it's kinda hard to see it, but in his own way he's right."

There was that patient smile again.

"Listen. In his eyes, you just a kid—ain't been nowhere, ain't seen nothin'. You got no right to try and tell him how to act."

"But Moss, how to behave, how to treat people, how to talk— that's just basic stuff. I mean, isn't it? I don't know how to say it, but aren't those things, like, independent? The filth he spouts all the time—that can't be right in anybody's book, can it? It's just common sense. Isn't it?"

Moss chuckled. "Nope. Ain't nothing common about sense. It's just the way of the dust, son. You can't judge a man that don't go by your book, and he won't listen to you anyway until he knows you been some of the places he's been. Look, Biggins ain't seen Vietnam in thirty years, but it still haunts him. You can't tell a man nothin' if you don't know his ghosts."

Jeremy chewed on this for a minute. "So like, you're saying I have to go fight a war someplace before I can relate to people like Biggins?"

"No," Moss laughed. "I'm saying you got to find some common ground before you can talk about common sense. If you went to live in a foreign country, would you learn their language, or expect all of them to learn yours?"

"I'm not just talking about language," Jeremy said.

"Neither am I. What makes you act the way you do? Where do you get that from?"

"It's how I was raised."

"So, if a man was raised different, then you ought to expect him to behave different, ain't that right?"

"But the Bible says watch what you say."

"That's *your* Bible, not his."

Jeremy stewed for a minute, frustrated. "Right's right," he finally said.

Moss chuckled, and his eyes were drawn to the flame across the yard, lashing at the night. "I remember when I was a little boy, my grandpa told me a story about *his* grandpa. They called him Sookie. He grew up a slave down in Cordele, but he never had the heart of a slave so he had scars all up and down his back from whippings, and the whippings made him mean as a chained-up dog. Even after he was free Sookie hated pretty near everybody and everything. Most of all he hated preachers."

"Preachers. How come?"

"Because when he was a kid they made him go once a month and sit up in the balcony of the white man's church and listen to a sermon. It was always the same one, always from the book of Philemon, about how he ought to be content with being a slave, how he ought to try and be a good slave. The white man's God said so."

"Wow. Did they really do that?"

"Yes sir, they did. All the slaves went once a month, sat up in the balcony. That's why all the old churches got balconies in 'em. Then after the war, when Sookie was free, he found out that a sharecropper, if he didn't know his place and mind his manners, was even hungrier and lower than a slave. Couple years after the war, some poor white preacher got lost and stopped at Sookie's shack one evening asking for a drink of water and some directions. Everything might've been all right if he hadn't made the mistake of asking after Sookie's immortal soul.

"They said it flew all over him. He nutted up—beat that preacher with his fists and then tied his arms up to the forks of a pecan tree, gonna horsewhip him. They said Sookie's wife and kids begged and cried and tried to hold him back, but he was crazy. They knew he'd get hisself hung, and they tried to stop him, only he wouldn't listen. *Couldn't* listen. He was out of his mind.

"Heh." Moss nodded, laughed a little reflective laugh and bit his lip. "They would have too. They would've hung him from that same tree, sure as the world, if he had went through with it and horsewhipped a white man. But he didn't. He pulled that preacher's shirttail out and flung it over his head to bare his back, and that's when he seen 'em. They say Sookie staggered back and sat right down on the ground, staring at that man's back."

Moss made a wiping motion with the flat of his hand.

"Scars, top to bottom. Whip scars. They said he sat and looked at that white man's back for a long time, then he got up and cut him down, set him up against that pecan tree and asked his wife to go get him a drink of water.

"When he asked him how he got them scars the preacher said Andersonville, but Sookie could tell by the way he talked that he wasn't no Yankee, and he said so.

"'Alabama,' the man said. 'Born and raised.'

"Then Sookie wanted to know how a Southern white boy come to be horsewhipped at Andersonville. Come to find out, the preacher was a guard, and they caught him taking corn from the company stores and giving it to a starving prisoner.

"They said Sookie and the preacher talked half the night, and from that day on he was a different man. Like somebody had just lifted the skin off of all that hate and stuck another man inside."

Jeremy pondered this for a while. "I don't get it," he said. "It sounds like you're saying you can't tell anybody anything unless you've been through the same stuff they've been through. Everybody's life is different, Moss."

Moss smiled. "In the details," he said. "But we all, sooner or later, go to some dark place, alone. A man like Biggins—or Snake, or any of them miners, as far as that goes—they look at you and they see a boy. They don't trust what you got to say because you ain't been where they've been. They don't see that what you know is any better than what they know. Even Jesus couldn't make His disciples understand what He was saying until after He got crucified and raised from the dead."

Jeremy snickered. "Yeah, well I don't think I'm exactly dealing with disciples here, if you know what I mean."

"Heh. Well, the people you work with most likely ain't no worse than the people Emilio meets every week in the federal pen, and he's makin' disciples out of them. It could just be, if the people around you ain't disciples, it's because you ain't Jesus."

Jeremy would've taken Eldon's advice and busted a move if he could have—but his mother wouldn't let him. Her letter held an undeniable power over him, but even that was weakening. He didn't know how much longer he could take it. And then, one Saturday morning, something happened that made him reconsider, made him rearrange his view of the wider world yet again.

He woke up at half past ten and Snake was gone—his truck missing from the lot, his slouch hat gone from the coatrack. Jeremy knew where he'd gone; he never went anywhere else.

It was a gorgeous fall day, spectacularly clear with a high, bluebird sky. Jeremy couldn't sit in the apartment on a day like this, so after he scrounged up some breakfast he hit the streets.

He followed the cracked sidewalk across from the apartment building, down the block and up over the next hill. He passed Kim's Grocery, the dingy old store with bars on the windows, Korean and Spanish translations on the sign, and a gutted pay phone on the pole out by the street.

Jeremy could still, at times, let his mind go free like a child and just see what it would see. He did so now, picking up a sawed-off broom handle from the weeds next to Kim's, using it for a walking stick for a while, then casually dragging the tip of it along a picket fence, then laying it across his shoulders and hanging his hands from it as he walked.

He passed a lot of little old clapboard houses, some with bars on the windows, and a mix of people—black, white, Hispanic, Asian—none of whom looked particularly prosperous, and yet, on the whole, no worse off than he was, or his mother before him. He crossed over a little foul-smelling creek and went up the rise on the other side into the shade of a string of live-oak trees. As the ground leveled off he came to a whitewashed wooden fence— not a privacy barrier like several other places he'd passed, but a country fence with boards running sideways like the ones around horse farms back home.

Inside the fence lay what he guessed to be a three-acre grove of pecan trees planted in neat rows. Old and thick in the trunk, the V-shaped trees joined hands with each other in the upper reaches, their slender leaves filtering the sun so that very few spots of light dappled the clear middle ground. The leaves of the pecan trees were still green, though the dogwoods had gone red, and the poplars yellow. Something about the pecan grove slowed Jeremy's step and made him utter, almost involuntarily, a soft "Wow." There was something ethereal in it, an otherworldly quality of light.

In the middle of the four-hundred-foot stretch of fence, a gated driveway ran through the heart of the grove back to a white two-story house with tall columns across the front porch. Jeremy stood at the entry gate and stared at the house for a minute. It was a pretty place, though it looked to be a little past its prime. Even from a couple hundred feet away he could see that it needed paint. One of the black shutters hung slightly askew, and the columns seemed too big for the house—or the house too small for the columns. The asphalt drive showed a crack and a dip here and there, and a scattering of leaves lay across it in places. Parts of dead limbs lay twisted on the ground, the combings of a squall that came through two nights earlier. But whatever its faults or ailments, the place enchanted him.

A tangled hedge of bamboo encroached on the far side of the grove, and over near the hedge a bent old man in a straw hat walked back and forth, dragging dead pecan limbs and adding them to the considerable load already on the back of his pickup truck. Jeremy had started to move on when a girl came around the corner of the house, carrying a glass of water.

He stopped walking. Stopped breathing. Stopped thinking. She was only a girl, in ordinary T-shirt and jeans, about his age. Her hair—hanging thick to her shoulder blades, with two narrow braids pulled from the front to join each other in back—was still tinged with summer around the edges, not quite blond but not brown. She was exactly the right amount of pretty. Any less would have been plain; any more would have been glamorous. And glamour would have been a detriment to this girl, for there was something about the way she carried herself. She possessed an innate grace, a perfection of form that seemed to collect the cathedral light of the pecan grove, intensify it, and reflect it.

He watched her. Unaware of himself, he watched her walk through the grove to the old man and hand him the glass of water. They didn't appear to speak, either of them. She waited, gathering her hair in her hands and tossing it back while he downed the water in one long pull, then she took the empty glass from him and walked straight back to the house. Jeremy watched her until she was out of sight and then moved on, his hands hanging limp from the ends of his broom handle, his eyes looking at the sidewalk but seeing a goddess.

He walked on, past any number of houses and people and trees and cats, but if he had been asked, he could not have played back a single detail of it. He saw nothing but the girl.

Eventually he looked up and realized he didn't know where he was, yet it didn't seem to matter anymore. Turning right, he crossed over a block and headed back roughly in the direction from which he had come, trusting that sooner or later he'd see something he recognized and find his way home.

CHAPTER 8

Looking both ways.

A crew, a team, a platoon, any trained group of men is an organism, and some organisms shed cells faster than others. That fall and winter would see an uncommon rate of attrition in the mining crew. It started with Travis. Jeremy was listening to snatches of conversation one afternoon as the men were filing into the hog house to dress out, when somebody said Travis wouldn't be back.

"What happened to him?" Jeremy asked.

"Well, you know," Geech said with a shrug, "some of us were up at El Paso Saturday night, and Travis got into the tequila."

"El Paso." Jeremy frowned. "Isn't that the dive up on Stewart Avenue? The one that was on the news a couple weeks ago?"

"Where those three dudes cut each other up," Luke said. "Yeah, that's the place."

Jeremy's surprise came out in a nervous bit of laughter. "Why on earth would you go in a joint like that? You could get killed."

"Nah, Germy," Griff rasped, unbuttoning his shirt. "We're the reason normal people stay out of places like that. We're the ones who start the fights." Glancing at Geech, he added, "Except when we're in the Pacific Northwest."

Geech cackled. "I heard that. Man, never pick a fight with a logger. Them guys got *wind.* I tell you what, Germy—a miner can hold his own with anybody for a little while, but when all that rock dust catches up with him and his lungs give out, he's through. Them loggers, they been workin' in the fresh air all their lives. When you're done, they're just gettin' started. They can beat on your head for a *while,* buddy. Trust me."

"So, what happened to Travis?" Nanny asked. Apparently Nanny wasn't there either.

"Oh, uh . . ." Geech scratched his head. "It was kind of an accident, really. See, when he got ready to leave, he went out to the parking lot and there was this guy sittin' in his truck, trying to get it cranked. So Travis goes up and jerks the door open and drags the guy out and proceeds to thump his head."

"Travis was Golden Gloves in Alabama," Ray Del explained.

"Yeah, the guy tried to throw a couple punches, but it just made Travis madder. He worked him over pretty good. Some of us started hollering and stuff, and the next thing you know there's a little crowd there, rooting for Travis. So he gives the guy a couple shots to the body to bring his hands down, then he drops that big overhand right and it's lights-out." Geech mimed the punches as he told the story.

"Then he looks up and sees the window's cracked and he figures the guy busted it trying to jimmy the door. So he rolls him over, pulls his wallet out, takes a twenty for the window and throws the wallet down in the guy's face, right? Man, everybody was cheering for him then. It's like he was Batman or something."

Tunk Morley had walked into the hog house in the middle of the story. "Well hey, if the guy was stealing *my* truck—"

"No, wait—I ain't finished," Geech said. "So Travis leaves the guy layin' there bleeding and climbs in the truck, right? Only the truck won't crank. Key won't turn. He looks over about three spaces, and there's another red truck."

"Oh no," Nanny said.

"Right. But does Travis panic? No sirree. He sees all them people standing there wondering what's going on, so he climbs back out of the truck, gives the guy a good kick in the ribs and says, 'If I ever catch you doing that again I'll *kill* you!' Then he walks over to his truck like nothin's wrong, gets in and drives off."

Jeremy's mouth was hanging open. "That's insane," he muttered.

"Word," Luke said. "He was still on parole for that assault thing at the stadium last year."

Geech nodded. "Yeah. They come got him yesterday for assault *and* robbery, on account of the twenty. He won't be back for a while."

The crew was shorthanded without Travis. Jeremy lobbied hard for the position, begging Snake to let him work underground with the rest of the crew so he could get out of the yard, away from Biggins, but Snake flatly refused. Wouldn't listen. Wouldn't even discuss it. For three weeks, the crew just had to work a little harder. Snake spent most of that time underground, taking up some of Travis's slack himself. Until Weasel arrived.

Weasel Truax came rustling in November, hauling a dinky house trailer behind an old GMC pickup, the bed of which was full of toolboxes and lawn chairs and a charcoal grill. He signed in with Meg and then set up his trailer out at the end of the parking lot, spending the afternoon leveling and tinkering, running a drop cord to feed a couple of lights, a mini-refrigerator, and a small electric heater, and putting out awnings and lawn chairs—the shallow roots of a nomad. He traveled light: his little round trailer held only a place to eat and a place to sleep. Nesting on jobsites where there was a hog house kept him from having to drag his own bathroom around with him.

A snowbird, Weasel preferred to winter in the deep South and spend his summers on jobs as far north as Canada when he could find them. He never stayed more than a few months in one place because he didn't pay taxes—he just filed "Exempt" whenever he signed on. He knew from experience precisely how long it took the government to catch up with him, and he always managed to pull up stakes just before they came looking. The mining companies ignored his eccentricities because he was a good hand and there was always a shifter or walking boss who would vouch for him. Everybody knew him. Nanny and Geech had worked with him before, drilling and blasting missile silos out in Nevada.

Weasel was a born instigator. The first weekend after he arrived on the job, Nanny invited him over for dinner, along with Geech, and while he was there he sat on the couch and watched a movie with Nanny's kids. Weasel's unique slant on the animated movie irritated Nanny, and his irritation turned out to be a ready source of entertainment for Weasel. That Monday, dressing out in the hog house, Jeremy met Weasel for the first time and was introduced to the running battle over the significance of The Movie.

"No, man, it wasn't your kids," Weasel was saying. "I told you I wasn't mad at your kids. I *love* your kids. They're terrific—"

"Especially Jesse," Geech said. "That boy's smarter than a lead mule, Nanny. In fact, all your kids are brighter than you are." Nanny's back stiffened slightly and he suppressed a father's proud smile.

"And Bobby Sue is a wonderful cook. That casserole was incredible," Weasel said. "I keep telling you, it was only the *video* I didn't like!"

Nanny puffed, rolled his eyes and yanked his locker open.

"What's not to like, Weasel? That movie's been around since forever, and I never heard nobody complain about it before."

Weasel tilted his head to one side to keep the smoke out of his eyes. He was smaller than Jeremy, though ropy strong, and his long graying hair and bushy beard made him look strangely impish as he squinted around the cigarette.

"It's elitist," he said, turning a sock right side out. "That story's grounded in feudal presuppositions that are an affront to any thinking man. You should be glad I set your kids straight."

Nanny frowned, unbuttoned his shirt, and took a couple glances in Weasel's direction. Leaning close, Geech translated:

"He says it's got a rich-guy attitude."

"That ain't true," Nanny snapped, glaring at Weasel. "It's just a fairy tale."

"It's an insidious way of indoctrinating your children in the fundamentals of serfdom is what it is."

Nanny turned to Geech.

"Teaching your kids to be slaves," Geech said, chuckling.

Nanny fumed, protesting that Weasel was making too much of the movie. "It's a *cartoon,* for cryin' out loud!"

But even Jeremy could see that The Movie was just an excuse. The mischievous glint in Weasel's eye said he was only beginning. Once he found an irritant, he was the sort who would worry it and add layers to it until it turned into a pearl.

And Nanny wasn't Weasel's only target. Luke's prize possession was a very fast 1000cc Japanese motorcycle he rode to work every day. Geech called it his "rice rocket." Soon after Weasel arrived on the job the bike appeared to develop an oil leak. Luke found a dark circle on the gravel underneath his bike and spent a few minutes on his back, looking for the source of the leak. The next day he parked in a different place, and when he finished his shift that night the oil spot was bigger than the day before. It drove Luke crazy for almost a week because he couldn't find the leak, until the night he happened to be in the right place at the right time so that he actually *saw* Weasel dip a cup of burnt oil from the reservoir on the threading machine, carry it out to the parking lot, and pour it under the motorcycle.

Nanny carried an old-fashioned steel lunch pail every night, and soon after Weasel arrived things started disappearing from it. At first it was only a bite or two; Nanny would open his lunch pail and there would be a large neat bite missing from his sandwich. He didn't mind. The truth was, he figured Geech was playing with him, and that was okay. But one night Weasel went too far. He must have been hungry, because when Nanny opened his lunch pail there was nothing left but a can of sardines and some empty baggies. He had even eaten the Twinkies.

Nanny lost it. After satisfying himself that Geech was indeed not the culprit, he stomped around half the night mumbling threats. "If I ever get my hands on that no-good, low-down, no-sardine-eatin' Twinkie thief, I'll *kill* him." This delightful nugget was overheard by the other miners and played back so many times that Nanny finally dropped the subject. No more was said about it, and his lunch pail remained undisturbed for nearly a week. The next time the Twinkie thief struck, Nanny got his revenge by means of an axle-grease and onion sandwich, pieces of which he found spit all over the trailing gear. His triumph was short-lived, though. The very next night, though his Twinkies and sandwich remained undisturbed, when it came time to go home Nanny snatched the handle clean off his lunch pail before he discovered that it had been welded to the deck. He couldn't prove it, but he suspected Weasel. Tino was no Twinkie thief, and Weasel was the only other guy who could weld.

Like most of the miners, Weasel spent the bulk of his time at the heading—the dead end of the tunnel, where the mining machine was—and since Jeremy stayed mainly topside, the two of them rarely crossed paths. But one night right after Thanksgiving the machine ran into bad ground and started dumping basketball-sized boulders onto the belt. Griff sent Nanny, Geech, and Weasel all the way back to the shaft to help cull the big rocks from the conveyor before they had a chance to jam the tray lift.

Biggins was holed up in his office that night, hung over, so Jeremy was in the bottom of the shaft mucking out around the tray lift when the three miners arrived from the heading. They had brought a small welding machine with them on the flatbed. Geech and Nanny fell arguing about whether to wrestle it up the steps into the man-lift or flag down the crane and have Eldon hoist it straight up the shaft. Nanny settled the issue by hefting the welder up against his chest and hauling it up the steps all by himself.

The landing for the man-lift sat five feet off the bottom, and the steps running up to it were apparently an inch or two narrower than the welding machine. Halfway up to the landing Nanny got it wedged between the cage and the handrail. He grunted and twisted, but he couldn't break it loose, couldn't go up or down. Watching him squirm and struggle, and watching Geech do nothing, Jeremy had to say something.

"Um, Geech, I think maybe your partner needs a hand."

"Oh!" Geech's eyes widened in surprise, as if his mind had been elsewhere. "Yeah, you're right." He carried a spud wrench—a big, heavy crescent wrench with a pointed handle for lining up bolt holes—in a wire hanger on his hip. Drawing it out with a swashbuckling flourish, he reached under the handrail and jabbed Nanny repeatedly in the backside with the pointed end. Nanny twisted and jerked, tore the welder free and went on up the steps with it. After he put it down in the cage, he wiped his brow and turned to Geech.

"Thanks, man. I was about to lose it," he said.

While Jeremy mucked out around the tray lift, Nanny and Geech lined up beside Weasel to pull boulders off the conveyor. Jeremy joined them when he was done.

Nanny looked irritated again, and Weasel was trying to hide a smile. The rhythmic clacking of the conveyor drowned out their words until Jeremy got close, and even then it took him a minute to figure out that Weasel was needling Nanny about The Movie. Again.

"Look, Nanny, it's cut-and-dried," Weasel said. "You got seven miners living out in the middle of the woods happy as clams until this dippy haybag with a Betty Boop voice decides to break in—"

"Break in? The door was open!"

"Well, hey, where I come from they frown on you for going in other people's houses while they're at work, even if the door's unlocked. That's B and E, open and shut, and they drop a nickel on you for it."

"Oh, come on, Weasel! She was a princess! She was noble! Who's gonna call the cops on a princess?"

"Right. She worked that princess angle right from jump street, and what's it worth? Listen, anytime a girl tells you she's noble, you better hide the silverware."

"But she didn't *do* that! She came in right away and started muckin' out the house. She didn't wear no fancy clothes and she didn't put on airs. She worked hard, like a cleanin' woman."

"Right," Weasel said. "She waved a little rag around while she was singing—while the raccoons and squirrels were doing the heavy lifting. I say put the skates on her."

Geech was looking the other way, his shoulders shaking with

laughter. The boulders were beginning to thin out a little on the belt, and Jeremy thought he could hear the distant rumble of the second loki returning from the heading.

"But they loved her," Nanny whined.

"Oh, right. Because she kissed them on the head. And you could tell she loved *them* too, by the way it ended. She gets her dumb self poisoned by a witch, right?" Weasel looked side to side, gathering agreement from Geech and Jeremy. "So then what happens?"

"They built her a glass box," Nanny said. He smiled, and there was a note of pride in his voice. He liked the glass box.

Jeremy definitely heard a loki coming back from the heading. The rocks on the belt were getting smaller, and the slag was taking on a lighter, more natural color.

"Right," Weasel said. "They build her a six-foot glass butter dish and pile flowers around it every day until springtime comes. Then some tall guy in leotards comes riding up, gives her a kiss and she's off. Wakes up, hops on the horse with him, and just rides off into the sunset."

Weasel's hand glided outward with his words.

"One can only assume her easy acquiescence is due to her instant recognition of the *prince's* nobility. And after everything those little guys did for her, did you catch what she said when she left? 'Bye.' That was it. No 'Been real,' no 'See you around the pool hall,' no 'Thanks for the potato chips.' Just 'Bye.' Noble is as noble does, I always say."

"Maybe they just weren't her type," Jeremy said. *Just friends* was what he was thinking. He'd been handed that one himself once or twice. He could see the approaching loki now, rounding the curve a quarter mile in.

"Not her type." Weasel rolled this one over in his mind, then asked, "You mean because they were a bunch of grungy miners, or because they were ugly?"

"Ugly," Jeremy said, grinning. "Definitely ugly."

"Okay," Weasel said, "I could maybe buy that, except for one thing. Every one of those little dudes had a pocketful of diamonds, and a diamond flush beats ugly every time. Let one of those guys go downtown flashing his diamonds around and those potato noses, missing teeth, and nappy beards disappear like the morning dew. It'd be *snowing* princesses, and you know it. The only thing that makes any sense at all is that she can't shake her medieval class consciousness long enough to consider these guys anything other than subhuman."

Geech leaned close to Nanny. "She's stuck up," he translated.

Nanny nodded, glancing down at Weasel's brown mining helmet, covered with decals from far-flung job locations. A smile spread slowly across his face.

"That ain't it," Nanny said. He said this with a proud air of finality, punctuating it with a nod, as if he'd discovered the fatal flaw in Weasel's philosophy of life.

"It wasn't because she was stuck up. And if she'da went after 'em for their money, well, she'd . . ." His big face twisted for a moment, trying to find words like Weasel used, words to fit the weight of his argument, but he didn't own any. "It'd make her worser, not better," he finally said.

The approaching loki geared down, brakes squealing as it stopped short of the pile of boulders on the tracks. Luke swung down from the cab and picked his way over the rocks.

"Okay. All right," Weasel said. "So why'd she walk? Why'd she take off with Prince Perfect Hair and leave her supplicants standing in the woods with their gap-toothed mouths hanging open?"

Nanny turned and moved a little closer so that he towered over the diminutive Weasel. Again, a triumphant grin spread across his face.

"It was because they were *short*," he said. He gave this momentous insight a few seconds to sink in, then added, "Women just don't like short guys. Nobody does."

"Yo, dude," Luke said, poking his head between them, "Snake wants Geech and Weasel up on the drill deck." He jerked a thumb at the large pile of rubble they had snatched off the belt, which now blocked the tracks. "I guess that leaves Nanny and Germy here to clean up the mess."

"So who's going to watch the belt?" Weasel asked.

Luke shook his head. "Won't be any more big rocks. We're into hard ground now, and the loose stuff's starting to come overhead. Somebody's got to get up on the drill deck and sink some bolts, and we're shorthanded."

Geech and Nanny normally worked together. Snake knew that. Everybody knew that, but Tino was out with the flu and Snake needed a welder at the heading. Weasel was almost as good a welder as Tino, and Nanny couldn't weld at all, which was why he had asked for Weasel instead of Nanny. Through no fault of his own—or Weasel's—he would live to regret the choice.

Geech and Weasel had been up on the drill deck of the trailing gear for less than ten minutes when it happened. They had already set up the drill and sunk two eight-foot bolts all the way into the dark, fractured rock, and Geech had started drilling the third one when the roof came down.

Snake was up forward on the control deck of the machine, fifty feet away. Later, he would not be able to remember whether he actually heard the rumble above the roar of the machine or merely felt it—but the earth shivered and the periphery of his vision sensed movement, a sudden change in the light from that quarter, and he knew even before he turned his head what had happened.

A rock the size of a small car lay on the drill deck where Geech and Weasel had been working. A couple of smaller boulders bounded and crashed to the bottom, and Snake's quick eye noted that they hadn't hit anybody. The quartz lamp on the drill deck had been smashed; he saw the scene in dark silhouette, backlit by tunnel lights. Through the haze he spotted the outline of Weasel picking himself up at the far edge of the drill deck. His helmet was missing, and he looked like he was straining to do a pushup.

Geech was nowhere in sight.

Snake absorbed all these things in less than two seconds. His gut tightened into a ball even before he turned back to wave his arms and give the operator the slit-throat sign, meaning "SHUT IT DOWN!" He'd seen it happen enough times to know—the rock usually follows the drill. Most of the time the guy on the drill doesn't stand a chance.

He vaulted a handrail, slid down a ladder, crossed the gap to the trailing gear and flew up the ladder to the drill deck before the cutterhead had stopped turning. A wailing moan poured into the void. Griff had climbed up from the back side and was kneeling next to Weasel, who had stopped trying to get up. At least he was moving—a good sign.

Geech's head and shoulders lay clear of the rock, face up, but the rest of him was under it. His left hand waved as his head turned slowly. Still alive. Snake bellied down next to the rock, shouting for a light. Somebody's head—it might have been Tunk—appeared above the ladder and tossed a flashlight to him. Snake caught it, snapped it on, and shined it up under the rock.

Geech moaned again. His bloodied face turned. His right arm flopped across Snake's shoulders.

"How bad?" he wheezed.

Snake peered under the rock. "Can you feel your legs?"

A weak nod, a hard wince. "Unfortunately."

"It's okay, pard. We're gonna get you out. Looks like you got lucky—the drill folded over onto the I-beam and made a little space. If it hadn't been for that . . ." Snake shook his head. The rock was precariously balanced on the body of the drill, which lay precisely on top of the main beam, which was the only thing strong enough to hold the weight. If the rock tipped, the metal grating on either side would never hold the weight. Any attempt to move the boulder might topple it, and if it went the wrong way it would make hamburger out of Geech.

Tunk and Ray Del appeared at Snake's shoulder with six-foot pry bars and shoved them up under the rock, feeling for leverage.

Snake shook his head. "No, don't do that. It's too heavy—the floor won't hold. Go below and wedge some steel underneath to stabilize it."

Snake's mind raced, working on the problem. "Griff!" he shouted. "Get on the horn and get some more jacks down here!"

Eldon had lowered a skip pan down onto the flatcar so Nanny and Jeremy could load the rocks into it, and they had almost cleared the tracks in the mouth of the tunnel when Jeremy heard the panicked shouts of Biggins coming from above.

He ran back to the shaft and looked up to see a cluster of pneumatic jacks descending, dangling at the end of the crane cable. Biggins stood on top of the jacks, holding on to the crane cable with one hand while leaning out to look for Jeremy, his face contorted with rage.

"GET THE FLATCAR BACK HERE! NOWWWW!"

Jeremy relayed the command to Nanny, who jumped on the loki and cranked it up. A moment later the flatcar hissed to a stop directly under the load, and the jacks settled neatly onto it. Biggins unhooked the sling, signaled the flagman, and the crane hook rose out of the way.

"LET'S MOVE!" Biggins bawled. "THERE'S A MAN DOWN!"

Nanny throttled up as Jeremy jumped into the cab with him. Nanny's face had turned to stone, his mouth a thin line, his eyes fierce.

"Here," he said. "You drive."

He climbed up onto the top of the loki, trotted to the front end and jumped onto the flatcar alongside Biggins, who caught his arm to keep him from tripping over the jacks and crashing into the skip pan full of rocks.

Nanny questioned Biggins for a few brief seconds, then looked away as if in disbelief. He snatched off his helmet, ran his fingers through his hair, put his helmet back on, asked another question. Biggins answered, Nanny shouted a word Jeremy couldn't hear but he could guess from the violence of the gesture, and then the big man squatted down right where he was, both arms folded up over his hat in despair.

Jeremy understood. Whatever had happened was bad, and Geech was involved.

The slow parade of lights rolled past until they cleared the last curve and the machine came into view. Even from a distance it was obvious that something was wrong. The rumbling of the loki's diesel echoed from walls alarmingly silent in the absence of the terrible, jarring noise of the machine. A cluster of men knelt atop the drill deck, up in the top of the tunnel, and a couple more waited at the back of the trailing gear.

And the air was clear. Always before, the machine had been shrouded in a haze of rock dust, but now Jeremy saw everything in crystalline detail. An uneasiness crept over him, a nebulous fear at the back of his mind as if some malevolent presence in this place, having struck, had now withdrawn again to escape reprisal, to regroup and relish the moment. Approaching the trailing gear, he throttled back. Nanny jumped off and sprinted ahead.

Ray Del and Tunk leaped aboard the flatcar before it stopped moving, shouldered a couple of jacks and jumped off again, running. Jeremy locked it down and ran forward, scrambling up the ladder behind Biggins.

Nanny had climbed up to the drill deck ahead of them, but he had stopped a few paces short of where Geech lay and was just standing there, staring. Somebody had rigged a quartz lamp so that Jeremy got a good look at Geech's face—ghostly pale and bloody, eyes at half-mast. Snake, on his hands and knees, shouted orders down through the grate, telling Ray Del and Tunk where to brace the jacks. Griff was squatting next to Weasel, who was now sitting up and rubbing the side of his head. Biggins bellied down next to Geech and peered up under the rock, assessing the situation.

What Jeremy witnessed next he wouldn't have believed had he not seen it for himself. Nanny, who had stopped at the edge of the drill deck, paralyzed by the sight of Geech under a couple tons of rock, seemed to shudder, then he burst into action. In two strides he reached the big rock, knocked Snake out of the way with a knee, and stepped over Geech's head. Grabbing Biggins's shirt in a giant paw, Nanny slung him aside like a doll. Planting his feet under the edge of the rock, he bent his knees, found a firm grip with both hands, threw his head back and grunted as he stood up, lifting the edge of the rock nearly three feet.

Jeremy inched closer, gaping at the impossible sight.

Nanny's whole body trembled, but he held it. He was locked in.

"Get him out of there," Nanny said through gritted teeth.

Griff and Biggins pounced on Geech, grabbing him under his arms and pulling.

Geech screamed as his back lifted clear of the grate, but he didn't come out.

"He's stuck!" Griff yelled. "His foot's hung!"

Nanny's legs shook, and veins bulged in the side of his neck.

Jeremy had seen the left leg of Geech's jeans tighten and pull down an inch when they tugged against him; he knew where the problem was. He flopped down and dove headfirst up under the rock, reaching deep in and grabbing a handful of denim and smashed leg, yanking ferociously until it ripped free of the steel grate.

"PULL!" he shouted, and Geech slid free. In the same instant, somebody grabbed Jeremy by the ankles and snatched him out from under the rock.

Snake said one clipped word.

"Clear."

Tunk and Ray Del, working on the lower deck, flung down their jacks and hustled out from under Nanny. The whole trailing gear shook and swayed when Nanny dropped the rock, and a metallic thunder reverberated up and down the tunnel.

When Jeremy rolled over, Snake grabbed him by the front of his shirt, hauled him roughly to his feet and held him there, nose to nose.

"Are you *trying* to get yourself killed?" he snarled, and his eyes spoke of murder. But before Jeremy could answer, shouts tore

Snake away and he turned to see about Geech.

Mercifully, Geech had lost consciousness and was still out. His left hip was badly distorted, but Biggins didn't attempt to do anything there. That would be for the doctors, later. He ran his hands up and down Geech's mangled leg.

"Busted up pretty bad," he said, and then his thumbs paused at a wet spot just above the knee where blood throbbed and pulsed against the fabric.

Letting fly with an oath, he unsnapped a leather pouch on his belt, flicked out a lock-blade knife and, with alarming speed, sliced open the leg of Geech's jeans from bottom to top. The leg was badly misshapen, bloody and bruised. A large gash ran side to side just above the knee, where blood spurted rhythmically from a severed vein.

Biggins straightened up, unfastened his own belt, whisked it out, wrapped it twice around the upper leg above the wound, tied it off, stuck a screwdriver under it and twisted until the bleeding stopped.

They managed to get Geech into a basket and lower him down off the drill deck without Biggins ever once losing his grip on the tourniquet. Weasel, who had only caught a glancing blow from one of the lesser boulders, had come around and appeared to be unhurt. He climbed down on his own.

An awkward silence settled on the men as they rode out of the tunnel. Geech lay face up in his wire stretcher, moaning, dipping in and out of consciousness with Biggins clamped to his leg, Griff and Snake hovering over him. When they passed under a waterspout Snake spread himself above Geech, using his body to block as much of the water as he could.

Tunk, Ray Del, Luke, and Weasel sat perched on the rocks in the skip pan at the rear of the flatcar with their backs to each other. They didn't speak, didn't look at each other. Occasionally one of them would sigh and look up at the ceiling or the wall, or another would crane his neck and stare ahead as if to look for the shaft, but their eyes never lit on another human being. Even the pretense of looking for the shaft was an affectation, a kind of pointless fidgeting done by men forced into an unaccustomed silence and solitude. They all knew the tunnel would curve left before the shaft came in sight.

Nanny drove the loki, putting himself farther away from Geech than anyone, having been the most grievously offended. Standing in the cab alongside Ruskie, he never so much as turned his head. When they reached the shaft he stopped the loki but kept the engine running, listening, as if he heard something wrong with it. But the truth was there, in his eyes: he just couldn't make himself stand next to Geech in the man-lift.

Jeremy, whose silence was perhaps not so profound as the others, whose young eyes were not so inured to the ravages of hell, felt a deep and childlike sympathy for them all. He alone stood apart from the band of brothers, far enough to sense, though he didn't fully comprehend, that somehow they had all been crushed.

Hardly a word passed between the miners as they bore the stretcher across the yard. They moved as quickly as they could while their feet made awkward allowances for Biggins and his screwdriver, and when the doors to the ambulance closed, they all scattered like quail.

Jeremy made himself scarce while Snake took care of business. It was a Friday night. Most of the crew bundled up their clothes and paychecks and went home early, but Snake still had a lot to do. He had to write the accident report, call the project manager and bring him up to speed, then later he had to go in with the graveyard shift to help with the cleanup. All this needed to be done before he and Jeremy could go to the hospital.

Graveyard shift came on after a couple of hours. Jeremy stayed away from them. Walking around in the dark, trying to stay out of the way, he found Moss standing by the flame at the foot of the slope, watching all the excitement from a distance.

Jeremy said nothing as he walked up and stopped next to Moss. Moss stood with his hands in his pockets, staring out across the project, and for a long moment didn't acknowledge Jeremy's presence. Then, without turning his head, he spoke.

"Wha'd they say?"

Caught yet again by the apparent sincerity of the question, Jeremy answered as best he could.

"The paramedics didn't know. They said it depends on how much internal damage there is. If he lives, it'll be a while before he walks again. How come you always say that?"

Moss leaned over to get a better look at Jeremy's T-shirt. It was the Deus Aderit one.

"You wear that shirt a lot," Moss said, changing the subject. Jeremy had gotten used to the man's little eccentricities, the way his mind skipped tracks without warning. Even so, he was never sure whether Moss did these things on purpose or if he was just plain crazy. In the end it didn't matter. Under the circumstances he took considerable comfort in the old coot's company.

"I like this shirt," Jeremy said. "My mom gave it to me. It's about all that's left of her."

He hung with Moss for a while as he made his rounds through the plant. Moss wanted to know everything that had happened, how the cave-in had occurred, how they got Geech out, and whether anything could be done to keep it from happening again.

Jeremy answered his questions as best he could, but there was a lot he didn't know.

Besides, he had questions of his own, and a renewed fear. When Jeremy opened up and told Moss how scared he was, the old man asked a pointed question.

"If you don't like your job, why don't you quit?"

Moss had stopped in a pool of light and struck a pose with his hands behind his back and his eyes fixed on Jeremy's face. The tilt of his head said it was a rhetorical question. His eyes said he already knew the answer.

Jeremy was here because of his mother's letter. He knew he was to stay with his uncle no matter what, yet he wasn't entirely sure about the job. The letter had said nothing about that. The job was something he needed to do for himself, and he understood such things least of all.

"I need the money," Jeremy said, but he shrugged it off without much conviction and he could tell Moss wasn't buying it.

"I see," Moss said. "It's about money. Well then, just come down here early Monday morning and you can pick dollars off the trash racks like peaches if you want to."

"Sure, Moss. Whatever."

Moss pointed to a low brick building down near the huge concrete diversion structure.

"I'm serious," he said. "See that? Those are the trash racks, where the raw sewage first comes into the plant, and they got conveyor belts with teeth, like big combs, that pull up all kind of limbs and trash."

"Yeah, so?"

"So take a peek at that building first thing Monday morning. The parking lot will be full, way before work time. Everybody comes in early and stays all day long, lined up shoulder to shoulder at the trash racks, pickin' dollars."

"Pickin' dollars?"

"Yep. People go into Atlanta on Saturday night to party, and they drop money in the streets, on the sidewalks, in the parking lots, in the gutters. Now, in Atlanta, it always rains on the weekend—*every* weekend, and all that money gets washed down the street drains and mixed with the sewage. Some of it ends up in the trash racks."

Jeremy's eyes widened as he realized what Moss was saying.

"You mean they pick money out of raw sewage, with their bare hands?"

"Oh yeah! It's like a big party. Man finds a twenty-dollar bill, everybody hollers. He's *somebody*. I seen guys come out of there with as much as a hundred dollars, free money."

"Yeah, but—whew!"

Moss chuckled. "Well, we all human. Everybody lines up at the trash racks, one way or another—it's just the way things are. Point is, if all you need is money, you ain't got to work *here*."

Jeremy took off his hard hat, stuck it under his arm and let the night breeze into his hair.

"So you're saying I should quit?"

"No, I'm just saying you should ask yourself why you are where you are. Hardly nobody does, and that's a mistake. You ain't here to pick dollars off no trash racks, I can see that."

They had come full circle in Moss's rounds and were now approaching the flame again. Jeremy watched it in silence for a bit, then said, "I don't know. It's like this is all there is, you know? There's something here I need."

"There you go," Moss laughed. "Now we're gettin' someplace. What is it you need?"

Jeremy shrugged. "I don't know. But I feel it. When I was a little kid my dad took me out fishing with him on one of those big boats in Panama City. I remember there were lots of other people. The only other thing I remember about being out there is that we went so far out we couldn't see land, and it really weirded me out. I still remember that lost feeling. That's how this place—this job—feels. As bad as it is, it's like land."

"Oh, now that's a pretty thing," Moss said, and his eyes shined. He gripped Jeremy's shoulders and talked straight at him. "Hold it up and look at it! But now let me tell you one more thing. I can't say things as pretty as you can—I talk best with my hands—but I know a bit about life. Now listen—when God takes you across a street, look both ways, 'cause there's gonna be something for you to *get* and something for you to *give*."

"Oooo-kay." Jeremy shot Moss a sidelong glance full of teen-age skepticism. The old man was definitely teetering on the brink.

"I mean it, son. God got His hand on you, whether you know it or not. I can see it, even if you can't. Keep your eyes open. Something to learn, something to teach. Every time."

CHAPTER 9

Snake's Law.

S nake had to put in an appearance at the hospital before he
could go home—whether Geech was conscious or not. He
had always spent a fair portion of his time and thought finding
ways to avoid the world, and of all the places in the world he'd
rather not go, hospitals were very near the top of the list. But
Geech was one of his men, and he had to see about him before he
could go home; it was an unwritten law. The smells of floor wax
and rubbing alcohol alone could send his blood pressure up
twenty points, but there were other things. Worse things.

He let Jeremy do the asking at the information desk, so he
made it to Geech's room without having to talk to anybody face-
to-face. At two o'clock in the morning the only people who were
not asleep were too busy to notice him.

Geech had already been through surgery and recovery and was
now sleeping the blissful sleep of the drugged. His left leg hung
from some sort of wire contraption while his hips were wedged
firmly in place with pillows to keep him from moving. He lay flat
on his back in a tangle of monitor leads and tubes. A plastic bag
of bloody stuff hung low on the side of the bed, with two bags of

clear stuff drooping pregnant from an IV pole near his head. His skin was pasty and pale. The slackness of his open mouth and wheezy snore made it plain he wouldn't be talking to anybody this night.

A nurse breezed in, a young girl wearing teal scrubs and gauzy nets over her hair and feet, smelling of Ivory soap. She brushed past Snake and then, too close, turned and looked up at his face.

She sucked a little surprised breath as her eyes dropped away from him. To fill the awkward silence, she struck up a pretend conversation with her unconscious patient—nurse talk, the same kind of prattle she might have used on a newborn baby. Snake was too familiar with it.

After she had fussed with Geech's pillows, checked his vital signs, and made sure the various bags were as full or empty as they needed to be, she sang to her oblivious patient that she would be back a little later. She turned to go, clearly avoiding eye contact with both Snake and Jeremy. Snake wasn't in a particularly sympathetic mood; it had been a bad day and the first cold beer was still a ways off.

"How is he?" he asked the nurse, timing his question to catch her just as she turned, so that it stopped her and she would be facing him. She talked to his third button.

"He's stable," she said, trying to smile, and failing. "Luckily, his spine was undamaged and he's not going to lose any major organs, although his left kidney took a beating. He has a fractured pelvis and his leg's broken in two places."

She would have delivered the whole speech to Snake's third button, but as she spoke he bent down, slowly lowering his face until his eyes met hers, mere inches away. As she listed Geech's injuries her voice trailed off and finally stopped.

"But he'll make it," Snake said, enunciating every syllable.

"He'll live, and he'll walk again. He's tough. If you're gonna be dumb, you gotta be tough."

He straightened back to his full height. The nurse whispered an "excuse me" and hurried from the room.

"You might have been a little hard on her," Jeremy said softly.

"*Life* is hard," Snake shot back.

He should have seen it coming, should have known from Jeremy's silence that he was thinking about it. The kid kept quiet until they were halfway home. Three o'clock in the morning, after all that had happened, everything pounding on Snake's brain, and Jeremy had to pick that precise moment to bring it up again.

"Tell me about my dad."

Snake kept his eyes on the road. The question wasn't very specific. Maybe he only wanted to know what Tom was like, not how he died.

"What happened?" Jeremy asked. "*How* did it happen?"

In a flash, in a flash. One brother to heaven, another to hell, all in a flash.

Misshapen fingers kneaded the steering wheel, waxy scar tissue stretching itself white over knuckles and tugging at the base of his fingernails. Snake shook his head.

"I don't know. It all happened so quick—"

"But you were there, weren't you? Mom said—"

Mom said. How much had Mom said?

"Yes! I was there. But it's . . . I . . . no, I told you, I can't talk about it."

He could feel Jeremy staring at him for a long time after that, but he refused to turn his head.

When he got home he went to bed. Shut the door. Turned out the light. Pulled the covers up over his head. It crossed his mind sometimes that he *looked* a little like a turtle. But even inside his shell he could never hide from Julie.

Tom's widow. Jeremy's mother.

She didn't come to the hospital in the dark, early days, when the swelling welded his eyes shut and the morphine held him under, allowing him near the surface only briefly, at odd intervals. He lost track of time. There had been voices then, somber and consoling, announcing themselves as if he were down a well, spouting empty platitudes, promising to offer prayers on his behalf to a God Aiden would never be able to face, even if he lived. Floating voices called to him from outside the vortex, but Julie's was not among them—an absence as conspicuous as the absence of Tom's name. There were only little silent spaces where news of Tom should have been.

If he were alive.

In rare lucid intervals Aiden wanted desperately to snatch out the tubes, willing to face a strangling death if only he could scream his frustration with his last breath.

Do you think I don't know Tom is dead? My brother laughed and played cards and went fishing and ate ketchup on his hot dogs, and he could always throw a football farther than I could, and I loved him. Does your silence honor him? Does it spare me? Do you think I don't know?

But the tubes rendered him mute. His charred lips would move, and yet no one could read them. Buried in bandages, suspended from poles, his hands were useless. Blind, mute, trapped and helpless—all that remained was his hearing, and the things not said made him regret even that.

The crisis came in the third night. The swelling peaked, fluids converged in his lungs, and his breathing tube began to clog. He was drowning. If he was very careful he could sip a tiny stream of air past the buildup in the tube, painstakingly, one agonizingly slow breath after another. He would do this sometimes for many

minutes, until a nurse would wander into the room, hear the rattling and shove some sort of vacuum down the tube to clear it.
Five minutes later the whole process would start again, and he
would brace his feet against the siren call of the morphine, clinging to consciousness because he knew he would drown if he lost
control. He didn't know exactly when it happened, but sometime
in the night the merciless, strangling tide in his chest took the
measure of his immense stubbornness, conceded defeat and relin-
quished its hold. He slept, and when he next awoke he could see
a sliver of light through his right eye.

By that evening he could see with both eyes. Four times that
day, and for several days afterward, he watched helplessly as the
nurses unwrapped him and the detritus slid away. His arms melted
before his eyes, and his hands shriveled into skinless claws.

Later—it must have been a week—after most of the swelling
subsided, after the doctors decided he was going to live, they sent
Tom's pastor to tell him.

"I'm afraid your brother, Tom, passed away the first night."

Aiden couldn't answer the preacher. He was still a prisoner,
bound and gagged and tethered. He could see, but he couldn't
speak or use his hands. A true captive audience, he was forced to
endure the absurdity of this polished professional, with his mellif-
luous voice and practiced graveside manner, talking about Tom's
"passing" as if he had drifted off to sleep and simply failed to wake
up.

*You weren't there, pard. You didn't see what I saw. I wasn't afraid
he was dead; I was afraid he didn't die quick.*

It was about that time, after they moved Aiden from the ICU
to a semiprivate room, that Julie started coming to see him,
accompanied by his mother. Martha Prine had been widowed
three years earlier when Aiden's father died in a farming accident,
and though it had never quite been said, they had laid that body

at Aiden's feet as well. Martha sold off the livestock immediately and went to live with Tom and Julie. She couldn't manage the farm alone. If she'd tried, she might have talked Tom into moving back home and running the place, but she never tried. She couldn't look at a hayfork without seeing her husband's knotted arms, or look at a drying barn without expecting him to walk out of it wiping his forehead on a tobacco-stained sleeve. And she never wanted to see a tractor again. Martha Prine once had a backbone as tough as a locust fence post, but her husband's death wilted it in a single heartbeat. She sold the place, furniture and all.

Aiden had drifted away from his family even before his father's death, and the guilt that came after drove him further away. He had not seen much of his mother since his father's accident.

Julie and Martha were dutiful, if nothing else. They would come and sit straight-backed in the hard chairs against the wall, rarely looking at Aiden even when they spoke, and they seldom spoke. Julie wore a simple black dress, always the same one, and her eyes were puffy. Aiden's mother wore one of a half-dozen interchangeable pastel double-knit pantsuits and kept her pocketbook on her lap. In those days she looked more bewildered than anything else, and her eyes, her thoughts, her halting words, deferred always to Julie. When she and Julie came to visit, their grief was so apparent, their widowhood so clearly shared, that Aiden began to understand. Three years in Julie's house, and Martha Prine had become more Julie's mother than his.

They came every afternoon for a week and sat for precisely fifteen minutes, then Julie would quietly excuse them by saying that visiting times were strictly limited and other people were waiting. She would rise to leave, and his mother would follow.

Aiden's tubes were out by then and he could speak, a sort of dry rasp to match his blast-torn body, his parched soul, but until that one memorable day, he and Julie exchanged little more than polite greetings.

The window laid trapezoids of afternoon sunlight across the room, a bright gulf between the three of them. Julie brought a Bible with her and kept it closed in her lap, her hands on top of it with close-cropped fingernails picking at the edge of the cover as if it were a guitar string. Never at rest, her hands fidgeted and fussed constantly, always finding something to adjust or clean or fasten or unfasten or straighten. She didn't seem to notice what her shiny, work-reddened hands were doing; they simply led her around and held her in place while her eyes scouted ahead for the next thing to do.

She spoke to him that day, starting with his feet. She usually avoided looking at his bandaged face, and he was never sure whether it was him or Tom she didn't want to see. But his feet stuck out beyond the bottom of the sheet—he still had an IV attached there, one of many minor aggravations at this level of hell—and they were dirty. Twice a day the nurses gathered him up with all his paraphernalia, hung his bags and tubes on a rolling IV stand and escorted him barefoot down to the tub room at the other end of the ward so he could soak his bandages off. It was a burn unit paradox—fastidious, germ-conscious cleanliness everywhere but the soles of the feet.

Julie spoke to his dirty soles.

"A friend of Tom's came by to see me yesterday," she said.

"Really? Who?"

"He told me what happened."

Julie's voice shook, just a little, and he saw his mother turn that bewildered look toward her. Awareness started at his toes and slithered up through him exactly like morphine, only cold. This was not to be a pleasant visit.

"Julie, I—"

Her hand shot up, palm out, and her eyes closed for a moment. She didn't want to hear it.

When she opened her eyes again her head tilted, staring at the soles of his feet as if she had just realized they were dirty. Her brow furrowed and she stood up, laying the Bible on her chair. Walking over to the little stainless steel sink near the door, she took a clean washcloth, soaked it in warm water, squeezed it out and brought it to the foot of his bed. His mother watched her every move.

Now that Julie's hands had found something to do, her voice steadied itself. "If they're going to let people walk around here barefooted they should keep the floors clean," she said, attacking the bottom of his foot with the washcloth.

"Julie, you don't have to—"

"Shut up," she said. Her hands didn't stop. Gripping his heel in her palm, she scrubbed as if it were bathroom grout. She looked up, staring him in the face for the first time, and her eyes were fierce. "You and I have never exactly been friends."

That was true enough. It had been an uneasy partnership; Aiden owned Tom's childhood, Julie everything else. Aiden and Tom, though utterly different, had always seen their differences as complementary and symbiotic. Julie saw this as a threat.

"I put up with you because you were Tom's little brother, and you put up with me because I was his wife, simple as that. You thought I was—what did you call me? Prudence Primrod?"

That was it, but he'd always been grateful that whoever quoted him had left off the rest of it, the "prune-lipped puritan church lady" part.

"Look, Julie, that was years ago. You and Tom weren't even engaged yet." This was true, and although they had not become friends, he had actually come to admire her in some ways since then.

His mother remained silent, hands propped on her pocket-book, eyes on Julie.

"It doesn't matter—now. I always thought you were arrogant and headstrong, way too conceited for your own good. I don't care what you think of me, but I want you to know I know what happened. I know it was you and your attitude that got Tom killed. He'd still be alive . . ." She hesitated, swallowed hard, and continued, "He wouldn't have even been there if it hadn't been for you."

Aiden's heart hurt. Given a choice, he would have preferred she set fire to the bed.

She switched to his other foot, yanked it up by the big toe and attacked it with the washcloth.

"I'm going to leave you his Bible," she said, glancing toward the chair. "He was your brother and he loved you. I don't know why, but he loved you to death. You should have something of his, so I'm leaving you that Bible. It's about half worn out—Tom put some miles on it—but it ought to last you the rest of your life and then some. It wouldn't kill you to take a look at it sometime."

Finished scrubbing, she dropped his foot, wadded up the washcloth and hurled it at the sink. Her eyes flashed. Her eyes said her hands were clean, that she had done her part by giving him Tom's Bible, while personally she hoped he didn't read it. Her eyes said she hoped he would *burn* for what he had done to her husband.

For countless dark hours in the years to come Aiden would wish she had said out loud the things her eyes betrayed in those few seconds at the foot of his bed that day. It would have given him something—some scrap, some ragged remnant of an enemy, however small—to hate, to grapple with, something to pit his formidable strength against and, in some measure, justify himself. He would have done it, *could* have done it, if only she'd left him something concrete to stand against, some solid words to defy. If only she had given in to her instinct and become, in the end, no different than he.

But she overcame it. She looked down at her red hands, closed her eyes for a few seconds, and when she looked up again she was calm.

"I forgive you," she said.

Her voice had shrunk. She spoke with a pained resignation.

"I know you don't understand this," she said, and the set of her chin told him she retained a small secret delight in his ignorance, "but I forgive you. Not for you, but for me. I *have* to forgive you, for the sake of my own soul." She shook her head slowly. "But God help me, I just cannot look at you anymore."

With those words, Julie stepped quietly out the door and was gone. His mother rose and walked very slowly, with the tiny steps of an ancient woman no longer in reliable contact with her extremities. She propped her pocketbook on the foot of his bed and leaned on it, curiously breathless, staring back and forth between the door and Aiden. Her bewilderment seemed to deepen, and her lip quivered.

"Aiden?" she said, in a very small voice. "What happened? What does she mean?"

Aiden turned his face to the window in defeat. He was so defeated he had no desire to live, let alone defend himself. Better his mother should go. It would be easier that way. He heard a few more sharp little breaths, and then she gave up and shuffled out the door.

It had been an execution. Julie's eyes condemned, even as her words absolved. Like a careful executioner, she would be neither friend nor enemy. He had witnessed it with a kind of hopeless detachment, like a condemned man smoking his last cigarette while the rifle was cocked and aimed by someone he had admired.

When he was alive.

CHAPTER 10

The walking wounded.

.

Snake slept fitfully, waking at dawn Saturday morning and creeping out, driving back to the job. The day crew was there already. They worked a lot of Saturdays because they were the maintenance shift and it was their job to put everything right, to get the machine and all the supporting gear in tip-top shape for the two mining shifts. On this day they would be repairing the damage done to the trailing gear and the number two conveyor by last night's cave-in. As he was walking toward the hog house Snake saw the shift boss and mechanic arguing with an electrician at the top of the shaft, and he knew the crew hadn't gone into the hole yet. Things were a little more casual on Saturdays. He stopped in the hog house to grab his helmet and jerk on a pair of rubber boots, and he caught up with the rest of the crew at the man-lift. To his surprise, Nanny was with them.

"What are you doing here?" Snake asked the big man as they stepped into the man-lift.

Nanny shrugged. His eyes were baggy; he hadn't slept much either. "I just wanted to get straight in my head what happened, before I go to the hospital. In case he asks me."

He refused to make eye contact. Something was bothering him, but Snake didn't take it personally. Nanny and Geech were like brothers, so he was bound to be upset. Snake let it go.

The repair crew—three miners, a mechanic, and a welder—ganged up on the flatcar with a load of bar joists and angle iron. Snake rode in the cab beside Bubba Turcott, the shift boss on days. On the way in, Turcott asked him a million questions about the accident. Snake answered as best he could, except he didn't feel much like talking.

He was thinking about deep-sea divers, the men who wore those lead-footed body suits and walked the ocean floor in cumbersome helmets and hoses back before SCUBA was invented, and how some of the older ones suffered from the bends. Their joints ached constantly, and they were twisted and gnarled from so many times having come up too quickly from the deep. In the old days nobody understood the cause of it. The divers knew only that they felt whole again when they suited up and went deep, where the pressure compressed the bubbles in their joints and eased the pain for a time. They were men living backwards, never comfortable in the daylight world, finding relief only in the dark depths where sane men would not go. Snake understood. He could relate. What bothered him this day, as he rode in on the loki, staring at Nanny's massive silhouette on the flatcar out front, was that this time the pain lingered, following him into the deep. It wasn't going away.

One of the lesser boulders had struck the conveyor halfway between the machine and the trailing gear and bent it badly. Three of the miners immediately set about dismantling the twisted rigging. Another set up a drill and found solid places to sink a couple of eye bolts, while another relocated the tugger and scrounged up some pulleys. It struck Snake then that it wasn't just him; all of these men seemed more comfortable underground. This crew, like his own, moved as a unit, with very little communication, each of them understanding his own place in the grand scheme and fulfilling his role with a surefooted economy of movement. They were at home here in a way that none of them would ever be at home in the real world.

The big rock was still perched precariously on the drill deck, though someone had shored it up from underneath as Snake had ordered the night before. Snake, Bubba, and Nanny stood side by side staring at the rock under the harsh glare of a quartz lamp.

"I gotta know, Nanny," Bubba said, pushing his hat back on his head. "Did you really pick that thing up all by yourself?"

Nanny shrugged. "They say I did. Tell you the truth, I don't remember. I remember most everything else, but not that."

"I do," Snake said. "I was right there. Wouldn't have believed it if I hadn't seen it."

Bubba looked Nanny up and down, appraising him the way a farmer might measure a draft horse. "Well, would you mind trying it again? You know, just to see."

Nanny shrugged, then peeled off his coat. He started to hand it to Snake—Snake was sure of it—then caught himself and turned the other way, leaving his coat with Bubba.

Nanny planted his feet, his toes just under the edge of the boulder. He spit on his hands, rubbed them together, bent his knees, gripped the edge of the rock with both hands, twisted his feet for purchase, and heaved. His whole body snapped taut—two hundred and forty pounds of gristle straining against the load until it seemed something would have to break. His head rocked back, his neck muscles bulged, veins stood out on his temple, his arms and legs quivered, but the rock did not rise. It didn't move. Not a wiggle. Nothing.

Nanny let go and relaxed, collapsing onto his forearms, resting against the rock.

"Adrenaline," Snake said. "I've read about this kind of thing, where a hundred-pound woman lifts a car to get her kid out from under it."

They tried again, with Bubba and Snake on both sides, and still the rock wouldn't budge. Bubba called his two strongest men up to the drill deck, but even the five of them could not lift it. In the end, they had to drill it into pieces and drag the pieces away with the tugger.

Snake got back to his apartment around noon. Despite the brightness of the fall day he had been unable to shake the gloom. It didn't help that Geech's truck was missing from the parking lot of the apartment building. The old wreck was still parked at the jobsite, because Geech wasn't there to drive it home.

When Snake opened the door he called out to Jeremy and got no answer, which was good; it was the first thing that had gone right all day. Jeremy was a decent enough kid, and he tried—really tried—not to cause ripples in the apartment. He didn't even complain about the chores like most teenagers would have done, but he was there. He was always *there*. He interfered with Snake's routine.

Snake's work was his whole life, all that remained. In working underground Snake had not only found relief, he had found his calling. He understood rock. He knew its personality, could read the nuances of a tunnel wall as well as any man alive. He could discuss point load and density with an engineer, add valuable insights about strike-slip faults, and interpret core samples and punch tests. His intense work ethic and proprietary interest in the job had gained him a reputation that allowed him to walk onto any hard-rock mining project in the country and sign on as a walking boss. And a walking boss, as Snake well knew, could hang around the job as much as he liked.

It was in his nonworking hours, the times when he was away from the hole and forced to hide, that the weight settled on him. Sometimes it crept onto him in the hog house while he was dressing out to go home; sometimes it found him as he drove through the gauntlet, trying to reach the safety of his cave without being noticed and pointed out, whispered about, or worse, dodged. By the time he reached home the weight was always on him, and all he could do was hide out—drink and sleep and carve, maybe listen to a little music.

It wasn't a perfect plan, but he could manage. He could function. He could eat and sleep in a more or less routine way, avoiding people most of the time, and function well enough to be fit when he made it back to work at the earliest opportunity.

But Jeremy had punched a hole in his routine, which was why Snake didn't mind finding him gone. Snake would take solitude anytime he could get it, especially when the weight was on him, when one of his men had been squashed like a bug. Coming home to an empty apartment on a day like this one was like getting back under the covers on a cold morning. He closed the blinds, grabbed a beer, and paused in front of the six-foot stack of shelves where his stereo lived.

Memberships in a couple of different record clubs over the years had resulted in a formidable collection of CDs and an even more formidable row of old vinyl records, most of which hadn't been main selections. Snake's taste ran toward the quiet, bluesy, acoustic stuff where he could understand the words; where smoky, knowing, broken-glass voices sliced neatly through muscle and bone to harmonize with the prisoner inside; where Lyle Lovett and Hank Senior and John Prine and Jackson Browne and a dozen other poets wielded words like scalpels; where Lacy J. and Emmylou sat down next to him and cried. Snake's music let him settle under the weight as if it were normal—never tried to lift or even lighten it, but let it be what it was and let him submerge himself in it. His music recognized the old familiar pain and justified it, rendered it as palpable and heavy and heartbreakingly reassuring as a pile of Grandma's quilts.

Flipping through a stack of CDs, he searched for something to fit the mood but found nothing. He had left a disc lying on the top shelf yesterday, and he put it away now. It was the only recording of classical piano that he owned, and it was mostly Beethoven sonatas. He had played part of it the day before because, like his other music, the *Moonlight* Sonata stroked the minor chords inside him.

Now he was undecided, wanting to indulge himself, yet fearing that he stood too close to the edge already. In the end he settled on a Bonnie Raitt disc—sort of jazzy, nowhere near as dark as his mood. That was what he thought when he put it on, only he'd forgotten about that one melancholy song. He hadn't listened to the song in a long time, and now it held a whole new meaning, opened a whole new wound. It wasn't long before the quiet desperation pounded him down.

"*. . . I can't make you love me . . . if you don't . . .*"

Sitting on the floor, he leaned back against the couch, elbows on knees, and clasped his hands behind his head. He was almost gone, sinking into the mire, when the first precise scales came crashing up through the floor to joust with Bonnie's voice.

"*. . . You can't make your heart feel something it won't . . .*"

The China Girl changed keys, climbing up and down the keyboard in a series of runs.

"*. . . here in the dark, in these final hours . . .*"

Scales clashed with Bonnie's smoky voice like a brass band.

"*. . . I will lay down my heart . . .*"

He punched a button, and Bonnie Raitt vanished in the middle of a word.

The China Girl's piano stopped a few seconds later, as if on cue. It appeared she shut it down in the middle of a run of scales, just chopped it off, as if she'd been waiting for him to turn off the stereo. There was a long silence, and then she began to play again, softly. Apparently finished with her warm-up, she started on a piece of real music.

Snake's hand shook when he turned off the stereo and put away the disc. His heart thumped as he groped for the arm of the chair and sank down onto it, because he recognized the piece.

The China Girl was playing the *Moonlight* Sonata, the same piece he had played on this same stereo only the day before. As if she'd been listening. As if she'd taken it as a request. It had not occurred to Snake that music traveled *both* ways through the floor. He considered for a moment that it might be mere coincidence, that she could have selected the piece by chance, but no. She was playing for him.

When Jeremy reported to the hog house on Monday afternoon Carl was sniffing at Geech's closed locker, whimpering, confused. Jeremy expected a shroud of gloom to lay heavily on the others because he felt it himself. He had assumed, since the miners were arguably human, that the same sense of fear and loss would subdue them all, leaving them quiet and reflective. It didn't. Instead, the accident seemed to have ignited a kind of bravado among them so that most of them were even more boisterous and belligerent—more *themselves*—than usual.

Griff, for instance, walked a little wider, stuck his chest out a little farther, and leaned a little harder on his men. He flung open the door to the hog house, stuck his head in and shouted, "Let's git it, grab it, and growl! We got to make up for lost time today, girls!" Then he disappeared, leaving the door open, the afternoon sunshine streaming in.

Griff was made of granite, though now, if anything, he was tougher than ever, and it was that extra layer that gave him away. That little extra grit in his voice, the fierce squint in his eye, the quickness in his step—all revealed that his defenses were up. Even Griff was not immune.

Luke McCluskey, young and full of himself, had always liked to talk, and today he talked nonstop about his weekend skydiving adventures. But his voice sounded a notch higher than usual, and his words came out in too much of a rush, as if the adrenaline hadn't worn off yet. At first, Jeremy was impressed with a guy crazy enough to work underground all week and then go jump out of an airplane on the weekend, but the pitch of Luke's voice and the furtive look in his eye leaked the truth: when the wind picks up, some people just spit into it a little harder. Jeremy began to understand. That, too, was a kind of fear.

"Yeah, one of these days we're going to read about you in the papers," Weasel said. "You'll be like a footnote at the end of your own life, a little spiky-haired asterisk in a pasture someplace."

Nanny, who was normally quiet in a crowd, was quieter than usual. In spite of this, everybody who came in asked him how

Geech was doing. After he got over being mad at Geech for getting himself hurt, Nanny had spent most of Sunday at the hospital, sitting in the room whenever the nurses would let him. Once or twice a doctor had come in while he was there, and Nanny had gotten up the nerve to ask a few simple questions. The doctors had answered him readily enough, but they didn't seem capable of using words Nanny could understand. Geech himself explained some of it when he could, when he was conscious and aware, and the nurses helped a bit too.

The other miners had meticulously avoided the hospital, knowing from experience that such a place—a place of cleanliness and order and exacting science—would naturally be hostile to them. Not that they were afraid of hostility; they had in fact been known to go looking for it on a Saturday night, but they didn't want to make trouble for Geech, and so they stayed away.

Nanny now answered their questions quietly, repeating the words he'd heard doctors say. Dark and sullen, he kept to himself as much as possible while he was dressing out, until Weasel started in on him.

Weasel always seemed like he had something to prove, like he needed to climb above somebody, and Geech's absence left Nanny virtually undefended. Weasel circled his prey.

"So give it to us straight, Nanny. What's the prognosis?"

Nanny was just starting to get undressed and he was picking at a knot in his bootlace. He didn't look up, but his brow furrowed and Jeremy could see his lips working over the word *prognosis*.

Ray Del, buttoning his shirt, looked sharply at Weasel and translated, "How long before Geech is back at work, Nanny?"

Weasel grinned a little.

Nanny shrugged. "I think they don't know, but maybe a couple months. It's just his leg's all busted up and they put pins in it."

"Ah, well then, they'll have him up and around before you

know it," Weasel said. "Is that the only thing wrong with him?"

Jeremy was watching Weasel's face. He was probing.

Nanny shook his head grimly. "They had to sew some stuff back together, but mostly everything's working right, now."

"Mostly. So what's eating you, Nanny? If Geech is gonna be okay, then why are you so down in the mouth?"

"It's just . . ." Nanny shook his head, yanked hard at the knot in his bootlace, straightened up and turned on Weasel. "They said his prostrate was crushed, all right?"

There was a little frozen silence then, as everybody absorbed the news.

"You mean pros*tate*," Weasel said. "Prostrate means lying down. I don't know why nobody can get that word right."

"You knew what I meant," Nanny growled. His chin jutted a little, and his breathing deepened.

Even Jeremy knew Weasel was pushing it. Weasel read books all the time and knew lots of words. That was okay, and nobody held it against him, but it was a clear breach of etiquette to go using his education against Nanny. Tunk Morley looked from Nanny's face to Weasel's as he cinched his belt, then exchanged a glance with Ray Del.

There was pain and embarrassment in Nanny's eyes, and he struggled with how to say the rest of it. Personal stuff like this wasn't usually discussed openly, especially with a wise guy like Weasel. Nanny tried to remember the word.

Finally he muttered, "They said he might be impudent."

Weasel choked off a laugh. Scratching his chin through his beard, he said, "You mean impotent. He was *already* impudent."

Nanny's left hand lashed out, grabbed a fistful of Weasel's shirt, whisked him off his feet and slammed him hard up against the lockers. His ham fist drew back, but Tunk and Ray Del both pounced, locking onto his arm.

Luke and Jeremy froze, staring at the tangle of straining miners. Nanny bared his teeth and growled like an animal, but his poised fist was stalemated by Tunk and Ray Del, both of them screaming and scrabbling for more solid footing with the bench in the way. Neither could let go because the other could never have held Nanny back by himself.

Weasel's feet kicked wildly at Nanny, and he couldn't utter a sound with his throat pinned to the wall. Jeremy saw the desperation in his eyes, caught the movement of the right hand burrowing into the pocket of his jeans and saw what was coming. He pictured Nanny staggering back, wide-eyed, with the handle of Weasel's lock-blade Gerber sticking out from his ribs.

But Jeremy couldn't move. He stood rooted to his spot. Luke, seeing the same thing Jeremy saw, burst past him, almost knocking him down.

Weasel's thumb flicked, and Jeremy saw a flash of steel as the blade snapped into place, but Luke clamped both hands onto Weasel's wrist before he could stab with it. Weasel squirmed and bucked and tried to yank his arm free. His knee flew up and hammered Luke's ribs, yet Luke held on. He, too, was stalemated. He wasn't strong enough to take the knife away; he couldn't let it go either.

"Jeremy, help!" Luke grunted.

Jeremy still couldn't get himself to move. Glued to the spot, he couldn't make up his mind. His mother hadn't taught him how to take a knife out of a man's hand. He wanted to bolt out the door and go get help, but that would leave Luke alone with the knife. Paralyzed with fear, he closed his eyes and started praying.

A shadow broke the sunlight from the door. Feet scuffled, and Snake was there. He bent Weasel's wrist inward, the knife came free, and he threw it clattering up under the toilet stalls at the other end of the hog house. He turned and slapped Nanny as hard as he could and then, gripping him by the temples, tilted his head down and shouted, "LOOK AT ME!"

Nanny blinked, and the wolflike snarl melted.

Snake's voice softened. "Let him go, Nanny. Ease up."

Finally Nanny's arms relaxed. Weasel crumpled to the floor and rolled up under the bench, gagging. Snake held on to Nanny's head, kept his eyes riveted while Tunk and Ray Del drug Weasel out from under the bench, helped him to his feet and hustled him outside onto the deck. Luke followed them, rubbing his ribs and glaring at Jeremy.

Slipping away, Jeremy eased quietly into the last stall and fished the knife out from behind the toilet. His hands shook as he held it, turned it over and examined it. He scraped the blade lightly along the back of his hand, and the pale hairs came away effortlessly. Unlocking the blade, he folded the knife and slipped it into his pocket before he stepped out of the stall.

Nanny was sitting alone on the bench with his elbows on his knees and his face in his hands. Snake had left. The door still hung wide open, and there were no noises coming from the deck. Jeremy stayed in the shadows for a minute because he didn't know what else to do. He started to move toward the door when his foot stumbled and made a noise and Nanny looked up. For a second or two he stared at Jeremy, and it was clear the anger was gone from his red eyes. He buried his face back in his hands without comment.

Jeremy fingered the knife in his pocket and pondered the strange sight before him. It scared him to see a bear of a man like Nanny sitting alone, lost and despondent. It scared him almost as badly as the fury he'd seen just moments earlier. He crept closer, stopping a few feet away from where Nanny sat.

"Are you okay?" he said.

Nanny spoke through his hands, "I shouldn't of went off on

Weasel like that. It was all Snake's fault. It's him I was mad at."

"Why?"

"If he hadn't of called Weasel up to the heading instead of me, I'da been there."

Jeremy shifted his weight from one foot to the other. "Nanny, I don't know anything about rock, but, well, I don't think it would have mattered."

"Maybe Geech woulda done things different. He don't watch what he's doing when he's got somebody *smart* to talk to. If I was there, at least he would of watched what he was doing."

"I don't know, Nanny. I think that rock might have come down on anybody."

Nanny raised his head, and his eyes were bloodred and accusing. "Me and him was *partners,* Germy! Maybe I don't read books like Weasel, but I can read rock. Me and Geech looked out for each other, and sometimes I seen things he didn't see. No rock never got him when I was there."

Later that evening, well after dark, after the night chill had fallen, Jeremy saw Snake patrolling around the slag pile in the circle of light cast by the quartz lamp on top of the stacker. The surge of granite chips clattering onto the growing pile appeared as strong and regular as waves breaking on a beach. Snake walked around the bottom of the huge cone of gray shavings, taking his time, poking at the edge of the pile, picking up a piece here and there, looking at it and tossing it back down. He turned and looked, as if he had felt Jeremy's eyes on him, then motioned for Jeremy to come.

When Jeremy trotted up to him he didn't say anything for a while. He stood there scanning the slag pile.

"You can tell a lot about what's going on by looking at the tailings," he said finally. "See how the pile gets dark near the top? Means they just hit a vein. According to the charts it's only a couple feet across, but you can see it in the pile."

Hands clasped behind him, he walked on a little ways around the pile, looking for something else. He stopped, brushed aside a couple of leaf-sized slivers of granite and plucked a piece of clear glass from the pile, a broken shard the size of a half dollar. He blew the dust off of it and held it up to his nose.

"Ray Del's drinking again," he said.

Jeremy didn't see any writing on the sliver of glass, or even a scrap of label. Nothing.

"How do you know it's from him?" he asked.

"That part of the pile is only about two hours old. Gotta be swing shift."

"Oh. Well, how do you know it's Ray Del?"

"He's the only one drinks vodka," Snake explained, sniffing the shard one more time to be sure. "Geech won't turn his nose up at it, but he's not here. The rest of them are just beer drinkers. Tino and Ruskie might take a toke of weed now and then but they don't do vodka."

"Could be Ripley or Biggins. Or an engineer." Jeremy was starting to enjoy the game.

Snake shook his head. "Ripley and Biggins both spend most of their time topside, and everybody knows you don't take glass of any kind in the hole. If they wanted to get rid of a bottle they sure wouldn't drop it underground. Biggins might be hammered sometimes when he gets here, yet I've never seen him drink on the job. And it couldn't be an engineer either—Perrier comes in a green bottle."

Snake took a few more steps, stooped to pick a piece of twisted metal out of the slag, tossed it away. He didn't say anything else about the vodka, and Jeremy was curious.

"So, what are you going to do?"

"About what?"

"The vodka. Ray Del."

"Nothing. I don't have to, now. What do you think I called you over here for?" A sly little smile crept into the corners of his mouth.

"What, you want *me* to say something to him?"

Snake nodded, shrugged. "You don't have to say it to *him*. If I catch him at it I have to fire him, and Ray Del's a good hand. If I ignore it, it'll get out of control, become an epidemic. But if you tell one of the other guys I suspect Ray Del's drinking, he'll tell Ray Del. Then Ray Del will get nervous and quit taking vodka in the hole, which is what I want."

"Oh. I guess I can do that."

"So tell me about the knife," Snake said.

Waves of granite chips surged onto the pile. The tray lift thumped.

"I gave it back to Weasel," Jeremy said.

"Not that. I want to know why you didn't take it away from him in the first place. I heard you froze."

"I guess I did." Snake didn't look at him, and Jeremy's uneasiness grew until he felt he had to defend himself. "I didn't . . . I wasn't sure what to do."

"When I came in, you were just standing there watching. Somebody could have gotten killed."

"I was praying," Jeremy muttered.

Snake looked up at the halo of rock dust around the quartz lamp.

"You were praying." He spit into the slag pile, and Jeremy

could see his serpentine jaw working. "I told you this was a hard place when you came here, Jeremy. This ain't Sunday school, but if I remember right, it says in the Bible there's a time for everything—a time to heal, a time to kill, and all that. In the real world you're going to find there's a time to pray and a time to take the knife away from the psychopath, and it's best not to confuse the two."

The tray lift thumped several times, waiting for Jeremy to explain himself.

"I was scared," he said.

"There," Snake said. "Now we're getting down to it. You were scared, so you did nothing."

"It was my first knife fight."

Snake laughed out loud. "Eighteen years old, and this was your first knife fight? Wow, you *are* a mama's boy!" He grabbed Jeremy by the shoulders and looked him in the eye. "I'm kidding. Look, there's nothing wrong with being scared. Everybody's scared of something, whether they'll admit it or not. But a man has to make decisions—sometimes tough decisions, and sometimes in the heat of battle."

Jeremy thought about it for a minute, then said, "I don't get it. When we were down there on the drill deck and I went under the rock to get Geech loose, I wasn't afraid, and you got mad at me. Then, when I don't take the knife away from Weasel, you get mad at me again. I'm wrong if I move, and I'm wrong if I *don't* move. You don't leave me a whole lot of choices."

Snake's eyes narrowed. "See, think, move. That's the drill. When you stuck your thick head up under that rock, at least you were seeing—you got that much right. You saw the problem. But you didn't know how long Nanny could hold that rock. He drops it, you're a waffle. You could have grabbed Geech's belt and done the same thing. You didn't think. When you needed to take the knife away from Weasel, you had time to think, but you got scared and didn't *do* anything. Didn't move. If you don't know what's going on around you, if you don't think, or if you can't move when the fear is up, you'll never make it in this place, do you hear me? You're going to have to grow up or get off my job before you get yourself killed, it's as simple as that. Do you understand me?"

Trudging back to the shop, Jeremy ran into Moss, making his rounds.

"Wha'd they say?" Moss asked.

CHAPTER II

The deer hunt.

Weak men, having clashed, will remain enemies for life out of one kind of fear or another, whereas strong men will often become good friends once the fight is over.

And so it was with Nanny and Weasel. They didn't speak to each other or look at each other for the remainder of the day, and the other miners kept the two men apart. At the end of his shift Weasel retired to his tiny trailer and holed up with a book. The book he was reading hinted that most men were fools, which made it all right, since he was not alone in it, to admit to being one himself. The next morning, long after day shift had gone to work, he ate a small breakfast, went to the hog house and took a shower, put on clean clothes, drove out to Nanny's place and, hat in hand, apologized for himself. He had no control over the words that came out of his mouth, he said. It had always been so. Some of the things he had read suggested that maybe it had something to do with his being small, but he wasn't sure. Nanny, being large, had left his anger behind and now wanted only to make Weasel feel a little less foolish.

"Men are ignernt," he confided sadly, looking over his shoulder at the house to make sure Bobby Sue wasn't listening, for he had stolen the very words from her. "And they do dumb and stupid things."

Weasel's careful timing paid off, and his arrival at eleven o'clock in the morning resulted, as he had planned, in Bobby Sue inviting him to stay for lunch.

"That's a good woman," Weasel said, and he meant it.

"I know. I couldn't make it a day without her takin' care of me. How come you ain't married, Weasel? Never found true love?"

Weasel chuckled, shaking his head, then stroked his beard and said, "Well. Once. Didn't work out."

"What happened?"

"Oh, I don't know. She had class." He said it the same way he would have said she had cancer.

Nanny nodded gravely. "I'm sorry," he said, and he meant it. It was mostly then, in that moment, that they became friends.

Weasel leaned back against the picnic table and blew smoke rings straight up at the sky. The twinkle crept back into his eye.

"I still say they should've tramped her out," he said quietly.

"Who?"

"The princess. In that movie. They should have tramped her out the minute she started calling them 'nasty little children.' Miners! That was rock dust under their fingernails, Nanny. Remember how she made them wash their hands before they ate?"

Nanny nodded cautiously.

"Yeah, well, did you ever see Miss Princess at the trough washing up?"

A shrug.

"And when she first got there, she was lost in the woods the whole night before, right?"

"I guess so." Nanny's memory had worn thin.

"And when they got home she was asleep in their beds, right?"

A perfunctory nod.

Weasel raged on, happily railing about how Little Miss Wash Your Hands jogged through the woods all night, sweating like a horse in her velvet dress, gathering bugs and worms, then broke into their house while they were at work and crawled her nasty self in their beds, under the covers, chiggers and all.

Nanny nodded and smiled, and let him run.

They feasted on red beans and rice, a recipe Bobby Sue had learned from Geech. Carl wolfed down a bowl of it too, after it had cooled. He had chosen to stay with Nanny in Geech's absence because he liked the kids—they played rough. After lunch, because Bobby Sue wouldn't let Weasel smoke his cigarettes in her house, he and Nanny sat outside where the cold air and falling leaves brought the conversation, inevitably, to deer hunting. Each of them was privately happy to find they had at least one thing in common. Somehow they both knew that the feud was completely behind them when Carl jumped into Weasel's truck as he got ready to leave. They didn't talk about it at all. No kind of permission was needed; Carl went where he pleased. But it was tacitly understood that Carl was family, and if he went home with someone, by extension that person was family as well.

The seed of the hunting trip was planted at Nanny's place that afternoon, and then it grew and flowered in the tunnel later in the evening when it was discovered that Ray Del had a cousin who owned a large farm down below Monticello, where the deer had multiplied like rabbits and made pests of themselves nibbling at his corn and sweet peas. By the time the shift was half over a kind of momentum had taken hold, and the hunting trip blossomed into an event that it seemed the whole crew had been looking forward to for years.

That same night Snake saw that the baloney cable would be running short after the next push, so he called up top to get Ripley to bring in another thousand-foot reel. The baloney cable, about the size of a man's forearm, was basically a giant extension cord designed to carry 7,200 volts—enough to power the machine. When Ripley and Jeremy pulled up to the back of the trailing gear with the big reel on the flatcar, the whole crew turned out to spool off the cable and figure-eight it into the cable tray. In the invigorating silence of the shutdown, the conversation immediately turned to the hunting trip.

What made the upcoming weekend so perfect was that both days were Doe Days. Normally, the Fish and Game people only allowed hunters to take bucks, but lately the deer population had been growing too fast, and the remedy was to open the season, for a few days, on does. The chances of bagging a deer improved greatly. Everybody was invited, though some declined.

"Lemme see," Tunk said, laughing. "Do I want to spend the weekend freezin' to death out in the woods with a bunch of beer-drinkin', gun-totin' white boys? I'd love to, fellas, but I got someplace I got to be."

While not sounding as enthusiastic as Ray Del and the others, Luke agreed to go. Snake figured he'd rather be skydiving, or chasing skirts.

"How 'bout you, Snake?" Weasel asked. "You want to come?"

"Oh, right," Luke sneered. "Kiss up to the man, Weasel."

Unfazed, Weasel heaved against the cable and shot back, "Obsequiousness ain't in my vocabulary, Luke."

Nanny straightened up, looked at Luke and nodded curtly. "Mine neither," he said.

"I don't know," Snake answered. "I'll have to think about it."

"What about Germy?" Nanny said, glancing at Snake for some kind of permission. Snake shrugged.

Jeremy stood on the flatcar, putting his shoulder to the big wooden reel. Nanny yelled back to him, "Germy! You want to go deer hunting?"

"Me?" Jeremy pointed to himself, surprised, then looked at Snake. Snake knew it wasn't permission Jeremy was asking for, it was an opinion. Jeremy would want to go; he'd be dying to go, but the cautious side of him would want to know if it would be a mistake, if he'd be getting himself into something he would regret.

Snake nodded. "Be good for you."

"Sure, I guess," Jeremy told Nanny. "I don't have a gun, though." This was no surprise either. Jeremy's mother wouldn't have allowed it. She sold all of Tom's guns the week after the funeral. Jeremy probably didn't even remember holding a gun, while Tom had always loved to hunt.

Nanny said, "Hey, Geech has got a old Marlin thirty-five he don't hardly use anymore. It ain't much in the open, but it's a pretty fair brush gun. I bet he don't care if you borrow it."

Luke rolled his eyes.

The morning sun lay across Geech's hospital room, a forgetful and purifying brightness. Jeremy had wanted to visit Geech anyway, but he also figured it would be a good idea to ask him personally if he could borrow the rifle, so he hitched a ride with Nanny the next morning.

"Sure!" Geech said, slapping his elevated leg. "If I can't get out myself, at least maybe my gun can do some good. You got a knife?"

"I got a pocketknife."

"No, I mean a real knife, a hunting knife, something with a little heft to it. Something you can strap on your hip and field dress a deer with."

Jeremy shook his head.

"Well, look, my keys are in that locker over there. My old Marlin is in the coat closet at home, right inside the front door. It's in the canvas case, not the hard case. Leave the hard case alone—nobody messes with my ought-six—but if you'll look up on the shelf there's a pretty nice old bone-handled bowie knife. You're welcome to use that too, only be sure to take good care of it. My daddy gave me that knife when I was about your age."

"You sure?" In Jeremy's present circumstances it seemed an extreme generosity, and he couldn't help letting his delight show.

Geech waved magnanimously. "Take it," he said, obviously enjoying the look on Jeremy's face. "And while you got those keys, how about swinging by the job and taking my truck home for me. You can drive it till I get back on my feet."

"You want me to drive your truck?"

"Yeah, why not? That old bucket's as pouty as my ex-wife. If you don't drive it every couple days it sulls up and won't crank. *Somebody's* got to drive it—might as well be you."

Suddenly the singing of angels welled up out of the sunshine, and a whole new world opened up with a wave of Geech's hand.

After Jeremy drove the truck home, he got Snake to go down to Geech's apartment with him. Snake drug out the old lever-action rifle and showed him how to use it, how to load and unload it, cock it, aim it, and fire it, but most of all how to carry and handle the rifle so he wouldn't kill anybody with it. Alongside the bowie knife on the shelf they found a box of bullets and a cleaning kit. Geech hadn't used the old rifle in years; it was dry and dusty, and there were a few tiny spots of rust on the barrel. Snake took the cleaning kit with him, and when they got back upstairs he showed Jeremy how to break the gun down, spread the pieces out on the kitchen table, clean and oil everything, and put it all back together.

Snake seemed to be enjoying himself. Jeremy watched his face as he sighted through the bore after ramming a rag soaked in cleaning solution through it. There was a new glint in his eye as he explained what he was doing, and a new animation in his voice. It was small, but to Jeremy's young eyes the complete darkness of the past turned even this small spark of interest into a bright flame.

"Your dad used to have a gun like this," Snake said, running his hand down the stock. "When we were just kids." He fell silent then, and stared out the window for a few seconds.

"Why don't you go hunting with us?" Jeremy said.

Snake flexed his fingers, looked at the waxy wrinkles webbing the backs of his hands. "It's hard on my hands." His voice had gone soft. "Scars don't keep out the cold—goes right through into the bone and my fingers lock up."

But there was something deeper, and Jeremy saw it. As quickly as it had come, the glint had gone from his eye. So it surprised Jeremy when Snake nodded and said, "I guess I could give it a try. Either I can pull a trigger or I can't."

Jeremy fretted over the hunting trip. Making the most of Geech's truck, he went and bought a hunting license right away, then picked up an old backpack from an army surplus store, along with a pup tent, an olive-drab sleeping bag, and a compass. Every morning he would get the Marlin out and handle it, loading and unloading, sighting along its barrel, smelling the oil and powder and wood. He kept the bowie knife in the backpack, but at least once a day he would take it out and feel the heft of the knife, wipe it off and put it carefully away. He tried to think of everything, except he had never been deer hunting and so didn't know what he would need. The morning of the hunt it finally occurred to him that he would need food, and he had an inspiration. He was pretty sure he was a better cook than most of the miners, so he drove Geech's truck to the grocery store and bought the things he figured they would forget. Once or twice he also cruised by the plantation house in the pecan grove where The Girl lived, but he didn't see anybody there.

A grayness settled in on the day before the hunting trip, leeching all the color out of the world so that even trees and buildings and thoughts turned gray.

"Wintertime in Georgia ain't always cloudy and cold," Moss said, "but it sure seems like it. Come spring, it's all I can ever remember. Cold and gray. Always cold, but it don't snow. Always damp, but it don't rain much. I think the sky stays gray out of pure boredom."

On the morning of that gray and ugly Friday, men who were normally sharp couldn't make a decision, and men who were not decisive to begin with hunched into their collars and waited for it to pass—this thing, whatever it was, that weighed on them.

Long before the weekend it had already been decided that they would all do without sleep on Friday night. It made perfect sense; if they were going to make the two-hour drive down to the farm, eat breakfast, find a camping spot, gear up and get to their places in the woods before daylight, they would have to be up by three o'clock anyway, and none of them ever got to bed before one. Two hours' sleep was worse than none, so they all brought their gear to work—tents, camping chairs, lanterns, stoves, tarps, ropes, groceries, insulated coveralls, boots, rifles, coolers, and long, razor-sharp hunting knives in leather scabbards.

Weasel had it easier than anybody else. He just tossed his lawn chairs in the back of his truck, hitched up his little trailer, and he was ready to go. He and Ray Del and Griff each brought a climbing stand, a rickety angle-iron-and-plywood contraption manufactured from spare parts in the machine shop, designed so a man could walk it right up the side of a tree, sit down, strap himself in, and hoist his rifle and thermos up with a rope. Weasel's climber even had a stool on it with a place underneath for a Sterno heater.

By the time everybody had showered and changed clothes, and the caravan pulled out onto the expressway, it was one o'clock in the morning. Somewhere near Jackson they besieged a Waffle House where they ate a prodigious breakfast, embarrassed the waitresses, hassled the truck drivers, left a meager tip, then piled back into their pickups for the last leg of the trip. Ray Del had been down to his cousin's farm earlier in the week to pick out a camping spot, so he led the entourage down an increasingly narrow set of county roads and finally to a rusty blue cattle gate with a NO TRESPASSING sign hanging on it. One corner of the sign had come loose and it hung at a forty-five degree angle.

Jeremy, dozing in the passenger seat of Snake's truck, saw the gate and thought they had finally arrived, but Ray Del led them another mile or so down an old logging road, across acres of open pasture, into the leafless hardwood forest, down to the edge of a creek, along the creek for what seemed like a mile, then up a little rise and into the edge of a dense pine thicket, where he finally stopped. Amazingly, Weasel's pickup managed to drag his little trailer through it all without once getting stuck or turning it over.

Grumbling engines fell silent. Ray Del and Nanny left their headlights on to light the little glade. Truck doors slammed; men grunted and stretched and hacked and spat in the shadows beside their trucks. Weasel pulled his trailer onto a level spot up against the wall of pines. When he opened his door, Carl popped out and did an immediate sniff check of the campground.

"I don't know, amigo," Tino said as he stepped into the light and arched his back. He called everybody "amigo," claiming he couldn't remember gringo names, though his English was better than most of the others. "If you try real hard I think maybe you can pick someplace a little farther back off the road."

"I been scouting this place," Ray Del said defensively, already pumping a Coleman lantern on the bumper of his Dodge. "There's about thirty acres of scrub pine here, with a pasture on the top end, a creek on the bottom and hardwoods on both sides. There's trails back in them pines runnin' every which way, where the deer go to hide and bed down. I figured this is a good soft place for a tent, and if the wind gets up, the pines'll keep it off of us."

Griff lit a cigarette, then stuck the lighter to Ray Del's lantern. The lantern woofed softly and came to life. "It's a good spot, Ray Del," he said quietly. "You did good."

Ray Del was still glaring slit-eyed at Tino.

"Hey, you need to lighten up, amigo. I was just makin' conversation, man." Tino was grinning. Tino was always grinning.

Ray Del had even cut up a blowdown for firewood when he had come down to scout the place, so Weasel built a nice big campfire while the rest of them pitched their tents. Within thirty minutes they had finished setting up camp and were sitting around the fire swapping lies and ragging each other. They had an hour to kill before it was time to head into the woods, so they drank coffee and checked and loaded rifles and warmed their insulated coveralls by the fire.

Listening to their stories, it slowly dawned on Jeremy that he had made a huge miscalculation: in his ignorance of deer hunting, he had assumed they would all march into the woods together and flush the deer like quail, taking shots at them as they tried to run away. That was how he had seen it in his mind. It simply had not occurred to him until now that he might have to go off alone in the dark, in unfamiliar woods, and figure it out for himself.

He waited for a lull in the conversation, then approached the subject gingerly.

"Um, what, exactly, am I supposed to do out there?" He peered into the dark outside the firelight. "I mean, I never hunted deer before."

"Gimme a break, man," Luke snorted. "What are you *doing* here, dude?"

"Hey, it's okay, kid," Tino said with a laugh. "Everybody has a first time, but I think you have fallen among some very bad men."

"Don't worry about it," Snake said, yet Jeremy thought he detected worry in his voice. "I'll take care of you. I'll put you in a good spot, just don't stray too far."

"Yeah, Germy," Luke added, "we got better things to do than spend all day looking for you. Bad enough we have to baby-sit during the week."

Griff shot Luke a hard look but didn't say anything. Jeremy figured tempers were a little short from lack of sleep, and Luke had been on him ever since the incident in the hog house.

"You ever shoot a rifle?" Ray Del probed, mostly to fill the tense silence.

"A couple times at a friend's house," Jeremy muttered. "We used to shoot bottles and stuff with his twenty-two."

Luke rolled his eyes.

"Yeah, well that ain't no twenty-two," Ray Del said, pointing at the Marlin. "You don't lock it into your shoulder, it'll kick you. Hard."

"Squeeze," Griff said. "Don't jerk. And take the chest shot. Just because it's Doe Day don't mean you got to play cowboy and make a head shot."

Jeremy's confusion showed on his face, so Snake explained, "Most of the time guys don't make head shots because they don't want to mess up the rack. But if you know what you're doing you can drop a doe quicker with a head shot." He pointed at Jeremy's Marlin. "But you're using iron sights, you don't know the gun, and you don't even know if you can shoot. Take the chest shot."

"And don't go running up on him after you shoot him," Weasel said, poking the fire with a long stick. "Give him time to get down. Most of the time a deer doesn't even know what hit him, and if you let him lay for a few minutes he'll bleed out and stay down, but if you get all excited and run up on him he'll take off."

"Yeah, he'll book," Luke said. "He'll get all adrenaline-amped and run, then *we'll* end up having to track him down."

Jeremy was about to say something back to him when Griff broke in.

"Luke's right," Griff said, flipping a cigarette butt into the fire. "You got to let it lay awhile. And when you go up to it, remember to take your gun with you."

Tino snickered loudly, as if he could identify with that particular mistake.

"I'm serious," Griff said. "Don't ever leave your gun behind. You might have to finish him off. I had one get up and run one time after I thought he was dead, and I couldn't do anything about it because I didn't have my rifle in my hand. I thought I'd *never* find him. He wormed his way up under a creek bank trying to stop the bleeding."

"They can be pretty smart," Ray Del said.

Tino laughed. "It's a good thing the deer they don't have guns. Say, amigo, you know how to field dress a deer?"

Jeremy didn't, so Tino proceeded to tell him, in great detail.

The lure of fire and talk held their attention for too long. From down among the pines they couldn't see the faint lightening of the sky in the east, and so didn't realize they were late getting started until they heard the crowing of a rooster in the distance.

Jeremy had already strapped the bowie knife to his leg, and he didn't own any insulated coveralls or cold-weather boots, so he tucked his sleeping bag under his arm, picked up the Marlin, switched on a flashlight and was ready to go.

Loaded like a pack mule with climbing stand, rifle, thermos, rope and stool, Nanny clanked off down the hill.

Snake cinched up his gloves, zipped his coat up around his neck, wrapped a heavy scarf around the bottom half of his face, picked up his rifle and headed out.

"C'mon, boy" was all he said.

Jeremy turned his back on the fire and followed him into the dark. From the start, he had a hard time keeping up with Snake, who followed the bouncing flashlight beam with a long, even, confident stride while Jeremy half-trotted, stumbling along behind.

"Any idea how far we're going?" Jeremy puffed, after what felt like ten minutes.

"Shhh," Snake said.

They crossed a creek, where Jeremy slipped and filled one of his boots with ice water, then marched on up the next rise for fifty yards or so. Snake stopped abruptly, pulled the scarf down and seemed to be feeling for the breeze with his nose.

Jeremy was already freezing, despite the hard walk. The low

was supposed to be near twenty degrees.

Snake turned right and took off again, parallel to the creek. After a couple of minutes he stopped and pointed his flashlight at the base of a huge white pine.

"Right there," he said. "Hunker down right there. Get comfortable so you don't have to move—and don't move unless you have to. Be still." He looked around, as if he could see the outlying terrain in the pitch-dark. "This is a good spot. If you don't see anything, don't wander off. I'll be back for you before lunch."

As Snake's footsteps trailed away over the hump to the left, Jeremy had one of those *What am I doing here?* moments. He was lost, freezing, a thousand miles from home, clueless, and utterly, completely, cosmically alone.

It was still dark, although once he settled in against the tree, wrapped the sleeping bag firmly around himself, and turned off the flashlight, he began immediately to see the shapes of trees and the outline of the pine thicket on the opposite ridge, black against a brightening sky. Dawn approached. Gradually, the broad shadow of the little ravine carved out by the creek fifty yards downhill came into focus.

Jeremy sat perfectly still, but not because his senses were attuned to hunting and he wanted to hear the crunch of a dry leaf that would betray the cautious tiptoeing of a deer, or even because he thought there was a chance he might *see* a deer. He held his breath and strained his ears because he didn't know the woods. Alone in the half-lit wild, he was afraid that any moment *he* might become prey. His eyes bored into the shadows, desperate to identify the source of every tick, every rustle, and he hated himself for being afraid.

He told himself that he was practically a grown man. Physically he *was* grown. Bigger and stronger than some men he knew, he was holding down a man's job and hunting deer on equal footing with men who feared absolutely nothing. Yet even as he told himself these things, he held his breath and listened, curling his fingers about the rifle, feeling for the trigger and memorizing the position of the safety so he could snap it off and be ready to defend himself in a second if something came out of the woods and pounced on him. Mentally he slapped himself, telling himself to buck up and to stop being so silly and weak, which may have even done the trick if a great broad-winged owl had not swooped a few feet in front of his face and pulled up to land softly, silent as death, in the lower branches of a tree just down the hill. The eerie absence of sound, interrupted by the sudden, evil blackness of the owl's passing sent him ducking under his sleeping bag while the rifle slid to the ground, forgotten. A moment later he raised his head from the folds of the bag, having realized too late that what he had seen was only a bird.

Daylight crept in under the cloud bank inch by inch, precisely matching the dissolution of his fear—most of it, anyway. For he was still out in the middle of strange woods with a bunch of people he really didn't know and, when he got right down to it, really didn't trust.

The frozen ground chilled him, even wrapped as he was in the sleeping bag. His wet foot began to go numb with a dull ache stretching up his calf. Taking off his boot, he dumped the creek water out of it, spread the boot open and set it aside so it would dry out a little, then stuck a twig in the ground and hung his wet sock on it. After wrapping his bare foot in a corner of the bag, he snuggled in to watch daylight seep into the shallow vale, and warmth gradually made its way through his bones.

Daylight chased his fears away and he became bored sitting in the woods with nothing to do, waiting for a deer he knew would not show itself. After two hours of fidgeting and wiggling and wondering what he was doing here, he finally heard a rifle shot a good ways off to his left. Thirty seconds later he heard another. At least *somebody* had seen a deer.

His neck was killing him from slumping against the tree, his left leg was asleep, and he had to pee. Discomfort finally outweighed the bitter cold waiting outside the sleeping bag so that he tossed the bag aside and forced himself to his feet. Lurching downhill on his bare foot he almost fell down twice before the pins and needles brought feeling back into his left leg. Eight or ten paces from his roost he stopped and wrapped an arm around a dogwood sapling to steady himself while he dispensed the morning's coffee.

From where he stood he had a clear view of the creek valley, blocked only on the left side by a little hummock, over which came charging—as he stood here indisposed, twenty feet from his rifle—a very large buck. The deer had a rack like a small tree and a neck like an Angus, and it never swerved, never granted Jeremy even a respectful glance as it leaped nearly over him, flew down the hill, vaulted the creek and bounded up the opposite slope, zigzagging, white tail flying, and disappeared into the pine thicket. A few seconds later there was more thrashing from behind the hummock, and Luke appeared over the rise, puffing from a hard run.

"Did you see him?" Luke asked when he first spotted Jeremy. Then he took in the sight: Jeremy, with one arm around a dogwood sapling, one bare foot held delicately off of the frosty leaves. Luke's lip curled into a smirk. "Man, what are you—!" He gulped a couple of hard breaths and then spat, "Where's your gun?"

Jeremy was at that moment discovering there simply was no surreptitious way to zip up one's jeans. He pointed over his shoulder.

"It's, uh . . . I was, um . . ."

Luke flung a hand up in disgust. "I swear, Germy. That was the biggest buck I've ever seen, and it ran right into your lap.

Right in front of you—broadside! And here you are takin' a leak! Dude, you blew it!"

"Well, how was I supposed to know?"

"You heard the shots, right? Deer are herd animals, Germy. Anybody with one eye and half-sense knows when you hear shooting close by, you lock and load—and you *hold* your water— because you don't know which way the *rest* of 'em will run. Man, what a moron!" Muttering a string of curses, Luke slung his rifle over his shoulder and stalked back the way he had come.

By the time he got back to camp, Jeremy profoundly regretted coming along on the hunting trip. There was no mercy, and no escaping the relentless roasting he took as the guys straggled in and Luke told and retold the story of how the world's biggest trophy deer had caught Germy with his pants down. He told it to Snake first, and then Tino, Nanny, Griff, and Weasel, and the story grew a little with each telling.

Fortunately, Griff came back with a small doe slung across his shoulders, which drew some of the attention away from Jeremy. Since the deer was small, they decided to go ahead and skin it out, cut up the meat and pack it in a cooler at camp rather than to haul the deer to a processing place. Weasel pulled a charcoal grill from a storage bin on the side of his trailer and started the coals while Griff took the backstrap and some of the choice cuts from the deer.

"Hey man, what are we gonna have with it?" Tino asked. "We can't just eat meat."

"Why not?" Luke asked.

Tino made a face. "Ain't good for you, gringo. Mess up your stomach."

"We got liquid grain," Luke said, popping open a beer.

Jeremy saw a chance to redeem himself. "I'll take care of it," he said. "I brought some stuff." He broke out his box of groceries and set to work peeling and slicing. Making three large foil packets, he loaded them with sliced potatoes and onions, then laced them with cheese, garlic, butter, salt and pepper, wrapped the packets up tight and laid them in the still glowing coals from the morning's campfire. He then made up two more packets with mixed vegetables in an Italian vinaigrette sauce and laid those in the coals.

It was a grand feast.

"Not bad," Griff said, shoveling down potatoes.

"Heard that," Nanny seconded.

Tino said, "Hey, this stuff is good, kid. Where you learn to cook like this?"

"My mother had to work a lot, so I had to do the cooking. No big deal."

"You're gonna make somebody a good wife someday, Germy," Luke sneered. "Long as they don't expect you to bring home a deer."

He was only half kidding, and everybody knew it so they only half laughed at what he said. Jeremy had put himself in this awkward place and he really had no defense. Anything he said back to Luke would only make matters worse. Men have rules about such things, and so they laughed at Luke's cheap shot and pretended not to notice that Jeremy didn't laugh with them. In fact, he never looked up.

At first he felt sorry for himself and wished he hadn't come on the trip, wished he hadn't come to Georgia, wished his mother hadn't died, and almost wished she hadn't left him the letter. But it was then, while thinking of the letter, that a small anger began to grow inside him. After all, he hadn't wanted to be here. He was a victim of circumstance, a victim of his mother's illness and her dying wishes. He was the victim of his hard-boiled uncle and his swaggering, semiliterate friends who didn't seem to care that he was really just a kid, a teenager trying to figure things out.

At the same time, somewhere in the recesses of his mind, he knew he was no more a victim than anybody else, and that ultimately it would be up to him to find his own way. It was the child in him that was the problem, the fact that the child was still *there*, not that other people couldn't see it. And so he turned, in his mind, to where he had always turned when he felt alone and trapped. Silently, inside his own little space, he prayed, *Help me. I don't want to be a boy anymore. I need to be a man.*

They hunted different ground in the afternoon. Snake led Jeremy on a long winding hike that turned him completely around so that, in the end, he thought maybe he was overlooking the same creek but from a totally different vantage point. It didn't occur to him until after Snake left him that he was completely lost; there was no way he would ever find his way back to camp unless somebody guided him. But he decided, quite consciously, to be a man, to think it through rationally and calmly, without fear, and figure out what to do.

Propping his rifle up against a tree, he scraped a patch of ground clear with his boot, then took a stick and drew a rough map of the campsite, the creek, and the path he believed they had taken, crossing over the creek and then making a wide arc to the left and eventually coming back around to the same creek. By following the creek bank he thought he could find his way back to the camp—if in fact it was the same creek.

Jeremy had dried out his boot and sock by the campfire, and in spite of the overcast sky, the afternoon had warmed enough so that he was comfortable with his sleeping bag wrapped around his legs. He laid the Marlin across his knees, checked the knife in the scabbard on his thigh, and once again reminded himself that he was a man, a hunter. But he was warm and comfortable, his belly was full, and he had slept very little in the last twenty-four hours.

"Please don't let me mess this up," he murmured, and it was his last coherent thought before he drifted off to sleep.

When he first woke up he wondered where he was, and why he was sitting against a tree—then he remembered. The light had changed; it had faded just a bit. He started to look at his watch, but then he froze and forgot all about the time because of the deer staring at him.

Don't move. Don't breathe, he told himself as his heart went from resting to racing in the space of a few seconds. He saw no antlers; it was a doe, and she was big—much bigger than the one Griff had shot that morning. She was standing broadside to him, at the edge of the little ravine at the bottom of the slope, and staring straight at him as if she couldn't decide what he was. Her ears twitched.

He waited, staring back, trying not to blink, his heart pounding and his mind darting, trying to remember all the advice he'd been given around the campfire. He held his breath until the deer finally lowered its head to nuzzle among the fallen leaves, then slowly, ever so slowly, eased his gun into position. The deer looked up twice more, still suspicious, but uncertain. He was careful to move only when it wasn't looking.

With the barrel lined up with his target, Jeremy sank the bead in the notch of the gunsight and aimed for the deepest part of the chest. *Squeeze, don't jerk,* he repeated to himself as he slowly increased the pressure on the trigger.

The gun wouldn't fire. The safety. Finding the button with his finger, he pushed it. There was just the tiniest *click* when it snapped off, but the deer's nervous ears heard it. The head came up, ears at attention. Jeremy was positive it would bolt and he would lose the chance before he could get off a shot, only it didn't. For whatever reason, the deer decided he was nothing, dismissed him and went back to grazing.

The rifle's blast split the quiet evening like a thunderclap, kicked Jeremy back against the tree and filled the air with smoke.

He didn't care. Righting himself, he was sure he would find the deer lying dead on the ground, for he knew he had hit it solidly.

It was gone. His eyes scanned the area, expecting to see his deer bounding away untouched, but then a rustling of leaves told him the deer had not run off after all. It had only fallen into the ravine, out of sight.

Wild with excitement, he dropped the rifle, whipped aside the sleeping bag and ran down to the ravine to claim his prize. He skidded to a stop at the edge and was shocked to see the deer still standing, almost under him. Its ears stood up, alert, but its head was lowered, its nose almost touching the ground. Mortally wounded, shocked and confused, it might not have even been able to raise its head. Jeremy was surprised it could still stand.

Standing at the lip of the ravine, staring down at the deer,

Griff's words came back to him—*"Remember to take your gun with you."* Slowly, he turned his head and peered over his shoulder. His gun lay fifty yards uphill, its polished walnut stock sticking up out of a pile of hickory leaves. He turned back to the big deer, still standing just below him in the ravine, and Luke's voice echoed in his ears.

"Man, what a moron!"

The doe had already stood still too long, tense and poised to flee. Any second it would raise its head, see him, and go flying off in a panicked rush to hide someplace where he would never find it. If he tried to get back to his rifle the noise would most likely flush the deer out, with the same result, and it would just as surely be Luke who ended up having to help him track it down after it had gone to ground.

"... gonna make somebody a good wife someday, Germy ... long as they don't expect you to bring home a deer ... bad enough we have to baby-sit during the week ..."

The little spark of anger flared up again, caught, and burst into a bright and heedless rebellion. The child in him fled, along with his restraint, as his right hand found the bone handle of the bowie knife and his fingers clamped around it. His lips curled back from his teeth and a primal growl escaped his throat as he leaped, the knife flashed in the air, and he landed astraddle the astonished deer's back.

Jeremy didn't even know at what point he dropped the knife, but it didn't matter. He would never have been able to turn loose with his right hand long enough to have finished the deer anyhow, for it exploded under him. The deer sprang forward bucking and bounding, a panicked fury of spring-steel muscle shot headlong through the woods like a drunken cannonball, bent on dislodging this strange, clinging predator from its back.

Jeremy grabbed fistfuls of hide under its neck and hung on in the grim conviction that the deer, mortally wounded, could not keep to this insane pace for more than a few seconds—that it must, if the laws of mortality held, fall down stone-dead. But the big deer kept going, in fact seemed to grow stronger and bolder in its terror, for what might have been seconds or hours, flying over rocks, hurtling through the hardwoods and careening wildly into the pine thicket.

Growling, fierce in his determination, Jeremy clung to his prize, grappling for purchase with his feet while the deer bashed him into tree trunks, raked him with pine boughs, and plowed through a dense bank of brambles. Breaking into open pasture, the deer put on another—surely the last—great burst of speed, and Jeremy closed his eyes.

Which was why he didn't see the barbed-wire fence coming. The deer sloughed sideways at the last second, skidding into the fence so that Jeremy caught the brunt of a post with his hip. Then his arms ripped free from the deer's neck and he flipped over, tangling himself in the top two strands of wire. He watched helplessly as his prize disappeared, white tail flying.

It took a good five minutes just to free himself from the fence. Plopping down heavily in the dry brown grass, he took inventory. Nothing was broken as far as he could tell. However, his hip was deeply bruised and his right knee hurt when he put weight on it. His jacket hung in tatters. He was bleeding from a three-inch-long gash in his calf, several barbed-wire puncture wounds on his back and arms, and dozens of briar scratches on his head and hands. His left ear still rang from a pine bough whipping across it, while his right eye was trying to swell shut.

As his heartbeat slowed and reason settled on him once again, Jeremy looked around and realized he was completely lost. Under the overcast there was no east or west, and colors started to fade quickly into purples and grays in the failing light. There were woods on both ends of the pasture, so he had no idea which way the deer had come. And it was getting colder.

He didn't know what to do. Somewhere out there his deer was probably lying down to die, and it would be lost to him—he would never find it now. But even the loss of his prize paled next to the thought of going into the twilight woods and trying to find his way back to where he'd left the gun, the knife, the sleeping bag—the *flashlight*. He could not, would not, face the woods alone in the dark without even a flashlight.

Staring at the barbed wire, it occurred to Jeremy that the fence was a man-made thing, and it seemed reasonable to assume that if he followed it he would find a road or maybe a house. His first instinct was to give it up and go home—just follow the fence line to the nearest road, hitchhike back to Tennessee and apologize to Walter and Anna. At this point, such a thing seemed infinitely easier and less embarrassing than going back to camp and facing the miners.

It took him a half hour to find the road, by which time darkness had fallen. Out here in the wide open country, there were no houses in sight. One or two cars passed him as he walked down the winding road, and he stuck out his thumb, but they speeded up when they got close enough to see him. He figured he must look pretty rough.

About a mile down the road he saw the black silhouette of a pole barn on a distant rise, but no other structures. Somehow, in his present circumstances, the pole barn—remote, silent, empty—made him think of God. "So, what am I supposed to do now?" he asked.

Limping, he pressed on in the near total darkness. He hadn't gone fifty yards farther when he noticed a cattle gate in the fence to his left. A few minutes later the lights of a passing car flashed by, and he saw that it was a rusty blue gate with a crooked NO

TRESPASSING sign hanging on it—the same gate they had driven through on their way in.

He looked back at the distant pole barn, then he bit his lip and walked through the gate.

Even in the dark Jeremy had no trouble following the deeply rutted logging road. Within another half hour he could hear Carl barking, and soon he was limping into the light of a roaring fire at the camp.

Weasel stood alone by the fire, drinking a beer. As soon as he recognized Jeremy, Carl stopped barking, trotted out to say hello, then went back and curled up next to the fire, having satisfied his guard duties. When Jeremy stepped into the light, Weasel looked him up and down, chuckling. He reached out and took Jeremy by the chin, turning his face to look at it.

"Okay, I give up," he said. "What happened?"

Jeremy shook his head, spread his hands out before the fire. "You wouldn't believe me if I told you. Where is everybody?"

"Out looking for you. Snake came back in saying he couldn't find you." He pointed at Jeremy's tent. "Found your sleeping bag and rifle, but no Germy. After dark, when you still weren't back, they got worried and went looking for you."

As he was saying this, Weasel reached inside the door of his trailer and pulled out his own rifle, a semiautomatic with a scope, and jacked a round into the chamber.

"I stayed here in case you wandered back into camp," he said, then pointed his rifle straight up and fired three rounds in quick succession.

Over the next fifteen minutes the others returned back to camp one by one, each in his turn doing a slow appraisal of Jeremy's face and clothes and wanting to know what happened. Jeremy wouldn't talk. Even Snake couldn't get the story out of him.

Luke was the last one in to camp. Cradling his rifle in his

arms, a black sock hat pulled low over his eyes, he walked up to Jeremy and tilted his head back, amusement crinkling his eyes as he considered the bruises and scratches and torn clothes. He swiped his red nose with the back of a gloved hand, sniffed, and said, "This has *got* to be good."

Jeremy wouldn't even look at him, but Luke wasn't backing off. "You gonna tell us about it, Germy, or do we have to use our imagination?"

"You wouldn't believe me."

"Try us," Snake said, leaning forward in a camp chair, warming his hands at the fire.

So Jeremy told them. He was still too sore, his wounds far too fresh, for him to have felt anything but dejected and humiliated. He was a long way from being able to laugh at himself. Even so, the further he went with his tale the harder the others laughed. Weasel spit beer into the fire and staggered away, choking. Griff doubled over in his chair, his shoulders shaking in silent, uncontrollable laughter.

Luke, standing next to Jeremy, just shook his head. The smirk was back.

"Great story, Germy," he said. "If it was anybody else I might even believe some of it."

"Hey, don't pay no attention to Luke," Tino said. "It's *your* lie, amigo. You tell it as big as you want to."

Nanny, who had remained silent until now, frowned at Luke and said, "If he's puttin' us on, how you figure he got so beat up?"

Luke kept his eyes locked on Jeremy's face, and the sneer never left his lips. "It got dark, he got lost, got scared, started runnin', dropped his flashlight, ran into a tree. I ain't buyin' the deer story."

"I heard him shoot," Nanny said.

"So? That don't mean he was shooting *at* anything."

It was one thing for Tino to make a joke out of it. It was quite another for Luke, who was not laughing, to doubt his word.

"You calling me a liar?" Jeremy asked. This was the gauntlet. Where he came from, it was an invitation to fight, a point of honor. Snake looked up from the fire to see what Luke would do.

Luke shrugged. "Yeah. I am."

Jeremy had finally had enough. His patience was exhausted, and he had faced enough fear already this night so that even a brawl with Luke seemed almost within reason, even if it meant— as it almost certainly did—that he would take a beating. It just didn't matter anymore. His fist curled, and he took a half step forward before Nanny caught his collar and yanked him back. Weasel stepped in front of Luke.

"There's no need for this," Weasel said. "If he shot a deer, we need to go look for it anyway, right?"

They all nodded, except Luke and Jeremy, whose eyes were still locked on each other.

"Weasel's right," Snake said. "Seems to me the intelligent thing to do is for everybody to load up and drive down to the pasture and see what we can see. Maybe we'll find out who owes who an apology."

"Or a stompin'," Luke said.

"Might as well go check it out," Griff agreed. "We got nothing better to do."

They piled into the trucks and drove down to the fence line. It took less than five minutes to cover the ground it had taken Jeremy an hour to cross on foot.

"There," Jeremy said, pointing. Nanny stopped the truck so that his lights shined on a stretch of fence where the wire was bowed down and the post leaned a little to one side.

Tino was the first to spot something snagged on the fence, a tuft of wool ticking that matched what was hanging from the holes in Jeremy's jacket.

"I don't know about no deer, amigo, but you can prove you rode this fence."

Weasel nodded. "You have a surprising grasp of forensic science, Tino."

Snake, Griff, and Nanny squatted on the ground a few yards away, looking at a bare spot between clumps of fescue.

"That's a doe, all right," Nanny said.

"And look at the size of it," Griff added. He placed his fist against the track for comparison.

"They got some corn-fed deer around here, that's for sure," Snake said.

Looking over Nanny's shoulder, Luke said, "There's tracks all over this place. That don't prove anything. If that's the deer Germy shot, where's the blood?"

They searched the ground with flashlights and Weasel's lantern. Not a drop of blood could be found anywhere near the fence.

"Sometimes a high chest shot don't bleed," Nanny said.

"True," Snake said, "but if that's what happened, the deer's lost. I don't think anybody here can track a deer over frozen ground at night without a blood trail."

Carl growled.

"Yeah, Carl probably could," Weasel said, "only he's too squirrelly. You'd end up chasing rabbits."

Carl ignored him and, with great dignity, went to water the fence post.

Griff nodded. "I guess that's that."

"What about Geech's knife?" Jeremy said.

"We can look for it tomorrow, in the daylight," Snake answered. His eyes and the subdued tone of his voice told Jeremy even Snake wasn't quite convinced he was telling the truth about the deer. "You're not even real sure where you lost it, are you?"

"Yes," Jeremy said. "I am. I dropped it in the ravine where I jumped on the deer."

"Yeah, right," Luke said, rolling his eyes, but Jeremy pressed the issue.

"If you can show me where I was hunting, I can show you the knife, and the place where I jumped on the deer."

Griff shook his head, blew an exasperated breath. "You took him there, Snake. You know which way it is from here?"

Snake nodded toward the black outline of the woods. "It's just down there a ways, on the backside of the pines. That's where I left him this afternoon." He shot a glance at Luke and said, "We might as well go take a look. It's obvious Luke ain't gonna shut up about it until we prove something one way or the other."

"Got that right," Luke said, glaring at Jeremy.

Snake took Weasel's lantern and led a ragged line of flashlights across the pasture and down by the tangle of scrub pine and briars. It wasn't long before they made it to the ravine. Instead of crossing over, Snake turned right and followed the near edge of the ravine for a hundred yards, finally stopping and shining a flashlight up the hill on the opposite side to pick out the big hickory tree.

"That's where I left him after lunch," he said. "And where he left his rifle."

The bank was steep where they stood, dropping ten feet to a flat sandy bottom probably twenty feet wide, with a little brook taking no more than six feet out of the middle during dry weather. The whole crew scrambled down the bank, and Jeremy immediately set about looking for the knife. While the bottom of the ravine had been swept clean by occasional flash floods, leaves had collected against the banks in drifts. It was among these roots and rocks and drifts of leaves that Jeremy kicked and raked, looking for Geech's knife.

Climbing down the bank, Weasel slipped and fell on top of

Tino, who rattled off a few words in Spanish, then laughed and helped Weasel to his feet. Weasel, Griff, Tino, and Luke all went straight for the bare, damp, sandy ground in the middle of the ravine where the tracks would talk the loudest.

"Well, I'll be," Luke muttered. "Something *did* happen here. Look at that."

"Yep," Griff's voice said in agreement. "It's pretty tore up, and it's a big doe just like the one up in the pasture." He knelt and measured the tracks with his fist, as he had done before. "Could be the same deer."

Jeremy's boot brushed aside some leaves and found the bowie knife caught behind a tree root. He saw the flash of steel and was about to bend over and pick it up when Carl started barking over near the opposite bank. The dog had apparently found something interesting. Nanny ambled over to check it out.

"Y'all better get over here and look for yourselves," Nanny said, his voice tinged with laughter. "You ain't gonna believe this."

Jeremy was the last one there, having stopped to wipe off the knife and shove it back into its scabbard. Each of the others, on joining the little circle, broke into surprised laughter. Even Luke.

"What is it?" Jeremy asked, stepping between them to see what Carl had found that was so funny.

"That there," Nanny said, pointing, "is a dead doe. Shot through the heart. And it's my professional opinion that this here doe was dead as a hammer before it hit the ground." He pointed to the top of the bank. "It fell from right there, slid down the bank, and knocked all these leaves down on top of itself, covering its ownself up when it stopped."

Jeremy was thoroughly confused. "But . . . but the deer I jumped on—"

"Was not the one you shot," Weasel said. "That's why we didn't find any blood. The deer you jumped on was perfectly healthy, and probably in a state of high anxiety."

"Duuuude," Luke said, reverently.

Snake stood there looking down at the deer, biting a corner of his lip, lost in thought. He said nothing.

Nanny crouched down and pressed a thumb into the bullet hole on the deer's side until a little puddle of dark blood welled up. Rising, he marked Jeremy's forehead with his thumb. "I reckon you're a hunter now," he said.

Jeremy couldn't help noticing that Snake didn't even look at him.

CHAPTER 12

In love and war.

Halfway through the shift on Monday night, Jeremy rode in on the loki with Biggins and Snake, who timed their arrival for the end of a push so Biggins could change out a frayed hydraulic line.

The machine was still and silent, emitting only the ticking and popping noises of hot steel, cooling. Luke and Tunk were laying out fishplates under the machine, bolting down twenty feet of new track. Using the flat steel fishplates as crossties, one of the miners' routine chores was keeping railroad track laid just ahead of the trailing gear.

Nanny and Weasel were busy extending the water line for the dust dampers in the heading, with Tino overhead welding some kind of rack to the side of the torque tube, showering sparks down around Biggins and Jeremy in the bottom. The sharp scent of molten metal hung in the air and the haze of granite dust left a sweet-sour aftertaste in Jeremy's throat and sinuses.

Up in the very front of the machine was the pressure plate, a wall of heavy steel that distributed over a million pounds of thrust against the cutterhead. Jeremy didn't even know it was possible to go forward beyond that point until he saw Griff open a heavy steel hatch on the pressure plate, and he and Snake and Ray Del crawled into the void in front of the machine. The cutterhead had been backed away from the rock face, leaving a six-foot gap, and the small hatch through which they had crawled was the only way in or out. Ray Del dragged a droplight in after him, trailing an orange cord.

Jeremy shuddered as he watched them disappear into the hole, into the narrow blackness between immovable granite and the irresistible iron monster waiting to eat it.

"Why are they going in there?" he asked Biggins.

Biggins rolled his eyes and spat tobacco juice at Jeremy's rubber boots. "Checking for flat cutting wheels," he answered. "Long as you been around here, and you still don't know the routine?"

Jeremy knew about the cutting wheels, but he'd never actually been here to see somebody crawl through the little hatch into the mouth of hell.

"I guess I just never thought about it," he said, then decided to spill what was really bothering him. "Has anybody ever got . . . *stuck* up there? In front of the cutterhead?"

Biggins rolled his eyes. "Not that I know of."

Jeremy eyed the hatch. "What would happen?"

"You mean if we was to crank her up with a guy in front of the cutterhead?" He bent down to pick up a sliver of granite the size of a leaf. "I reckon he'd come out on the belt in pieces about like this," he said. "And there wouldn't be anything he could do about it either, 'cause once the machine cranks up ain't nobody gonna hear him scream." A sinister gleam lit his eye when he spotted Jeremy's terror and decided to feed it a little. "'Course it'd be all right. It'd take a minute or two for the cutterhead to close up the gap. He'd have plenty of time to make his peace before he got tore into little bitty pieces."

Luke was lining up a bolt hole with his spud wrench, listening. "It's no big deal, Germy," he said, eyeing Biggins. "It's routine. You're supposed to check the cutting wheels between every push. *Supposed* to," he said significantly.

Nanny was listening in too. "I heard there was a half-dozen cutters dumped in the sludge pond from graveyard shift. If you don't check 'em every push, you're gonna tear 'em up where you can't never get a ring on 'em."

"Yeah," Biggins snorted, "but you can bet Griff'll watch 'em close. He's keepin' his nose extra clean these days—don't want another black mark on his record."

"Word," Luke said.

"What do you mean?" Jeremy asked. "What did Griff do?"

Everybody laughed. Jeremy was the only one who didn't know why. "You haven't heard about the train?" Weasel asked. "Man, Griff's a legend."

"It was up in St. Louis," Luke said. "About three years ago now. He was walking boss on swing, and a good one—Griff *knows* how to run a job. It was a hole kind of like this one, except it wasn't good ground for a mining machine, so they were drilling and blasting. I think it was a two-mile hole, and it ran under a railroad yard."

"They hit a void," Weasel said. "That's what caused the problem."

"That's right. The drill steel went in a few feet and then just punched air. Griff wasn't sure what to do, so he called up top to the project manager and asked him. The PM got all huffy. 'Pack it and shoot it,' he says. Griff explained it to him, how they couldn't find the back of it, and he thought it would be a good idea for the PM to come down and take a look at the situation.

'Pack it and shoot it,' the PM says again. Griff tried one more time, but the boss just told him either do his job or get out of the way and he'd find somebody else to do it.

"So, Griff packed it. And packed it, and packed it, and packed it. Then he pulled his crew out."

"All the way out," Weasel added, for Jeremy's benefit. "Normally you just pull back a few hundred yards when you set it off, but he took his crew all the way back up top before he lit it up."

"Yeah," Luke said. "That's how come they were all standing in the yard watching. They felt the rumble when it went off and then, about a mile away, they saw a little puff of smoke—*above* ground, in the railroad yard. The whole crew got to watch while six boxcars on a siding just sort of folded up in the middle and went down like a torpedoed ship."

"*Large* void," Weasel said, laughing. "Made Griff a reputation, it did."

Given Luke's talent for exaggeration, Jeremy was weighing the story in his mind, trying to figure out what percentage of it might be true, when Luke brightened suddenly and rocked back on his heels.

"Hey, Biggins, speaking of reputations, did Germy tell you about riding the deer?"

Biggins glared. "Say what?"

"Aw, man, it was unbelievable! You shoulda been there. I swear, that deer was as big as a horse, and Germy rode him like he owned him. Stayed on him for like a mile! Didn't he, Nanny?"

Nanny leaned up against the rib of the tunnel, cranking on a pipe wrench, tightening a new length of water pipe. He stopped for a second and grinned at Luke. "It's *your* lie, Luke. You tell it big as you want to."

Tunk shook his head, laughing to himself. "Y'all crazy," he muttered.

Luke beamed. "I'm serious, man! I had Germy all wrong. The dude's about half psycho." He spun the whole story again for Biggins, adding to it, embellishing where he could. Biggins didn't pay a whole lot of attention.

Neither did Jeremy, for that matter. He kept staring at the square of steel in the pressure plate, where three men had disappeared. The heavy hatch had swung slowly closed again after they went through, and now was held open only a half inch by the orange cord trailing out of it. Over time, Jeremy had grown more comfortable with the tunnel itself, with the idea of being underground. The terrible power and noise of the machine didn't bother him as badly as it once did, but something about that dark one-way hole still shivered him. He looked up through the grate to the control deck where Ruskie sat kicked back in his ragged desk chair. He could just see Ruskie's face, all nose and glasses, reading a paperback in the yellow glare of a bare light bulb, and Jeremy's imagination followed the coaxing of his darkest fears. How small a switch had to be thrown, how small a lever had to be pushed to set the great malignant mechanism spinning, crushing, ripping? A trickle of sweat ran down the bridge of his nose. For a split second, in his mind's eye, he saw himself in that void, saw the machine coming for him, and his knees almost buckled.

A bolt broke loose unexpectedly, and Biggins smashed his fingers with a wrench. He let fly with a string of obscenities, dropped the wrench, stuck a knuckle in his mouth, then examined the blood blister forming on it. He glared at Jeremy.

"Germy, you need to wake up and start helping me, you little—"

"Man, Germy didn't do nothin'," Tunk said. Tunk was checking the spread on the rails, almost at Biggins's feet. "The wrench slipped, that's all. You need to ease up, old man."

"Old man?" Biggins grunted. His eyes narrowed. "Old man? I

don't think you want to get in a name-calling contest with me, Tunk."

Rage flashed across Tunk's face for a second, then he shook his head and dropped the subject. Jeremy watched the exchange and saw the look in Tunk's eye. He'd seen it before whenever Biggins ran his line on one of the black guys. It wasn't even anger; it was something colder. Tunk switched him off, and it was plain on his face: he knew that mixing it up with Biggins wasn't worth the trouble that would follow. There were laws about fighting underground; a man could actually get locked up for it. Tunk could have snapped Biggins like a twig, but instead he let it go.

Snake and Griff appeared alongside Biggins while Weasel and Tino climbed out of the hatch behind them, dragging the droplight.

"Cutters look okay?" Biggins asked.

"Yeah," Snake said. "Couple of them are getting close, but they'll make another push or two before we have to change them."

"You ought to bring Germy in and let him help change out the cutters sometime," Biggins suggested, twisting Jeremy's knot a little tighter.

"Jeremy's yard help," Snake said. "'Fraid you're stuck with each other."

Luke stood up, holstered his spud wrench and hitched up his jeans. "We really could use another hand down here, Snake. You could hire another grunt for the yard and let Germy work with us." He glanced at Jeremy, and the half grin on his face spoke volumes—Luke had become an ally.

Snake shook his head. "I talked to Rico this morning. He's been wanting to switch over to swing shift so his wife can take a job. He'll be coming with us tomorrow. Jeremy stays in the yard."

"Listen, Uncle Aiden, I think I could probably—"

"I said no. And don't call me that."

Nanny put in his two cents. "It'd be all right, Snake. I could look after—"

"Nobody asked you, Nanny!" Snake shot back. "I think I can figure out who needs to work where." He turned around and stalked off through the trailing gear before anybody else could get a word in. Jeremy hefted Biggins's toolbox up to his shoulder and followed him to the loki.

Biggins sat down on his toolbox on the flatcar while Jeremy and Snake stood side by side in the little waist-high cab of the loki on the way out. The diesel had throttled up to a steady rumble, and the twinkling lights of the machine had shrunk into the distance by the time Jeremy got the nerve, but he finally spoke up.

"What have you got against me?"

"Nothing. Why?" Snake's voice was stone.

"Because you keep treating me like a kid."

A snort. "You *are* a kid."

"You're the only one who thinks that. The rest of the guys seem to think it would be okay if I worked in the hole. How am I ever gonna learn mining if you keep me up top doing grunt work for Biggins?"

Snake looked at him in the passing glare of a light, and a thin smile parted his lips. "I see," he said. "You think you're one of the guys now. You're some kind of hero because you pulled that stupid stunt in the woods."

"It wasn't a—"

"It was a bonehead stunt! You're lucky you didn't get stomped to death! It was a dumb thing to do, and you know it." He jabbed himself in the chest with a thumb. "*I* have to watch these guys, and think for them, because most of them aren't capable of making rational decisions for themselves. About anything! Oh, they're good hands—they're amazing hands. Give them a foothold and they can move the world, as long as there's a grown-up there to keep them from killing themselves. But don't go staking your life on their judgment. Right now you're the *man,* because it's fresh in their minds that you did something to prove you're as crazy as they are, but that's not exactly a recommendation in my book."

Jeremy had lost, at least for now, and the tension remained between them the rest of that night. It was a cold ride home at the end of the shift, and when they got there Snake pretty much drank himself to sleep. They didn't exchange three words the whole time.

By the time Snake woke up, Jeremy was gone, the sleeper sofa folded away, the blankets stashed in the closet. Snake's head pounded, and disjointed images kept slapping him in the face—pictures of Tom, pictures of Jeremy, overlapping—so different, yet so very alike. Gritting his teeth, he muttered and grumbled at himself while he downed coffee and Tylenol to chase away the headache.

The boy just didn't get it. Even now, after what had happened to Geech, he didn't seem to understand what he was asking. Jeremy did not belong here—didn't belong in the hole, didn't belong in the company of miners. He was just a kid—an innocent, pimple-faced child. Worst of all, Snake saw flashes of Tom when Jeremy smiled that sheepish Stan Laurel smile, stuffing his hands in his pockets and shuffling his feet when he walked, all gangly, like his joints were too loose. At mealtime, Jeremy would bow his head for a few seconds, eyes closed, lips moving slightly, and the profile of Tom's lowered face would hit Snake so hard he would have to turn away.

Sometimes it was Tom's ghost who haunted him, sometimes

Julie's. Right in the middle of saying something, Jeremy would use one of his mother's pet expressions and Julie's face would flash across Snake's mind. The face he saw was always the same—grim and accusing—the way she had looked the last time he saw her.

Julie had come to the door of Aiden's room in the burn unit one final time, a few days after she had "forgiven" him and told him she couldn't look at him anymore. It was midmorning, after he had been to the tub room and soaked his bandages off. His pins were out by then, and every day brought more flexibility to his ravaged fingers as he imposed his iron will on them.

They brought him back to his room with his hands and face exposed, but that morning they left him bare instead of wrapping him back up immediately as they usually did, because the doctors wanted to look at him. It was a teaching hospital, and they were making their rounds with a group of interns who would want to study his hands and face while he was unwrapped and clean.

The nerves were starting to grow back, and raw nerve endings, like microscopic cauliflower heads, found themselves exposed to the air without the protection of salve and bandage. As the minutes passed, the discomfort intensified. At first delicate and penetrating, the needles of pain gradually ran together into a swelling symphony of raw agony. He lay on his back in the bed, bare claws pointed straight up, and writhed. Grinding his heels against the mattress, he gritted his teeth and waited.

It was between visiting hours, so he hadn't expected anybody to come. He heard nothing, and his eyes were shut tight against the pain, but he felt a draft coming from the door. It was only a slight movement as the door opened just enough to admit a face, and it was more than ten feet away; still, his raw nerve endings felt the breath of it. Opening his eyes, he expected to see doctors. Instead, it was Julie's face peering at him from the crack of the door. He didn't know whether the revulsion on her face was because of the sight of him without his bandages or from what she had to say. He would never know.

"Your mother's had a stroke," she said, and seconds later the cadence of her words repeated itself, puffs of air drumming lightly against the raw nerves of his hands and face, the echo of the final indictment.

"I think all this was just too much . . ." she began, and then hesitated, looking away.

"It's bad, Aiden. She's paralyzed. They don't know how much she'll recover—or *if* she'll recover. I thought you should know."

Her words hammered, one at a time, against the iridescent pain in his face and hands. The door swung softly closed, and Julie was gone. She had come back one last time, his executioner. It was a coup de grace, clean and cold. He never saw her face again.

He couldn't take the chance on it happening again—not for Jeremy's sake, but for his own. He simply couldn't risk it. He didn't want Jeremy on the project at all, though at least here he could keep an eye out for him and see that no harm came to him. But he had no idea how much longer he could go on protecting Jeremy, as every day he wrestled with the temptation to just tramp him out and send him back to Walter and Anna.

On this particular morning it was not Jeremy's presence, but his absence, that angered Snake. He wasn't really worried about where the kid had gone—Jeremy, after all, was almost *too* straight-laced—but he needed to make a bank deposit, and he had come to depend on Jeremy for running his errands. Over the last couple of months Jeremy had saved him any number of trips out into the real world, where he'd rather not go, and today the deposit had to be made or checks would bounce, so of course this was the time Jeremy picked to skip out. Snake strapped on his boots, put on his sunglasses, jammed his hat down, went out the door and down the stairs, glad at least for the cold wind that gave him an excuse to wrap a scarf around the bottom half of his face.

He saw the China Girl as soon as he stepped out the front door of the building, hurrying across the lot toward him, eyes downcast as usual, hands shoved into the pockets of that shapeless black overcoat she always wore. She didn't see him, or if she did, she didn't show it with her silky black hair hiding most of her face, points curving together and almost touching under her chin.

But he saw *her*. It was the music. The same aloneness that poured from her fingertips when she sat at the piano radiated like an aura from the tilt of her head and her steady, no-nonsense, unwomanly walk. She wore white ankle socks and penny loafers— he'd never noticed that before—and just before they passed each other he saw something else. It was the tiniest thing, and yet it broke his heart. At the very last, perhaps in the last two strides before she passed him and trotted up the steps to the door, he saw a flash of white through the toe of her right shoe. The seam was torn, and the white sock showed through when she started to lift her foot.

He passed her without any sign, any acknowledgment. He didn't nod, nor did she. He did not break stride nor look back after he passed her, and anyone watching would have thought he hadn't seen her at all. But the man who walked away from the China Girl was not the same man who had walked toward her. That flash of white had imbued her with a noble poverty and, piercing him like a sword, had filled him instantly with a noble pity. Something in him awakened and wanted to hold her—*his* China Girl—to protect her, to see that she didn't have to wear worn-out shoes anymore, shoes with holes in the seams where her socks showed through. All of this came to him instantaneously, without reflection, without conscious thought, as if, when they brushed by each other and he caught the faint soap smell in the warmth of her passing, his heart had simply fallen out of him and shattered like glass on the asphalt.

Lost in thought, he was barely aware of going through the drive-in window at the bank over near the big shopping mall. On the way back he passed any number of stores, yet they were all the same to Snake, all beyond the walls of his prison, until Burchman's Music caught his eye.

Music, yes.

He turned into the little plaza lined with stores on three sides and parked in no-man's-land, out away from the other cars. He sat for a few minutes watching the store. The wind had lain down, and the sun had warmed the sidewalks a bit. People took their time sauntering up and down the walk in front of the shops, free to go where they pleased and do what they pleased. Because of the glare of sunlight on the front of the store he couldn't really see what was going on inside Burchman's, so instead he kept his eye on the door. The store didn't seem very busy when he first pulled in, but as he sat there watching, a young couple pushing a stroller fumbled their way through the door into the music shop, a gaggle of teenagers straggled in with Cokes in their hands from the burger joint on the corner, and then a clutch of middleweight women entered the store laughing like a sisterhood of escaped housewives.

Way too crowded.

It was just not his day. He cranked up and pulled back out onto the street, heading home. It had been years since anything like this had happened to him, since there had been anything in the outside world he actually wanted badly enough to consider braving a crowd in the light of day. But the China Girl had made contact. She'd broken through and projected her image into the heart of his fortress, and now he desperately wanted to find a way to confirm the contact, to establish a relationship, however distant.

CHAPTER 13

Fragrance.

Defining moments, the points on which people's lives turn, seldom come announced and planned and accompanied with all the fanfare and celebration of a wedding or a birth. Most of the true turning points in a man's life can be seen only in hindsight, and then only through the prism of his own skewed valuation of the outcome.

Jeremy awoke before daylight that morning, restless. He had taken Geech's truck and gone for breakfast, then spent two hours just driving around, going no place in particular. He was about to head back to the apartment when he passed by the plantation house that was set back in the pecan grove where The Girl lived, slowing as he drove by on the off chance that he might see her. There was a stark emptiness about the place since winter had stripped the pecan grove of its leaves and mystique. Studying the trees and the old house, he almost passed the driveway before he noticed the hand-drawn cardboard sign posted beside the gate.

Garage Sale
Sat–Sun 10–6, Behind House
Designer clothes—collectibles

A cold terror gripped his heart as he drove on. He shivered involuntarily because he knew he had to go back, because he knew *she* might be there. There would be tables of junk he could pretend to look at, bicycles and books and secondhand clothes, and The Girl would be there watching; he just knew it.

A few blocks down he pulled off and turned around on the cracked, weedy pavement of what must have been an old gas station long ago. Painted brick columns held up a little portico in front of a tiny, boarded-up, whitewashed building. He stopped for a minute before pulling back out into the road, checking his hair in the rearview mirror. Not good. He dug under the seat and came up with a navy sock hat, which he thought would go well with the pea coat he was wearing—the good kind of pea coat, bought at a surplus store. He checked his breath and then wondered why he'd done it—he could never smell his own breath. Carl, sensing something was up, had planted his front feet on the dash to get a commanding view over the hood, ears pricked, spoiling for a fight in a strange neighborhood. Jeremy huffed a breath at him and said, "What do you think?"

Carl granted him a quick glance and a low growl.

"Thanks for your honesty. You know, your breath ain't no picnic either, pal." He scrounged through the trash in the glove box and found a pack of gum. It was old and brick hard, but he chewed two pieces anyway.

Approaching cautiously, he turned in at the gate and crept nervously down the long driveway, passing under the naked arms of the sleeping pecan trees and following the curve around the right side of the house, which, as he could now see, really did need paint.

In back, he saw that a paved courtyard separated the house from a long four-bay garage. One bay sheltered a Cadillac; the other three held long tables full of odds and ends and the racks of used clothing common to all garage sales. A few people were already there, poking among the tables and racks.

Jeremy parked off to the side, killed the engine, and hesitated. For a long moment he sat muttering to himself—"I just wanted to look . . . I just thought I'd see what you had in . . . I was just driving by and saw the sign . . ." Nothing sounded right. Anyway, he knew perfectly well that if he met The Girl he would do well to remember his own name; a clever opening line was out of the question. He decided to wing it.

When he opened the door Carl jumped out and took off, and Jeremy let him go. The little deserter knew where to find the truck, and he could certainly take care of himself.

Although he wasn't aware of it, Jeremy had changed. Months of hauling pipe had broadened his shoulders and stripped the baby fat from his face. The shadow of a two-day beard chiseled his features. He stuffed his fists into his pea coat and strode into the courtyard with the confident bearing of a man, but his awkwardness was so newly gone that he had not yet missed it. In his mind he was still just a kid.

Assuming a casual air while scanning like a radar for The Girl, Jeremy strolled past a long rack of hanging clothes, behind which two matronly ladies argued over a dress. "I *know* it's a designer dress, Carla, and it's beautiful! But it's a *six*! I couldn't get one of these hams into a six with a shoehorn!"

An old man in coveralls picked through a table full of woodworking tools. There was a table with books on it and a long table covered with all sorts of glass stuff.

Then he saw her. In the back of the garage, at the end of the table with all the glass on it, stood The Girl. She was placing small colored bottles in a curio cabinet against the wall. He could only see her back, and she was dressed differently than the last time he saw her, but there was no mistaking the hair—light brown with touches of blond and copper, silky, and perfectly trimmed across her shoulders. She still had those tiny braids pulled around to meet in the back.

He couldn't think; he had to force himself to breathe. Desperate for a prop of some kind, he stopped at the book table, picked up a hardcover volume and flipped through it, consciously donning a look of intense intellectual curiosity in case she looked around, except the book had no jacket, no synopsis on the outside, so left him without a clue as to what sort of story it was. His foggy memory of high school English proved to be of little help either, though he questioned whether the author's name was a match for the title.

She closed the cabinet and turned around. When she spotted Jeremy she smiled, a perfectly natural and friendly smile, yet one that charged through him as if a switch had been thrown.

"Oh!" she said, pulling her hair back from her face as she approached, her eyes appraising his pea coat, sock hat, jeans. "Are you a Henry James fan?"

Her eyes were the color of the sea, and he learned close up that what he had seen from a distance was true: she was exactly the right amount of pretty. She appeared to be somewhere near Jeremy's age, but it was hard to tell. She looked like a Kennedy or something, the way she dressed—the layers of blouse and sweater, the cut of her slacks. Jeremy didn't know the first thing about style. He didn't know anything about a Rolls Royce either, but he knew one when he saw it.

"Uh, no," he said, closing the book and laying it back on the table. "I never really got into James."

"I see." Her face tilted down a bit, and the smile morphed into something vaguely teasing as she made a little plucking motion at his pea coat. "More of a Hemingway kind of guy, right?"

"Well, no. I'm not really much of a . . ." His voice trailed off, his eyes casting about for an escape route. "Hey, what are all those little bottles for?"

"Those are perfume bottles. It's kind of a hobby. You want to see?"

It wasn't really a request; she had turned back to the curio cabinet even before she finished asking. He followed, happy to have dodged the book questions.

Taking a key from her pocket she unlocked the cabinet and, very gently, holding it with both hands as if she expected the thing to shatter, she took down a squat little bottle with some kind of fancy blue top that looked like a bunch of flowers or something.

"Muguet," she said. He couldn't have reproduced the pronunciation at gunpoint. "That's the name of the bottle, not the perfume. This one held Femme by Rochas." Gently she lifted the lid, twisting it slightly, and waved it under his nose with an expectant half smile.

"Nice," he said. It smelled like flowers. This, at least, was easier than Henry James. All he had to do was remember not to hyperventilate.

"A classic chypre," she added, waving the stopper under her own nose and closing her eyes for a second to savor it. "My favorite family of fragrances. Fruity top notes that give way to a heart of everlasting flower, with oakmoss and sandalwood underneath that. Potent!" she said, and her eyes flashed.

"Wow. You can really smell all that?"

"It's just a matter of training the senses. Here, look at this one." She put the flower bottle back and took down a tall, slender one with palm leaves drooping down the sides. She held it out to Jeremy, but he declined to take it. It looked way too fragile for his hands.

"I've forgotten," she said, frowning, and then she gently lifted the stopper and passed it under her nose. "Ah. Patou's Sublime—

a floriental. Mother wears it in the summer."

She waved the stopper under his nose. It smelled like flowers.

"Nice," he said. "But the bottles are empty. You're selling empty bottles?"

"Yes. They're Lalique, some of them quite expensive. They're worth hundreds of dollars."

"Each?"

She giggled, maybe a little more than she meant to. "Yes, each."

"Wow. And you got, like, a couple dozen of them."

"Yes," she said, and a wistfulness came into her eyes as she gazed at the bottles lined up in the curio. "We have a rather nice collection. Some are my mother's and some are mine. But Daddy's business isn't doing as well as it once did." Her voice grew weaker with this last, and she let it hang without elaborating. "Oh! Here, let me show you this one."

She took down another bottle, slightly larger and sort of jug-shaped, with a plain stopper, and made of pink glass with little balls molded into it. On closer inspection Jeremy saw something he thought to be weird for a perfume bottle.

"Are those *lizards* crawling around on there?"

A smaller giggle. "Salamanders. I love this bottle. I kept my very favorite fragrance in it. Here, see if you can guess." She waved the stopper under his nose. It smelled like flowers.

He couldn't help it. The Stan Laurel *I don't know* grin slipped out and she saw it. She laughed.

"I really don't have a clue," he said.

"Yes," she giggled again. "I gathered. It's Cuir de Russie. It hints of leather, and Mother says it's a bit masculine, but I don't think so. At least it doesn't smell that way on me. Here, what do you think?" She leaned into him, raised herself on tiptoe, pulled her hair back, and presented the side of her neck for him to smell.

Very slowly, perhaps too slowly, for he was afraid his knees would betray him, he brought his face near her neck and took the daintiest of whiffs, then straightened up and tried to remember the question. He knew there had been a question, although he seemed to have gotten away without answering it; at least he didn't *remember* answering any question. She was talking, still smiling, but he caught only bits of what she was saying, as if it were English phrases lost among long, convoluted French sentences.

" . . . never rub it between the wrists . . . bruise the fragrance—"

"It's beautiful," he finally said, interrupting her. He had suddenly remembered the question. "Not the least bit masculine. On you."

She smiled, tilted her head a little. "Why, thank you!" she said. "You're sweet."

"But then, you could probably wear coal tar and I wouldn't, um . . ."

Coal tar? He panicked, pictured himself retreating to the truck while being pelted with perfume bottles, and then trying to explain to the guys how he got lizards imprinted on his forehead.

But she laughed! *Thank you, Jesus.* She laughed out loud and then said, in a conspiratorial whisper, "You know, the base notes of Cuir de Russie are balsam and birch tar. So you're not that far off, actually. My name is Kearston, by the way."

"I see." He pointed to the gold necklace she wore with the name KEARSTON dangling from it, block letters running together. "Odd spelling," he said. "I don't think I've ever seen it that way before."

"It was my grandmother's maiden name," she explained. "She used to hyphenate it, but they gave it to me without the hyphen. Kearston Manning." She held out a slender hand for him to shake.

"Jeremy Prine. Would that be Manning as in Manning Transport?" He'd seen the signs at the trucking place out on Moreland.

"My father," she said while nodding. "You have rough hands. What do you do?"

"Uh, I work for a mining company." *I dropped out of high school so I could wear a blue hard hat and tote pipe for a crazy alcoholic in a sewage treatment plant.* "I'm a miner."

"That sounds exciting. I could never do anything like that, I'm so claustrophobic." As she spoke, she removed yet another bottle from the cabinet and held it very gingerly. The top looked exotic and delicate, flowing into some knobby looking stuff that cascaded down the sides of the round bottle.

"This is our rarest one. Blackberries. There aren't many of these left. A clear one like this isn't worth as much as the blue, but it's still worth a thousand or so."

"A thousand dollars?" Carl appeared from nowhere, trotting briskly into the garage.

"Uh-huh." The dog sat by Jeremy's feet and scratched at an ear.

"But why? Why would anybody want to pay—I mean, it's just a chunk of glass!"

"Well, yes, but it's an antique. It's quite rare." She put the bottle back in the cabinet, and when she turned around, Carl caught her eye. "Is that your dog?"

"No, he belongs to a friend of mine who's in the hospital, so he sort of bums around with whoever."

"Whomever," she said, squatting down to scratch behind the dog's ears. "He's a Border terrier, isn't he?"

"Well, yeah—so I'm told. His name's Carl. Boy, you know your dogs, don't you?"

Carl raised his head to accommodate her when she scratched under his chin, and his stump of a tail wagged vigorously.

"Mom used to show Goldens, so I spent my formative years

hanging around dog shows. These little guys are very bright," she said.

Jeremy nodded. "I don't know about the rest of them, but that one's smarter than most of the people I know."

The old man in the coveralls shouted something from two bays over, and Kearston excused herself to go see what he wanted.

Jeremy wandered around, looking at things that didn't really interest him—picture frames, pewter dishes. The old guy talking to Kearston started to raise his voice. From overheard bits of conversation, Jeremy figured out that he wanted to buy a whole set of high-grade carving tools for the price marked on a single chisel, and Kearston wouldn't budge. Jeremy stopped at a table of used sports equipment, picking over it just so he could stand close enough to hear her voice. The old guy suddenly tossed the set of carving tools back on the table and stalked off, swaying on bowed legs, muttering to himself, fishing for his car keys. Kearston turned around and came straight over to Jeremy. She was smiling.

"Thank you," she said.

"For what?" Jeremy wasn't aware he had done anything at all.

"Oh, right," she said, laughing. "You didn't do anything. That old coot saw us talking and he must have thought you were my boyfriend. He was giving me a hard time until he saw you standing there smacking that baseball bat in your palm. Did you see the look on his face? It was priceless." Her laughter was pure silver, and she touched his arm as she spoke.

Jeremy looked down at the Little League bat he still held in his hands and gently laid it back on the table. "I'm sorry. I really didn't—"

"It's all right," she said. "I thought it was hilarious."

"Hey, how much is this boom box?" He hadn't noticed it before, but it was right there on the end of the table with the baseball stuff.

"Oh, that's my brother's. It's twenty dollars."

"That's pretty cheap," Jeremy said, picking it up. "What's wrong with it?"

"The radio's broken. The CD player still works, though, and the speakers sound great."

A stack of CDs beside the boom box caught his eye, and he picked up a handful. "Are these yours?" he asked, shuffling through them.

"Some of them. I went through the stuff in my cabinet and took out whatever I haven't listened to in a while. I'll be going off to college in the fall anyway, and Mother said I needed to lighten ship."

What he saw surprised him. "These are Christian groups. Are you into Christian rock?"

"Well, yes, but I kind of prefer the slower stuff. Quiet stuff, ballads. I guess Deus Aderit is my favorite, because they do a lot of that. You won't find any of their stuff out here because I won't part with it."

"No way," Jeremy muttered. He was stunned. This couldn't be happening. Things like this never happened to Jeremy, and he quickly convinced himself it wasn't happening now either. A girl like this—those eyes, that hair—who listened to the same music he did? Who was he kidding? She was just being nice. It made for a wonderful moment, and he would remember it, but he just couldn't invest in it. He kept shuffling through the CDs as a memory crept out of him, quietly, almost accidentally.

"My mom hated Christian rock, and then one day she finally broke down and went with a bunch of us to a Deus Aderit concert in Knoxville—more than a year ago now." He spoke reverently, and he was careful to keep his eyes on the disc in front of him. "I think she really liked it. She was happy that day. That was after she found out she was sick. I think it was the last time I ever saw her face the way it was before. After that, you could always see it in her face. She just knew."

"I'm sorry," Kearston said softly. She understood, seeming to know without being told that his mother had passed away, and she didn't try to say too much. A girl like this was far too good to be true.

"It's okay," he replied with a shrug. "I still have the T-shirt, as the saying goes. Got the name right across here." He swiped his hand across his chest. "The guys are always asking me what it means."

"What, Deus Aderit?"

"Yeah. I guess it's Latin or something."

"It means 'God is present.' They borrowed it from Carl Jung's tombstone."

She'd delivered the explanation pleasantly, without a hint of condescension, as if she simply didn't know how it deflated him, how it sent his self-image staggering backward, as if she couldn't see his ears turn red. Jeremy straightened himself and pulled out his wallet, avoiding her eyes. He carried away the boom box and a bunch of CDs for less than forty dollars.

As he started to walk off she said, "Are you in that old rusty truck?"

He stopped, thought for a second, turned and said, "It's an antique. It's quite rare."

She laughed, and he tucked away the sound, saving it in a special place so he could pull it out and listen to it again later.

He and Carl and the boom box got into the old truck, and as he cranked it up he waved one last time, to be polite. Backing the truck around, he couldn't help thinking it would have been nice if she hadn't been so out of his league, if she hadn't known what the Latin words on Carl Jung's tombstone meant, or maybe had a wart in the middle of her forehead or something. But when he shoved it into first gear and glanced in the rearview mirror for one more glimpse of her, she was looking at him. Holding a fist up to her ear with a thumb and pinkie finger extended in an unmistakable sign, she mouthed the words, "Call me."

He froze. She nodded, smiled.

He dropped it into reverse, eased off the clutch, and the truck crawled backward until her face appeared beside him. He rolled down the window.

"Can I have your number?" he asked.

"Do you have something to write with?"

"I don't need it." This was true. "Just tell me."

She told him her number. He repeated it to himself, nodded rather numbly, then said, "Okay," and started to drive away. When he eased off the clutch, the truck lurched back, and a lady who happened to be crossing behind him let out a warning yelp. Kearston bit back a smile, and Jeremy grinned sheepishly as he found the right gear and drove away.

He practically floated home. Snake wasn't there when he got back, so Jeremy naturally figured he had gone to the job because it was daytime. If the sun was shining, Snake would either be at work or behind the locked door of his apartment. The first thing Jeremy did when he got inside was go to the desk and write down the number. Twice. He tore off one piece of paper and stuck it in a desk drawer, then put another in his wallet, just in case. He had to fight back a serious urge to call her right then; the only thing stopping him was that he knew it would make him look like a jerk. The second thing he did was to set the boom box he'd bought from her on the end of the desk, plug it in, and put on a Nicole Mullen CD.

As the first song started up, he noticed the carving on the little shelf above the desk. It was the one Snake had been toying with for so long. It appeared he had finally finished. It was, indeed, a hand and forearm rising from the rough half log, and now that the carving was done it didn't seem so curious, so purposeless. The forearm widened and lost its shape near the bottom, merging naturally into the log, but where it tapered toward the hand the slightest shading of bone, sinew, even veins, stood out in intricate detail. The hand itself was a work of art, and as he studied it closely he noticed that the fingernails looked odd. Then he saw the subtle webbing at the base of the fingers, the swirling scars along the side of the wrist, and the careful etching of snakelike partial-thickness graft across the back of the hand.

Holding the carving at arm's length, Jeremy studied its form and began to see. It was clearly Snake's own hand, which seemed to be saying something. The palm faced neither up nor down, neither giving nor receiving, the fingers shaped to be separate and distinct. The wrist bent backward just a bit, as did the fingers. He replaced the carving carefully on the shelf and took a step back. Now that he had looked at it—*really* looked at it—he didn't see how he could have missed it before. The hand was reaching out, not grasping or grappling or cupping itself to receive some gift, but reaching blindly, almost desperately, out of the earth. Out of dust.

CHAPTER 14

To soothe the savage breast.

Snake heard two things as he climbed the stairs to the third floor. The first was the China Girl's piano, playing a song he didn't recognize. And like most of the stuff she played, it killed him. The second thing he heard was music coming from his own apartment, so he took the last flight of stairs two at a time.

Jeremy was kicked back in the recliner with a lottery-winning smile on his face, eating a sandwich and listening to some woman sing from a boom box sitting on the end of the desk.

"What is that?" Snake shouted over the music.

Jeremy grinned. "Nicole Mullen. Good, isn't she?"

"Turn that thing off," Snake said, and went into his room. When he came back out Jeremy was still in the chair, still eating a sandwich, still listening to his music.

"Where did you get that?" Snake asked.

"I bought it from an angel." Jeremy beamed. "The most amazing girl I've ever seen, and she wants me to call her."

That was all it took. Anger bubbled near the surface. The rage was barely restrained under normal circumstances—if anything in Snake's life could be called a normal circumstance—but now, just now, coming back from the parking lot of the music store, frustration sat in the front of his mind.

"Turn it off," he repeated, and this time he raised his voice a little. He did *not* want to hear about Jeremy's dream girl, and he did *not* want to listen to any Jesus rock. He *did* want to be able to hear the piano downstairs, which, as far as he was concerned, was being played just for him.

Jeremy gave him a puzzled look and said, "In a minute."

Snake felt the warning tremor inside himself and stepped into the kitchen. Carl scrambled out of his way. The dog had more sense than Jeremy, who smiled, closed his eyes and mouthed the words to the song, blissfully unaware of how close Snake was to a meltdown. The music from the living room stopped for a moment, and he heard the piano downstairs clearly in the silence between songs. Pure ambrosia. Then the woman in the boom box started singing again. Snake got a beer from the refrigerator, opened it, and tried to reason with himself, his arms shaking, leaning on the sink. But finally he couldn't take it anymore and he stormed back into the living room.

"Turn it off," he said, through gritted teeth.

Jeremy's eyes opened. He was lying back in the recliner so he was looking almost straight up at Snake, and he frowned.

"No. I was here first."

"Turn it off."

"No!" Jeremy repeated, nodding the word emphatically and pulling the recliner upright. Gripping the arms of the chair, he glared at Snake. "You won't let me touch *your* precious stereo, so I got my own. You can't stop me from listening to it. It's mine!"

Snake's thin lips curled into a smile. He allowed Jeremy to stare him down for a few seconds.

"Okay," he said calmly, and his eyes went to the boom box. It was solid black, with CD player, radio, and tape deck stacked in the middle, and two medium-sized speakers mounted on the ends. He didn't know boom boxes, but this one appeared to be as good as any.

"It looks like a pretty nice outfit," Snake said. "Decent sound, for something that size. How much did you pay for it?"

"I picked it up at a yard sale for twenty bucks," Jeremy said proudly. "The only thing wrong with it is the radio's busted."

Snake nodded and walked over to the window, behind Jeremy's line of sight. The woman on the boom box was showing off her powerful voice, belting out something about her redeemer, so Snake was pretty sure Jeremy didn't hear the window sliding open. When he passed back by the chair he held out a twenty-dollar bill and let it flutter down into Jeremy's lap. In one fluid series of motions he reached down and unplugged the boom box, picked it up by its handle, took two steps and sailed it out the window. The long black rectangle tumbled through a high, lazy arc with its power cord trailing behind, plummeted three stories and hit precisely on the edge of the steel dumpster, disintegrating into a shower of plastic and metal and wire. Snake gently closed the window and latched it.

Now it was quiet. He could hear the piano.

He heard Jeremy get up and walk across the room, but he didn't turn around to see what was going on until he heard noises coming from the direction of the stereo shelf. Jeremy stood at the shelf with his arms extended over the top of the receiver, snatching wires out of the back of Snake's vintage McIntosh 1900. His intention was clear.

By the time Snake got to him, Jeremy had yanked out all the wires, grabbed the receiver and started to pull it off the shelf. Snake managed to wedge himself in between. With brute force, he separated Jeremy from the receiver and slung him backward across the room, where he tripped, stumbled, and landed on the sofa.

Snake was settling the receiver back on the shelf when he heard Jeremy approaching. He stepped aside just in time to avoid the first wild swing, but the second punch landed. Jeremy's hard fist bit his lip, except the kid didn't know how to get his shoulder behind a punch, so there was no real harm in it. Snake sidestepped the flurry and landed a hook to the sternum. Jeremy reeled backward, then quickly regained his footing and charged back in headfirst, low and hard. The two of them crashed over the recliner with Snake hitting flat on his back, his head slamming hard against the floor. Momentarily dazed, he rolled over and staggered to his feet, holding his left arm out to block whatever might come.

Maybe it was the growl. Maybe it was just the grainy, swirling, uncertain vision that hadn't entirely cleared. Maybe it was only the heat of battle that brought it back, but when Snake raised his head, the boy he saw standing before him was not Jeremy. He saw Tom—the upper lip quivering in a snarl, the coiled-spring posture, the fiery, tensely focused eyes that said, "*Enough!* Do not cross this line!"

He blinked, and Tom was gone. The face looked nearly the same, only the hair was longer, and the figure in front of him held a weapon. Jeremy had grabbed the carving from the shelf above the desk and now held it poised to strike, gripping the carved hand in his own, ready to swing the half log like a club. Snake's fist, the one he held in front of him like a shield, opened slowly, palm out—calling for a truce. He leaned back against the wall and slumped to the floor.

Running his fingertips up the back of his head, he could feel a goose egg rising. Seconds passed, marked in three-quarter time by the piano downstairs, and his head started to clear. Opening his eyes, he saw Jeremy's feet and the heavy bark-covered half log dangling by his knee, held loosely in his fingers, no longer poised to strike.

Jeremy placed the carving back on the shelf, and the wooden hand seemed to reach out to him when he released it. "I'm sorry," he said. It was almost a whisper. "Are you all right?"

Snake nodded.

"I'm sorry," Jeremy repeated. "I don't know what I was . . . I'm sorry."

Snake waved once, then his hand went back to his forehead. "I had it coming."

Jeremy lowered himself to the floor, folded his legs and leaned back against the recliner, facing Snake. Carl appeared and padded softly up to Jeremy. Standing on his hind legs, putting his fore-paws on Jeremy's shoulder, he licked his face once, just to make sure everything was okay, then curled up next to him and laid his head on his paws.

"This isn't working out very well, is it?" Jeremy said. "Maybe I should just go back home."

Snake sighed, rubbed the knot on his head. "It's my fault," he said quietly. "Everything's my fault."

They stared at each other for a moment, and then Jeremy said, "Yeah. It is."

His words were followed with impeccable timing by a series of heavy chords pounded out on the piano downstairs. This drew first a trace of a smile, followed by a chuckle from each of them, which broke the tension.

"When I was about your age I bowed up at my old man," Snake said, "and it went just about like this." He waved a weak hand at the overturned coffee table. "He won the fight—my old man was a bull—but he lost me." Drawing a deep breath, he looked up at the ceiling. "He had to control everybody, every*thing*. If he could have just once put a little slack in the reins, we might've got along. But he couldn't do it."

Making a fist so that the scars stretched waxy white over his knuckles, Snake said, "He squeezed so hard I slipped right through his fingers, and he never forgave me for it. Then Tom followed me, and the old man ended up all alone with his farm."

Jeremy nodded. "That's how he came to be working a field by himself after dark." Everybody knew the story. When Tom decided to marry Julie, he left home to take a good paying job in the tunnel alongside his brother, and their father had blamed that on Aiden too. So when neighbors went looking for his father in the wee hours of the morning and found him tangled in the power take-off behind his own tractor—lights still on, engine still running—the family laid his twisted body on Aiden's pile of guilt. Nothing was ever said, exactly, but for Aiden it was a cold and silent funeral. Everybody knew his father would not have been working a field alone in the dark had his two grown, healthy sons not deserted him.

"Yeah," Snake said. "And then Tom died, and it was just too much for Mama."

"I know about all that too. My mother went up to the home every couple weeks to see about her." Jeremy's hand rubbed absently behind Carl's ears as he spoke.

"There's more," Snake said, "but what I'm trying to say is, it all started right here." He tapped the floor with a forefinger. "I just didn't see it coming. Jeremy, do you know how long it's been since I had somebody else to worry about? Since I looked past my own skin? For ten years I haven't had a family. No mother, no father, no brother, no wife . . ." He paused, grinding a fist against his forehead. "Not even a girlfriend. I guess when you're that isolated, maybe it takes a thump on the head to get your attention. I swore, I *swore* I would not become my father, but here I sit, rubbing my sore head and wondering how it came to this. It's so easy. All you have to do is forget."

A slow, enticing melody flowed quietly through the floor, one note at a time, and Snake nodded his head sadly.

"I don't really understand any of this," he admitted. "I've never had a son. But I've *been* one. I'll try to remember that."

Jeremy nodded, stroked Carl's back.

"Sorry about the boom box," Snake said quietly.

"I still didn't have any right to throw a punch at you," Jeremy said. "I was all wound up on account of Kearston—the girl I met this afternoon—so when you chunked the boom box out the window I just lost it. Anger isn't supposed to rule me; I'm supposed to rule it. Mom raised me better than that. I'm a Christian."

A wry smile crept onto Snake's face. "Even a Christian's gotta be a man. Jesus was a construction worker—hung out with a bunch of commercial fishermen, and He was known to get mad and fight. David was a warrior, a giant-killer, a man of violence, but the Bible says he was a man after God's own heart. I could name a half dozen others."

Jeremy's head tilted and his eyes narrowed. "I didn't know you knew any of that stuff."

A nod. "I grew up in the same house as your dad. Sat in the same Sunday school classes, went to the same revival meetings, walked down the same aisle, got baptized in the same creek. Oh, when I was little I was just as much a church boy as Tom was."

"What happened?"

A shrug, a smirk. "I don't know," Snake said. But then he began to talk, softly, thoughtfully, about his childhood. Whatever religion he'd owned as a child, he'd inherited the way a man gets his father's nose or his hairline, without thinking about it or ever feeling like he had a say in it. His family's religion just *was*. It was what they did on Sunday morning and Sunday night, and most of the time on Wednesday night. It was their society, their circle of friends, a fountain of gossip and an encyclopedia of judgment. Always it seemed to young Aiden that his parents passed judgment constantly on each other and on everybody and everything around them, pronouncements held forth with a firmness of chin and sharpness of tone that brooked no opposition—but then, they were never uttered in the presence of anyone who might pose opposition. After years of hearing these pronouncements it suddenly came to Aiden as a teenager that the absolutes from whence the judgments came were in fact quite malleable and fluid, that creative interpretation could be applied to almost any edict to make it possible to praise one's friends and condemn one's enemies for precisely the same attribute. Two men could argue vehemently—one a friend and the other an imagined enemy—and the friend would invariably be judged a tenacious defender of right principle and true faith while the other, who had done no wrong as far as Aiden could see, was pronounced an ignorant, bullheaded heretic. Sometimes a hatred born thus would live for years, unspoken but for small slights and whispered remarks. Aiden watched, and listened, and made judgments of his own.

"By the time me and Dad had our little falling-out," Snake said, "I was a long way from the church boy I used to be. But not Tom. Good old steadfast Tom. He never looked too deep into anything. He was always just simple enough to be happy."

"You don't believe in God?" Jeremy asked.

"I don't know. I did, once. Now, sometimes I think maybe men create God in their father's image, and then add to Him out of their own experience."

"Experience. You mean like getting burned beyond recognition," Jeremy said quietly.

"Or losing both your parents. That's the stuff gods are made of. So where was He? If God's around, shouldn't I be able to summon a miracle in a pinch? Or maybe I should call it a miracle that I'm alive. Should I thank God I'm still here, or should I be upset because I don't have a face? Why didn't He stop this from happening, or make it go away. If God *is,* then where are the miracles?"

"There are miracles," Jeremy said.

"Show me one." Snake spread his hands and looked around the room. "Call down a miracle. Make it rain frogs, and I'll be convinced."

"God's timing, and His reasons, are His own. It's not room service." Jeremy was quiet for a moment and said, "What *do* you believe in?"

Snake paused, then laid out his best argument. "When I was in the burn unit, after they moved me to semiprivate, there was a guy named Ross in the same room with me. Ross believed in miracles. His face was okay but his hands and arms were burned about like mine. He spilled a grease fire down the front of his pants and then burned all the skin off his hands trying to beat it out. He had a big family. I watched them gather around his bed every day and wave their arms and shout prayers over him. They brought him all the latest herbal remedies, had him drinking aloe and all that stuff. Every night, before they left, they joined hands and said one last prayer over him and claimed all kinds of promises from the Bible and told him when he woke up in the morning he'd be healed. Just like that. All better. Not a trace. Told him he didn't have to do a thing, just lie there and wait. God would handle it."

Snake sighed heavily. "I admit it—I asked for help myself, more than once. I actually prayed, on the off chance God would remember who I was—or maybe hoping He'd forget. But as far as I can tell, He wasn't listening.

"Me and Ross both had pins in our hands. Early on, they bend your fingers hard down, drill holes through the bones and put steel pins on a forty-five through the backs of your hands, so when the scar tissue forms you'll have enough of it to make a fist. They pin the thumb down too, so your hand looks sort of like a duck head."

He used his own hand to illustrate.

"First thing in the morning they'd always take us to the tub room to soak off the night's bandages, and Ross would just sit there in his tub and mope. Every morning, it broke his heart that he didn't wake up healed. Me, I saw the tip of my thumb and forefinger sticking out of the bandages, and I learned that if I concentrated really hard and ignored the pain I could strain against the pins hard enough to make my thumb and fingertip come together. I could pinch the end of the bandage and unwrap it myself. It was hard. I would grit my teeth and sweat blood for five minutes, just bringing these two fingertips together. Ross said I sounded like I was lifting weights. I told him lifting weights would've been easier. But in *here*," he said, and tapped his chest, "I never felt so strong in my whole life as I did then."

He splayed the fingers of his right hand, flexed them twice, then made a fist. He turned his fist, studying it from different angles.

"It isn't pretty," he said, "but it works. I can use it. When I left the hospital, Ross's hands were almost useless. He couldn't grasp anything." He leaned forward a little and looked Jeremy in the eye.

"I believe in my own strength," he said. "I believe in my own will. I never saw God lift a finger."

The afternoon sun slanted through the window, lighting Jeremy's face, and the China Girl's piano danced on the light.

"*Your* strength," Jeremy said. "I was little, but I still remember one or two things about that time. I remember Mom sitting on the cushions in the bay window, looking down the driveway and crying. All day. I remember Dad's casket, and I remember wondering why they didn't open it like they did at Grandpa's funeral. It always felt to me like Dad left without saying good-bye. You were in the hospital then, but they never took me to see you, and

Mom never talked about you. Except once. I remember because it surprised me. It didn't sound like Mom. I asked her if she prayed for you and she said no. She just said no, and I couldn't believe it. She knelt down and took my shoulders—she had this hurt look in her eyes—and she said there were twenty-three churches full of people praying for you, and she thought maybe that was enough."

Snake swallowed, tilted his head back to stare at the ceiling.

"Twenty-three, she said. I remember the number. I don't know how she knew it, but I guess there was some sort of prayer chain for when something really bad happened. Twenty-three churches full of people praying for you."

"What's your point?"

"I don't know if I can explain it but it's about how God works. Look, you remember the Bible stories they told when you were a kid, right?"

A nod. The China Girl had begun a new piece, deep and stirring, spinning effortlessly through places inside Snake where no one had gone in years.

"Remember the three guys in Babylon who wouldn't bow down to an idol, so the king threw them in a furnace? And it was so hot it killed the guards around them. Next thing you know, the three guys are walking around in the fire, unhurt, and somebody's in there with them."

"I remember the story," Snake said.

"Well, that's kind of how I see it. God won't keep you out of the fire, but He'll go in there with you. He won't make your problems go away, but He'll give you the tools you need. All you have to do is use them."

"Tools."

"Yes, tools. When you were in the burn unit, there were hundreds of people praying for you, every day. I've heard you talk about it. There were people who said it was a miracle when you recovered the use of your hands, didn't they?"

"Some did."

"God can be pretty subtle," Jeremy said. "You were burnt beyond recognition. You were hurt about as bad as a man can be hurt and live, and they were feeding you morphine around the clock, but in spite of all that, you felt stronger than any other time in your life. Isn't that what you said?"

Snake gave him a cautious nod.

"Where did you think that strength came from?"

Snake sat staring into space, his head leaning back against the wall in the shadow of the desk. There was nothing for him to say. This new level of responsibility had painted him into a corner. Jeremy's way of looking at things, of assuming a God first and then arranging the facts to fit, was interesting, but it required a child's tacit acceptance of God to make it work. Snake wasn't ready to go there. He couldn't agree with Jeremy's way of seeing without some proof—at least something—a sign, a clue. A miracle. But neither would he argue with the kid, because somewhere in the mists of his childhood memories lay a warning, something about how it was better to be cast into the sea and drown than to offend a child. Like it or not, some of the ancient Sunday school admonitions still cast their shadows.

The beautiful, flowing melody poured freely into the silence. Jeremy closed his eyes, and his face relaxed into a smile of deep contentment.

"Wow, Rachmaninov," he said. "I was beginning to think she didn't play anything but Chopin."

Snake leaned forward, focused.

"You *know* this stuff?" he asked.

"Oh, yeah. Mom played classical all the time. You knew she taught piano, right? I took lessons from her for a few years, but I never was—"

"But you *know* this stuff."

"Classical? Well, yeah, a lot of it. 'Course, even Mom couldn't hang with Swan. Swan's probably the best I've ever heard. They're gonna have to *burn* that piano when she gets—"

"Swan?"

"Yeah. You know, the Chinese girl downstairs. I thought you knew she was the one playing the piano."

"Her name is Swan?"

"Something like that. I can't pronounce it the way she does."

"How do you know her?"

"I see her sometimes when I do laundry. And a couple times I gave her a lift to the grocery store in Geech's truck. What's wrong?" Jeremy stared hard. "You got a thing for Swan?"

Snake didn't answer him. Wouldn't look at him. He personally had never run into the China Girl in the laundry room, because before Jeremy came he had always washed his clothes at two o'clock in the morning.

"You do!" Jeremy said, grinning. "You got a thing for Swan!" And then his face lit up as the whole picture came to him all at once. "So, all this time when you wanted it quiet in here, it was just so you could hear the piano? *That's* why you got so bent about the boom box! Man, why didn't you just say so?"

Snake finally found his voice. "Hey, it's not like I'm asking her for a date or anything. I just like to hear her play."

"Why not?"

"Why not what?"

"Ask her out."

Snake shuddered. "I don't go out."

"Okay, so ask her up for dinner. I'll even cook."

"I think her husband would probably object."

"She's not married. Oh, you thought . . . No! That's her *brother*. Her family sent her with him to look after him, to cook, clean house, and keep his clothes washed and stuff while he goes to school. She's his big sister. Look, I'm telling you we're friends. I can introduce you. Really. What have you got to lose?"

Snake coiled himself back into the darkness where the desk met the wall.

"Dignity," his voice said, out of the shadows.

Snake was shattered. Her situation was even worse than he had thought. Lonelier. That intense wave of compassion rolled over him again, but even so, he knew he could never bring himself to face her. A distant, nebulous relationship was the best he could hope for. Six inches of concrete was a fragile barricade against rejection.

"I don't want to meet her," he said flatly. "I just want to know more about the music."

"I saw the Beethoven disc on the stereo shelf the other day. Is that what you were doing? Trying to learn something about classical piano?"

He nodded.

"Okay," Jeremy said. "If that's all you want, I can help you with that. It'll cost you, though. I'm going to need to borrow your truck."

CHAPTER 15

The snake charmer.

The Saturday of Jeremy's first date with Kearston dawned deep blue and bitter cold. Puddles froze solid, and exposed patches of red clay spewed up little stalagmites of ice on the sides of the road. In the middle of the afternoon Jeremy pulled Snake's truck into the loop in front of her house and shivered in his new jacket as he hurried up onto the porch. He'd bought the gray tweed blazer, along with a new dress shirt and shoes whose names he couldn't pronounce, all for this date. From talking to Kearston on the phone he'd come to realize she thought him older and more sophisticated than he really was, and he desperately wanted to keep up the illusion.

He rang the bell. A couple of freezing minutes passed before an older lady opened the door and met him with an apologetic smile.

"You must be Jeremy," she said, extending a delicate hand. "I'm Kearston's mother." He wouldn't have guessed it. Though she was impeccably attired—she was the dark dress and pearls type, with not a single silver hair out of place—she looked too old to be Kearston's mother. "Sorry to keep you waiting, but I went to the back door. Nobody ever comes to the front. Please come in. Kearston should be down in a minute."

She seated him in the formal living room and offered him something hot to drink, which he declined, then excused herself, saying she would just go and let her daughter know he was here.

He sat on the edge of the sofa with his clammy hands clasped in his lap, fearful of touching anything. The space surrounding him looked to have been professionally decorated twenty or thirty years ago, full of heavy brocaded furniture. Mirror-cut walnut judge's paneling covered the walls, and an ornate chandelier hung from the high plaster ceiling in the center of the room. Jeremy stared at it, feeling small and intimidated—out of his league. Now he wished he'd sprung for a new pair of slacks instead of wearing jeans with his new outfit, and the suspicion grew in his heart that his best wasn't good enough. Raking his hair back, he chided himself for not getting a haircut. He felt like a short, ugly miner waiting for the princess to arrive, painfully aware that he hadn't any diamonds in his pockets.

But when Kearston walked into the living room wearing a simple sweater and jeans, her smile went all through him and his fears began to fade. A heavy wool topcoat was draped over her arm, and she smelled like flowers.

"I'm sorry," she said. "Have you been waiting long?"

He looked at his watch, shrugged. " 'Bout an hour and a half. But it was worth it." It had been less than five minutes; it only *seemed* like an hour and a half.

Her laugh melted the remainder of his tension. "Come on. You have to meet my dad."

Taking his hand, she led him to the back of the house, to a much more comfortable den where an old man sat slumped in an armchair, dull eyes focused on a television. Jeremy was pretty sure it was the same bent old man he'd seen months earlier wearing a straw hat and picking up limbs in the pecan grove. He didn't move, didn't look up until Kearston touched him.

"Daddy?" She shook his shoulder, and he jerked, looking up at her in surprise. Then he spotted Jeremy and frowned.

"Daddy, this is Jeremy. We're going out."

"I'm not hungry," the old man grunted.

"No, Daddy. Jeremy and I are going out. We're going to David's concert, but you don't have to go. I just wanted you to meet him."

"Who?" He spoke gruffly, as if he wasn't even sure who Kearston was.

"Jeremy," she answered patiently. "We're going now. We'll be back later, okay?"

"I don't want to go," he said, watching Jeremy, and his gruffness seemed to morph into worry.

"Okay," she said. "You don't have to."

Something was not right about Mr. Manning, but it was clear that Kearston knew how to handle him so that he answered her tenderness with a kind of childlike trust.

An oblique winter light cast spider-web shadows under the leafless pecan trees as Jeremy eased out the long driveway, and Kearston explained that her father had Alzheimer's.

"There are good days and bad days," she said. "But the trend is pretty much downward. It's getting so we have to watch him all the time—Mom worries about him wandering off."

"Yeah, and it's kind of a rough neighborhood."

Kearston looked out the window, watching run-down houses and weed-ridden yards roll by. "It wasn't always. Mom says when I was little it was pretty nice around here, but then the airport expanded and everybody rushed to sell out, to get away from the noise. The price of real estate went down fast. Now we have an alarm system and she's thinking about bars on the windows."

"Why didn't your folks sell out when everybody else did?"

"Well, it was the house they built together, and they wanted us to grow up there, so they waited. Now it's too late. Nobody's going to buy it now—not for what it's worth."

"Yeah," Jeremy said. "It's a nice house."

"It used to be a *grand* house, when I was a kid. Now all the new houses out in the suburbs are bigger than ours. Times change."

"Yeah." Jeremy nodded slowly. "Everything changes."

Kearston glanced back and forth suddenly, and frowned. "Where are you going?"

"The college. Your brother's concert."

She laughed. "No, no, no. He goes to school there, but that's not where the concert is. The concert's at the Ironworks, up on the north side."

Jeremy swallowed hard. He could feel his ears turning red.

"North side?"

"Uh-huh. You mean you've never been to the Ironworks? It's an awesome place. I'm sorry, I thought I told you where we were going."

"The north side," he said, and he couldn't hide his concern. "Of Atlanta."

"Well, yeah. Northwest—you know, the old industrial district. People are converting all sorts of stuff there now—"

"I'm not a real big fan of the city," he muttered, panic rising in his throat. *"You go down there by yoself alone, you gid yo butt whupped and yo chicken took."*

"That's okay," she said, in a voice too bright and cheerful. "I can get you there. Take a right at the next light."

She guided him onto the expressway, where he spent the next twenty minutes threading his way through the hurly-burly insanity of Atlanta traffic, clinching his jaw, holding his lane, and feeling a bit like a duck in a gator pond. When she realized he was a newcomer to the city, she started pointing out familiar places.

"You're easy to talk to," she told him, after he'd managed to survive the gauntlet and was pulling off on the Fourteenth Street exit.

Attempting a casual grin while trying to loosen his death grip on the steering wheel, it occurred to him that silence served him well.

"It's because I don't have anything to say."

"Uh-huh." Skepticism twisted her lip. It was clear from her expression that she took it for a lie, which pleased him immensely.

She guided him right back through the same part of the city he'd covered on foot that first day, back in August, only now it seemed very different. There weren't as many people out walking around because of the cold, and only the junipers and magnolias remained green. Yet it also made a profound difference that he was now in the company of this girl—this magical girl who knew everything about the world and yet was still unafraid. So it never occurred to him not to follow her lead. His greatest fear was that his fear would show.

Sitting on a side street in the industrial heart of town, the Ironworks had been a wrought-iron manufacturing plant for a hundred years or so, but now the place had been purchased and renovated by a group of progressive entrepreneurs who recognized its radical chic potential.

Immediately, Jeremy saw that the owners had taken some liberties with the term *renovated*. They had removed the machinery, painted the floors, swept out the cobwebs and dust, and brought in a bunch of folding chairs, but the warren of connected buildings retained their industrial personality. Uneven concrete floors, rutted and grooved by a hundred years of blacksmiths having dragged steel over them; two-foot-thick walls of ancient brick, sandblasted and unpainted; huge old multi-paned factory windows spilling natural sunlight on exposed beams; the original heavy industrial roll-up doors with chains tied off to one side, all tastefully lit by a system of indirect lighting and swagged here and there with vast swatches of what looked like cheesecloth, the place had undergone a striking transformation with a minimum of remodeling. The new Ironworks consisted of a large concert hall, an expansive atrium with wrought-iron tables and a glass wall looking out onto a garden, two gourmet restaurants, a coffee shop, and a smaller concert hall, sometimes rented out for weddings, and sometimes, as it was today, loaned gratis to college groups who needed a place to perform. Wandering around before the concert, Jeremy overheard other people—people who looked and sounded like they knew what they were talking about—using words like "texture" and "ambience."

"I just love this place," Kearston said, settling into a folding chair in the lesser concert hall. "It is *so* cool."

Jeremy's head tilted back, mouth open, examining the elaborate sound and lighting system draped and tied and bolted to the girders, and he nodded, careful not to smile. "Yes," he said, pensively. "It has a certain ambience. Has to do with texture, I think."

The concert was as unique as the building, at least to Jeremy. In front of a crowd of no more than a hundred people, twelve college kids trooped out onto a stage of rough-sawn oak planking and tore into an Irish jig. He hadn't thought to ask what sort of concert it would be, and was delighted when they proved to be an accomplished Celtic ensemble complete with bodhran and penny whistle, squeeze-box and flute, fiddle and mandolin. They played an astonishing array of reels, jigs, waltzes and Irish drinking songs with equal zest and a contagious humor.

Kearston's older brother's name was David. Tall and serious, despite the Harpo hair and Groucho glasses, he played cello and sometimes blended vocals with a pale wisp of a dark-haired girl whose lilting voice nailed those haunting ballads Jeremy found so unutterably sad, even though he didn't understand a word. Kearston told him the thin soprano was David's girlfriend, an anthropology major.

After the concert the ensemble hung around for a while, breaking down, and Kearston dragged Jeremy up to meet them.

"And what do you do?" David asked, with a glancing appraisal of Jeremy's too-new coat and shoes.

"I, uh . . . I'm in mining," Jeremy said, squaring his shoulders, raking his hair back.

"Ah." David flashed a small condescending smile at his sister.

"You play an excellent cello," Jeremy offered, anxious to change the subject.

"He's really good, isn't he?" Kearston said, beaming.

"You bet. Where I come from, he'd be the finest cello player in town, hands down." Where Jeremy came from, he would have been the *only* cello player in town.

"Ah well, my little sister's into political science, so it's left to me to carry on the artistic tradition in the family," David said.

Jeremy frowned, looked to Kearston. "Artistic tradition?"

"Oh, he means Dad. Our father made a bit of a name for himself in tempera."

"Tempura? He cooks Japanese food?"

"Temp*er*a, not temp*ur*a," David said, and Jeremy was sure he detected a trace of a smirk. "It's paint made with egg yolks."

"Oh," Jeremy said, and feeling his face flush, he retreated into silence once more.

Kearston gave his arm a meaningful squeeze and interceded with a brief dissertation on the history of egg tempera. "Oil only came into vogue about five hundred years ago. Before that, tempera was the main medium of . . ."

Jeremy's attention trailed away, torn between embarrassment at his own ignorance and euphoria over Kearston's casual embrace. She had come to his rescue. He said very little after that, and Kearston clearly covered for him.

Leaving, they turned up their collars and lowered their chins, forging out the door into the brunt of the cold. Once in the truck, Kearston looked at her watch and said, "There's a place near here where they have a few of Dad's pieces on consignment, if they're still open. I haven't been there in a while, and I'd like to see them again myself if you're interested."

Tobias Galleries was down a hill off of Peachtree Road in Buckhead, an upscale part of the city Kearston said was populated by doctors, interior decorators, and stockbrokers. Lining both sides of the slope down to the cul-de-sac in front of the galleries was an eclectic array of artsy shops with exotic names advertising Persian rugs, antique furniture, bathroom fixtures, Italian tile, interior design services, and custom upholstery. Jeremy cringed as he parked his uncle's pickup truck between a Porsche and a Jaguar, wondering how much further he could get from his comfort zone.

Once inside, he found not the art museum he'd expected but something resembling a mini-mall with perhaps twenty storefronts, selling all sorts of original art on consignment. Kearston went straight to one of the smaller stores in the middle of the promenade. Beside the door stood a rectangular plaster monolith as tall as Jeremy, bearing the name *Temperal Images* across the top, and beneath that a column of a half-dozen names in bold raised letters—the names of artists whose work was featured in the store.

The bottom name on the list was Manning.

The manager of the store, a portly gentleman with a pure white crew cut and an expansive sand-colored cable knit sweater, hailed Kearston immediately and talked to her like a favorite niece.

Jeremy followed along as the manager led them through an elegant maze of false walls, each one displaying the works of a different artist, and each piece spotlighted by track lights hanging from the ceiling. They stopped in front of a wall bearing a dozen small paintings clearly done by the same hand. They were rustic scenes—a barn in a state of gray collapse, a barefoot boy and a calf on a footpath, a vacant dinner table with dishes still in place. Jeremy was struck by the colors, the extraordinary warmth exuded by nearly all of the paintings.

"This is amazing," he said. "How come he didn't do this for a living?"

"Oh, he didn't start painting until he was in his forties, right before I was born. The doctor told him he needed a hobby, so this was how he learned to handle stress. His stuff really only started selling a couple years ago, just about the time he was diagnosed."

"Wow," Jeremy whispered. "What could he have accomplished if he'd been doing this all his life?"

Kearston shrugged. "I asked him that once. He said if he'd been an artist all his life he wouldn't have been the same man, wouldn't have seen things the same way. 'You are what you are,' he always said. 'Bring what you got, do what you do, and be who you are.'"

The manager, standing behind them, added, "Some people said his work was too derivative of Wyeth. I know your father, and he was never derivative of anybody. But he just shrugged it off and said their opinion of him was none of his business."

Kearston seemed drawn to a painting on the far end of the

wall. Jeremy went to look over her shoulder. It was a simple scene, what appeared to be the front room of a small and spartan country house. The door stood open, with no one in sight. The photographic detailing of a polished wood floor bathed in sunshine from the open door, the slight bulging of a breeze-ruffled curtain, the brightness and warmth of the afternoon light—all conspired to leave an aftertaste of absence and sadness.

"He painted this when I was four," Kearston said softly. "It's my favorite. He did it right after my grandmother died. I don't remember her at all—I was too little. I don't think her death had anything to do with the painting, but when I look at this piece, it's always the same, as if she left suddenly, and I just missed her." She sighed. "Now Dad doesn't remember her either."

Jeremy had to know. "Why on earth is it for sale? How come it's not hanging in your house?"

She smiled, and there was a pained resignation in it. "Well, pretty much everything's going. If we don't sell the trucking business soon, our accountant says we're going to be in real trouble."

The manager cleared his throat. "Kearston," he said quietly, "have you seen the new Ethier exhibit over here?" There was a kindness in his manner that made Jeremy suspect he was trying to take her mind off of things.

"No, I haven't! I *love* his stuff." She hurried off with the manager, and Jeremy started to follow, but as he turned he happened to glance out through the front, across the promenade, into the store directly opposite. Two men were talking in front of a huge painting of some water lilies done in bold splashes of bright color when one of them glanced over his shoulder in Jeremy's direction.

He recognized that face—the perfect hair, the chiseled frame, the expensive clothes. It was Perry, the man who had picked him up on his way down from Tennessee. The man who had disappeared with his duffel bag.

Kearston's voice came from behind him. "Jeremy, come here. I want you to see this."

He ignored her. Slowly at first, almost unconsciously, he began moving toward the face across the hall.

"Jeremy?" she said as he pushed open the heavy glass door. An old anger gripped him, fueled by helplessness and frustration, and he gained momentum. He jerked open the door across the hall and strode up to Perry.

Perry turned at the last second, arms crossed, a forefinger aside his tanned chin. His eyes looked Jeremy up and down, and there was no trace of recognition in them.

"I want my bag," Jeremy said, flexing his fingers at his side.

"Excuse me?" Perry's eyes widened, uncomprehending.

"I want my bag," Jeremy repeated, a bit louder. A slight hiss from the door told him Kearston had followed him in.

"I'm afraid you have me confused with some—"

"My name is Jeremy. You gave me a ride late last summer. White Lexus. Chatsworth. You drove off with my duffel bag, and I want it back." His voice shook.

Kearston tugged at his arm. "Jeremy, what's going on?"

He pulled away from her, glaring at Perry. "He knows," Jeremy said.

Perry flashed an exaggerated shrug of comical confusion at the salesman next to him, who stared blankly at Jeremy.

"I've never seen this man before," Perry said, then to Jeremy, "I'm sorry, but I can't help you. You *must* have me confused with someone else."

Jeremy reached out to grab him by the shirt, but the salesman, who looked like he might have been a linebacker in a former life, shot an arm out to block him, then stepped in front of him as Perry backed away.

"Young man, I'm afraid you're going to have to leave. If you persist, I *will* call the police."

Jeremy allowed Kearston to drag him away, but his angry eyes stayed locked on Perry until he was out of sight. She walked him to the coffee shop in the corner of the mini-mall and held him at the counter while she ordered cappuccino for both of them. Sitting across from him at a little café table, she waited. He fidgeted for a minute, kept leaning over and checking the long promenade, one knee bouncing nervously up and down.

"He knew who I was," he said, and his jaw clinched. "The man's wacko."

"Back there," she said, pointing a thumb, "he wasn't the one who looked like a wacko. What happened? What was that all about?"

He stared at his cup. He wasn't about to tell her that it was the first time he'd ever tried cappuccino, or that he didn't like the taste.

"I was hitchhiking last summer, on my way here," he finally said. "He picked me up outside of Chatsworth, gave me a ride all the way into Atlanta. Then he hit on me, and when I said no, he put me out and drove off with my duffel bag. All my clothes and stuff." He puffed a frustrated breath, looked Kearston in the eye. "I mean, what kind of guy picks up a high school kid on the side of the road and hits on him, huh?"

Her eyes narrowed. "High school? I thought you were like twenty-one."

It was too late and he knew it. He'd already hung himself—made the noose, cinched it tight, and stepped right off into oblivion.

"No," he said, and his shoulders sagged. "I'm eighteen. Almost."

She sat back in her chair and just stared at him for a full minute. "So, are you really a miner? Or did you make that up too?"

He met her stare. "I didn't make up *anything*. I never told you how old I was, and you didn't ask. And yes, I really do work in a tunnel. When my mother died I had to do something. I quit school and went to work for my uncle—mining."

"You never finished high school? I figured you were just working to save up enough money for college."

He shrugged. "I can't do college. I'd never make it. It's too hard."

"Harder than what you're doing now?"

Now *there* was something to think about. He had forgotten all about Perry and was staring at his cup, twisting it on the table, when he heard Perry's voice beside him.

"I'm sorry," Perry said, and it sounded like he meant it. He was just standing there, hands in the pockets of his hundred-dollar slacks. "I would have sent your bag to you. Really, I would." A shrug. "But there was no address. I dropped it in a Salvation Army bin."

He stood there a moment longer while Jeremy said nothing, didn't move, didn't look up.

"I'm sorry," he repeated, then turned and walked away.

Jeremy sat waiting for Kearston to unload on him. He had it coming. After a few minutes passed in silence he finally heaved a sigh of resignation and said, "Well, I guess you want me to take you home now."

She tilted her head and gave him the oddest little grin. "I was just about to say I'm getting hungry. Maybe we could go somewhere and have dinner."

A charge went through him, and he made no effort to hide it. "You still want to be seen with me?"

"You are what you are," she said with a smile.

"Okay, then." He rose, pushed his chair in. "But could we

please just go someplace where they have *normal* food?" He flung a hand at his still-full cup. "No . . . funny-tasting coffee, no snails, no raw fish—just *food,* all right?"

"Daddy Mac's," she said, shrugging into her overcoat.

"Huh?"

"Daddy Mac's. It's where all the truckers eat. Best soul food on the south side of town—or any side, for that matter. Beans and corn bread kind of place."

Headed back south on the expressway, he finally gathered his thoughts enough to talk to her.

"You're different," he mused. "Not like I expected at all. The girls I know play a lot of games and never, ever, say what they really think. You just lay it out there, don't you?"

She stared ahead for a bit, then said, "The last couple of years have been rough. I haven't been out much because I have to help watch Dad, and there are a million things that have to be done around the house—things he used to do. I used to be into perfumes and clothes and boys—I played the games." She sighed. "But I had to grow up. It wasn't a matter of choice, really. You do what you have to do."

She craned her neck suddenly and scanned the inside of the truck as though she had just noticed it. Snake's truck still smelled like new leather, and it was by far the best ride Jeremy had ever driven on a date. His mother had only owned two cars in his whole life, and either of them would have made Geech's old raggedy truck look good.

"This is nice," she said. "Whatever happened to your priceless antique?"

"Oh, that wasn't mine. I was taking care of it for a friend. Actually, this one isn't mine either. It belongs to my rich uncle. He lets me drive it in exchange for music lessons."

"Really. So now you're a musician?"

"No, I'm kidding. He did buy the boom box from me, though. Good thing too. It quit working right after he bought it."

"Oh no! I should give you your money back, then."

"Nah, it was his own fault—he kind of dropped it. Why don't you look through the console and pick out something you want to listen to? Sna . . . um, Uncle Aiden's got a lot of CDs in there."

When Kearston opened the console and started flipping through jewel cases, her perfume wafted across Jeremy and made him nervous all over again.

"This is bizarre," she said. "I don't even see anything I recognize. Who *are* these people?"

"Yeah, I forgot. Sorry. Voices from the dark side. Uncle Aiden's got strange taste. Tell you what, it's right on the way—I'll swing by the apartment and pick up a couple of my discs. I've even got some Deus Aderit."

"That would be nice," she said, and he could hear her smiling.

"I'm not taking much," he told Snake. "I just need to borrow a couple of the classical discs I got for you the other day. Maybe Liszt and Mozart. And I'll take the Christian rock. You don't like any of that anyway." He had left Kearston waiting in the truck while he ran in to pick up some music. She wanted to come up, but he wasn't about to let her meet Snake. After everything he'd been through today, he didn't want to risk losing her now.

"There must be twenty CDs in my truck," Snake said. "She couldn't find anything she liked out of all that?"

"She couldn't find anything she'd ever *heard* of." Jeremy ran his finger down a long rack of jewel cases looking for something, anything, that Kearston might be interested in. "I mean, look at this! Leon Russell? Neil Young? Who listens to George Strait?"

Snake shrugged. "Somebody with culture? Somebody with an open mind? Who is this illiterate haybag, anyway?" As he spoke, he picked up a Lyle Lovett disc, put it back in the case and jammed it into its place in the rack.

Jeremy could tell by the force of the movement, Snake was on the brink of a mood. But of course he was. He'd been holed up for ten years, and managing to live with it—until Jeremy moved in. Now, with Kearston waiting for him in the truck, Jeremy looked at himself through Snake's eyes for a moment and saw just how brutally unfair life could be.

"She's a really nice girl," Jeremy said, apologetically. He was about to congratulate himself for not bringing her up to the apartment with him when he looked over Snake's shoulder and saw her standing there, wide-eyed, hugging her overcoat about her.

"Pardon me," Snake said, oblivious. "Did I say illiterate haybag? I meant airhead debutante, but it's a subtle distinc—" He saw the warning in Jeremy's eyes and stopped, too late. He turned around and looked her up and down.

She held up the truck keys, pointed to the door and stammered, "I got scared. It was a little, um, spooky, you know, in the . . . in the dark, um, by myself. You know." She had trouble making herself stop talking, as her eyes remained, against their will, on Snake's face.

Snake closed the distance between them, stopping a breath away from her. He raked the side of his distorted nose with a thumb.

"Kearston, this is my uncle Aiden," Jeremy blurted. He knew it was too late, but silence was unendurable.

Snake kept his eyes riveted on Kearston. Her head retreated

the least little bit, and she was breathing through her mouth, but she stood her ground.

"My friends call me Snake," he said, and he fairly hissed the name. This was his den, and he wasn't backing down for anybody.

Jeremy saw it happen. Something came over Kearston's face: her left eye quivered and then narrowed just a fraction, from the bottom, like Clint Eastwood. She reached up very slowly and gripped Snake's chin with her fingertips, turned his head gently this way, then the other way, studying the damage. She let go and looked straight into his eyes.

"Because of the skin graft," she asked, "or the personality?"

The air crackled with tension for a moment, and then Snake couldn't keep from grinning.

He broke first, but the laughter was contagious.

CHAPTER 16

Soul food.

After Geech had been in the hospital a little over a month, in Nanny's words, "They got their fill of him and throwed him out." Nanny saw to it that Geech's homecoming was a major event. The day before Geech was to be released, Nanny took Bobby Sue and the kids over to muck out the apartment, dusting and mopping and scouring and disinfecting until the place smelled like a hospital room; then they hung a big *Welcome Home* banner across his living room and left bouquets of Mylar balloons all over the place—the silver kind, with silly messages on them. Jeremy and Snake showed up to help, and the kids even gave Carl a bath. When it was over, Carl looked about the same, while the kids and the bathroom showed signs of a major skirmish.

On the big day Nanny took his truck to the hospital because it had a camper shell. Weasel, Jeremy and Carl all came along to help. They hoisted Geech, wheelchair and all, into the truck and rolled him up against the cab and tied his chair down like a piece of freight. The cast, from ankle to hip on his left leg, stuck out like a battering ram, and Carl, in his boundless joy, kept jumping into Geech's lap and using it for a springboard.

They didn't make it home for quite a while. Geech insisted on stopping someplace for a real breakfast, saying he was "bone-tired of rubber eggs, turpentine coffee, and leather biscuits." So at Jeremy's suggestion, Nanny drove them all to Daddy Mac's. They hunched their shoulders against a sharp January wind that parted their hair and reddened their cheeks while they rolled Geech across the parking lot. There were people waiting, but Geech played the wounded warrior, shaming the hostess into moving them ahead of a young couple with a toddler and into a newly vacated booth by the windows where the sunlight slanted across the table. It was one of those crisp winter mornings where the oblique light penetrated everything—the heavy white cups, the saucers and spoons—and cast blue shadows that took on a shiny, hard-edged clarity. A glass of ice water became a diamond.

The crowded restaurant was full of the smell of coffee and bacon, and a cafeteria murmur cluttered the air, interspersed with the tangled sound of laughter and the clinking of plates and forks. Yet each voice, each clink, each chuckle seemed separate and distinct.

"This is heaven," Geech said reverently.

"We been in lots nicer places than this," Nanny said. "One or two, anyway."

Weasel turned up his nose, turned down the corners of his mouth and feigned a blue-blood accent. "I believe the gentleman is referring to the atmosphere—that certain *je ne sais quoi.*"

"He don't even *speak* Spanish," Nanny mumbled.

"No, I don't mean just this place," Geech said. "It's everything. After laying up there in a hospital bed—"

"Ah. Sensory deprivation," Weasel said, nodding.

"Nah, it's not that either. I don't know how to say it."

Jeremy had remained silent until now, hearing Geech through an eerie prescience because he had heard the same secret knowledge laid out before—in his mother's letter.

"Things look different to you now," Jeremy said softly. "It's like you can see forever."

"Yes," Geech said, and his face lit up. "Yes! That's it! That's exactly what it's like. Why is that?"

Jeremy shrugged. "Maybe because when you've been close to death all the unimportant stuff goes away and you know what's real?"

Weasel's mouth opened, his brow furrowed, and he gazed at Jeremy with a kind of puzzled frown. Nanny tried to spin the salt shaker on the table and slung salt all over the place.

Frowning, Geech said, "You know, Germy, you can be a little scary sometimes. Where does a kid like you get something like that?"

"Must've read it someplace." He kept his eyes on Nanny's big hands, watching him rake salt off the table. He knew where he'd read it, but he didn't want to go there.

They ate like kings, all of them, because it was a feast and a celebration. A homecoming. Geech was alive. In the middle of their feast, there came a scraping of wooden chairs on the linoleum floor and a burst of spontaneous laughter as five tables in the middle of the restaurant emptied at once. Jeremy looked the group over while they put on their coats and counted out tips—an even mix of boys and girls not much older than he was. Obviously, they belonged to the charter bus in the parking lot, a college group going someplace. They took their time, laughing, talking, lining up at the cash register by the door, checks in hand. The fat man at the register ran a hand through his hair and blew a harried breath through puffed cheeks as his sausage fingers began ringing up the separate checks.

Jeremy paid them no more attention until he heard the voice. It was one of the two girls standing at the back of the line with her coat on, a pocketbook hanging from an elbow. She was singing. In a voice as clear as water, she sang softly at first, as if to herself. Her eyes were closed and her face lifted a little. Jeremy cocked his head, listening intently, and through the murmur of the crowd he made out the beginning of an old song called "Seven Bridges Road." He had heard it on one of Snake's old vinyl albums.

The voice grew more distinct, and Jeremy realized that the girl had not gotten louder, but the crowd in the restaurant had quieted. A moment later, a second girl leaned close to the first and blended in with perfect alto harmony. In the space between lines, Jeremy saw that everyone in the place had fallen silent, listening. Even the waitresses had stopped what they were doing. He laid his fork down beside his plate and turned sideways in his chair, careful not to make a sound. More of the kids in line, a girl and two boys, turned around and crowded against the duet. As the girls began the last verse, three more voices blended smoothly with them, and the volume grew. All was in perfect balance, no voice louder than any other. Not a note sounded out of place, not one note clipped too short or held too long. The five sang as a single unified voice, in flawless harmony. By some strange magic, even the acoustics of the restaurant conspired to make it seem as though the music were being projected telepathically to a fine point inside Jeremy's head, and he could see by the others' faces that everyone, each in his own space, felt the same way.

Nanny, Geech, and Weasel looked enraptured, completely swept away and unaware that their mouths were open. Nearing the end of the song, the little group slowed and cradled the last note, held it for an excruciating moment, and ended it precisely together.

Weasel was the first to recover himself. He pressed a napkin to his lips, then dropped it carelessly on top of his unfinished breakfast and slid from his seat. As he stood, the word "Bravo!" spilled from him in a coarse whisper and rolled across the silence like a train. He began to clap, and the applause erupted as everyone followed his lead.

The two girls covered openmouthed grins with their hands and put their foreheads together in delight, then took exaggerated vaudevillian bows in all directions, and the spell was broken.

"Wow," Nanny said.

Jeremy nodded. "That was awesome."

"It was perfect," Geech echoed.

Weasel shook his head. "No, it wasn't perfect. It was inspiring. It was extremely good, and it was *close* to perfect—probably as close as those two girls will ever get. But it was not perfect."

Geech was puzzled. "Now that's interesting, Weasel. You were the first one on your feet. There was tears in your eyes, buddy. So, what was wrong with it?"

Weasel shrugged. "Nothing that I could see. It was wonderful. But they're human, and humans are incapable of perfection."

"Okay." Geech studied him for a moment. "And why, Wise One, should we lug this particular nugget of wisdom around with us?"

Weasel leaned back in his seat and tapped the edge of his plate delicately with a fork. "Because it's possible, while you're looking for something perfect, to let something very good slip away. And it's a shame when that happens, because what you're looking for doesn't exist. Perfection is an absolute."

"God's perfect," Nanny said, proud that he'd followed the conversation, more or less.

"Whatever," Weasel said, smiling patiently.

Geech's face darkened and he said, "I never thought much about religion until I was in the hospital."

"If I was God, we wouldn't need no hospitals," Nanny said,

and it struck Jeremy that it was the most profound thing he'd ever heard Nanny say.

Weasel's eyes crinkled as he studied Geech, and he said, "Everybody wants to conjure a god after they get squashed. It's a human weakness."

"That doesn't mean He isn't there," Jeremy said. He felt small, and he spoke haltingly, but he spoke. "Maybe the weakness isn't that we believe there's a God when we're in a bind, but that we don't believe the rest of the time. If there was no God, then making one up would be weakness. But if there is, if God really exists, then the weakness is pride."

"Interesting way of looking at it." Weasel sipped his coffee. "Okay," he said, "I'm open-minded. So, Geech, did you find God? Was He there?"

Geech frowned, toying with a napkin. "All I know is I wanted real bad to live, and I'm alive. And it's true, what Germy said before—you get to thinking about what really matters. I see things different now."

If Geech had been married, or even if he'd had a roommate, he wouldn't have gotten half the attention he did. But since he couldn't get around very well with a cast almost up to his hip, everybody tried to take care of him. Through most of January his apartment was as busy as an airline terminal. Weasel and Nanny came by to check on him nearly every day, and in the evening sometimes Bobby Sue and the kids would bring supper, muck out the apartment, and either haul away a basket of dirty laundry or bring back a load of clean. Coming off shift and getting home around midnight, Snake and Jeremy would knock on Geech's door if his lights were on, and most of the time they'd end up hanging around for a while.

But despite all the attention, Geech just got more depressed. Embarrassed by the loss of his independence, and increasingly weighed down with the sheer grayness of winter, he became uncharacteristically morose and irritable. Nanny was afraid his depression might be due to impotence, but when he finally asked the embarrassing question, Geech reassured him that the dreaded malady had not materialized. So Nanny's final diagnosis was cabin fever. Geech had been stuck, first in the hospital, then in the house, in the dead of winter with nothing to do, for weeks. In the end, it was Snake who knew what to do about it.

They were listening to Mozart on the way home from work one night when Jeremy brought it up. Snake had developed an overview of classical piano in a few short weeks by listening to CDs Jeremy had bought, and had even gotten to the point where he could distinguish between Mozart and Bach, even if he hadn't heard the piece before. On several occasions he had managed to broadcast a piece he particularly loved until Swan played it. It had become a strange kind of cat-and-mouse game between Swan and Jeremy whenever they ran into each other in the laundry room, because neither of them would bring it up, but both of them knew—she played sometimes just for Snake. Later, Jeremy figured it was the sudden brightening of Snake's own life that prompted him to suggest the fishing trip for Geech.

"There ought to be something we could do to cheer him up," Jeremy said.

"We need to take him fishing," Snake said.

"We?" Jeremy was shocked. "You want to go fishing? Wow. Seems like kind of a public thing, for you."

Snake shrugged. "Not really. It's not that different from

hunting. You're out there alone, away from people. It's people I don't like being around. Fish, I have no problem with."

There was nothing in the world Geech liked better than fishing—any kind of fishing. Growing up close to the bayou, he had learned to entertain himself by fishing for whatever happened to be in season—bass, crawfish, catfish, bream or crappie. Crappie, he said, had an identity crisis; they were called crappie in Georgia, croppie in Alabama, and *sac au lait* down on the bayou. Depending on what he was fishing for, he'd learned to use a fishing rod, a cane pole, trotlines, jigs, and sometimes he had even gillnetted big things like alligator gar. He had always known how to think like a fish; knew what they would eat at any given time of year and where they'd go to get it.

Jeremy was in Geech's kitchen at lunchtime one day and he asked casually, "You got any butter-bean jigs?"

Geech was sprawled on the couch in his bathrobe, his cast propped up on a footstool. His hair was clumpy greasy, and he hadn't shaved in a few days. He was playing with a knife, flicking the blade out with his thumb and snapping it back in.

"Yeah, I got jigs. Why?" he said, without looking up.

"Griff says his neighbor told him the hybrids school on top this time of year at West Point. Especially on cloudy days."

Geech flicked his knife, didn't answer.

"Tomorrow's Saturday, and it's gonna be cloudy."

Geech flicked the knife open, then used the tip of it to scratch his whiskery chin. "Butter-bean jigs?"

Jeremy nodded. "Big schools, a hundred yards wide, right on top. Eight or nine pounders, Griff said."

Geech's cast thumped to the floor and he stood up. "Germy, why don't you bring in the battery from the boat? I'll get the charger out of the closet and top it off." He looked down, blinked, appraised himself. "Man, I need a bath."

Neither the schools nor the fish were as large as advertised, but this was the way of fishermen and nobody really expected them to be. Still, Geech's instincts led him to a bend in the lake where schools of hybrid bass did indeed surface from time to time. When they first started chasing schools Geech was standing in the carpeted bow of the nineteen-foot bass boat, propped up against a "butt seat," which was not much more than a bicycle seat mounted on a pedestal. Feeling pretty secure, even with a full-length cast, Geech pointed and sang out like an old whaler when he spotted the telltale splashing where hybrids had trapped a school of shad against the surface and gone into a feeding frenzy. Snake throttled up and threw the wheel hard over, trying to get into position before the splashing died and the school submerged again, but the wild maneuver spun Geech off his prop and dropped him hard against the windshield. Only then did it occur to them that if Geech had fallen over the side, his cast would have taken him down like a greased anchor, even with a life jacket on. From then on he stayed low in the middle and did the driving, standing up to fish only when the boat was idle. Snake took the front.

"Pound for pound," Geech said, "hybrid bass are the hardest tuggers I've ever seen. They don't come up and dance like a largemouth; they dive straight down and try to wrap you up in a tree."

Jeremy landed a five-pounder once—the biggest fish he'd ever caught. Geech was right. It was like pulling a German shepherd up a ladder.

Geech forgot his troubles for a while, for the day turned out to be a raucous, happy time such as Jeremy had never seen—dashing and casting, bending rods, tangling lines, shouting, laughing at themselves and each other while Carl zipped back and forth between their feet, barking at the fish. They pulled out of the lake at dusk with a live well full of fish and a whole new stock of lies to tell at work.

Snake was exhausted by the time they got home, yet it was a fine, satisfied exhaustion such as he had not known in a long time. After they unhooked the boat, Geech took Snake and Jeremy around back of the building, past the dumpster, where he showed them a castoff two-by-twelve plank and some concrete blocks that they quickly turned into a worktable—a little rickety but quite serviceable for cleaning fish. They set about filleting a cooler full of hybrid bass and dropping the remains into a five-gallon bucket. The evening had gotten cold, and though he'd had a wonderful day, Geech seemed to have slipped right back into his depression during the long ride home.

Snake couldn't help noticing that Jeremy had fallen silent too. The boy listened while Snake showed him how to fillet a fish, cutting behind the gills, slicing the meat away from the dorsal bones, trimming it from the ribs, flipping it over and separating the fillet neatly from the skin. Jeremy paid attention, and he picked it up immediately, always happy to learn a new skill. But he kept watching Geech, who had drawn up an old rusty lawn chair and plopped himself down in it to rest. He could get around, albeit clumsily, with his cast, but he wasn't used to being on his feet and the day in the boat had worn him out.

After he had filleted a half-dozen fish, Jeremy started to grin for no apparent reason, and then he started chuckling to himself.

"I'm gonna do it," he said. He laid his knife down and took off running, back around the building toward the parking lot.

When he came back he was carrying a fishing rod—the big bait-caster he'd used all afternoon—and a crowbar from the back of Geech's truck.

"Watch this," he said, laughing, and grabbed a large hybrid by the lip, hoisting it out of the cooler. Trotting across the back lot, he went right out into the middle of the street, in the glow of the streetlight, laid the fish and the rod down, and used the crowbar to pry the lid off of a manhole.

A look of awe came over Geech. "He's not really . . ."

Jeremy sat down facing them on the other side of the open manhole and patiently worked the line through the fish's lip.

"I think he is," Snake said, and crossed his arms to watch.

Jeremy picked up his rod and lowered the six-pound hybrid bass down into the hole. He didn't have long to wait. A car topped the hill, and when its headlights shined on the boy in the middle of the street, its engine backed down and its nose dipped as the driver hit the brakes.

Jeremy played his part well, hauling back on the rod, jiggling and dipping and cranking the reel. Just as the car came to a complete stop twenty feet away he hefted the big fish up out of the manhole, grabbed its lip in his fist and held it up, grinning like a schoolboy, to show off his prize.

It was about then that the row of blue lights on top of the car began flashing.

Schoolboy grin turned to schoolboy panic as Jeremy dropped everything and took off down the street with the cop shouting in hot pursuit.

"My money's on the cop," Geech said.

A couple of minutes later Jeremy trudged back into view, head down like a condemned man, hands cuffed behind him with the cop trailing, holding on to the cuffs.

Geech shook his head. "Man, what was he thinking?"

"He was trying to cheer you up." Snake smiled, and his eyes were lit with a new kind of pride.

"Wow," Geech said softly.

"It's scary. I'm starting to understand how he thinks," Snake said, letting out a deep breath and heading for the street. "I guess I better go bail him out."

The cop, for his part, was amicable about it. Once he established that Jeremy wasn't drunk or dangerous, and since he couldn't think of anything else to charge him with, he made him put the manhole cover back, wrote *Fishing in a restricted area* on a warning ticket and let him go. But he kept the fish.

The next morning, Jeremy got himself up and dressed, wolfed down a bagel and headed out the door to go to church. He'd grown accustomed to Moss's church. He'd made friends there, and he had come to love the strangeness, the unpredictability of it. He bounced down the stairs and almost ran over Geech in the lobby. He was waiting at the bottom of the stairs all scrubbed and clean-shaven, wearing a new pair of sweats over his cast.

"I figured maybe I could go with you, if you don't mind," Geech said. He stammered a bit, shrugged and added, "Probably do me good. 'Course, you'll have to drive."

CHAPTER 17

Bad ground.

Snake was torn. After the boom box incident, Jeremy had lobbied harder than ever for the right to work underground with the miners. The kid was right about one thing: Snake had worked a mining machine when *he* was eighteen, and he'd seen lots of other guys do it. It was entirely possible that Jeremy came across as a mama's boy only because he'd never had the opportunity to be anything else. And it wasn't Jeremy's fault that he had to grow up without a father.

It was Snake's. That was what made him nervous.

But Snake's dilemma became a non-issue when the young, overeager shift boss on graveyard did something that changed everybody's plans. Looking at the race chart on the project manager's wall and seeing that graveyard had fallen behind swing shift by two hundred feet, he started pushing harder. The pressure had rolled downhill and landed squarely on the shoulders of the shift boss, so he had his electrician crank up the voltage on the step-down transformer to give him a little more juice, and started skipping time-consuming maintenance rituals. When the machine ran into bad ground around three in the morning, he could hear big rocks breaking loose in the heading, but he told his operator to keep full pressure on it.

"It's a skinny little fault," the shift boss said. "Push on through it."

The operator raised an eyebrow. It was against his better judgment, but a boss is a boss, so he watched the gauges and poured it on. A huge slab of granite sheared off and slid down on one side of the wheel, wedging itself like a doorstop and locking down the cutting mechanism. With the drive motors running flat out, a million pounds of torque had to go somewhere. The ring gear cracked. The great circular gear which transferred all the torque from the drive motors to the cutterhead broke in two.

They lost most of February and part of March. Working around the clock, all three shifts labored as hard as they would have labored had they actually been gaining footage. Instead, they were breaking down the machine, completely dismantling the digging apparatus from its front, hauling out the broken ring gear, then reversing the whole process when the replacement came in.

The main reason Jeremy wanted to work underground was to get away from Biggins, but when he finally got there it was on Biggins's coattails. Everybody pitched in at the heading, except Eldon, who stayed up top with his crane and his loader. Biggins, being the chief mechanic, practically lived down there.

And he rode Jeremy harder than ever. Helping Ripley change out a switch one night, Jeremy put his hand in the wrong place and got a 277-volt jolt up his arm. The shock startled him so badly he pitched off the ladder and landed flat on his back in six inches of greasy water in the bottom. Biggins, who happened to be working right over his head, leaned off the end of the control deck to stare down at the stunned kid in the blue hard hat, who lay there staring straight up while brown water swirled and eddied around him.

"Well, Germy," he said, and spit tobacco juice off to the side, "did you learn anything?"

Jeremy picked himself up and went back to work, but the others had seen what happened. Weasel and Rico both saw the whole thing, heard what Biggins said, and thought the entire little comedy was enormously entertaining. The phrase "Did you learn anything?" became the gibe du jour and was instantly aimed at anybody who made a mistake, particularly if he managed to stub a toe in the process, and *most* particularly if the guilty party was Jeremy, since the not so subtle reminder of his greenhorn status clearly embarrassed him.

Geech got his cast removed in early February and right away returned to work, assigned to light duty. Jeremy was with him when he made his first trip back into the tunnel. The two of them had stayed behind to bring in a rebuilt drive motor and a new acetylene rig.

Geech was at the controls when the loki rounded the bend and the dark place came in sight. It was about a hundred yards long, the stretch where Geech had gotten crushed, and his miner's eye recognized the place immediately. Unlike most of the tunnel, which was a hard, seamless tube of granite covered in chalky white dust, this part was dark and damp, marbled with cracks and fissures. Water spouted from the walls in thumb-sized rivulets here and there. A half inch of grime and damp dust clung to all the surfaces, coating boulders with the color and texture of modeling clay. As he approached it, Geech throttled back. The loki slowed and grumbled to a halt in the middle of the dark place, and he killed the engine. The only sounds were the whining hiss of the big round air duct supplying fresh air to the heading and the faint splashing of water on rock.

Geech climbed down off the loki, with Jeremy following him. Jeremy hung back a little as Geech stood in the middle of the tunnel, a stream of water running around his rubber boots, his mining hat tilted back as he looked up at the crown. The hole was still there where the rocks had turned loose, although now it was covered with chain link fencing and pinned profusely with big, thick bolts. Heavy steel washers six inches square held the chain link in place and kept smaller rocks from falling on the tracks below. Geech shined his flashlight up at it.

"I never saw it coming," he said softly, shaking his head.

"Does anybody?" Jeremy asked. "Ever?" Jeremy thought he was talking about reading the rock, but he found out differently.

"Sometimes. Lots of people have a pretty good idea when they're gonna die. It doesn't happen like that down here. You don't get any warning, most of the time."

Jeremy nodded. "My mother saw it coming. I'm not sure that's a good thing."

"It is if you're not ready to go," Geech said. "Makes you think. Gives you time to look at yourself."

Jeremy said nothing. Geech was staring intently at the hole left by the boulder, remembering. His breathing deepened perceptibly, and the struggle was plain on his face.

"You sure you're ready for this?" Jeremy asked.

He nodded. "Yeah. It's part of it. I'll always come back to mining because I love it, and this right here is part of the reason. I can't explain it, but the other guys know. I never could explain it to my ex-wife either. She thought I ought to get out when they found spots on my lungs, only I just can't." He took his hat off and wiped his forehead with his sleeve.

"See, I was never any good at school. I was never any good at anything, much. My folks said I wouldn't ever amount to nothing, and I spent a couple years proving them right. But when me and Nanny stumbled across the mining job, we knew we'd hit on something, you know? It's like, all my life I never was able to do anything special, something nobody else could do. But the first summer we spent drilling and blasting, we figured out we could do something nobody else *would* do. And we were *good* at it. They say this is the second most dangerous job there is, right after commercial fishing. That makes me *somebody*," he said, and there was a glow of fierce pride in his eyes.

"Yeah," Jeremy said softly. "Yeah."

Geech turned and shined his light up and down the fractured walls. A few yards up the tunnel he found a narrow crevice bisecting one whole side, top to bottom, and shined his flashlight into it.

"Hey, look at that," he said, pointing with the flashlight.

"What?" Jeremy poked his head into the crevice. The walls wore the same brown floury paste as everything else.

"There." Geech aimed the flashlight beam.

Almost out of sight in a cleft, the light flashed across something startlingly white. Quartz crystals—a whole slab of them. Most of it was covered by muck, but Jeremy could still make out a cluster the size of a dinner plate.

"Looks like some decent crystals," Geech said. "Don't know how the guys missed them. Shame I can't get to it. I can't climb with this hip."

Jeremy studied the crack, sizing it up, looking for handholds. His fear surged again. This time, standing beside Geech, his fear made him angry and ashamed. Maybe it was what Geech had said, maybe it was something deep in the sap of his own soul, but more than anything, more than survival itself, he wanted to push beyond the fear.

"I could reach it," he heard himself saying. "You got a hammer?"

Geech produced a rock hammer from the loki and held the light while Jeremy wormed his body into the crack. He found solid ledges for his feet, stabilized himself, and struck the top of the crystal slab timidly the first time, managing only to shatter a few crystals. He almost dropped the hammer. He got a better grip, and the second blow landed hard in exactly the right spot. A slab of crystals broke free and clattered down into a notch within easy reach. He tossed out the hammer and wriggled back out of the crevice with his prize, hoping Geech wouldn't notice the panicked haste in his movements.

Geech rinsed it off under a waterspout and shined his light on it. Quartz crystals of various sizes huddled together—little pyramid-tipped spires crowding together like a miniature city, cracking the light into a thousand rainbow shards. The whole thing was evenly salted with pinpoints of iron pyrite, glittering like tiny stars. Jeremy had never seen anything like it, and said so.

Geech held it close to his face, studying it under the flashlight. Finally, he handed it to Jeremy. "You can have it. I already got one of these."

"Cool! You find stuff like this all the time?"

"Nah." Geech swept the fractured ceiling with his flashlight. "Only in bad ground."

CHAPTER 18

Secretary of State Weasel.

$\mathbb{A}$ t the end of his first week back, Geech invited Jeremy, Nanny, and Weasel out to eat at a local barbecue restaurant as a way of thanking them for taking care of him. Snake was invited too, but everybody knew he wouldn't show up. Nanny brought Bobby Sue with him, and Jeremy brought Kearston. He didn't want to bring her; he was reluctant to expose her to the guys, except she really wanted to meet the people he worked with. He warned her as best he could.

Weasel, whose free spirit and big mouth had been Jeremy's biggest worry, actually seemed rather docile when they first sat down. Jeremy thought maybe he was trying to behave himself because there were ladies present, but after a while Weasel explained that he'd been here before and was afraid the staff might remember him. It turned out that he had visited this same restaurant months earlier, right after arriving on the job, and he'd had an altercation with a couple of plumbers, resulting in what Weasel referred to as an "untimely, unjustified, and altogether undignified defenestration." Nanny and Jeremy both looked to Geech for a translation, who offered only a shrug—he didn't know either.

They were seated around a long, heavy pine table. It was one of those country-style barbecue places where the waitresses wore cowboy hats and brought everybody quart-sized plastic glasses full of over-sweetened iced tea, whether they ordered it or not. The paneled walls were hung with steer horns and saddles and sepia pictures of bad guys of the Old West. About the time the bowls of Brunswick stew and the plates of barbecued pork and beef and grilled half chickens started arriving at the table, Geech did something totally unexpected and unprecedented.

He stood up and waited until all the table talk died down and all eyes were on him before he began. He spoke haltingly, as it clearly made him nervous to do something that so closely resembled the making of a speech.

"I don't know how to go about this," he said, "but it needs doing. I feel like I could have not been here today. Real easy. I could have died right where I was that night if Nanny and Jeremy hadn't got me out of there, or I could have bled to death if Biggins hadn't been there and knew what to do. Must have been a dozen times that first week in the hospital I could have died, a dozen different ways, but the whole time I felt like everything was gonna be okay. I felt like there was something there, something a lot bigger than me, holding me up, keeping my heart beating."

He paused briefly, trying to find words, and glanced briefly at Jeremy. "I don't know. I don't know much about God or how to explain what I do know, but I came out of the hospital knowing—*knowing*—that there is one. I look at all of y'all and I see people who care, who went out of their way to look after me when I couldn't take care of myself, and I *know*. Why would anybody risk his life, or even waste his time and energy to help somebody else, if he didn't deep down know there's a God? Anyway, I just thought . . . it seemed like the right thing to do, to get all of you together and, kind of formal like, to say thanks. To you and to God."

He cleared his throat and continued. "Now, I've done about all the speechmakin' I'm inclined to do for the rest of my natural life. I wouldn't have a clue how to go about doing this myself, but Jeremy, if you'd give thanks for this meal before the food gets cold, I'd be honored."

It felt like a milestone to Jeremy, a moment when the shadow of something great and deep had passed silently over them. He bowed his head and offered a simple prayer of thanks for the bond of brotherhood made possible by Christ, for the day that God had made, and for the meal He had provided.

It turned out to be a most unusual evening, especially for Weasel. He spent most of his time talking to Kearston, which worried Jeremy at first, but after listening for a while he realized the two of them had gotten into a serious dialogue about the philosophy of government. Weasel was enjoying himself immensely, pontificating about how freedom and equality were natural enemies, how the tension between the two opposing interests had driven every political conflict in history, and how it was not likely to ever be resolved by man. Weasel appeared genuinely surprised when Kearston calmly pointed out that, of all people, the French seemed to have gotten it right when they recognized in their motto that the third leg of the tripod was brotherhood and that, yes, as long as the problem was left to man alone, the kind of brotherhood necessary to engender peace was not likely to be achieved on any grand scale. Weasel listened with growing fascination, his eyes lighting up, clearly taken with her.

It couldn't have been anything more than pure coincidence that former president Jimmy Carter and his wife arrived, along with a sizable entourage of casually attired Secret Service agents, while Weasel and Kearston were debating political philosophy.

People waved at them, and the Carters waved back, smiling yet not stopping on their way to a separate room at the back of the restaurant. The Secret Service agents fanned out all around the place, taking up prearranged strategic positions.

Weasel, who could see Mr. Carter through the distant doorway, became distracted and eventually lost track of the conversation he had been engaged in with Kearston. There were things he'd been wanting to say to President Carter for years, and he reasoned that he would probably never have a better opportunity, so he excused himself, slid his chair in, straightened his denim jacket, ran his palms down his graying, shoulder-length, unkempt hair, and marched to the back of the restaurant.

"He's fixin' to get shot," Nanny said absently, biting off a piece of Texas toast.

"I hope he gets to say his piece before they shoot him," Geech answered.

Two men closed in on Weasel and stopped him in the arched doorway to the private room where the Carters sat. Weasel was obligingly placing his hands on top of his head when Mr. Carter looked at him and, smiling that polite smile of his, said a word or two, motioned with his hand, and Weasel was allowed through. Jeremy and the others watched in openmouthed astonishment as Weasel stood across the table from the ex-president and started laying out his views. Mr. Carter motioned for him to sit, and Weasel never stopped talking as he turned a chair around and sat astraddle of it, knifing his hand on the table for emphasis. Jimmy Carter smiled and nodded while he ate, and Rosalynn's shoulders shook with silent laughter once or twice. When, after about five minutes, Weasel had said his piece, he calmly replaced the chair, shook hands with Jimmy Carter, bowed his head sedately to Rosalynn, and marched back to his table.

They were shocked. Weasel's rhetorical skills were legendary, but he was, after all, Weasel. Nobody's mind could quite wrap around the picture of him sitting there having casual dinner conversation with Jimmy and Rosalynn Carter.

"And on top of that, he made it back with nary a bullet hole," Nanny pointed out.

"Wha'd they say?" Jeremy asked, and he heard the echo of Moss.

"They said I was probably right," Weasel answered. "I told him his whole problem was that bunch of dirtbags he had working for him. I told him he should've just tramped them out—the whole low-down, backstabbing lot of 'em. If he'd done that early on, he probably could have gotten himself reelected." Weasel puffed his chest out, riding the moment like a wave. "He said I just might be right, and if he ever ran again he was going to call me about a cabinet position."

It made for a wonderful memory of Weasel, a story they would all tell many times over in the future, for it was the last time they would see him. As the evening wore on, he grew quiet and thoughtful, troubled. Before they left the restaurant he started talking about his tax-rebel status and how he had probably already stayed in Georgia longer than he should have. Walking out of the restaurant, picking at his teeth, Weasel casually scoured the place with his eyes and counted all the Secret Service agents.

"By morning," he whispered to Jeremy, "those guys are gonna know what brand of shorts I wear. Listen," he said, looking over Jeremy's shoulder to make sure Kearston couldn't hear, "before I leave, I wanted to talk to you about that girl you're running with. She's got class, and she's got it bad, but don't you hold it against her, you hear me? All things considered, she's a decent kid. You got to overcome your prejudices. Nobody's perfect."

The next morning Weasel was gone. He had folded his life into his little silver trailer, hitched it to his truck, and headed for Canada.

CHAPTER 19

Crazy birds.

Early March in Georgia can be fickle and treacherous, and yet there are days when God smiles, and the earth smiles back. The Bradford pears were on the backside of full bloom, turning bright green and snowing little white petals, like trees out of a fairy tale. The redbuds along the creek were starting to show a fine sprinkle of deep pink, and the dogwoods out in the open were beginning to blossom—buds of off-white scattered like strings of popcorn along the thin branches.

Snake had been walking around the job in his shirtsleeves, basking in the bright, warm spring day. Nearly a month behind schedule, the machine was almost ready, and he had just come from a little heart-to-heart with the project manager.

As he approached the concrete apron in front of the shop where his crew had collected to chow down on Ripley's chili and catch the last rays of daylight, he caught a flurry of movement on the edge of his vision. A budding dogwood stood by a window on the side of the shop, a small, neglected tree, doomed by its location but for now struggling to bud like all the others. A male cardinal—a bright red clot of color against the gray industrial backdrop—lit on the very tip of a delicate limb and chirped loudly, once. Snake stopped to watch. Bobbing up and down on the flimsy twig, the bird hacked again, a sharp single note of warning, and then flung himself against the window, stuttering across the three bottom panes, pecking at the glass. He dropped, flapping, almost to the ground, then fought his way back up to the limb, where for a few seconds he bristled and yipped his territorial frustration at the redbird in the window while he marshaled his strength for another charge. Obsessed, he attacked his own reflection again and again. Snake shook his head sadly and went on into the shop.

Ripley had parked the big pot of chili on a worktable in the open door of the shop, and somebody had brought a stack of styrofoam bowls and a little box of plastic spoons. Snake ladled himself a bowlful and sat on a big wooden wire reel to eat.

"Hurry up, girls," he said. "We got work to do."

"What's up? Somebody light a fire under you?" Griff asked. There was no official dinnertime for swing shift, because the machine dictated when the crew could take a break and when they had to hustle. They had all come up to help load a new conveyor onto the loki, and Griff had timed it so they could take a dinner break.

"Sonny's on my back," Snake said, then his eyes widened with the first taste of Ripley's five-alarm chili. "Good chili," he wheezed.

"A bit bland," Geech said. "Luke, toss me the cayenne."

A little cardboard shaker of red pepper flew through the air.

"Sonny getting nervous?" Griff asked.

Snake shrugged, wincing as he watched Geech dump more fire into his bowl. "He's a little uptight. The clock's ticking. Headquarters turns Sonny's crank, Sonny turns mine—"

"Yeah, then you turn my crank, and it rolls, as the saying goes, downhill."

Snake nodded, frowning, exhaling through pursed lips. "You remember the guy we called Poindexter?"

Griff frowned, trying to recall. "Chunky little guy? Tortoise-shell glasses, big lips?"

Snake nodded. "Nerdy looking."

"Yeah, what about him?"

"Got smoked the other day. Working on a loader tire and the ring blew out. Took the top of his head off."

"Well, if that don't just beat all," Griff said. "Old Poindexter. He was a good hand. Was he still up in Chicago?"

Snake nodded. "Six Mile."

Nanny had the pepper shaker now and was busy piling it on. "Ain't he the same guy that lost his big toe last year, workin' a jumbo?"

Griff nodded. "He always was a little accident prone."

"How did he lose his toe?" Jeremy asked.

Rico wiped his mouth on his sleeve and explained, "You know how the drill steel skips and jumps all over the place when you first set it down on the rock? You just sort of steady it with your foot till it finds a notch and gets a hole started? Well, once in a while it'll kind of stutter and take a great big bounce, and if you're not paying attention it'll come down on your toes."

"Couldn't they sew it back on?" Jeremy asked.

"Nah," Nanny said. "Wasn't enough left."

"Now that's more like it," Geech said, his eyes watering. He had finally gotten his chili hot enough to suit him. Carl sat at his feet lapping chili from his own styrofoam bowl.

The staccato tapping from the window asserted itself during a lull, and half the crew looked up at it.

"Somebody need to shoot that loco bird," Tino said, nodding

at the window. "He been doing that all day long. Wha's wrong with him? Nanny, let me see that pepper, man."

"He's stupid," Luke said. "Birds are just stupid. Couple years ago this girl talked me into taking her to Austria skiing—"

"D'ja see any kangaroos?" Nanny asked.

"Wrong continent, ace. Think Alps. So we're up on top of the mountain and we come across this little restaurant—little A-frame kind of thing sitting right up there on the summit. It's like eight degrees or something, and about a forty-mile-an-hour wind. There's smoke coming out of the stovepipe, and the wind's blowing so hard the smoke don't even go up; it just bends back and curls under, swirling around behind the building. There were these black specks flitting around in that smoke, and I thought it was ashes until we got close. Turned out to be six or eight little black birds—looked like martins or swifts or something—playing around in the smoke behind that building. Probably the only place left where they wouldn't freeze to death." He took another bite of chili, sniffed, wiped his eyes, reached for the pepper. "Man, what were they thinking?"

Jeremy was perched up on a steel worktable outside the ring of miners. "They probably didn't know any better," he said with a shrug. "Just doing what they were designed to do."

"Maybe they were penguins," Nanny offered, but nobody acknowledged him so he let it drop.

Luke waved his spoon and continued. "I mean, they were like a couple hundred miles from the Riviera, right? They got wings, and it's downhill all the way. So tell me why they're freezing their little tails off on a glacier when they could be hanging out at the beach. Were they too lazy to fly south when all the other birds did, or did they stay there on purpose? Either way, I'm telling you man, birds are stupid."

"Maybe they got used to getting free food out of the trash can behind the restaurant and forgot how to work for a living," Biggins said, glancing at where Rico and Tunk sat together on a gangbox. "I've knowed people like that."

Rico and Tunk paused and looked at each other. Rico smiled ostentatiously; his gold tooth gleamed. "Now, Daddy, you know Mama don't like it when you cast aspersions on our less fortunate brothers and sisters," he said. Weasel had taught him well. Biggins got stuck on the word *aspersions* and stalled out. A smile of pure admiration lit Tunk's face.

"I ain't your daddy" was all Biggins could say.

Snake stayed out of it, his gaze drifting frequently to the window. The cardinal had gone away, finally, and didn't return. He thought at first the bird might have come to his senses, but then he realized the light was failing. Once the light outside grew dimmer than the light inside, the bird could no longer see its own reflection and gave up the fight. Snake understood the cardinal. He knew it would be back at first light, and it would keep hammering away at its reflection until one of them was dead.

Carl's bowl, licked almost clean now, began to skid away from him on the concrete. He stood up and walked after it, his face pressed into the styrofoam while licking at the corners. The harder he chased the bowl the faster it moved, so he was trotting by the time he broke out of the little circle of miners, and nearly at a gallop when he ran into the wall. He yelped once, then turned around, sat down quickly, belched and looked off to the side as if nothing had happened.

"Look at him," Luke said, grinning. "Too cool. Positively too cool."

When the crew headed back into the hole, Snake made an excuse and stayed behind. He took his time, waiting until he heard the man-lift trundling down into the shaft, then strolled over to the hog house. He came back with a can of shaving cream and used it to frost all three panes across the bottom of the window on the side of the shop, smearing it into a thick film with the flat of his hand.

"That ought to do it," he said. "Now maybe you can quit acting like a fool and go build a nest someplace."

Snake came to work early on Monday, hoping the machine would be up and running. He found Griff sitting on the steps in front of the hog house, sat down next to him and filled him in. Day shift had finally gotten the machine all buttoned up on Sunday afternoon. On Monday morning they had run their tests, aligned all the conveyors and even mined a little, making a couple of pushes to see that everything worked properly. The engineers signed off on it, and by the time swing shift showed up Monday afternoon, everything was primed and ready. They were finally going to make some hole.

"I know you're still a little short of help," Snake said, "but Geech is almost back up to speed, and Travis gets out of jail in a month or so. I'm thinking we can get by till then."

"There's just one little problem," Griff said. "We lost Luke over the weekend."

Alarm trilled up Snake's spine and onto his face. He hadn't heard about any accident. "What happened?"

There was a tired smile on Griff's face and he rubbed the back of his neck. "He went skydiving."

"Oh no."

"Aw, he ain't hurt too bad. It wasn't a . . ." Griff made a spiral motion with a forefinger and chuckled. "He just had a wreck—

totaled his motorcycle. He called me this morning and told me about it."

Snake raised an eyebrow. "Wait a minute. How do you total a motorcycle and not get hurt too bad?"

"Well," Griff said, and then stopped to think how to put it. "He was coming home from the airstrip where he goes to jump. Made four jumps during the day and repacked his chute before he went home. So he's riding home on his bike, carrying his chute on his back, right? You know how Luke's mind works. He got to thinking about drag chutes—you know, like on dragsters?"

"No. He didn't—"

"Yeah, he did. 'Bout a mile from the house he hit a long straightaway and decided to try it out. He figures he needs to be doing eighty to make it work, so he looks around to make sure nobody's watching, then lays his ears back and pulls the cord."

"You've got to be kidding."

"Scout's honor." Griff held up two fingers. "Said the next thing he knew, he was two hundred feet up in the air watching his bike go on down the road without him."

Snake shook his head, chuckled. "That's gotta be the dumbest thing I've ever heard."

Griff nodded. "It's world-class stupid, all right. He said that big Kawasaki never even slowed down, just eased off the road, center-punched one of those big brick mailboxes and folded like a wallet. When it was all over the wheels were side by side."

"So how'd he get hurt?"

A shrug. "Came down on a stop sign. Cracked his wrist and put a gash in his cheek. Couple stitches. He'll probably be back in a week or two with a short cast."

Snake sat looking down between his feet, elbows on knees. "Griff, is it just me, or is everybody here nuts?"

Griff pulled a weed from beside the steps to chew on, then

said, "It ain't just you. But who else is gonna do this? I mean, look around. If I wasn't nuts I wouldn't be here." He turned and looked long and purposefully at Snake's scarred head. "And neither would you."

Snake sighed heavily. Even after Weasel split they were able to function well enough as a crew of mechanics, but now that the machine was up and running they would be under a lot more pressure. Luke's absence was going to leave them extremely short-handed. Again.

"Well," Snake said, "unless you know somebody that's rustling, I guess we don't have any choice right now but to bring Jeremy in and try to find somebody to help in the yard. Is he gonna be okay down there?"

Griff winced. "I don't know. Boy's stubborn as a mule."

Snake nodded. "Yeah, but apart from that he doesn't have much going for him. You think he can handle it?"

Griff twirled the weed between his fingers, watching it spin. "Maybe. He's been down there most of the time anyway, this last month."

"But we weren't making hole. It's different when the mole's running."

"Aw, he'll probably be all right. He's come a long way," Griff said. "The guys'll look out for him."

Walking back down to the shop to talk to Biggins, a flash of red caught Snake's eye. It was that same cardinal, still attacking the same window from the same tree. Snake had only frosted the bottom row of panes; the cardinal had simply moved up to the middle and continued his assault. Snake went back to the hog house and got out the shaving cream, this time frosting the entire window, taking pains to blot out every corner. The cardinal watched from a power line, chirping at him occasionally. After Snake backed off, the bird returned to the little dogwood and flitted from branch to branch, looking high and low for his imagined rival, then flew away without once attacking the glass.

Jeremy rode in to work with Geech that day, since Snake had come in early. An hour or so after talking to Griff, Snake caught up with Jeremy at the door to the hog house and told him he was being promoted to the mining crew. The kid actually jumped up in the air and whooped, then high-fived Geech and took off down the road to tell Rico and Tunk.

Geech scratched his chin and watched Jeremy run off. "Poor kid," he said. "I think he misses Biggins already."

CHAPTER 20

The valley of the shadow.

Jeremy was at the tail end of the trailing gear adjusting rollers on the conveyor when he heard the change. The roar from the heading died down abruptly as the grinding stopped. The cutterhead still turned while backing away from the wall, and the flow of gravel petered out on the conveyor. A few minutes later the wheel stopped turning, followed by an alarming silence. Jeremy's teeth and skin continued to vibrate, even after all the noise had abated and the air stood still. Carl had curled up asleep on a gangbox in the trailing gear, but the silence awakened him. He raised his head, looked around, and woofed once. Jeremy figured he was saying thanks.

Jeremy went forward, under the belly of the machine and up to the front, to find out what was going on. Snake, Griff, and Nanny were there, along with Biggins, who was working the hole for this one shift to make sure everything started up smoothly and there were no leaks in his hydraulic systems.

Griff twisted a handle and opened a man-sized hatch on the pressure plate in front of the machine. Peering forward into the blackness with a flashlight, he said, "Yeah, we're lined up. Germy, look in the gangbox on the trailing gear and bring the droplight and the come-along."

He climbed through the hatch and disappeared. Snake and Biggins followed him, and the hatch slowly swung shut, all by itself.

Jeremy was back in thirty seconds, plugging in the droplight, tugging the hatch open. He looked inside. Apart from the dripping of water and the ticking of hot metal there was no other noise, and he could barely make out the rock face through the darkness in front of the cutterhead. He waited, not even sure they were still in there. Alone, staring into the black hole, the lump returned in his throat, and his breath came a little quicker. *Be anxious for nothing,* he thought.

Biggins's face appeared in the hole. "Git in here, boy! We got a dollar waitin' on a dime!"

Suck it up, Jeremy. Push through it. It'll pass.

He clambered through the hole, dragging the light and the come-along. The hatch eased shut behind him. The cutterhead had been backed away from the rock face for a space of six feet so Griff and Biggins could check the cutting wheels for signs of wear. They looked like giant glass-cutting wheels mounted on heavy steel yokes welded to the front of the cutting mechanism, each one the size of an engine block. There were fifty of them, scattered seemingly at random around the cutterhead, but one look at the tracks on the rock face told Jeremy there was nothing random about the placement. Etched deeply into the granite at precise three-inch intervals were concentric circles. This was the business end of the machine, the part where tempered steel met solid granite, and the granite shattered. Such was the force of the machine.

Droplights seemed frail and puny against the ominous darkness of the tight chasm in which the four men stood. Jeremy's heart pounded, standing in the jaws of hell itself, two hundred feet under the earth. He fought the urge to bolt, to scramble through the hatch and run till he found daylight and fresh air.

Biggins shined the light on a cutter halfway up the right side. "That one's gotta go. The rest can wait, but that one's shot." The cutting edge was severely flattened. It could be repaired if they changed it now, but not if they waited.

Biggins turned to Jeremy, shining the flashlight at his feet. "Where's the toolbox?"

"What toolbox?"

"I told you to bring the toolbox, Germy! It was right beside the come-along."

"I . . . I didn't hear you."

Biggins stepped close, tobacco breath in Jeremy's face. "It's like this, Germy—it's costin' us a hundred dollars a minute to stand here and jaw. You best git the taters out of your ears and GIT THE TOOLBOX, BOY! NOW!" He raised his hand as if to strike. Snake didn't interfere, didn't even act like he'd heard. Jeremy was on his own now.

He scrambled out and returned in less than a minute, shoving the heavy toolbox through the hatch.

For the moment, Jeremy's fear of the dark, tight place yielded to his fear of Biggins. He worked feverishly, monkeying up the cutterhead and placing the come-along where Griff told him to, then handing Biggins tools as he needed them. The whole switch took less than ten minutes.

When the job was finished, Biggins climbed down and went out the hatch without a word.

Griff handed Jeremy the flashlight and followed Nanny out the hatch. Snake spoke for the first time, after the others had left.

"You did good, Jeremy. Best way to handle Biggins is ignore him, but I guess you know that better than any of us by now." He clapped Jeremy on the back and turned to go. "You need to get all this stuff out of here. Let me know when you're clear, then go topside and get a load of rail and fishplates."

Jeremy's terror returned, mushing through him in a great soft wave as soon as Snake disappeared out the hatch and left him alone in the black void. Wild-eyed, he flung the droplight and come-along out the hatch, then tumbled out after them as if he were being chased.

He stood in the yellow light at the front of the machine, leaning back against the cool steel of the pressure plate, collecting himself. *You're a fool, Jeremy, acting like a scared little kid. You can do this. Grow up.*

He stood there alone for a couple of minutes, letting his heart rate return to normal. Carl trotted up next to him, wagging that stump of a tail and barking at the hatch.

"What is it, Carl? What's up?"

Then he remembered the toolbox. At his feet lay the come-along and drop cord, a big hammer and an impact wrench, but Biggins's toolbox was missing. Jeremy flicked on his flashlight and slowly, reluctantly, crawled through the hatch one more time, into the void in front of the cutterhead. The hatch swung softly closed behind him.

Waiting at the trailing gear, Snake checked his watch. "Where is that kid?" he said aloud. Griff, standing next to him, bent down and looked under the belly of the machine at the heading. The drop cord was out and the hatch closed. Snake looked back up the tunnel and saw the loki pulling out with the silhouette of a lone man on the engine. The silhouette spotted him, threw up a hand

and waved. Snake waved back. All accounted for.

He put two fingers in his mouth and whistled at Ruskie, who was kicked back in his chair at the control console, as usual. When Ruskie looked up from his book, Snake twirled an index finger in the air. The operator leaned forward, flipped a switch, and the wheel began to turn, snuffing out all other sound. With the pull of a lever, four great pistons inched out of their sockets. It would take a few minutes for the cutterhead to make contact with the wall, but the rumble would let him know.

Jeremy stood with his back to the face, hands splayed out against the rock, screaming—but above the monstrous roar of the spinning cutterhead he could not even hear himself. The flashlight lay at his feet. Loose rocks ricocheted and flitted past his face. His vision narrowed; a grainy static choked his consciousness. Death crept toward him, laughing, and he was paralyzed in the face of it. His voice gone, still every muscle poured itself into a futile, sound-less scream.

A fist-sized rock hummed out of the darkness, shattered his blue hard hat, and drove him to his knees. Momentarily stunned, all sensation fled from him for a few seconds before the horrific sights and sounds came rushing back in.

But he had stopped screaming. A single clear thought fought its way through his blind panic: *I am alone. No one is coming.*

He pressed a palm against his forehead and it came away cov-ered with blood. His blood. This was real, it was happening, and he was utterly alone in it. The whirling cutterhead had closed to within four feet. In another minute it would be upon him, would tear him into little bitty pieces and spit him out on the conveyor belt. The thought flashed through his mind that whatever happened now was entirely up to him, but in the next millisecond Moss's voice gently corrected him.

"You can find God—especially in the low places. . . ."

From the eye of the storm, Jeremy sent the simple message, "Show me."

When he looked up again, his mouth was closed, his jaw set, his eye clear. He shined the flashlight into the bottom of the maelstrom where rocks jumped like popcorn. There. Just there. In the bottom, behind the cutters, he could see the blades pass—the eight blades of the mechanism that scooped up shattered rock and fed it to the conveyor belt at the top of the machine. His mind raced, flying over facts at warp speed, searching for something, anything. Stepping to one side for a better look, his foot struck the toolbox.

Snake stood alone at the back of the trailing gear watching the silhouette of the loki disappear into the distance. Something wasn't right; he could feel it in his gut. He turned and looked up toward the heading. Griff had gone under the belly of the machine to talk to Biggins, while Tunk was up on the drill deck helping Nanny. Everything *looked* normal, yet something was not right.

He sighed and had started to turn away when he sensed a movement. The rock hadn't started flowing yet. Only a smattering of loose gravel rattled and danced along the belt. He wasn't sure—he hadn't been looking directly at it—but the limits of his peripheral vision sensed something the size of a large rat tumbling over the end roller of the number one conveyor, up high, and disappearing into the hopper of the next belt. The oddness of it, the peculiarity of the movement, made him pause. He was already standing beside the long conveyor, the one that ran all the way out to the shaft, so he waited for whatever it was to come to him. He thought maybe somebody had dropped a tool or left something behind in the heading.

Ten seconds later the object dropped onto the long belt. Bobbing toward him was what looked like a grit-saturated mop of cloth, but when he plucked it from the belt he found the rag was twisted around a large box-end wrench. Part of the wrench was missing, pinched off cleanly halfway down the handle, with the cloth knotted firmly to the business end. Letting the wrench dangle, Snake pinched the corners of the cloth and fanned it out.

Two words leaped out and went through him like a hot sword.

Deus Aderit

He hit the emergency shutdown switch and raced toward the heading, bending low under the belly of the machine, wild-eyed, muttering, "No no no no no no . . ."

Silence flooded the tunnel as the machine ground to a stop, leaving only the ringing in Snake's ears—and the barking. Carl was there, had been there all along, barking furiously at the hatch in the pressure plate at the very front of the machine. Snake flung the hatch wide, roared to the operator, "Back it off!" and plunged headfirst into the black hole.

He didn't have a flashlight with him but he didn't need one; he knew the cutterhead like the back of his scarred hand. Even as the pistons retracted and the sound of tortured metal ripped the air, he located Jeremy by the keening sound he made, flattened against the wall an arm's length from the hatch. Groping for him, calling his name softly, Snake knew from the brush of hot steel on his sleeve that the cutters must have stopped a mere hand's-breadth away from Jeremy's face. The boy didn't seem capable of moving on his own; Snake had to pull him out by an arm and lift him bodily when he collapsed. Stunned faces appeared in the hatch, and Griff and Nanny moved to help. Snake hefted the boy off his hip and up to the opening so they could drag him out by the shoulders. Snake climbed out after him.

Jeremy's bare chest heaved, and a strange keening sound came from his throat. When they let him go he dropped to his knees, leaning on his fists in the thin stream running from the headwall. His hard hat and shirt were gone. Hair hung in his face, with blood dripping from the end of his nose. Nobody moved. Even Snake froze in place; for once, he simply did not know what to do.

Biggins elbowed his way through the men until he stood over Jeremy. A smirk twisted his sallow face when he realized what had happened.

"Well, Germy, I guess the important thing is, did you *learn* anything?" Biggins glanced around to measure the effect of his little joke, but the men ignored him. They were all staring at Jeremy, each of them mired in his own unholy contemplation. They knew where he had been, what he had seen.

They knew, and they shuddered.

Jeremy put a shaky hand against the pressure plate and tried to pull himself to his feet. Snake tried to help him up, but Jeremy jerked his arm away, stumbled backward, spun around and caught himself on the lip of the hatch. Then, before anyone realized what was happening, he lunged through the hatch and disappeared into the blackness.

Snake had started after him when two sounds from the void stopped him. He could still hear Jeremy's keening, only it was different now: it came through gritted teeth. Snake knew the sound of his brother's growl, and he knew what it meant. The other sound he heard was the jangle of a toolbox being hefted to a shoulder. A thin smile curled Snake's lip as he backed away from the opening. Nanny took a step toward the hatch, but Snake put an arm out and shook his head.

"Wait," he whispered.

Jeremy shoved the red toolbox to the lip, crawled over it and fell heavily out of the hatch. He pulled himself to his feet, then lifted the toolbox, cradling it across his bare chest.

He staggered over to Biggins.

Biggins had to do a quick shuffle to keep his toes from being crushed when the fifty-pound toolbox crashed at his feet. Gray water splashed up to his face, spattered the front of his clothes, speckled his glasses.

Jeremy bent over, hands on knees, breathing deeply, gathering himself. He coughed, spat, swallowed, and stood up straight, raking a clump of matted hair back from his face, his wet fingers leaving stripes in the grime and blood. The keening had stopped, his breathing steadied. The white eyes he fastened on Biggins were as sharp as knives.

"My *name*," he said, his cracked voice bricked with a dangerous resolve, "is *Jeremy*."

CHAPTER 21

What about a man?

Snake watched Jeremy closely while driving him out on the loki, asking every so often if he was okay. Once the adrenaline abated, Jeremy gripped the rail and didn't say much—only that he was sick in the stomach. When Snake shined the flashlight in Jeremy's face, he winced, said the light hurt his head, and pushed it away. The jacket he had borrowed from Griff swallowed him, it was so large. Still, he seemed content to melt into the jacket, to dissolve away to some secret place. Snake couldn't tell if he was reliving what he had seen or trying to hide from it. Jeremy stumbled twice getting to the loki, and if Snake hadn't been there when they got to the top of the shaft he would have fallen down the steps coming off the man-lift.

Walking across the yard toward the hog house, Snake said, half to himself, "Well, that was a short career."

Jeremy stopped, and Snake, still holding his arm, was pulled up short. The steady metallic thump of the tray lift counted the seconds.

"What do you mean by that?" Jeremy asked.

Snake's eyebrows went up. "You don't seriously think you're going back in there, do you?"

"Right now, no. But when my head quits hurting—maybe tomorrow or the next day—yes, I *will* be going back in there. Soon."

"You're delirious." Snake laughed and tried to take hold of his arm again, but Jeremy shrugged him off. If the near disaster hadn't been so fresh in Snake's mind it might have been comical—Jeremy's grimy, bloodied face peering out of a jacket four sizes too big.

"You want to keep me safe," Jeremy said, and there was a note of accusation in it. "Just like my mother. Same thing. Now I get it. Now I know what she meant. She held me too close, and she knew it. You really think she sent me here to be *safe*?"

A shock wave went through Snake.

"Julie *sent* you here?"

Jeremy didn't answer. He just stared, his mouth open slightly in surprise at what he had let slip out.

Snake stared back, even more shocked than Jeremy. *Julie had sent him here?* The Julie that Snake remembered would have died before she let her only son fall into the hands of the man who had killed her husband. The fact that she *had* died before Jeremy came here had only served to reinforce Snake's impression that Jeremy had acted on his own. What could she have been thinking?

"Why?" he asked. "Why would she send you here?"

"I'm not sure I can explain it," Jeremy said, rubbing his neck and turning away for a minute. When he turned back he looked strained and confused, like he couldn't remember. "She said you have something for me. Something she couldn't give me."

Snake waited. "And. . . ?"

"And what?"

"What was it? What did she want from me?"

"My head hurts," Jeremy said. His eyes roamed, and he waved a hand vaguely toward the hog house. "It's in my locker. You can read it for yourself."

"What's in your locker?" He was being maddeningly obtuse, but Snake had already figured out that he had suffered a concussion. Frankly, he was surprised the kid was still on his feet.

"The letter," Jeremy mumbled. "I guess it doesn't matter now."

Snake looked at his watch. "We need to get you to the emergency room."

Jeremy stood his ground, wagging his head drunkenly, eyes at half-mast. "I'm okay. This isn't about me. It's about you. It's about control."

"Jeremy, I told you the first day you came here—that hole is no place for a kid."

"Right," Jeremy slurred. "But what about a man?" Waves of granite chips rained onto the growing slag pile from the end of the stacker conveyor.

Snake took his hat off and stuck it under his arm. He refused to take part in the argument. Control was part of his job description, and the kid was half out of his head anyway.

"It's tough being responsible for everybody and everything, isn't it?" Jeremy said. "You have to drink yourself to sleep every night just to get out from under . . ." His words trailed off and he teetered uncertainly.

Snake had heard enough junior league psychoanalysis. He closed in so that their faces were inches apart.

"We're going to the truck now," he said, too calmly. "I *really* don't want to have to knock you out and drag you there."

But he wouldn't have to. Jeremy wobbled twice and his knees buckled. Snake caught him, and wrapping Jeremy's arm around his own neck, he half drug, half carried him to the truck. While he was fastening Jeremy's seat belt the kid managed to get in one last shot.

"Might want to put a little slack in the reins," Jeremy muttered.

Jeremy managed to remain conscious on the way to the hospital, but he didn't talk, and Snake was glad. His heart hurt. The words had hit him like hammers. *A little slack in the reins.* Snake's own words, thrown back in his face. Once again he had forgotten, and turned into his father.

He felt drained, and more than once it occurred to him that he could really, really use a drink.

CHAPTER 22

Three kinds of people.

The doctor studied the scan, checked Jeremy out very thoroughly, said his concussion was relatively mild, and pronounced him extremely lucky. Nevertheless, he was held overnight for observation. He looked okay, apart from the three stitches right at his hairline and an assortment of scratches and bruises, but even the prescription stuff didn't do much toward easing his headache. He lay asleep on the couch when Snake went to work the next day.

Late that afternoon he was awakened by a knock at the door. He stumbled over and opened the door, half awake, one hand jammed in his wild hair pressing a palm over his bandage. Moss Fisher stood there in his uniform with a foil-covered plate in his hand.

"I heard what happened," Moss said, raising the plate. "Pearl sent you some dinner."

Jeremy motioned him in, closed the door behind him.

"Aren't you supposed to be at work?" Jeremy mumbled, navigating back to the couch.

Moss answered from the kitchen, having stepped inside to put the plate in the refrigerator. "Yeah, but when you been there thirty years you can take a couple hours now and then. Wha'd they say?"

"They said I'll be fine." Jeremy sat gingerly on the couch, still holding his head. "Soon as this headache goes away."

Moss came in and sat on the edge of the recliner for a few minutes, watching.

"How you doin'?" he finally asked.

"I told you, they said—"

"I can *see* your outside. I want to know what's going on *inside*. You saw the devil last night—face-to-face. So, how you doin'?"

Jeremy took his time. He lay back on the couch and crooked an elbow over his eyes. "I'm okay," he muttered.

"Really?"

Unable to get comfortable, Jeremy sat back up, pinched his eyes. "I always thought if something like that happened to me I'd go crazy with fear, even after it was over. I figured I'd never stop shaking." He smiled, and his shoulders shrugged a little. "But it's not like that. I guess there are always gonna be things I'm afraid of, but they'll never freeze me again. I couldn't even dream up anything worse than what happened last night. There can't *be* anything worse." He looked Moss in the eye. "But I'm still standing. More than that, I know now that I'm not ever really alone. No matter what."

"That's good," Moss said, nodding. "That's *real* good." He had spotted the carving of Snake's hand, picked it up and was holding it in his lap, looking at it, running his finger over it, feeling the details.

"What's up with Snake?" he asked quietly.

"What do you mean? Is something wrong?"

Moss set the carving down on the desk. "He was kind of ornery this afternoon. Worse than usual, I mean. On the way to the hole, Geech asked him when you were coming back and I thought Snake was gonna hit him."

Jeremy opened his eyes and scanned the room, frowning. He got up, shuffled into the kitchen, rummaged around for a few seconds, then came right back to the couch. "I don't see any beer bottles anywhere," he said. "Not even in the trash can. He gets cranky when he's out of beer."

Moss laughed. "Maybe that's it. He even snapped at me a time or two when I was askin' about last night. That's one scared man."

"Snake? Scared? You gotta be kidding. You haven't been underground with him, Moss. Snake's not afraid of *anything*."

There it was again—that old, patient laugh. The lines around Moss's eyes smiled. "You're young, son, and you see everything from ground level. Just because a man's brave don't mean he ain't scared."

"Is this gonna be another philosophy lesson, Moss? Because my head already hurts."

"The only philosophy I know is grace, but the Book says a scared man don't know nothin' about grace. Grace beats fear, every time."

"What makes you think he's scared?"

"Heh. Well, the truth is, there's only three kinds of folks. See, most folks are either chasing after something or running from something." He ticked off two fingers. "Take Luke McCluskey. He's chasing thrills. Weasel? He's hiding, running scared."

"From the IRS. He just wants to keep his paycheck," Jeremy said.

Moss smiled, shook his head. "It's a lot deeper than that, but Weasel's beside the point. We're talking about Snake, and Snake *lives* underground, even when he's not at work."

The old man fell silent for a minute, waiting.

"Okay, he's hiding," Jeremy agreed, "but only because of his face."

"I don't think so," Moss said, reaching out and casually running his middle finger along the carved hand sitting on the desk. "You're right, it's *eyes* he don't like—he can't stand people looking at him, except his brothers, the people he works with. Why you think that is?"

Jeremy shook his head. He really didn't know.

"That kind of fear, the kind that makes a man hide, is always about punishment," Moss said. "About judgment. Always. A man can face just about anything as long as he's sure it ain't his fault. You see a brave man like Snake hiding, you can bet he's full of guilt."

"I never looked at it like that," Jeremy said. "I just always figured he was hiding because of the way people look at him, and he's mad all the time because he doesn't have a life."

But he knew the truth. Deep down, in a dark place, Jeremy knew the truth: Snake was marked like Cain. He decided he'd have to think about this some more before he was ready to talk to Moss about it.

"So, what's the third kind?" he asked, mostly to change the subject.

"Huh?"

"You said there are three kinds of people." He counted fingers. "Chasing something, running from something, and . . . what? What's number three?"

"Heh." Moss looked out the window and his eyes shined. "Standin' still," he said wistfully. "Man learns to stand still, the whole world opens up."

"Yeah," Jeremy whispered, nodding slowly. "And he can see forever."

Like that time up at Eagle Rock.

Snake made sure the machine was on-line and everybody was doing their job in the hole, then went up top to check in with Sonny before the project manager left for the day. A few minutes later he walked out of Sonny's office trailer with a piece of paper in his hand and headed toward the hole.

Moss Fisher came from around back of the offices and fell in step with him.

"Wha'd they say?" Moss asked.

"Oh, this? It's just a CYA addendum from the manufacturer of the ring gear. Probably doesn't mean a thing, but Sonny wants me to read it. I guess it's real important for me to know how their lawyers think."

Snake stopped, shaded his eyes against the westering sun and looked up at the stacker conveyor, finally pumping out bursts of slag again after almost a month.

Moss stopped too and clasped his hands behind his back. "You seen that bird?" he asked.

"What bird?" Snake hadn't noticed the cardinal at the shop window anymore, so he assumed he had saved it from itself.

"There's some fool redbird keeps peckin' on a window around back of the offices. I think he's crazy."

Snake sighed. "He was down by the shop earlier, doing the same stupid thing. I was hoping he had left."

"Nope, he's still at it. That bird's nuts."

"Yeah, well he better stop soon. I'm running out of shaving cream."

Moss peered in the direction of the soaped window on the side of the machine shop and a knowing smile grew on his face.

"That was you? I wondered why that window was soaped. You can't save him, you know."

Snake shrugged. "I can try."

Moss shook his head. "That old bird's gonna do what he's gonna do, and you ain't God. I know God, and you ain't Him."

Moss went on with his rounds and left Snake alone, but his words continued to eat at Snake. He couldn't have explained why to anybody, but he couldn't shake it. For some reason it had become his mission to rescue this one silly bird. It mattered to him.

When nobody was looking, he started up toward the office trailer thinking he might just do a casual walk-around. If anybody had said anything, he would have told them he just wanted to watch the bird do his thing. But before he got to the trailer he spotted Carl trotting briskly across behind the hog house with his head up, and there was a flash of red at the corner of his mouth. Snake thought he heard a sharp chirp just before Carl disappeared behind the trailer.

"You got no right to squawk now, pard," he muttered. He started to say, "If you're gonna be dumb, you gotta be tough," when he checked himself. It would have been eulogy enough for a lousy redbird, but he stopped short of it. He stood out in the yard for a long time as the sun set, staring at the flame across the way and wondering why he felt as if he'd lost something, as if he'd been defeated and diminished somehow. The flame flickered on, unchanging except that it seemed, as always, to brighten with the oncoming darkness.

By Wednesday morning Jeremy's headache was gone and he felt almost human again. That evening, since he was still off of work, he called Kearston and went with her to church. He didn't have access to a truck, so she had to pick him up, but she didn't seem to mind. When she asked him about the stitches in his head he shrugged and said, "I got hit with a rock." She didn't press the issue, and he was glad.

Thursday morning he pulled on his jeans and told Snake he was going to work that afternoon. He had prepared all his arguments and braced himself for a fight, but Snake just nodded and said, "Okay. If you're up to it."

When Snake wasn't looking, Jeremy peeked at the trash can. Still no beer bottles. He had said very little to Jeremy since the accident. At least he didn't seem angry anymore.

After they got to work that afternoon and parked the truck, they were walking past the office trailer when Meg stuck her head out the door.

"Jeremy Prine, could I see you in my office?"

Her words were clipped; she sounded mad, the way his mother had sounded whenever she used his full name like that. Snake shrugged. He didn't know what it was about.

She was back at her desk by the time Jeremy got there, peering through reading glasses, checking over an application sheet, looking very much like a teacher grading papers.

"Sit down," she said, without looking up.

Jeremy sat and waited for a full five minutes. When she was through with what she was doing, she closed a folder, leaned back in her chair and regarded him sternly over the top of her reading glasses.

"The hospital called yesterday," she said, and then she waited as if she expected him to figure out what she was up to. When he didn't, she continued.

"They needed to verify your personal information. The girl said you filled out the papers yourself and that they were afraid you might have been a little confused. You left a couple answers off of the admissions form and wrote a couple others in the wrong places. She had to call me for the insurance information anyway, so she just went over everything while we were on the phone." Meg waited again, but Jeremy didn't flinch.

"The date of your accident was March twelfth," she said. "So when you wrote March twelfth as your birthday, they wondered if maybe your *head injury* caused you to get things mixed up."

She'd accented "head injury" as if she would like to cause one, and Jeremy suddenly knew what this was all about.

"It's right, isn't it? The date. You got confused and wrote down the truth, didn't you?"

He nodded, staring at his feet.

"March twelfth, the day of the accident, really *was* your birthday. And if the year you wrote down was correct, it was your eighteenth birthday."

"Yes, ma'am."

"Do you have any idea how much trouble you could have caused us—caused *me*?" she asked.

He shook his head. He was busted, and there was nothing to do but tough it out.

She stewed for a few seconds and then said, "But you *are* eighteen now, are you not?"

He nodded.

"You're lucky I don't have a rock handy," she said, and it sounded like she meant it. "If you ever lie to me again, I will find a rock and I will hunt you down and I will finish the job, do you understand me?"

"Yes, ma'am."

"Get out of my office."

He was almost to the door when she called his name again. He stopped and turned around.

"Yes, ma'am?"

"Happy birthday, Jeremy. I'm glad you're all right."

Stepping out of the trailer, Jeremy saw that Carl was waiting for him. He ran up and laid a freshly killed rat at Jeremy's feet, sat back and grinned.

"Thanks, pard," Jeremy said. "But if it's okay with you, I think I'll save that for later."

Eldon was standing in the road talking to Moss as Jeremy and Carl walked by on their way to the hog house.

"Yo, Jeremy!" he called out, and met him with a high five. "Good to have you back, dude."

Moss nodded toward the office trailer Jeremy had just come out of, and asked, "Wha'd they say?"

Jeremy saw the gleam in his eye and knew he didn't need to answer. Moss already knew what Meg had said. Moss always knew everything.

"Meg's got a mean streak," Jeremy said, and Moss laughed.

Tino arrived at the hog house at the same time as Jeremy, trotted up the steps and threw an arm around him.

"Hey, Jeremy, it's good to see you! I'm really glad you din' get smoked, amigo. That would have been very bad. How's your head, man?"

"Feels good, now," Jeremy said. And it did. Hanging back after Tino went in, he looked around at the sudden burst of springtime, the profusion of new color. A Japanese magnolia had blossomed. The leafless tree leaned over the deck, loaded down with magenta and white tulips. The grass on the banks of the treatment plant across the way had turned achingly green almost overnight, accented by random patches of violets. Bright yellow sprays of forsythia spewed waist-high from the bases of the tanks. Jeremy felt very glad to be alive. Tilting his face up to gather the warmth of the afternoon sun, he closed his eyes.

"Thank you," he whispered.

Heavy footsteps disturbed his reverie as Rico clomped up onto the deck.

"Jeremy!" he boomed. "You're back, huh?" He placed his big hand on Jeremy's head and pulled the hair up with his thumb so he could inspect the stitches.

A gold tooth flashed in the middle of a wide grin, and Rico said, "Hey, that's gonna leave a good scar, bro!" Then he opened the door and swept Jeremy into the hog house.

They were all there, dressing out for work—Griff, Geech, Nanny, Tunk, Tino. Even Ruskie was hanging around talking, though the mole operator never dressed out with the rest of the guys. There was some new kid who looked even younger and greener than Jeremy, flame-red hair and freckles adding to a perpetually embarrassed look. His name was Logan Snitker, and Geech was already calling him "Stinker." Faces lit up when Jeremy stepped inside. They all pounded him on the back, shook his hand. Nanny wrapped him in a bear hug, lifting his feet clear off the floor.

He didn't even notice at first that they were all watching him when he opened his locker. Inside, he found a brand-new miner's helmet—brown Bakelite, with a brim all the way around. Riveted to the front of the hat was a little brass plate with a name stamped neatly on it: JEREMY PRINE. Only then, staring at that nameplate, did it register with Jeremy that on this day he had not heard the name Germy, even once, since walking onto the jobsite. But then, he hadn't seen Biggins yet.

He ran his finger around the brim. He started to talk, then had to stop and clear his throat.

"Who did this?"

"Well," Geech said, looking around, "Snake got the hat—but we all chipped in. It wasn't much."

"More than you know," Jeremy said.

"The nameplate was, uh . . . well, Biggins made that for you."

Jeremy glanced over their heads, not seeing Snake or Biggins anywhere. *No, they wouldn't want to be here,* he thought. But it was all right.

"You din' see the T-shirt, amigo," Tino said. "Geech had to get your girlfriend to buy it because nobody knew how to say the name."

Jeremy plucked the new T-shirt out of his locker, held it up by the corners, and pronounced the name for them.

"Day-us Ah-dare-it," he said, very slowly.

"What does it mean, amigo?"

He stared at the words for a moment, remembering. The corners of his eyes smiled, and he said quietly, "It means everything's under control."

Jeremy found Snake out in the lay-down yard taking inventory of the pipe. Alerted by the crunch of footsteps on the crush-and-run, Snake looked up and saw him coming.

"Looks good on you," Snake said. "Looks natural."

Jeremy pushed his new mining helmet back on his head. "Yeah, I like the hat. Thanks. I went by the shop and thanked Biggins too. He said—well, I can't really repeat what he said, but as far as I could tell it was a compliment. What made you change your mind?"

Snake kicked at a rock with his toe, dug it up out of the crush-and-run, pressed it back in.

"I found out I'm not God."

"Really?" Jeremy smiled. "How'd you figure that out?"

Snake's eyes wandered to the flame, pale and thin in the bright daylight. "A little bird told me."

CHAPTER 23

Church music.

Jeremy took Kearston with him to church that Sunday to see Geech baptized. She'd gone with him before, though not often enough to get completely comfortable with the controlled chaos. He'd been to her church too—the only one she'd ever known. It was a mahogany-and-stained-glass refuge where things were orderly and neat and polished and sedate and predictable, where the pastor wore a robe and sometimes spoke in another language. Growing up in the hills of eastern Tennessee, Jeremy had never heard the word *liturgy*. But it was, after all, the same God. Kearston wanted to see Geech baptized because she had never seen an actual dunking. She would see several new things on this day.

The first major surprise was when Nanny showed up with his family in tow. They trooped in all together during the singing, while everybody was standing, and took up most of the row behind Jeremy. Nanny had put on his best work jeans, freshly ironed, and apart from the slicked-down hair he looked normal. Geech had invited them all to watch his baptism.

Emilio took prayer requests, then got down on his knees on the dais and remembered every one of them, just like always.

When the prayer ended, Jeremy looked up and Snake was standing next to him, holding his hat in his hands. So great was Jeremy's surprise that it didn't immediately dawn on him that this was the first time he'd ever seen Snake in a public place with his head completely exposed.

Snake leaned close and whispered, "Geech asked me." He seemed to think he needed to explain his presence. Emilio stepped down and disappeared through a side door while Nguyen, the young music director, picked up an acoustic guitar and stepped up to the mike stand alone. The rest of the band and the little choir of backup singers were absent on this day, so Nguyen had the job to himself. As he slipped the guitar strap over his shoulder, he looked up and saw all the new faces.

"Oh, hey! You know what?" he said, obviously having just thought of it. "Let's all say hello to each other."

People boiled out of their pews shaking hands with each other and introducing themselves to people they didn't know—a nightmare scenario for Snake, but it happened so fast there was nothing anybody could have done to stop it. Jeremy tightened involuntarily, expecting trouble. There must have been a dozen people who came up to Snake, gave his scarred hand a firm shake, smiled into his hooded eyes and treated him exactly the same as they would have treated anyone else. Jeremy couldn't help noticing that when they said their names to Snake, he always answered with "Aiden Prine." A couple of them made the connection and he had to explain that, yes, he was Jeremy's uncle.

A familiar melody poured from Nguyen's acoustic guitar, and people drifted back to their seats to the tune of "Jesu, Joy of Man's Desiring."

Snake sat listening intently. "Boy can play," he muttered.

Donny Flippen, the mentally challenged man-child, and his dad were sitting a couple rows in front of Jeremy. The whole time

Nguyen was playing, Donny kept trying to get up for some reason, but his dad held his arm and restrained him.

By the time Nguyen had finished, Emilio and Geech had stepped down into the baptismal pool up front, behind the choir loft.

"Belton Peek came to us several weeks ago when he got out of the hospital after a near fatal accident," Emilio said, and then he told a little about Geech and what he had been through.

"Belton?" Jeremy whispered.

Snake nodded. "Now you know why he don't mind being called Geech."

Jeremy and Snake and Nanny all watched solemnly as Geech made his confession of faith, was symbolically buried, and rose to new life.

Jeremy heard a quiet, subdued "Hoo-ahh" from Nanny when Geech came up out of the water, and he understood. It was just Nanny's way of saying amen.

Then Nguyen had everybody on their feet and singing an old hymn, accompanied only by his guitar.

After the hymn was over and everybody sat down, a plump lady wearing a floor-length skirt and with a pile of frazzled gray hair on her head hobbled up the two steps to the dais and stood facing the microphone. Her name was Vangjli Logoreci, and in a thick accent she told a little of her background. She was nervous and kept stopping to breathe.

"For many years, in Albania, we did not speak of Christ," she said, working each word carefully in a dry, frail voice. "There was price. Seven years prison, only to say name of God." When she was a child, the Communist regime tore down all the churches and mosques. Later, when she married and began to raise children of her own, though she herself was raised, and remained, Christian, she could not speak of God to her own children. Every third person was an informer. The schools taught children that there was no God, and if a child repeated the name of God in school, *both* parents would be sent away. Her homeland became a spiritual wasteland where, for fifty years, no one spoke of God. She was happy that her daughter had been able to come to the United States, and happier still that she herself had been able to obtain a visa so she could make this visit.

"Is lovely country. Is free," she said. "But *beware*. You must never forget who give you this gift."

As she opened the English Bible she had borrowed from her daughter, she spoke again of the fears she had faced while trying to raise a family, and how she had learned to face life unafraid because God commanded it. And then she read a short passage from Isaiah.

"'Fear not, for I have redeemed you; I have summoned you by name; you are mine. When you pass through the waters, I will be with you; and when you pass through the rivers, they will not sweep over you. When you walk through the fire, you will not be burned; the flames will not set you ablaze. For I am the Lord, your God, the Holy One of Israel, your Savior.'"

Jeremy was mesmerized. Sitting next to Snake, the words had sent a chill up Jeremy's spine. But the thing he would remember best, the thing that would stay fused in his memory, was the way she'd said the name Isaiah in her Albanian accent, with a deep and quiet reverence. "E-*sigh*-ya."

As she made her way carefully back down to her seat, her daughter and seven or eight people from the front rows got up and crowded around her in a spontaneous show of love and support. While they were still on their feet, Emilio came back in through the side door, followed by Geech, whose hair was still wet and slicked back.

Geech strolled down the aisle grinning and slapping hands like a football player. Nanny rose and stepped out into the aisle to meet him with an exuberant high five. Snake, thinking maybe the high five had become a standard greeting in the long years since he'd been in a church service, stood up and followed with a high five of his own. Then Jeremy. One of the teenagers in the little clutch of people down front saw the mini-celebration going on in the back and turned around to high-five Emilio as he started up onto the dais, and within seconds everybody in the church was standing and high-fiving each other. Everybody except Kearston, who remained seated with her mouth hanging slightly ajar. This was a long, long way from sedate.

When the impromptu party died down and everybody had returned to their seats, Emilio began to speak. He first thanked Vangjli Logoreci for her willingness to stand up in front of a strange group and speak from the heart in a foreign language. It struck Jeremy that Emilio didn't seem to notice that he too was speaking to a strange crowd in a foreign language, had in fact made a vocation out of it. Moss Fisher, as always, sat down front, facing the crowd, and translated every word into sign language.

Emilio started talking about deserts, when they appeared in the Bible and the significance of them, but he hadn't gotten very far when a commotion in the crowd stopped him. Donny Flippen struggled to his feet and made a little grunting noise as he tore himself from the restraining grip of his father. He tripped over somebody and almost fell while stepping out into the aisle, then he lumbered down front, past Moss, and straight up the steps onto the dais.

Smiling, Emilio stepped aside as Donny headed for the piano. Donny's father stood, apologizing profusely, and started to go after his son, when Emilio held up his hand and said simply, "Wait. It's all right."

The old upright piano sat off to the left side of the dais with its lid closed and the bench tucked under, for it was not in use this day—Nguyen played only the guitar.

Donny pulled the bench out, sat down heavily, raised the lid and launched without preamble into a lively and intense piece of classical music. Bending low over the keyboard, he did not play perfectly, for he had no sense of nuance. Yet the notes were all there, and the timing was dead-on.

Geech, who had seated himself next to Nanny in the row behind Jeremy, leaned forward and whispered, "That ain't church music, is it?"

Snake shook his head. "I think it's Mozart."

Raising an eyebrow, Kearston said, "In *church*?"

"He gives what he's got," Jeremy said. "It's church music to Donny."

As soon as he had played the last chord, Donny stood up, unceremoniously shoving the stool aside, and tromped back to his seat, blissfully unaware of how he looked—the unkempt hair, the heavy eyes, the pugnacious set of his protruding lower lip.

"That's amazing," Snake muttered.

"I've seen it before. He's a savant." Jeremy had gotten to know Donny and his father over the last few months and had, a couple of times, seen him pound out a complicated piece, by ear, note for note. His dad said he'd been doing it since childhood, needing to hear a piece only once in order to imitate it. For a guy who couldn't even talk, it was astonishing. Donny didn't seem to even notice when Emilio laid a hand on his shoulder as he passed.

Emilio took up right where he had left off, unperturbed, as if nothing had happened, as if this was the natural order of a worship service. In a way, Jeremy thought, maybe it was.

"Joseph," Emilio pointed out, "was thrown down a well, sold into slavery, unjustly imprisoned—all to strip away the attitude of a spoiled child and forge in its place the character of a patient, wise and merciful man who would guide a great nation through a famine and rescue the very brothers who betrayed him."

He spoke of Moses, forty years banished before he went back to free his people, and how those same people, after they proved they were not ready to enter the promised land, were made to spend years wandering in the desert, learning whose hand it was that fed them. He talked about Jesus, and how He spent forty days in the desert focusing and honing himself, divesting himself of all that was not essential before He went back, like Moses, to free *His* people.

"It was in a prison that I myself found God," Emilio said.

Lastly, he spoke of Vangjli Logoreci's Albania, and how "her memories of a spiritual desert contrast so sharply with those of you who were brought up in a land where the water of religious freedom and the endless sunshine of prosperity make it easy to *say* you are followers of Christ."

His eyes roamed over the crowd for a moment before he closed, letting silence have its due.

"But I am only a man," he said, "and I cannot judge the motives of the heart. So Vangjli was right. *You* must beware. It falls to you, each of you alone, to be alert, to watch for the subtle hand of God when you enter the desert in your own life. Whom God would use, He will shape and mold and fire in His kiln."

Jeremy figured Snake would bolt before the service was over, to avoid the crowd, but he didn't. In fact, though he was sitting near the back and could have gotten clean away, Snake didn't move immediately. He stood there staring at the piano on the dais until everybody else had clogged the aisle. By the time he remembered where he was, he was hemmed in.

When Snake and Jeremy and Kearston did finally manage to squeeze themselves into the throng inching down the aisle toward the back door of the church, Snake found himself pressed up against Donny Flippen. Jeremy saw him lean over and mutter something to Donny, but Donny didn't respond right away.

From the other side of Donny, his father caught Snake's eye and said, "He don't talk. But he understands most of what you say if you talk slow."

Snake nodded and said nothing else. Jeremy noticed as they neared the back of the church that Donny had become agitated. He snorted a couple of times and slung his head, frowning, his upturned lower lip looking more pugnacious than usual.

"He's frustrated about something," his father said. "He gets this way sometimes. It'll pass."

In the back vestibule, Donny stopped. Despite his father's prodding he refused to budge, and instead started rocking his upper body and grunting as if he wanted to say something but the language wasn't there. He grew more frustrated by the second.

Then he did a strange thing, or a series of strange things. He did them so quickly that Jeremy might not have noticed if he hadn't been looking directly at Donny for the few seconds it took. Donny chucked his own chin with a thumb, then clasped his hands together, jerked them apart, and knifed his right hand between the fingers of his left. His father hadn't seen it because he was talking to the pastor at the door, while Jeremy had turned around to see Donny's little rocking episode.

"What was that?" Jeremy asked. "Kearston, did you see that?"

She hadn't. Neither had Snake. And Donny didn't do it again. Whatever he had done, it had satisfied him. He straightened up, stopped rocking, and a bright smile replaced his frustrated grimace.

Moss stood waiting out on the sidewalk to talk to the group of miners—Geech, Snake, Nanny, and Jeremy.

"I had to get out of there fast," Moss said. "Four of y'all in one church building? I was afraid the roof was gonna cave in."

Jeremy wasn't paying attention. He was watching Donny and his dad walk away, and he couldn't stop thinking about what he had just seen. On an impulse, he broke away from the cluster of people around Moss and ran after Donny.

"Wait! Hold up! Mr. Flippen? Listen, would you and Donny mind coming back here for a minute? Some of my friends want to meet you."

Mr. Flippen was nice enough about it. He turned Donny around and steered him up the sidewalk toward the crowd. When Donny was finally standing next to Moss, Jeremy waited for Moss to finish talking, then said, "Uh, Moss, could I just ask you something?"

"Sure, Jeremy. I know pretty much everything. What would you like to know?"

"Well, I don't know how to say it, and I could be wrong, but . . ."

"Spit it out, boy."

"I think Donny was trying to talk."

"He can't talk," his father said. "He just grunts and points."

It was Jeremy's turn to be frustrated. "No, I mean, with his hands. Like Moss." He took Donny by the shoulders, looked him in the eye and said, "Donny, show them what you did with your hands back there."

Donny stared blankly. He opened his mouth, folded his bottom lip into it and scrunched up his face.

"He don't talk," Mr. Flippen repeated, and he glanced up the sidewalk toward home.

"He went like this," Jeremy said. He tried to imitate what he thought he had seen Donny do.

Moss stroked his chin. "That thumb thing—that could be *not*. But the rest, I can't make out. Show me again."

Jeremy tried again, but it had happened so fast he didn't catch it all, and he knew he didn't have it right. Donny must have been paying attention, however, because all of a sudden he did it again, very rapidly—a quick flurry of movement. This time Jeremy wasn't looking at him. He caught the movement from the corner of his eye, but he couldn't miss the look of complete shock on Moss's face.

"He's signing," Moss said. Then he said to Donny, "What did you say?" His hands flew over the words as he spoke them.

Donny did it again.

"Not out through," Moss translated. "He said, 'Not out through.' It doesn't make any sense."

"He can't talk," Donny's father said, but his voice was losing some of its conviction.

Moss tried again. "Donny, why do you say 'Not out through'?"

Donny looked at Snake, and his hands flitted through more signs.

"Smooth man says out," Moss translated. "Did you say something to him, Snake?"

All eyes turned to Snake when he didn't answer right away. He couldn't; he was that stunned. Slowly, his serpentine mouth began to work.

"Up there. Before we came out. I . . . I told him it was very surprising to hear such beautiful music coming out of him."

Jeremy still didn't see whatever it was that Snake saw.

Snake's voice shook. "What he's saying is two sentences, not one. Not out, period. Through."

"Oh, mercy," Moss said. "Mr. Flippen, your son *can* talk."

"But how could he . . . how did. . . ?"

Moss took Donny's face in his hands. Donny smiled because he liked the contact, and he liked Moss.

"He's been watching me sign," Moss said. "Every Sunday for seventeen years."

Snake turned and walked away, putting his sunglasses on, snugging a rumpled hat on his head and reaching into his pocket for his car keys.

Jeremy watched him go. Tilting his head back to look up into a bright blue spring sky, he held his hand out, palm up.

Kearston squeezed his arm, followed his eyes.

"What is it?" she asked.

He smiled. "I think it's raining frogs."

CHAPTER 24

What Julie couldn't give.

In the spring, when the sun returns from the south and once
again warms a man's back, when the dogwoods and azaleas
explode, when a field of new grain bursts out of the ground so
green it hurts the eyes, when pollen turns the horizon yellow and
lays a skim of paisley swirls on standing water, a man, if he is a
man, must go fishing.

Snake and Jeremy borrowed Geech's boat, and first light found
Snake backing the trailer into the water at a local reservoir. Within
minutes they were afloat—tackle boxes tucked away, trolling
motor lowered into the water, fishing rods in hand, eyes searching
the calm surface off the nearest point of land for signs of movement.

A thin blanket of mist lay in patches on the water. In the half-
light at the edge of a small cove, two young deer that had come
down to drink raised their heads and pricked their ears, watching
the boat slice through the mist. A pair of ducks, startled from
sleep, made a great clumsy racket, quacking and pedaling and flapping into the air.

"Put the motor down," Snake said, keeping his voice low.

Snake was in the front of the boat, leaning on the butt seat and working the electric trolling motor with his foot.

"The big motor?" Jeremy asked from the back. The little three-hundred-acre county reservoir forbade the use of gasoline engines.

"Yeah, lower it," Snake answered. "We can't run it, but it'll stabilize the keel, keep the back end from swinging. It's that black switch right there."

As the boat slowed approaching the first point, Jeremy rummaged through the tackle box. "What should I use?" he asked.

"Water's flat," Snake said. "Why don't you tie on a Rapala and see if they're hitting top water? I'm throwing a plastic lizard. We'll bracket 'em—find out what they want."

Jeremy was pleased that he at least knew what a Rapala was, and he started to tie one on the end of his line with a granny knot.

"Wrong," Snake said. "Let me show you. You gotta leave a loop."

Jeremy stepped up to the front and watched while Snake tied the lure on so that it dangled freely from a half-inch loop of line.

"See? It's got to be able to move or the action is all wrong."

Jeremy made his first cast, dropping the lightweight lure within a couple of feet of the shore. He started cranking, and as soon as the line tightened the lure dove down and swam, shimmying like a minnow, back to the boat.

"You ever use one of those before?" Snake asked.

"No." Jeremy waited, knowing he was about to learn something.

"Throw it back out there."

He made another cast, dropping the lure near the bank again. His hand went to the crank, but Snake said, "Wait. Let it sit for a second. See the rings? Let the splash rings get away from it before you move."

"Okay. Now what?"

"Your line's too tight. Drop slack. Right, that's it. Now jiggle the tip of the rod. No, that's still too tight. You don't want to pull it under like that."

"You don't?"

"No, not yet. Jiggle the slack line. That's it. You see the way the lure dances on top like a dying minnow? That's what you want. And be ready, because if he hits it he won't hold it long."

Jeremy's technique improved with every cast. Working down the back side of the point, he cast his lure close to a stump and made it dance. The water boiled up around it, and the lure disappeared. He hauled back, set the hook, and reeled in a yearling bass. The first fish of the day.

Holding it up by the lip, he said, "That's a nice fish. What, maybe a pound and a half?"

"Maybe," Snake said, flipping his plastic lizard expertly into a little creek mouth. "Not what I'd call a big fish, though. Me and your dad used to catch crappie with bigger bass than that in their stomachs."

Jeremy laughed. It was an excellent lie, and he wondered if Snake had made it up on the spot. "Was my dad a pretty good fisherman?" he asked.

"Best I've ever seen." Snake raised his rod tip slowly, jigging it three or four times, then dropping it back down and cranking twice. "Your dad fished rings around me. He knew how to think like a fish."

They talked a lot about Tom that morning. Snake opened up more than he ever had before, reliving childhood memories of Jeremy's father. At the same time, Jeremy learned things about bass fishing that his father would have taught him if he had lived. By the time the sun had risen clear of the treetops, he had switched over to a bait-caster, with Snake teaching him how to work a plastic lizard. There were long spells when neither of them said anything, and Jeremy noted that fishing was good for that. Men needed something to occupy their hands so they could talk when they wanted—and be silent when they wanted.

After one such silence, Jeremy spoke quietly as his arm swept through a cast.

"Uncle Aiden, tell me what happened to my dad," he said. "You were there. I need to know."

Snake pulled a deep breath and let it out, staring off into the woods in quiet resignation. "I guess you got a right."

It took him a minute to begin. "Life hangs from the smallest *if*," he finally said, his voice weak and tinged with regret. "Any little breeze can shove a gnat into the path of a windshield."

He'd had ample time to ruminate on this simple notion, he said—to digest it, to learn to hate the aftertaste of ashes. If he hadn't eaten Buffalo wings for lunch that day, ten years ago, he wouldn't have been late coming out of the hog house. If he hadn't had to make an emergency stop he wouldn't have been lagging behind the other miners heading into the hole at shift change. Some other straggler would have been picked off by the walking boss and told to stay behind and help Tom bring in the pump.

Some other gnat.

Aiden found Tom in the machine shop, putting another impeller in the sump pump. If he had been on the loki with the others he wouldn't have been in the shop with Tom when the yellow light started flashing on top of the electrician's trailer and that obnoxious buzzer went off, signaling some kind of problem underground. Cribbs, the electrician, the one who normally manned the emergency phone, had gone in on the loki with the miners, so nobody was home to answer it. Tom reacted first, racing out of the machine shop, sprinting the ten yards to the electrician's trailer and bounding up the steps to answer the hot line.

Good old Tom—always ready, never able. Tom's problem, as Aiden had pointed out on countless occasions, was his complete inability to make a decision. The last such lecture had been delivered only the day before, when the two of them were driving back down through the wooded hills of home. It had been an unusually dry winter and the squirrels constantly crisscrossed the roads in search of food and water. Inevitably, one of them ran out in front of Tom's truck. When the squirrel saw the truck he stopped, started back, changed his mind and reversed course again. Tom jammed the brakes and whipped the steering wheel first right, then left, perfectly matching the panic of the squirrel. The short dance ended with a double thump and a squirrel flip-flopping in the wake of the truck.

Aiden, who had grabbed on to the dashboard, cast a wry grin at his brother. "Well, you taught *that* squirrel to break-dance, didn't you?"

"I didn't mean to" was Tom's sullen reply.

"Oh, I know that. It wasn't *you* killed that squirrel, Tom, it was indecision. I mean, look—there's a little gray pile of fur every hundred feet on this road, and if you watch what they do you can see why. They can't make up their tiny little minds. They go this way, that way, this way, that way—and then thump-thump, it's over. If that squirrel had just kept right on running in a straight line, or if *you* had, he'd still be alive right now. But what really drives me nuts is I can't figure out why anybody in his right mind would run off the road trying to miss a lousy squirrel in the first place!"

Tom chewed on this for a while and then said, in his affable way, "I figured it was kind of important to the squirrel."

Tom. He was as good a hand as anybody—better than most—but somebody had to tell him every move to make. If he could see an alternative it would stop him cold every time, which was precisely what happened the day of the accident.

By the time Aiden got to the electrician's trailer, Tom was already doing his usual foot-shuffling routine. He had a finger in his other ear trying to block out the screaming of the compressor in the yard, and he was staring at his boots with that confused frown on his face. Aiden snatched the phone away from him.

"What's the problem?" Aiden shouted into the phone, noting the offended set of his brother's jaw.

"We're leaking high voltage from the main." It was the shift boss, an ex-naval gunnery officer, top dog on the mining machine, and he sounded shrill. There was no mistaking the deafening roar of the mole in the background, still grinding away. "We got blue lightning running up and down the cable tray and all over the control deck. Where's Cribbs?"

"He's on his way in with the crew. They started in about fifteen minutes ago—ought to be there any minute. Why don't you just kill it and wait?"

"We can't get to it! You can't touch anything! The mole's running wide open and we got no way to shut it down. We can't even get to the breakers. Besides, it's the incoming high voltage that's leaking, and that's gotta be shut down from the switchyard."

Aiden shrugged. "I can do that."

"You can?"

"Yeah, no problem."

"You sure you know how?"

"I can handle it. I've seen Cribbs do it enough times. It's just a big switch."

It was true that he had seen it done, and Aiden rarely forgot what he saw. But if Cribbs had been there he would have told him you never open a high-voltage switch of that type without first taking the load off of it.

Ever.

Aiden grabbed the keys from a hook near the door and headed for the switchyard next to the shop. Tom stayed right with him. When Aiden popped the lock, Tom shoved through the chain link gate and took the lead. It was a big gray cabinet the size of a dumpster with a weather-sealed steel door on the front. Tom unlatched the door, swung it out of the way and stopped to stare at the main switch, a heavy three-foot lever leaning forty-five degrees to the right and pointing to the word *ON*. Forty-five degrees left of center was the word *OFF*. It seemed fairly cut-and-dried to Aiden, but Tom pushed his hard hat back and took a moment to study it.

"You sure about this?" He was wearing that confused look again.

Aiden pointed. "On. Off. It ain't that complicated, Tom. Here, move."

But Tom stood his ground. He planted a hand firmly against Aiden's chest. "I can *do* it," he growled. His lip curled, his eyes narrowed, and his body tensed. Everything about him said, "Enough! Don't cross this line."

"Then do it, bro. Lock and load," Aiden said, spreading his hands. He knew his brother well. He was the nicest guy in the world, except he did have a limit. When Tom growled, if those around him were smart, they backed off. Aiden backed off.

If Aiden hadn't prodded him, he never would have done it. If only. If only Tom had argued a little longer. If only he had waited, had listened to his innate caution instead of reacting to Aiden's goading; if only they had seen the miner drop the phone in

Cribbs's trailer and turn toward the switchyard waving his arms, screaming, his lips forming the word *NO!* If only they could have heard him over the high-pitched whine of the compressor. There were a thousand *ifs*.

Tom gripped the lever with both hands and shoved it hard left. There was a resonant *THUMP* from inside the mammoth switch, accompanied by a low, vibrating hum that swelled instantly to a loud buzz, then an evil, grating roar.

Tom's horrified face started to turn. Words tried to form, but "Oh, n—!" was as far as he got before the switch exploded with a thunderclap and the white light leaped at him like a sprung trap, quick as thought, merciless as a snake, erupting, shattering reality.

Aiden's mind, instantly shifting to short scale, captured a series of snapshots: Tom's hard hat silhouetted black against this new sun like a photographic negative, first tilting, then airborne, then flying past like a feather in a hurricane. Aiden's left arm flew up, and his mind snapped more pictures—white-hot blades of armor-piercing heat overtaking the hand, the elbow, the shoulder. Aiden closed his eyes. His feet twisted for purchase as Tom slammed into him and they both hurtled backward, launched by the adrenaline rush of panic, boosted by the force of the blast.

Aiden crashed shoulder first into the gravel and rolled onto his back, pushing, digging with his heels to put more distance between himself and the volcano. Blinded by the flash, he kept his eyes closed tight against the flames, but a rapid-fire succession of Technicolor replays exploded behind his eyelids. His nose was seared shut, the acrid memory of charred flesh and molten metal fused into his nostrils. A jumble of discordant noises assaulted him—the thunder of secondary explosions, voices shouting first in the distance and then nearer, the sound of feet running, crunching, the clang of the gate. He heard his own heels grinding furiously against the gravel, and closer, a sibilant whisper from his clothes and hair and skin, and he knew, though he could not see, that most of his upper body was in flames.

A chilling scream ripped the air. Recognition came to him only on the tail of the echo, as out of a dream: the scream was his own.

Voices clashed above him, shouting orders, cursing. Hands grabbed him under armpits, behind knees, dragging him away as other hands slapped out flames on his arms, chest and face. A narrow spot of vision returned to his right eye, filled with the bearded grimace of a miner. As they lifted him and hauled him through the gate, Aiden looked back into the switchyard and caught a glimpse of Tom—a last hellish sight he would forever wish he could un-see. But the picture seared itself into his memory, stark and clear, and would return at odd moments throughout his life, unbidden, to rake charred fingernails across his soul. In that snapshot, Tom's body was arched, his head thrown back, his mouth yawning wide, blackened teeth grinning in agony, fighting for a breath that his ruined lungs would not process. His arms bent at the elbows; black claws pointing skyward, shaking violently, burnt flesh peeling like brittle paint from his arms and head. Smoke curled casually from the cracked ebony roundness where his hair had been.

Aiden's fire-blasted throat croaked out Tom's name and he stretched a twisted hand in his brother's direction, but his bearers wouldn't stop; they carried him swiftly away, through the gate, away from his dying brother. He hadn't prayed in years, but now his tortured heart cried out to any god who would listen, begging first for this atrocity to be undone, to somehow be a nightmare from which he could awaken. When his senses denied that possibility he prayed for deliverance from unimaginable reality. He almost prayed for Tom to live, but the snapshot intruded for the first of a million times and he thought better of it.

The pain began to climb. Mercifully, Aiden Prine lost consciousness.

Jeremy sat numbly in the back of the boat, staring into space.

"Are you all right?" Snake asked.

He nodded thickly. "I think I understand now," he said.

"Understand what?"

"What Mom meant. What she said in the letter."

"The letter. I never got back to it the night you got hurt. I never read it."

Jeremy pulled out his wallet, took the letter from it and handed it to his uncle. "Be careful," he said. "It's starting to tear on the crease."

Snake reeled in his line and laid the rod down on the carpeted deck. Carefully unfolding the brittle pages, he leaned back against the pedestal and read.

When he had finished, his gaze wandered away for a minute, then he read it a second time. Jeremy pretended to fish.

Staring at the second page for a moment, Snake read out loud, "'You have something I couldn't give him, and he has something I couldn't give you. I won't tell you what—you'll just have to find out from each other. When you find it, you'll know.'"

Jeremy let the silence hang between them.

"This is what you were talking about the other night. After you got hurt. So you think you've figured this out?" Snake asked quietly. "What she meant?"

"I think so. I wouldn't have shown you the letter if I hadn't."

Snake's eyes roamed in an abject poverty of confusion. "I don't get it," he muttered. "What could you have needed from me? What could I possibly have that Julie couldn't give you?"

Jeremy jiggled the slack in his line, slowly working it upright and keeping his eyes on it. "I needed to know how to fish a plastic worm. I needed to know how to skin a deer, and how to work hard and take pleasure in it. I needed to know it's okay to make a fool of myself sometimes, that grown men do stupid stuff every day, and sometimes they get beat up for it. I needed to know how to get up and dust myself off and keep going, how to stand up for myself, and how to face the dark. How to be a man. The things my dad didn't get a chance to teach me."

He stopped, swallowed hard, and continued in a diminished voice, "I guess most of all I needed my dad to look at me, all grown up, and tell me I'm okay. That he's proud of me. But he wasn't there."

Snake sat for a long moment, staring at the words Julie's hand had forged. Aiden Prine, in his youth, had not known that his sister-in-law possessed such wisdom.

"Jeremy," he said, but Jeremy didn't look at him.

"Jeremy," he repeated, very softly, and this time Jeremy looked up and met his eyes.

"You're okay, Jeremy Prine. And I am *proud* of you."

Jeremy pondered this for a second, then nodded gravely. It was only a nod, a slight tip of the head, but a palpable consent had passed between them.

Jeremy reeled in his bait and flipped it behind the boat, parallel to the bank. The boat had drifted too close in. Snake stepped on the pedal, the trolling motor purred, and the prow veered outward as the boat eased back to where it should be. The plastic lizard hadn't yielded a fish lately, so he tore it loose and tossed it overboard.

"And what about the other?" Snake asked, busying his hands

tying a crankbait to his line. "The hard part. You think you know what it was that Julie couldn't give me?"

"Yeah, I do now. I know it for a fact. If you could see yourself, Uncle Aiden, if you could hear yourself, you'd know too. You've dug yourself into a corner where you got nothing left but pain and guilt. You think my dad died because of who you are—or were—and you're killing yourself over it."

"I was there," Snake said. "I know."

"Dad was there too. His death was no more your fault than his. You were confident; he was cautious. Personalities. It was just as much his personality that put him in front of that switch as it was yours. If the situation had been different, he might have gotten *you* killed."

"Might have. Didn't."

"You said it yourself, Uncle Aiden—you're not God. Other people live and die and make stupid mistakes all the time without asking you, and sometimes people do great things, all on their own, without your help. God will see that the world keeps spinning, even if you stop pushing. Not everything is your fault."

"Yeah, well I don't think your mother saw it quite that way."

"Maybe in the beginning, but you didn't see her after she got sick—those last months. She changed. She went to a whole different level, like she said in the letter. I was there," Jeremy said. "I know. But I guess in the end it doesn't matter whether I think you did something wrong, or even if my mother thought you did. What's killing you is that *you* believe you did."

Snake nodded. This was a true thing.

"The trouble is," Snake said, "it's airtight. Tom would still be alive if it hadn't been for me. Julie said that herself. And I can't bring him back. I would trade my life a thousand times if it would bring Tom back, but it won't. What's done is done."

Jeremy smiled. "Weasel used to say perfection is an absolute.

Nobody's perfect, Uncle Aiden. We're all dust, and the one thing we have in common is that we can't save ourselves. But *listen*—" he turned to face Aiden and captured him with his eyes before he continued—"we're blood—you, me, my dad—but we're all busted up, all split apart by what happened, and I want to be family again. I'm Tom Prine's only son, and he's *in* me—I believe that. I believe I know what he would do, and I'm the only one left who has the right to speak for him. Uncle Aiden, whatever part of my father is in me, every ounce of it loves you. Every ounce of it wants nothing but good for you, wants you to live, wants you to be free of what haunts you. Every ounce of my father forgives you, free and clear. I think that's what my mother wanted me to give you."

Aiden Prine took a deep breath and held his fishing rod very still. He couldn't say anything. He didn't dare twitch his lure for fear a fish might strike at it, and at the moment he couldn't see it very well.

CHAPTER 25

A miner's prayer.

I just need a couple days," Snake said. "I can be back by Friday."

Sonny chewed on the stub of a cigar. The springs under his chair creaked as he leaned back, kicked his feet up onto the desk, put his hands behind his head, and glanced at the race chart on the wall.

"I guess you've earned it," he said. "I just wish you had brought this up last month when the machine was down. You could've had all the time you wanted then. Now that we're running again—"

"Griff can handle things. It's just a couple days."

"I know Griff *can* do the job; I just don't know if he *will*."

"Water under the bridge," Snake said. "He's solid."

"So what is it? What have you got to do?"

Snake shook his head. "It's personal. Just some personal business I need to take care of."

Sonny sighed, nodded. "Okay. I guess I can hang around in the meantime and keep an eye on things. You *will* be back Friday."

"I'll be here."

Driving home that night, Snake told Jeremy about the trip. "I have to go see my mother," he said.

"Wow. You haven't seen Granny since—"

"Since she had the stroke, right. So tell me, what's she like?"

"She's gone."

"What do you mean, 'gone'?"

Jeremy shrugged. "She's just gone. She swallows when they put food in her mouth, and she breathes on her own. That's about it. Granny's not there anymore. I think she moves a little now and then, but there's nothing in her eyes. Nobody's home."

"I still have to see her. To talk to her. If not for her, for me."

"Okay," Jeremy said, and the calm tone of his voice told Snake he understood. His nephew understood a lot of things.

Snake had forgotten about the Bible that Julie gave him. It didn't even peek out of dusty memory until he got home and started to pack for his trip. He pulled down the small suitcase from the top shelf in his bedroom closet, saw the cardboard box hiding in the corner, and then he remembered. He took the box down, set it gently on the bed and bent back the flaps.

Books. Old paperbacks—mysteries, spy stories, horror— mostly second-rate stuff he would never read again yet couldn't make himself throw away. One by one, he pulled them out and dropped them on the bed. In the very bottom of the box he found what he was looking for.

It was thick and heavy in his hand compared to the paperbacks. He ran his palm over the leather cover, then touched a fingertip to the name stamped into the lower right-hand corner in small gold letters. *Tom Prine.*

He had never opened it. Not once in ten years. When Julie left the Bible in his hospital room he refused even to touch it. It lay for days on the chair where she'd set it, until a nurse picked it up and stashed it in the cupboard with the rest of his personal effects. The day he left the hospital someone else packed up his stuff so that he didn't have to touch it then either. Tom's Bible was a hateful thing to him then, a reminder of Julie's accusing eyes, Aiden's passport to pariah-hood. The only time he'd ever actually put his hand on it was when he buried it in this very box.

Now it felt warm in his hand.

Things had changed in the last twenty-four hours. From beyond the grave, Julie had sent her only son to offer him forgiveness—and this time it was genuine. The symbolism was not lost on him. After ten years in the desert he had seen the hand of God, and he knew it for what it was. Tom was right. God was real.

But it was one thing to learn after all these years that Julie and Jeremy—and Tom—had forgiven him. Of all the people whose lives he had destroyed, only his mother remained. She, at least, he could see. He could look at her face while he said the words and accept whatever closure came from it.

God, however, was another matter.

Over the years Snake had hardened to his own hopelessness, had become almost comfortable in the stomach of despair, but the glimmer of light Jeremy shined on him had made the darkness intolerable. He wanted to cry out, only he didn't know what to say, didn't know if there were even words capable of reaching God from where he stood, or whether God would listen. He stood at the foot of his bed and literally shook, like Donny Flippen, with frustration.

Jeremy hadn't gone to bed yet, hadn't even folded out the sleeper. He was sitting on the sofa eating an apple when Aiden handed him the Bible. His reaction was identical to Aiden's. He ran the flat of his hand reverently over the cover, then touched the name printed in the corner. He just sat and held it and stared at it for a long moment, speechless.

"Your mom gave it to me right after Tom died," Aiden said.

Jeremy opened the Bible, stuck his face in it and inhaled. "I don't smell anything anymore," he said, flipping pages, "but it's covered with his tracks. Thanks, Uncle Aiden. You don't know what this means to me."

"It means a lot to *me* just to give it to you."

A faint smile crossed Jeremy's face. He closed the Bible and held it edgeways in front of him, then parted his palms and let the pages separate by themselves.

Aiden's head tilted. "What are you doing?"

"Looking for the dirty places. Mom used to say you could know somebody by the dirty places in their Bible."

The Bible fell open naturally to a place in the middle.

"I guess they *both* had a thing for Psalms," Jeremy said. "Look at this. Dad wore this spot out coming back to it again and again. There's this little crocheted cross hanging here to mark the spot, and the edges of the pages are all brown and smudged with fingerprints."

"Yeah, Tom wasn't big on washing his hands," Aiden said. "Can I see that?" Reaching down, he gently lifted the delicate cross from the crease of the Bible and laid it on his palm. Only a few inches tall, the cross was intricately woven, attached by a short string to a tassel.

"I remember this," Aiden said, and his voice came out distant and rusty. "Your grandmother always had a needle in her hand—sewing, knitting, crocheting, cross-stitch, you name it. She made this cross for Tom when he was fourteen and he had hepatitis. He always claimed it had healing properties. Can I have it?"

"Sure," Jeremy said, his eyes still focused on the Bible. "You should have something that reminds you of Granny, of who she was before the stroke. All I have left of my parents is the memory."

"Julie didn't leave you anything?"

"Yeah, a couple things, but I lost them on the way down here. I really hate that I lost her Bible. It was in my duffel bag. Everything else in that bag was just stuff, but Mom's Bible meant something to me."

"I'm glad I saved this one for you."

Jeremy's face lit up suddenly. "Look at this, Uncle Aiden! This is too cool. Look what Dad underlined here. See, that's what Mom was talking about—these are *Dad's* marks. It's like he's sitting here with us, showing us something with his own hand. Listen to this.

"'Out of the depths I have cried to Thee, O Lord.
Lord, hear my voice!
Let Thine ears be attentive
To the voice of my supplications.
If Thou, Lord, shouldst mark iniquities,
O Lord, who could stand?
But there is forgiveness with Thee,
That Thou mayest be feared.
I wait for the Lord, my soul does wait,
And in His word do I hope.
My soul waits for the Lord
More than the watchmen for the morning;
Indeed, more than the watchmen for the morning.'

"Now that's beautiful. I can see why Dad liked it. It's like a swing shift miner's prayer, don't you think? Uncle Aiden?"

But Aiden had turned away and was padding toward his room.

"Good night," he said softly, and closed the door without looking back.

Aiden wrestled with pillow and blanket for three hours before he went to sleep, so he made up for it the next morning. He waited for the Atlanta rush hour to dissipate before leaving the apartment.

Near Cartersville, well north of the city, he stopped for gas and got lunch at a drive-through. On his way back to the expressway he passed a little shopping square and saw the words *New Life Bookstore* on the sign.

Ten minutes later he was back on the expressway with the miles clicking away underneath him and a new Bible lying on the seat beside him—New American Standard version, just like Tom's. Only then did he recall that he had gone in and bought the Bible without covering his face and head, and no one seemed to have noticed. A piece of paper bearing a handwritten prayer was now taped to his sun visor—a swing shift miner's prayer. By the time he finished the drive he would have the words etched permanently in his mind.

Later that afternoon, outside Sevierville, he stopped and called Anna to let her know he was in the neighborhood, and where he was going. She insisted that he come over for dinner, wanting also to put him up for the night.

He already had a hotel reservation, but he couldn't turn down a home-cooked meal. With evening coming on he figured it would be better to wait and go see his mother in the morning, and then head back.

Anna's girls weren't even born the last time Aiden visited their house. Norman didn't remember him; he could tell by the initial horror as Norman's face seemed to retreat in a kind of porcine wince. The fourteen-year-old did manage, reluctantly, to shake hands when he was introduced. The twin girls could hardly be faulted for hiding behind Walter, though in the true spirit of five-year-olds, they were the first to recover. Within an hour they were climbing on Aiden's shoulders and burning his scalp with their knuckles, asking him if it hurt.

Anna was desperate for news of Jeremy, and more than a little put out that he hadn't come along with Aiden.

"He's filled out a little," Aiden said. "He's got shoulders now."

"How's he dealing with, you know . . . Julie's death?"

"Pretty well, I guess. I think it was good for him to get away— new surroundings, new people. And he started work as soon as he got there, which kept his mind—"

"Oh, Aiden, you didn't let him go to work on the mining project!" Anna was horrified. Her face was a little rounder than Julie's and not so austere, but the deeply furrowed look of consternation was strikingly reminiscent of her sister.

"I didn't have much choice," Aiden said in his own defense. "I figured I'd have more control if he was around where I could watch him. Turns out I'm not in control of much anyway. He's grown up a lot. Trust me, Jeremy can handle himself." He wasn't about to go into detail, especially sitting on Anna's couch with the twins climbing on him. Well, one was climbing on him; the other was patiently removing the laces from his boot. He'd never thought about it before, but watching them in the same room with Norman, the age difference seemed peculiar.

"You had your kids an awful long time apart," he said to Anna.

She gazed with loving affection on the little monster absconding with Aiden's right boot, and said, "Yeah, I'm not exactly in control either."

Ignoring the other little blond dynamo, who had climbed up onto his shoulders to inspect the graft on his head very closely, and sensing that he would have to leave soon or bite one of the children, he pressed for information.

"Anna, have you been up to see my mother?"

"Yeah, I've been up there a couple times since Julie died. Julie was all she had. She used to go up there at least once a month."

"Why?"

"Well . . ." Anna looked around as if she were searching for an answer written on the furniture, then said, "Because. I mean, you don't just abandon somebody like that."

"But Jeremy said she was gone. I mean, you know—not there anymore. Just a shell."

Anna gave a strained look and said, "I . . . well, you never know. I've never personally seen anything, but Julie said she just had a feeling Martha was listening to her sometimes when she talked. I don't know why, exactly. Just small stuff, I guess. I never saw her move at all."

"She moves?"

"Julie said she did. A little. Once or twice. You know, now that I think about it, I remember about six years ago—I was pregnant with the twins—she came back from up there all excited one time because she was just so sure Martha had moved her hand on purpose. I think the only reason I'm remembering it now is because of what she said triggered it."

"You mean something Julie did caused her to move?"

"Yes. I remember it now."

"What was it?"

"She was talking about you."

The dust was thicker than usual that evening because Jeremy and Tino had the ventilation duct shut down. They were adding a twenty-foot section to the galvanized, corrugated, heavy-duty air duct, fitting it onto the previous section and securing it to the steel pins driven into the wall. When they were done, Tino would spot-weld it for good measure, and then they'd call somebody up top and tell them to turn the big blower back on.

The machine stopped, which was odd because they were only about twenty minutes into the push. A minute later it started up again, ran for thirty seconds, then stopped again. Luke flashed by, hurrying toward the ladder up to the control deck. Through the dense haze of dust, Jeremy identified Luke mostly by the bright green cast he sported on his forearm.

"Luke! What's up?"

Luke hooked one foot on the ladder and turned. "Don't know. Somebody said something about gas." He went on up the ladder.

Jeremy glanced at Tino, saw that he had the duct secured and was putting on his hood so he could weld. He clambered down from the wall and followed Luke.

Ruskie, Griff, and Luke were standing in front of the control console staring at the gas meter mounted above it. The dial on the meter looked a lot like Ripley's voltmeter—just a red needle against a broad arc of marks and numbers under a piece of clear plastic—except that it was bigger, and there were holes in the metal box behind it.

Looking vaguely professorial with his thick glasses, prominent nose and receding chin, Ruskie reached out and tapped the face of the meter.

"See?" he said. "It goes back down."

"I've never seen anything like that," Griff said.

"Me neither," Luke agreed.

Jeremy watched over their shoulders as the needle bled slowly back down to the left side. While they watched, it bottomed out at zero and stayed there.

Griff scratched his chin. "Do it again," he said.

Ruskie flipped a switch and the great churning tornado sounds rumbled out of the heading. The red needle on the gas meter moved, slowly at first, and then faster as the noise swelled, finally pegging the right side of the meter. Griff made the cutthroat sign.

Ruskie killed the switch, and the cutterhead ground to a halt. Against the silence, Jeremy could hear the ticking of hot metal in the heading. The walls flickered with the blue glare of Tino's welding.

Griff nearly knocked Jeremy down rushing past him. "TINO!" he roared.

Across the way, Tino stopped welding, lifted his hood and peered innocently at Griff, who shook his head and made the cutthroat sign again. Tino nodded once and took the helmet off. Griff squeezed back into his place next to Ruskie.

Again the needle slowly dropped back to the left side of the meter. Griff shook his head, puzzled. "I don't like this."

"Something's not right here. Methane doesn't go away like that," Ruskie said, glancing up. "Especially with the ventilator down. Doesn't make sense. It acts more like an electrical problem of some kind."

"We never had any trouble with this meter before," Griff argued.

"It might not be the meter," Luke said. "Could be feedback off of something else."

"I don't smell any gas," Jeremy said, but he knew he should have stayed quiet when they all gave him a look.

"Methane's odorless," Luke explained, rather tersely.

Ruskie shook his head. "That meter's not acting right. I've seen gas before, and this isn't how it behaves. I don't think it's gas; I think there's something else wrong."

Griff took a deep breath and blew it out, staring at the meter. "I just don't feel good about this," he said. "I think we better get a geologist down here, just to be sure."

Luke nodded. "Ruskie's right. It don't act like gas, so it's gotta be an electrical problem."

"Then we'll get a geologist *and* an electrician, okay? But we're pulling out until we know something for sure."

When Griff called Sonny to let him know he was pulling the crew out, Sonny argued with him. Griff won. It was a fact that nobody in the hole at that time had the expertise to know for certain if the meter had spiked because there was gas in the tunnel or because of an electrical back-feed. It was a judgment call, and Griff had the right to pull his crew if he believed the tunnel to be unsafe. But at a hundred dollars a minute, and with the job running a month behind schedule, he had better have a very good reason.

The ride out took twenty minutes—two thousand dollars in downtime—and Sonny was waiting for them at the top of the shaft by the time they got there, flanked by Biggins and Ripley. Sonny's cigar was puffing like a train. Griff lit a cigarette, and only then did Jeremy realize he hadn't seen anybody light up since the trouble started.

Without the background rhythms of the tray lift and the

stacker, an eerie silence hung over the yard. Jeremy could hear the crunch of every footstep on the crush-and-run as Griff and his crew met up with Sonny and his technical troubleshooters.

Sonny crossed his arms on his chest. "So tell me exactly what it's doing, Griff, and this better be good."

Griff clenched his cigarette in his teeth while he hitched up his jeans. "It's simple. The minute we start mining, the gas meter pegs. When we stop, it goes back down."

"Fast or slow?" Ripley asked.

"Slow. Takes maybe ten, fifteen seconds to bottom out. Comes up about the same. Look, it's easy to solve this. We got any badges?"

Sonny shook his head. "I didn't order badges because the geological survey didn't indicate a need. There's not supposed to be any gas here. Couldn't the meter just be busted?"

Biggins shrugged. "It's a mining machine—*anything* can be busted. I seen a meter do something like this once before."

"What's the ground like?" Sonny asked. "Is it solid?"

"No, we ran into a fault about an hour ago, but it's small and diagonal. Hasn't slowed us down any. You can see it starting to come past the left side of the plate."

Jeremy had enough experience to know that the presence of a fault would complicate things. It was a variable. There *could* be gas.

Sonny chewed his cigar for a minute. "Listen, the one thing I do know is that methane doesn't dissipate when you shut the machine down. This sounds electrical to me. What do you think, Ripley?"

Ripley shrugged. "Sounds like it. The meter pulls low voltage power from the control console, and it doesn't take much of a back-feed to mess it up. It worries me a little that it comes up and down slow like that, though. If it's electrical, it should go on and off with the switch. But I guess you could be getting motor feed-back, maybe through the ground wire, and then it might wind up and down with the motor. The only way to know for sure is to go in and put a tester on it."

"Can you do that?" Sonny asked.

"Sure."

"Good. There you go, Griff. Take Ripley and Biggins back down there with you and let them figure out what's going on. It doesn't sound like gas to me."

"Me neither," Biggins said, and his years of experience out-weighed Griff's.

Luke put in his two cents' worth. "I'm game. I thought it was electrical all along."

"I don't like it," Griff said. "We don't have another gas meter, or badges—nothing to tell us if there's gas."

"There's no gas!" Sonny said, eyes flaring. "Take Ripley and Biggins and *get back to work.*"

"I still don't like it," Griff said, bristling. "Can't we just get a—"

"You can get back to work is what you can do!" Sonny jabbed his cigar at Griff. "You can get down there and make some hole, or get out of the way and I'll find somebody who will!" His eyes flashed for a second in Luke's direction, and even Jeremy knew what would happen if Griff refused. Luke was young and crazy. He would jump at a chance to take the crew, and they would end up going back into a bad situation without Griff's experienced head to guide them.

Griff looked around, took a silent poll. Everybody nodded, shrugged. The debate with Sonny was above their pay grade, and Griff didn't need another blemish on his reputation. Not now.

"All right," he said, flipping his cigarette butt away. "We'll go back in." His men parted for him when he turned around, while

Sonny grinned his minor triumph around his cigar.

Griff stopped. "Jeremy and Stinker," he said, finding the red-headed new kid with his eyes, "get up a load of water and air line."

Jeremy had brought in a load of pipe an hour earlier. He thought maybe Griff just forgot.

"Boss, we already got more than enough—"

"Jeremy!" Griff snapped, cutting him off. He swung around and came face-to-face with Jeremy, then spoke slowly. "I *said,* you and Stinker get up a load of water and air line." He glanced at Sonny's back, heading toward his office. "And take your time."

"Yes, sir," Jeremy answered. Without another word, Griff led his crew back into the hole, and a deep sense of foreboding washed over Jeremy. He trusted Griff's instincts, even if Sonny didn't, and he devoutly wished Snake was here.

Aiden had finished eating, Norman had polished off a second plateful, and the girls were still playing with their food when the phone rang. Anna jumped up to answer it and immediately broke into that squeaky, excited, what-a-surprise voice.

"So, how've you been, you little rat, and how come I haven't heard from you?"

Her face darkened suddenly, and she said, "Yeah, he's here. Hold on." Frowning, she held out the phone to Aiden. "It's Jeremy. He wants to talk to you, and he's in a big hurry."

Rising from the table, he took the phone and wandered into the kitchen to lean back against the counter.

Breathless, Jeremy was talking too fast for Aiden to follow.

"Slow down, pard. What is it?"

Jeremy took a deep breath, and then explained the situation with the gas meter. "Have you ever seen anything like that?" he asked.

"Never seen it myself, but I remember an old guy out in Arizona talking about something like that once. It wasn't methane; it was something else, some other ane . . . hexane or heptane, something like that. It's pretty rare, but it—"

"How come it falls off the meter?"

"Because it's heavy. Heavier than methane. Heavier than air. When they crank up the machine it stirs up the gas so the meter can read it, but when they shut her down it all goes straight to the bottom."

"Well, this hexane—or whatever—will it blow up?"

"Oh yeah," Aiden said. "You bet it will. If somebody drops a cigarette butt in the wrong place it'll go off like a shotgun. Let me talk to Griff."

Silence.

"He's gone," Jeremy finally said. "I'm sorry, I thought I told you. The crew's on the way back in. Griff got into it with Sonny about the meter, then he told me and Stinker to stay here and get up a load of pipe."

"How long have they been gone?" Snake gripped the phone a little too hard.

"About fifteen minutes. They should be there anytime now."

"Where are you?"

"I'm in Ripley's trailer. Hey, I can just call Griff on the hot line. It's right here, so I can keep you on the line at the same time."

Mentally, Snake replayed everything he knew. Griff didn't like Sonny in the first place, and if Sonny forced him to go back in against his better judgment . . .

"Was he mad?" Snake asked.

"Who?"

"Griff. Was he mad at Sonny when he went back in?"

"Oh yeah. You could've fried an egg on his helmet."

"Then he won't answer the hot line. If he's mad, he'll go straight in and fire it up, then push like a demon till he cools off. You don't want to try to talk to him when he gets like that. I know Griff. If the phone rings, he'll think it's Sonny and he won't pick it up."

"Then what are we gonna do? If they start up the machine, won't that set it off?"

"Sooner or later, yeah. And it'll kill the whole crew."

It was at this precise moment, even as he spoke the words, that Aiden put it all together and saw, clearly and for the first time, the choice he was facing. Slowly, his knees gave way and he slid to the floor, clutching at the kitchen cabinet. Walter and Anna stopped talking and turned to stare at him.

Jeremy was saying something, but the words flew past Aiden like a cloud of birds, the flapping of many wings. In the last ten years, Aiden Prine had learned almost everything there was to know about mining, with the exception of one area that he had intentionally bypassed, one place he could not make himself go. In ten years, he had not set foot in a switchyard. Now, when the lives of his whole crew depended on it, he would have gone in and thrown the switch himself, even *knowing* what would happen, if only he were there. If only.

"Jeremy," he said, and his voice rang hollow against the pounding in his ears, "somebody has to kill the power."

Jeremy didn't answer. There was a brief silence in which Aiden thought he heard a sharp intake of breath, and then he heard the *fa-dump* sound of Jeremy's handset being tossed onto the wooden desktop.

"JEREMY!" he screamed, but no answer came. He pressed the

phone hard into his ear, flattened his palm against the earless side of his head to blot out the squabbling of the twins, and listened intensely. Seconds passed, and he could have sworn he heard shouts, then nothing. Half a minute later, when he dared to hope everything would be all right, he heard a distant, muffled explosion. The phone slipped from his grasp, clattered to the floor, and his head drooped into his hands.

"What is it? What's going on?" Anna asked, rushing over and grabbing up the phone.

"Hello? There's no one here," she said, putting a hand over the mouthpiece, her eyes searching. "I hear people shouting."

"So do I," Aiden whispered, and his fingernails bit into his scalp.

Still holding the phone to her ear, Anna knelt beside him, reached out gently and squeezed his shoulder. He flinched sharply, recoiling from a horror Anna could not know, *should* not know— *screams and lightning, the smell of molten steel and charred flesh and . . . Please, God, not again!*

"Aiden?" she said, but he didn't look up. The pitch of her voice rose in desperation. "Aiden, *please!*"

He couldn't speak, couldn't raise his head, couldn't make the flashes go away. Anna's voice called to him from the distance, from beyond the thunder, and only the touch of her hand held him to the earth.

She pulled back suddenly and switched the phone to her other ear.

"Wait, no. Hel—hello? Yes! Hang on a second!"

Against the pain, Aiden forced himself back, forced his eyes open, and looked up.

She covered the mouthpiece again and said, "It's somebody named Moss—"

He snatched the phone away from her. "Moss! This is Snake. What's going on? What hap—"

"It's Jeremy," Moss said. "Boy's gone crazy. I saw him come runnin' out of here, and then he jumped in the Grove and went tearing across the yard, lowering the bucket. Ran right into the baloney cable—cut it clean in two with the bucket."

"That was the explosion I heard? He blew up the baloney cable with the loader bucket?"

"Sure did."

"Is he all right?"

"Oh yeah, he's fine, but he blowed a hole in the bucket big enough you could throw a cat through it. Sonny's gonna kill him."

Aiden was laughing now, and Anna looked at him as though he had lost his mind.

"Moss," he said, "you go tell Sonny that boy—that *man*—just saved his job, and he saved the lives of the whole crew. You tell Sonny that Snake said to get down on his knees and kiss Jeremy's boots, and then tell him to come to this phone and talk to me. I'll wait."

"Snake?" Anna said. "Who is Snake?"

Spring hadn't quite made it up into the mountains of eastern Tennessee yet. Advance platoons of jonquils sprouted here and there like tiny periscopes, but nothing else. In the parking lot of the nursing home, a cold March wind swayed the pine tops and rattled the bare limbs of hardwoods against each other like antlers. Aiden hurried inside.

The front lobby of the home seemed warm and cozy despite

the polished tile floor, mainly because of the overstuffed sofa and chairs, the indirect downlighting, and half a dozen huge pots full of oversized houseplants—tea plants and yuccas and a couple of weeping figs with flocks of deep green corrugated leaves brushing the ceiling.

"Can I help you?" a thin voice said, and Snake turned around to find a petite woman who looked plenty old enough to have been a resident of the home. She was maybe five feet in height, all of eighty pounds, with a perfectly coifed cloud of pale blue hair, a white cardigan wrapped about her shoulders. When he turned to face her, she said, "Oh!" Frail fingers rose to cover her mouth, and a shock registered in her eyes.

"I'm sorry," Snake said, ducking back into his rumpled hat. But there was no way to hide his face.

"No! Oh, no!" she said, reaching for his forearm. "It's all right. It's just, I *know* you. I know who you are, anyway. You must be Martha Prine's boy, the one who got burned."

"Aiden. My name's Aiden. You know my mother?"

"Oh, yes! I'm Zelda, by the way. I know everybody here—and everything about them, pretty much." She leaned close and whispered, "There's not much else to do."

"Is it okay if I go see her? I mean, I don't know what the visiting hours are, but if—"

"Aw, honey, visiting hours are anytime somebody comes. Come on, I'll take you there."

The corridor was wide and clear with handrails down both sides. There were rooms on the left side, and he glanced into them as he passed. Pictures of family members hung on walls, greeting cards and plants and books rested on dresser tops—the rooms reflecting the occupants. The right wall of the corridor was all glass, facing what appeared to be a small park. He saw that the facility formed a square around a large central courtyard where brick-lined pathways wandered through a manicured garden with benches, where the residents could walk or sit and read.

"The garden is our best feature," Zelda said. "Some of our guests forget where they are sometimes, and it's so nice to have a place where they can get outside without us having to worry about them wandering off."

She talked the whole way, for which Snake was grateful. "Julie's sister—what's her name?"

"Anna."

"Anna, yes. She's been up a time or two, but I don't think anyone else has been in to see Martha since Julie died last summer. Oh my! Has it been that long already? Such a shame about Julie. She was a sweet, sweet girl."

"Yes, she'll be missed."

"I visit with Martha almost every day. I like to just sit and talk to her." Grinning mischievously, she added, "Martha's a real good listener. And you never really know what goes on inside a person's head, do you? Well. Here we are."

Zelda ushered Snake into the room and introduced him in a loud, cheery voice that suggested his mother was not absent at all, just hard of hearing. Then she left, and Snake stood before what remained of his mother. He would not have recognized her. Wearing a faded terry-cloth robe and slumped in an overstuffed armchair, she seemed as small and fragile as a child. Her face, once strong and purposeful and ruddy from working her garden in the sun, now hung slack and pasty and peculiarly smooth, the wrinkles having fallen out from lack of use. The left side of her face drooped a bit, and the left eye seemed to slope. Her hair had gone white. When he last saw her she'd had a full round head of brown hair with gray creeping up the sides. Now it was cut fairly short, brushed severely back from her face with no discernible style, and solid white, tinged with an unnatural yellow stain. Her eyes stared straight ahead, blank. He hadn't understood what Jeremy meant when he said "gone," until now.

Apart from the wheelchair in the corner there was only one chair, and she was sitting in it. He sat gingerly on the edge of her bed, crossing his ankles and clasping his hands, wondering what to do now. Her room looked almost sterile. The only pictures on the wall were the stock landscape prints put here by the staff, and the top of the dresser was clear but for one small framed picture of Julie and Jeremy together. From the age of the Jeremy in the picture, he guessed it was five or six years old.

He looked out the window at the gray day, the gray trees swaying, and sighed. There were things he wanted to say, to expunge, even if she couldn't hear him, but looking at her like this was almost like facing a corpse, and it hushed him. Anything said to those dead eyes would doubtless bounce back and clatter to the floor like so much loose change. Finally, he sat down on the carpet and leaned back against the edge of her chair. He found it easier to remember her than to look at her.

"Ma," he said, for that was what he had called her, even as a child, in subtle mockery of the stereotype foisted on people from the hills, "I want you to know I'm sorry. It seems like everything I ever did destroyed you in one way or another, and I never meant for it to be that way. For what it's worth, I want you to know I won't hurt you anymore." A brief sardonic laugh fell out of him then, because he couldn't imagine anything short of death getting through to her, and even death would not seem a great hurt.

He sat listening to his own breathing for a minute or two, then took the crocheted cross from his pocket and spread it against his palm. He felt the texture of it with his fingertips, toyed with the little tassel. "Lord, hear my voice," he whispered.

"Ma, it just seemed like nothing ever moved unless I pushed it. So I pushed, and I pushed—and the more I pushed, the more life pushed back. Tom, he was different. It wasn't in him to push. He just stood still and waited for life to come to him, and it crawled up in his lap like a puppy. At least it did until that night."

Rubbing his thumb against the cross in his hand, Aiden closed his eyes. His lips flew, almost silently, over the words, "'If Thou, Lord, shouldst mark iniquities, O Lord, who could stand?'"

"I'm sorry, Ma," he said. "There's not a thing I can undo, not one single thing I can change. All I can do is tell you I'm sorry from the bottom of my soul."

In the end, he knew, there was nothing more to be said. He couldn't bring Tom back, or his father. Even his mother was beyond his reach, but he knew the words needed to be said anyway. He sat there in complete dejected silence for several minutes, until he heard the faintest little scratching, like a fingernail on cloth.

He turned to see where the sound was coming from and caught a slight movement of his mother's hand, resting on the arm of the chair near where he'd been leaning his head. As he watched, her middle finger moved—haltingly, and very slowly, but it moved. The fingertip went out, stopped, and came back along a slightly different path. Inches away from his eyes, the pale, liver-spotted finger described a small circle, and then another.

He looked into his mother's face. Her eyes had not changed; they still looked like the eyes of a cadaver, and yet he could have sworn they glistened, ever so slightly, at the bottoms.

Turning his back to her again, he leaned his head against the arm of the chair and very gently reached up, lifted her hand, and placed it squarely on his head.

Her middle fingertip moved in a slow circle on his scarred, bald scalp, precisely as she had done with a hank of hair when he was a child.

"'But there is forgiveness with Thee,'" he whispered faintly, "'that Thou mayest be feared. I wait for the Lord, my soul does wait, and in His word do I hope. My soul waits for the Lord more than the watchmen for the morning.'" He held his brother's crocheted cross in his palm and kept his eyes fixed on it as his lips moved over the words.

"'Indeed, more than the watchmen for the morning.'"

CHAPTER **26**

Dream of love.

Aiden was stretched out in the recliner watching the Braves' season opener when Jeremy came and blocked his view.

"Well, how do I look?" The kid spread his arms, showing off his new navy blazer and slacks. The shoes were new too. He'd even gotten his hair cut short and styled, if that was what it could be called. Aiden, liberated as he was from hair, had watched with a detached curiosity in recent years as hairstyles evolved into meticulously tended non-styles.

"You need to comb your hair," he said.

"I *did* comb it."

"With what, a brick?"

"Hey, this is what hair is supposed to look like these days, Ancient One."

"Well, then I guess you're all right. You look like a male model, if that's what you're shooting for. Or an engineer. I'm not sure which is worse."

Jeremy's shoulders slumped. "Thanks for the encouragement."

"Hey, I'm your uncle, not your wife." But the beginnings of a smile crept out, and he relented. "I have to admit, you look pretty sharp. Special occasion?"

"Kearston's birthday. We're going out to eat. Nice restaurant—you know, where the waiters don't wear hats." Jeremy said this while disappearing into the kitchen. As his voice faded, Aiden heard the piano downstairs start into a quiet melody. He picked up the remote and muted the ball game.

Jeremy emerged with a gift-wrapped package and a dozen red roses, long-stemmed, arranged in a vase with baby's breath and a big bow.

"What's in the package?" Aiden asked.

"Oh, this? It's a birthday present for Kearston. A painting."

"Sounds expensive."

Jeremy sort of grinned and winced at the same time, just like his dad. "Well, you remember the car I was saving up for? It's gonna take a bit longer now."

Aiden shook his head. "And what if she doesn't like your taste in paintings?"

Jeremy held the package out and smiled at it as though he could see through the wrapper. "She likes it," he said.

He looked at his watch and turned to go, then stopped in the middle of the room, staring at his uncle. Lost in the music drifting up through the floor, Aiden had forgotten himself for a moment and let the loneliness onto his face.

When he saw Jeremy watching, he felt compelled to explain. "*Pathetique*," he said. "Breaks my heart every time."

The vase full of roses slowly lowered to Jeremy's side.

"Go see her, Uncle Aiden. Talk to her. Trust me."

Aiden shook his head, said nothing.

Jeremy gently laid the package down, then tugged one of the roses out of the vase and held it out to him.

Aiden took the rose and looked at it as if he had never seen one before.

"Just go," Jeremy said. He hesitated, standing there and looking like one waiting for a tip, then picked up his package and left without another word, closing the door softly behind him.

Aiden didn't know how long he sat there with his forehead in his palm, the rose dangling from his other hand, Swan's fingers playing up and down his spine. Finally, after the piano had fallen silent for a few minutes, he stood up, took a deep breath, steeled himself and went out quickly before he changed his mind.

When he knocked on her door his whole life seemed to gather itself for flight, and he unconsciously held his breath.

Footsteps, followed by a slight rustle against the door as she looked through the peephole. His heart pounded. A deadbolt slid back, a chain dropped. The door swung wide and Swan stood before him. He was sure that she had seen him before, though never without his hat and sunglasses or a scarf wrapped around his face. Her mouth opened slightly as she looked at him now, yet he saw none of the revulsion he had expected in her eyes. Instead, there was a trace of a smile.

He held out a fist with the rose in it. Like a schoolboy.

She took it delicately in her fingers, then cupped her other hand around the bloom as if she was afraid it would fall and break. Crimson reflected from her porcelain skin when she brought it to her face. She turned abruptly and walked away, leaving the door wide open, Aiden still standing outside. He waited, wondering.

A minute later she came back into view, standing in the middle of the living room, with the rose in a crystal bud vase. With two fingers she beckoned him into the room.

He stepped inside cautiously, leaving the door open.

"Sit, please," she said, and he eased himself into a sagging corduroy armchair. Placing the vase delicately on top of the old upright piano, she sat down without a word and began playing a beautiful, flowing waltz.

Even the rose leaned toward Swan.

Aiden was afraid to look at her for fear of tarnishing the moment, and he was grateful for the little starburst of sunlight that drew his eye to the vase. Like an elongated teardrop, clear and unadorned, the bud vase captured a tiny upside-down picture of Swan in its belly.

She cradled the notes with heartbreaking insight. The piano loved her, and it poured out a soulful richness far beyond the sum of its tired wood and strings and pegs.

"'Liebestraum,'" Aiden whispered. A knowing smile curled the corners of his lips, and he closed his eyes to listen.

ACKNOWLEDGMENTS

First, last, and always, I thank God for showing me the keys. I would also like to thank:

My wife, Pam, who owns half of all I do.

All the miners, electricians, pipe fitters, carpenters, brick masons, concrete finishers, and ironworkers who haunt this book in a thousand places.

My friends Lori Patrick and Larry McDonald, for their unwavering support.

My folks, for watching the kids now and then so I could write.

Luke, Carol, Dave, and all the others at Bethany House who make all this possible.

Janet Kobobel Grant, the best agent in the business.

Joanie Grimm, for a name, and Tom Swafford, for another one.

My friends and family at MCC.

My sons, who I hope are as proud of me as I am of them.

And Claudia King, wherever she is, for a crocheted cross that really did have healing power.

ABOUT THE AUTHOR

W. DALE CRAMER lives in Georgia with his wife and two sons. *Bad Ground* is his second novel.

For more information visit *www.dalecramer.com*, or you may write to Dale at P.O. Box 25, Hampton, GA 30228.